Whatever

Gets You

Through

the

Night

Whatever

Gets You

Through

the

Night

♦

TERI DENINE

St. Martin's Griffin

New York

WHATEVER GETS YOU THROUGH THE NIGHT. Copyright © 2008 by Teri Denine. All rights reserved. Printed in the United States of America. No part of this book may be used or reproduced in any manner whatsoever without written permission except in the case of brief quotations embodied in critical articles or reviews. For information, address St. Martin's Press, 175 Fifth Avenue, New York, N.Y. 10010.

www.stmartins.com

Library of Congress Cataloging-in-Publication Data

Denine, Teri.
    Whatever gets you through the night / Teri Denine.—1st ed.
        p.   cm.
    ISBN-13: 978-0-312-36429-8
    ISBN-10: 0-312-36429-6
    1. Advertising executives—Fiction. 2. Newlyweds—Fiction. 3. New York (N.Y.)—Fiction. I. Title.
PS3604.E5844 W47 2008
813'.6—dc22   2007048965

First Edition: March 2008

10 9 8 7 6 5 4 3 2 1

This book is dedicated in loving memory of:

My father, Haskel Cleveland—it is your strength that I continue to draw from. Your encouragement from the early years has inspired me to become the person that I am.

And my sister Patricia Inez Cleveland—I wish that you were here to see that I really was listening to your every word.

Acknowledgments

First and foremost, I give thanks to God: that I am, and for blessing me with a strong circle of family and friends who have engulfed me with endless support and never stopped believing in me.

To my mother, Betty Cleveland: It was you who planted the seed, nurtured it, then stood back and watched it grow. You are the example by which I live. Thank you.

Pamela Patino: You are my never-ending sounding board, my emotional support and "third eye." Thank you for making me laugh when I wanted to cry. You told me that I could when I was convinced that I couldn't. You're my sister, my heart, and, of course, *my girl!* Keep doing what you do!!

Sylvia Walton, you know I rely on you for those all-day talks—for all the advice and all of that sisterly "stuff."

Sharlene Cleveland: Thank you for the fights that gave me the inspiration. Thank you for the laughs that gave me hope and thank you for being you. Don't ever lose that.

Rickey, Reggie, and June—the Cleveland boys—I love you guys forever!

Tasha Gilroy: Thank you a trillion times over for allowing me to *hear your voice.* Your words of encouragement and constructive criticism helped me make it all make sense.

Nadir Renée Cleveland: Thank you for always keeping it real with me. You are definitely the President of Peanut Gallery. (Lol.)

To my spiritual sisters, Annie Page-Taylor and Tryphena Greene: Thank you for feeding me all of those wonderful meals of wisdom. Your spiritual kindness is truly a blessing from God.

My editor, Monique Patterson, and Kia DuPree, you ladies are on it—you rock!

To film director Lawrence Page, my heart. Thank you for being forever next to me through the tough times and the good times. You keep giving me my dreams. I love you for that!

And finally, thanks to all of the wonderful readers who will take the time to read my story and get lost in my dream.

Whatever

Gets You

Through

the

Night

Prologue

AT FIRST, NOTHING could be seen. Just the fog. A low, thick fog that covered everything. And everything was black and gray. Dark. The faint sounds of the song became clearer. The words sounded slow and muffled at first; then they became more deliberate and quicker. *"Ring around the rosy."* The dead, adults and children alike, were lying in a mass grave. Their mangled bodies could be seen through the fog now. The fog hadn't lifted, but it was moving all around in swirling circles. Moisture beads covered everything that it touched—including the dead bodies, making them wet and soggy. *"Pocket full of posies."*

Little Bari and Franki spun and spun all around with their small hands joined tightly together, making an unbreakable chain that would seal in their chant forever. Round and round they went, faster and faster, over and over. *"Ashes, ashes!"*

A gunshot rang out. *Pow! "We all fall down!"*

"DADDY!" BARI YELLED as she was jolted awake. She had fallen asleep in the old red rocking chair that was tucked in a corner in her living room. "Daddy?" she said again. It was a whisper this time. Bari took a deep breath and put her hand to her chest as if that would stop her heart from beating so fast. She knew that one day she would probably have a heart attack from that dream. The same dream that she had been having over and over for the past few years. No matter how much praying she did or how many remedies she tried, the dreams continued.

Bari looked all around the room. Everything was still. The only sound she could hear was the squeak from the rocking chair. Her grandma Greta had left her that chair when she died. It didn't fit in with any of the other furniture in the room but she kept it there anyway.

Nobody said it, but the family knew that Bari was Granny's favorite. Bari spent a lot of time in her grandmother's room tucked in beside her and sleeping through the night or just listening to her grandmother's stories. It was no wonder that when Granny was on her deathbed she called Bari to her room.

GRETA'S BEDROOM WAS like a place that was frozen in time. A four-poster nineteenth-century cherry-wood bed was pushed against the left wall. A matching bureau was placed opposite it. The bed, the bureau, and the two bed tables had been handed down to her by her mother, who had gotten them from the family that owned her and later freed her at the abolishment of slavery. Cream-colored lace doilies covered the tops of all the furniture. Black-and-white photographs from days long ago stood ageless in their silver frames. A porcelain-faced doll dressed in plaid knickers under a pink velvet dress with lace at the end of each leg and a matching lace-collared jacket that Greta had since she was a girl stood atop the dresser, seeming to watch over her. A small wooden jewelry box with hand-carved swans painted along its sides held her precious trinkets on the bed table.

Bari had pushed open her grandmother's door slightly at first. She peeked inside; then she opened the door all the way and went into the room. Greta's mouth turned up into a faint smile when she saw Bari. Bari was wearing a pair of Hazel's spike-heeled pumps and a long string of pearls that hung down to her waist, and she carried a beaded handbag. Heavy rouge covered her cheeks, and tomato red lipstick was smeared across her mouth.

"Granny?" Bari called out as she approached her grandmother's bed. "Granny, I'm here. Are you awake?"

"Yes, baby." Greta spoke in a raspy whisper. "Why, Miss Bari, how lovely you look."

"Why, thank you, madam. I brought you a flower." Bari handed her grandmother the yellow daffodil that she had pulled up from the backyard.

"Bless your heart, child."

"Granny?"

"Yes, Bari?"

"Did I tell you I love you today?"

Greta struggled but she adjusted herself so that she could hug Bari. "Oh, Bari, I love you, too. Did I tell you how special you are today?"

"No, Granny."

"Well, you are a very special little girl," Greta said. She lay back down. "And you're flyin' on angel's wings." Greta was weak. She spoke so low that Bari had to move even closer to her to hear her better. "I know that you're gonna touch a lot of people's lives as you pass through this here journey we call life. I want you to listen to me, Bari, 'cause I mean what I'm sayin'. . . . I want you to keep your head high and always trust in the good Lord, 'cause he'll provide for you. You hear me? You just have faith no matter what. And Bari?"

"Yes, Granny?"

"Be happy, you hear? You only got one life, so be careful of the choices you make. You have a good soul and you deserve nothin' but the best so don't you go settlin' for less. I know you're just a little girl, but you're smart. You may not understand all what I'm tellin' you right now, but I think that you'll remember later on when it counts. And it won't hurt to use a little bit of the 'help' I told you all about." Greta was breathing more heavily now and she was starting to cough. "Look over there in that drawer for me and pull out that little brown paper bag." Bari walked over to the dresser and took out the brown paper bag and brought it over to the bed. "Open it up," Granny told her. Bari opened the bag and took out a small white handkerchief with a red ribbon tied around the top of it. She took it out and held it up.

"I want you to keep that," Granny said. "You take good care of it and it will take good care of you. Your momma never cared much about this stuff. She didn't want to know nothin' about it. But don't you shut yourself off from it. You take my posies and use them whenever you need to. They will protect you from evil and bring you all the luck you need."

"Okay, Granny." Bari put the talisman in her pocket. "Can I read you a story? It's your favorite; it's *Mabel the Whale*."

"Of course, baby, that sure is my favorite," said Greta.

Bari settled down on the bed next to Granny and started reading the story to her grandmother. Bari was far too young to understand the power that she had just been given. In her grandma Greta's day, putting posies in your pocket was potent enough to ward off the bubonic plague. And as far as Granny could see, nothing had changed.

one

Brooklyn, New York, 1959

THE SCREAMING BABY woke Hazel up for the second time that night. "Oh, my God," she whispered, "please just let me get at least one hour of sleep. Jesus." Hazel looked over at Jimmy before she got out of bed. He was as still as a dead man as usual, every time the baby cried during the night.

"I hate this," she said, rolling out of bed.

Hazel rushed through the darkness and went next door to the baby's room and quickly gathered him into her arms before his crying woke up everybody else. Even as Hazel held the baby close to her chest and gently patted his back, he continued to cry. She slipped one hand under his diaper to see if he was wet. He wasn't. Hazel paced back and forth frantically trying to quiet the baby.

"What's the matter with you, boy? Don't you know you done already caused more trouble than I ever seen? Lucky for you I can't do nothin' about it." Hazel shook the baby a little harder now. "Come on now; stop cryin', you little devil you. What's the matter with you?" Hazel sniffled. Before long, she was crying right along with the child. "Lord, what's wrong with my baby?" Hazel cried, laying one hand on the child's forehead. The overhead light in the room was suddenly switched on. Hazel nearly jumped out of her skin. "Oh, Momma, you just 'bout scared the mess outta me," she said, turning toward the door to face her mother.

"What are you cryin' for?" Greta asked.

"Momma, I think somethin's wrong with this baby," Hazel said.

"Ain't nothin' wrong with that baby; he's hungry. When was the last time you fed him?" Greta asked.

"I just gave him four ounces of milk not even two hours ago, just like the doctor said."

"That child is four months old, he's big as the dickens, and he's hungry. Give him to me," Greta said, reaching for the baby. "I don't care what them doctors say; I know what my grandbaby needs." Greta gathered the child into her arms and almost immediately his screams lessened to a whimper while his granny carried him down to the kitchen to get a full bottle.

Hazel followed them down the steps. "What would I do without you, Momma? I know I couldn't do this by myself. Thank you for letting Jimmy and me stay here."

"This is your home," Greta said, as she put the baby's bottle in a small pot of water on the stove to warm it. "You don't have to thank me for letting you live here."

"I know, Momma, but we do appreciate it. Even though it's just temporary until we can afford a place of our own."

"Y'all are welcome to stay here for as long as you need to. I just appreciate all the help I get from you with your daddy. That diabetes done tore him up. Them sores on his leg ain't goin' nowhere."

"Talk to him, Momma. Make him listen to the doctors and let them cut off his leg or he's gonna die."

"There ain't no more talkin' to him. You heard your father. He said that cuttin' off his leg would be like cuttin' off his manhood. Said if he couldn't function like a normal person and take care of his family, then he would rather be dead."

"But, Momma . . ."

"Just pray, Hazel; just pray."

Hazel was silent. She stuck her finger into her baby's palm and watched him squeeze it. She looked at his big, round face while he lay on Greta's lap feeding and she couldn't help but see her father's face in his. She couldn't help but think that they should have named him Henry, after her own father, instead of Jimmy's deceased brother Ricky.

With all of Henry's stubbornness, he refused to have his leg cut off. Exactly four months and a day later, he died.

"WHAT ARE WE gonna do now?" Hazel asked Jimmy, one night as they lay in bed after Henry's funeral. "Daddy paid most of the bills and Momma ain't got no money. The little money I bring home from my job ain't gonna help much. And you're havin' such a hard time finding work."

"We'll get by. We'll be all right. At least we'll eat and have somewhere to live."

Hazel reached over and held Jimmy's hand. Finally, he drifted off to sleep.

Hazel couldn't sleep, though. She lay awake in the wee hours of the night, staring at the ceiling. Then she tossed and turned until Jimmy woke up. "Would you lay still?"

"I can't sleep."

"Well, try," Jimmy said, turning over on his side.

"Jimmy, I'm worried about us."

Jimmy didn't answer. He only sighed and stuck his head deeper into his pillow.

Hazel continued to talk. "I don't know how we're gonna get by on just one income."

Jimmy lifted his head up off the pillow and looked at Hazel. "What are you talkin' about, woman? Who said you're gonna be the only one workin'? I'm gettin' up and I'm goin' down to Webber's first thing in the mornin' to see if they're hirin'. But right now all I wanna do is get some sleep."

Jimmy buried his face down into his pillow again.

"Okay, Jimmy," Hazel said quietly. She turned over on her side, facing the wall. Eventually, sometime around sunrise, she fell asleep just as it was time to get up to go to work.

WEBBER'S WASN'T HIRING, and it seemed like nobody else was, either. Jimmy went out every day, and every day a door was slammed in his face. He didn't give up, though. He couldn't. Jimmy was sitting next to Hazel on the living room couch. Hazel had a cardboard box in her lap and a pair of scissors in her hand. She was cutting the cardboard into the shape of a foot.

"See," Jimmy said. "It eats me up inside whenever I think of what my momma and daddy said to me. They told me I had to lie in the bed that I made for myself, without their help. They cut me off, Hazel. I can't go to them, no matter how bad things get. I got somethin' to prove."

"I understand, Jimmy." Hazel stuffed the cardboard inside one of Jimmy's shoes to cover the holes in the sole. "I ain't askin' you to go to them. I'm askin' you if I could get a second job. My job at the airport cafeteria ain't enough."

"I won't hear of it. I'm gonna find work. I *will*."

But seven months later, Jimmy was still looking for work. He scouted every day. But after seven months of not being able to find a job and several months of backed-up bills and mounting stress, Hazel took a second job working at night at the Clean Towels Factory.

"HI, JIMMY," HAZEL said when she walked in the door from working her second job the next day. She was wearing a big smile on her face. "I bought us a treat." It had been a very long time since they had one of those. She held up the brown paper bag with the ice cream in it. When she took the ice cream out of the bag, Jimmy's smile ignited something in her. That night they ate their dinner of pinto beans, fatback, and corn bread. Then they had their ice cream. Hazel cleared up their dessert dishes, then put the baby down to sleep. When she was done she returned to the table. Hazel pushed her chair farther under the table and sat face-to-face with Jimmy. Her smile reappeared but her heart was palpitating.

"What are you grinnin' so much for?" Jimmy asked.

"I ain't really grinnin' like you think I am—I mean I'm really a little nervous."

"Nervous about what?"

"About what you're gonna say."

"What I'm gonna say about what?"

"About our new baby. I'm pregnant, Jimmy."

Jimmy didn't speak. He just stared at Hazel. "A baby?" he said finally. "We're gonna have another baby, another mouth to feed?" Jimmy looked down at his clasped hands. He gritted his teeth, then looked up at Hazel again. "How, Hazel? How in the hell can I be the man I'm supposed to be when you just keep throwin' bricks in my way?"

"Jimmy, I . . ."

Jimmy pounded his fist on the table. Hazel jumped.

"I don't wanna hear it!" Jimmy said. He got up from the table, pushing his chair so hard that it fell backward onto the floor. He stormed through the kitchen. Hazel watched his back as he walked out the room and went through the back room to the enclosed back porch.

Hazel didn't know what to do with herself while she waited for Jimmy to come back into the kitchen. She tried to think of what she would say to him. How she could convince him that they would be okay. It was after ten o'clock when she decided to turn in and wait for him in their bedroom.

IT WAS THE chirping birds and the sunlight filtering through the shades that awakened Hazel the next morning. Jimmy still hadn't come to bed. Hazel got out of bed and went down the stairs and out to the back porch. Jimmy was asleep on the bench. Hazel nudged him awake. "I'll be in in a minute," he mumbled. But by the time Hazel showered and got dressed to leave for work, Jimmy still hadn't come into the house.

It was a sad time in the house. And money was tighter than ever. Especially when the baby was born. Hazel thought that Jimmy would be happy when she named their daughter after his brother Frank, even though she altered the spelling to suit the child's gender. Their daughter would be called Franki.

Jimmy started staying away from home more and more. Hazel didn't mind, though, because it gave her a chance to do what she had to do around the house and tend to the kids without getting on Jimmy's nerves. Hazel and Jimmy used to get away from the house every now and then to visit their friends Butch and Francine, or they would take in a movie. Now they barely spoke. That was because Hazel was at work most of the time and when she did come home either Jimmy was asleep or he wasn't home at all. That's why Hazel was shocked when baby Franki was nine months old and Hazel was pregnant again. She was petrified this time. It took her best friend, Francine, two and a half months to convince Hazel to tell Jimmy.

"What's the worst that could happen?" Francine asked. "He can't kill you."

"I guess you're right," Hazel said, and with the little courage that she managed to muster up, and on the verge of a nervous breakdown, she told Jimmy. A lightning bolt flashed in both her eyes and pain spread over the side of her face when Jimmy slapped her. Hazel was stunned. She couldn't move or speak. She stood there holding her cheek and staring at Jimmy. Her chest heaved up and down while she fought back tears.

"How could you do this! Is this what I gotta do, slap some sense into you? Huh?" Jimmy raised his hand to slap Hazel again. Hazel cowered in fear. Jimmy put his hand down and pushed her instead. Hazel stumbled backward and fell onto the living room couch. Jimmy took a couple of steps back. He was swollen with anger.

"I'm gonna go out now . . . and I don't know when I'm comin' back."

When Hazel saw Jimmy two days later, she didn't know if she smelled him first or saw him first. He was drunk and disheveled as he stumbled through the kitchen and went into the living room and passed out on the couch. Hazel went in behind him after a while. She bent down and untied his shoes and took them off of him. Then she struggled as she lifted his legs and pulled them onto the couch so that he could lie there more comfortably. This would be their routine for the next six months.

Hazel worked her two jobs, coped with the kids, and took care of herself until she gave birth. It was another girl. Hazel named her after Jimmy's baby brother, Barry, who died right before she met Jimmy. Jimmy used to talk about Barry a lot since he missed him so much, so Hazel hoped that this would please him.

Hazel learned how to deal with Jimmy's fits. She kept her mouth shut and agreed with everything he said. That worked for the most part but Hazel worried about her kids. She kept a stiff upper lip and she worked hard. She started to work as many extra hours as she could to earn extra money. Hazel figured that maybe if they had more space to move around in, it would lessen the tension around the house. And so it was set. Hazel had a goal in mind. She would somehow, someway, buy her family a bigger and better house. She scrimped and saved and stretched their meals. She would put wet bread and flour into the ground-beef mixture when she made hamburgers or meat loaf. She put milk or water in the scrambled eggs to make more. Every extra dime went toward her mission.

two

T HE NEW HOUSE was a mess. Hazel and Jimmy Hunter had just finished entertaining every single friend that they could think of to help them celebrate the purchase of their new home. Hazel was tired, but she was happy. It had taken ten long and tumultuous years for her and Jimmy to scrimp and save up enough money to buy their house. Finally, their kids wouldn't have to share the one bedroom that they had anymore. Now they each would have their own room. The kids were growing up fast. Ricky was almost twelve. Franki was nine; and Bari, eight. The bigger they got, the smaller their old place had become. Hazel and the kids had spent hours cleaning the old house before they moved out. They scrubbed the bathroom and the kitchen and mopped the floors in every room. Hazel wiped out cupboards and washed down the woodwork along the base of each wall. Everybody complained. They couldn't understand why they had to clean up a place where they wouldn't be living anymore. Hazel told them that they were doing it because she said so. But she knew the real reason they were doing it was because she didn't want the new owners to think that they were nasty.

The housewarming party had started at 4:00 P.M. It was almost midnight and the party had just ended, which was why Hazel couldn't understand why Jimmy insisted on dragging his running buddy, Frosty, out with him to their usual spot, the Redwood, to play poker like they always did. What she really wanted was for Jimmy to help her clean up the house. Hazel shooed the kids upstairs to wash themselves up and get to bed. "It's my house, so I don't see why I have to go to bed just because Mommy said," Bari complained as she sulked her way up the stairs. Ricky had convinced Bari that since they moved into the house on her birthday their new house belonged to her.

"Well, just because Mommy told us to go to bed doesn't mean we have to go to sleep."

Bari's eyes brightened up and a smile crept across her face as she looked at Franki. That was how it went with the two of them. It never took much for Bari to do whatever it was that Franki wanted her to do. "What do you want to do?"

"I don't know; we could play a game or something."

"What game?"

"I'll think of something. Let's wash up first so Mommy won't yell at us."

"Okay."

When the girls were done, they tiptoed out to the top of the stairs to listen to see if Hazel could hear them. She was somewhere in the back of the house. The girls scurried into Franki's room. They joined their little hands tightly together and slowly they began to swing around and around in a circle.

"THIS FRESH AIR sure smells good. I guess we better take it all in right now, 'cause we're gonna be stuck in that smoky shit hole for a long time," Frosty said. And he was right. Their visits to the Redwood's cellar sometimes lasted at least twelve hours. Jimmy had developed a fierce reputation as "Big Man Jimmy Hunter." Nobody messed with him. He had figured out how to beat the house mercilessly and reap a tremendous payday for him and his buddies on any given night. It wasn't that long ago that he had figured it all out.

One night when Hazel had settled in for the night, Jimmy came home and went straight up to their bedroom. Hazel had just gotten into bed when Jimmy pushed open the door and turned on the light.

"Hazel, are you up?"

"Yeah."

Jimmy walked over to the bed. He looked down at her. His eyes locked with hers for a fleeting moment. He reached into his pocket and pulled out a wad of money. "Here," he said, tossing the money onto the bed.

Hazel sat up, picking up a handful of the bills. "Where did this come from?" she asked, her eyes opened wide.

"I earned it."

"How?"

"Let's just say I finally figured things out."

"What do you mean you finally figured things out?"

"Just keep that safe for me."

Jimmy walked out of the bedroom and went into the bathroom and showered. When Jimmy came out of the shower, Hazel grilled him until he told her that he had been playing poker and that he had figured out a way to mark the cards so that he could win. Hazel didn't like it and she was scared for Jimmy, but she put the money away and kept it safe just like he asked her to do. She added it to the savings that she had already accumulated.

JIMMY AND FROSTY were almost four blocks away from the Redwood. Jimmy was the first one to turn around when a car screeched up behind them. The Redwood's most reputable bouncer, Lopez, had been tailing them. His headlights were turned off. Suddenly the car shifted into high gear, and the headlights were turned on high beam as it drove up onto the sidewalk. The lights blinded them as the car cut them off.

"What the . . . ?" Jimmy said. He was about to reach down into his sock for his knife but he couldn't have done it fast enough.

Lopez jumped out of the car with his gun already drawn. He was a burly, hooked-nosed man dressed all in black with a ponytail. "Put your hands up!" he yelled. "Don't nobody move!"

Jimmy put up his hands. Frosty did, too.

"You Jimmy Hunter?" the man asked.

"Yeah, that's me." Jimmy didn't recognize the man but he had a feeling he was one of Fats' men. Fats owned the Redwood and ran the poker games.

"You and me need to talk." Lopez used his gun to motion Jimmy to step forward.

"All right, all right, take it easy," Jimmy said, easing forward, keeping his hands over his head. "We could talk . . . but whatever this is about, Frosty ain't got nothin' to do with it. It's just you and me." Jimmy knew he would have to think fast and take this guy out. Whatever it was that he wanted to talk about, Jimmy wasn't interested. He took a couple of steps toward Lopez.

"That's close enough," Lopez said. "You're up to somethin', Jimmy. All I wanna know is what you're doin' and I want you to give Fats back the money you been takin' from him and nobody'll git hurt."

Jimmy let out a cynical laugh. "Nobody'll git hurt? Nobody'll git hurt?" Jimmy repeated, still laughing. Suddenly his face hardened. "You threatenin' me! Huh? You threatenin' me?" Jimmy asked, taking two steps forward.

"Stop! Don't make another move or I'll blow your fuckin' brains out!" Lopez said.

Jimmy stopped. "You still threatenin' me, motherfucker? I don't like nobody threatenin' me!"

Jimmy lunged forward, pushing Lopez backward. The gun fell out of his hand and flew into the street. Frosty ran into the street and picked up the gun. He rushed back over to Jimmy and Lopez, keeping the gun pointed at Lopez. Jimmy threw Lopez up against the car and they wrestled to the ground. The chalk cube that marked the cards fell out of Jimmy's pocket and broke in half. His house keys fell out, too. Frosty was braced and ready to jump in if he had to, but Jimmy was in control of the situation. Lopez managed to get back up on his feet but Jimmy was still holding on to him. Jimmy pinned Lopez up against the car; then reached into his sock for his knife. He took out the knife and plunged it into Lopez's stomach, sending him into shock immediately. He fell back onto a parked car. Jimmy tried to pull out the knife but it was stuck in between one of Lopez's ribs. Jimmy braced his foot up on the parked car for leverage, and he yanked it out. Lopez's body slumped to the ground.

"If you're gonna shoot, asshole, shoot." Jimmy kicked away the limp leg that had landed across his foot when Lopez's body fell.

Frosty and Jimmy looked around to make sure that there were no witnesses. Frosty lagged behind Jimmy as they rushed around the corner. Jimmy hadn't noticed it when Frosty picked up the broken cube and slid one-half of it into his pocket. When they were in the clear, Frosty gave the other half of the cube and the house keys to Jimmy. Jimmy put the broken chalk cube into his pocket. He looked at his watch. It was 1:30 A.M.

"Look, we need to make this look good. We're gonna go into the Redwood like nothin' ever happened. I don't know who sent that gorilla after us, but since he won't be around to tell nobody, nobody has to know that it was us that did him in. If anybody asks us about it, we'll deny it. Be natural until this thing blows over. Nobody will suspect us if we still show up as usual."

"Us? What you mean, us?" Frosty said. He laughed nervously when Jimmy ignored him. "I-I'm only jokin'. I don't mean no harm. I gotta hand it to you, though, Jimmy; you are one crazy motherfucker to walk up on a gun like that. You coulda gotten yourself killed. Shit, you could've gotten us both killed!"

"That fool wasn't nothin' but talk. I could see that a mile away. And you know damn well I don't like nobody threatenin' me. I just don't like that shit at all. You go ahead of me. Let's make it look good. I'll be there soon."

THE MUSIC WAS loud and the crowd was thick as usual at the Redwood. It was a chilly Saturday night. The rain had finally subsided but the air was still damp.

Frosty kept a low profile when he walked into the club. His eyes darted around the room at everybody. He was looking to see if anybody was looking at him suspiciously or otherwise. He stood against the wall for a while, and when he was convinced that nobody noticed him he made his way to the bar.

"Hey, hey, Frosty, what's new, cat?" Inky Dink, the bartender, called out to him.

"Ain't no thang. Give me a scotch and water. How are the games?" Frosty asked.

"The games are good," Inky Dink said. He moved in closer to Frosty as he mixed his drink. Inky Dink lowered his voice so that only Frosty could hear him. "You know, I heard that there was some trouble a few weekends ago. They say one of the bouncers, a cat named Lopez, was tailin' some dudes and ended up gittin' offed. Now, I don't know who did it but I sure know that Fats is pretty pissed off. He's lookin' to get revenge."

"Is that right? And they don't know who did it?" Frosty asked.

"Oh, I'm sure Fats has a pretty good idea of who did it but he's keepin' it quiet for now. I guess he's gotta play his cards right. Ha! Ha! Play his cards right. Git it? I'll tell you what, though, I pity whoever did it. Lopez was not only Fats' best bouncer, but from what I hear they was like family . . . real close like."

"Well, then he has my sympathy. I'll see you around, Ink." Frosty downed the rest of his drink; then he got up from the bar stool and made his way through the crowd and down the cellar. Halfway down the stairs, he took the broken white cube from his pocket and rubbed some of the chalk onto his right thumb. In the cellar, Frosty watched the dealer for a few minutes. When a seat became available, Frosty took it. He wasn't nervous anymore. If Fats or any of his gorillas knew who killed Lopez, they would have made a move by now. He was in the clear. Tonight he was going solo. If Jimmy could do it, he could do it. Hell, he could bring the whole goddamn house down if he wanted to. As a matter of fact, he figured he could make as much money as he could before Jimmy got there.

There was no way in the world that Inky Dink could have known that last night Fats and his two most trusted cronies had spent half the night going through every deck of cards. They even used a magnifying glass to see if Jimmy Hunter had done something to the cards. Surely, if Inky Dink had known that he would have told Frosty. But Inky Dink didn't know because Fats didn't tell him. Fats trusted Inky Dink about as far as he could piss. The only reason he kept Inky Dink on the payroll was because he knew how to keep the customers drinking.

The first two rounds were good for Frosty. He pulled his winnings in front of him and didn't take notice when Tiny, the dealer, glared at him.

Frosty played on. Round three was his, too. Frosty was unstoppable.

After three hours, two of the players announced that they were out of cash. Frosty grinned and offered them carfare. They declined. He wasn't about to quit. He was just warming up. Now Frosty knew what Jimmy felt like making people shit bricks. What it felt like to be in control. Frosty remembered being on the losing end. He remembered it clearly. Those days were over now. Right now he was in charge and he was calling his own shots. Hell, he didn't need Jimmy at all. Big Man Jimmy Hunter was just paranoid. Why should he split the pie with Jimmy when he could have it all to himself?

Fats walked over to Frosty's table, stood directly across from Frosty, and gave him a barefaced stare. His eyes were dark and unblinking. Frosty didn't notice Fats at first and when he looked up and nodded in Fats' direction, he didn't nod back. Fats continued to stare Frosty down. Frosty tried to appear cool. He decided to play another round, then call it quits. He didn't like the vibes that he was getting.

When the round ended, Frosty announced that he was out and he went to the bar and ordered himself a scotch and water. He sat at the bar and looked around the room to make sure he wasn't being watched. He ordered another drink and waited. When all was clear, Frosty left the Redwood. He walked out into the night air and welcomed the breeze that touched his face. His eyes were red and burned from the cigarette smoke that had danced around his head all night. Frosty felt good. He fingered the money that was stuffed in his pant pocket. He figured with all the extra cash he could afford to buy Gracie the rabbit fur that she had been asking him for. He could see her face light up when he told her to go shopping for it. That would keep her quiet for a while.

The two men appeared out of nowhere. The bouncers had followed Frosty when he left. They followed him for three blocks; then they caught up with him. They walked up on either side of him. Frosty turned to look at the man on his right side. He was shocked by the dark, wide keloid that crossed from the man's forehead straight through his eye and down across his nose. It was amazing that he had gotten such a slash and his eyeball was still intact. His nose looked like it had permanently swollen from the wound and it never quite returned to its normal state. Frosty likened the man to a monster. The man on Frosty's left was shorter and smaller than he was. He figured he could take the man down easily if he had to.

"This was your lucky night, huh?" the monster asked.

Frosty tried to appear cool. "Yeah, I was pretty lucky, heh, heh."

"Even without your friend?" the smaller man on Frosty's left asked.

"I don't know what friend you're talkin' about."

The smaller man grabbed Frosty by the collar. "Don't try to play dumb with us, man!" He shoved Frosty against the parked car.

"Hey, hey, take it easy, man; what's the problem?" Frosty asked.

"The problem is that one of our friends got killed and we have reason to believe that you and your friend had somethin' to do with it. You wanna tell us what you know about that?" the monster asked.

"See now, you done got yourself the wrong man, 'cause I have no idea what you're talkin' about."

"Oh, you don't know what we're talkin' about? Well, maybe this will jog your memory," said the smaller man. He pulled his gun out from behind his pant waist and pointed it at Frosty's temple, then hit him over the head with the butt. Frosty fell back against the car again. Blood gushed from the side of his head.

"Do you know now? Huh?" The smaller man punched Frosty in the stomach. Frosty doubled over.

"Are you ready to talk now?" the monster asked him.

"I done told you I don't know nothin'," Frosty insisted.

The smaller man took over again. "I think you do know. But maybe you need some more help rememberin'." He gave Frosty a kick to the ribs. Frosty doubled over again. He heard a cracking sound and knew that his ribs were broken. He groaned in agony as he stiffened and grabbed onto his side.

The smaller man punched Frosty in the eye. "Did you say somethin'? I didn't hear you."

"I ain't got nothin' to say." The side of Frosty's mouth was badly cut and his left eye was swollen shut.

It was the monster's turn again. "What about the games? Are you and your buddy pullin' a scam on us? How did you git so lucky? Maybe you could tell us somethin' about that."

Frosty was openly crying now. "How many times do I have to tell you? I don't know nothin', man."

"Maybe you just wanna keep gettin' the shit kicked outta you," the smaller man said.

Breathing was difficult for Frosty. He spoke slowly in between breaths. It was hard to tell where the blood was coming from.

"If you kill me, don't think Big Man Jimmy ain't comin' after you. Jimmy is crazy. He'll take *all* of you down," Frosty threatened.

"Oh yeah?" asked the little man. "If Big Man Jimmy is so tough why don't we give him somethin' to git pissed off about so we could see just how tough he really is."

"You mess with me, you mess with Jimmy." Frosty moaned.

"Yeah, well, I got a message for Jimmy. I'm sendin' him your ass in a body bag," the monster threatened.

"Man, shoot the fucker and get this over with," the smaller man said impatiently.

Both men beat Frosty down to the ground. They used their fists and their feet. When Frosty was on the ground, they stomped him. The smaller man bent down next to Frosty and pounded him in the head over and over again until his skull cracked. Frosty lay there on the ground. Lifeless. A stream of blood had flowed from his mouth as he took his last breath.

The smaller man rifled Frosty's pockets. He found the wad of money in one pocket and the small white peculiar-looking broken cube of chalk in the other pocket. The man stuffed everything into his jacket pocket, and the two of them rushed back toward the Redwood.

ABOUT FORTY MINUTES later, Jimmy Hunter walked into the Redwood. His eyes squinted from the thick smoke that hung in the air. When his eyes adjusted to the darkness in the room, he made his way to the bar.

"Hey, hey, Big Man Jimmy Hunter," Inky Dink called out to him.

"Inky Dink! What's good, man?" Jimmy asked. The men shook hands.

"Ain't nothin'. Scotch on the rocks, right?" Inky Dink didn't wait for an answer. He turned around and fixed the drink for Jimmy.

"Do me a favor, Inky Dink, put that drink on ice for me. I'll be right back. I gotta make a pit stop." When Jimmy turned to head toward the men's room he bumped into Judy. She was standing right behind him on her tiptoes and was just about to kiss him on his neck.

"Hey, baby, I was hopin' you came down here tonight," she said, kissing Jimmy on his lips instead.

"Not right now, Judy." Jimmy waved her off.

"Well, excuse me for livin', I fell out the hearse! I just wanted to tell you that I have reason to believe that your friend is in trouble."

"What friend? What are you talkin' about?" Jimmy asked.

"The white-headed one. He's bein' followed. He left here just about an hour ago."

"Are you sure?" Jimmy had both his hands on Judy's shoulders now.

"Do ducks quack?"

"Thank you." Jimmy kissed her forehead and ran outside through the back door. His eyes darted left and right as he rushed in the direction that he figured Frosty went in. Jimmy saw no sign of Frosty. He focused on the car that was coming up the street toward him. He couldn't see who was driving the car, but he was on his toes just in case he needed to be. The car stopped. Jimmy did, too.

BARI AND FRANKI continued to hold hands and spin around in their circle. *"Ring around the rosy,"* they sang as loud as they could.

"I'm tellin' Mommy!" Ricky yelled at them from his room across the hall.

"So?" Bari and Franki yelled in unison.

"Stop singin' that stupid song!"

"JIMMY HUNTER!" THE man with the ugly scar called out as he climbed out of his car. The smaller man got out on the other side. "You look like you lost somethin'. This look familiar?" The monster was standing at the door of his car holding up the broken chalk cube. "Or maybe you lost a friend. A white-haired little runt? I could show you where his body is."

"You son of a bitch!" Jimmy rushed toward the car, reaching for his .45. He pulled it out and fired a shot. It hit the smaller man in the neck.

"POCKET FULL OF posies." The girls ignored Ricky and continued to sing. *"Ashes, ashes!"* Round and round they went, faster and faster

THE MAN WITH the scar pumped a bullet straight through Jimmy's chest at the same time. Jimmy's body flew backward against a brick building. The man with the scar walked over to Jimmy as he fell.

"This is for Lopez." He pumped bullets into Jimmy point-blank. He stopped shooting when the gun clicked empty.

"ALL FALL DOWN!" Finally, Bari and Franki let go of each other's hands and fell onto the bed dizzy with laughter.

HAZEL WAS IN Ricky's room nursing his cold when the doorbell rang. "Who in the world would be ringin' my doorbell this time of night?" Hazel asked no one in particular. She switched on the hallway light and cautiously walked down the creaky steps to answer the door. She looked through the peephole and didn't recognize the redheaded woman who stood outside her door at first.

"Please, Hazel, open the door. It's me, Judy."

Hazel wasn't going to open the door. Francine had found out about Jimmy's affair with Judy earlier that night at the housewarming party and didn't hesitate to tell Hazel about it. Seeing the red-haired woman at her door brought back all the anger she had felt when she first found out. Hazel pulled open the door. "What the hell are you doin' at my door? You got a lot of goddamn nerve showin' your face here. Get the hell off my property!" Hazel shoved Judy and tried to slam the door.

Judy stumbled backward, then caught her balance and rushed back up to the door to try to keep it from closing. "No, no. You don't understand. I'm here because of Jimmy. Jimmy's dead, Hazel! They shot him and killed him. They killed his friend Frosty, too," she cried.

Hazel froze. It took about a minute for the words to sink in. Her world started spinning all around her. The sickness that formed in the pit of her stomach rose up and gathered in her chest, then in her throat, and it stayed there. Darkness surrounded her. It comforted her when she fell.

three

I T HAD BEEN four days since Jimmy died, and Hazel was still looking haggard and peaked. Her eyes were swollen and red from too much crying, and dark circles appeared around her eyes from not enough sleep. Her body was numb. She no longer had any control over the crying spells. They came on without warning and she wasn't even aware when they stopped. Hazel told herself that she was dead, too, but she was just too damned tired to lie down. Francine held Hazel by the arm as they walked over to the coffin, which was now ready to be lowered into the ground. They each took a turn placing a single rose on the coffin, the kids first, then Hazel, Jimmy's parents, Eva and Jules Hunter, and the rest of the guests. Eva and Jules walked over to Hazel. Eva lightly touched Hazel's arm. "Take care of yourself" was all she said. Jules tipped his hat to Hazel, and together he and Eva walked off toward their car.

Francine kept hold of Hazel's arm as they walked away. Butch caught up with Hazel and Francine as they walked up the narrow path to the waiting limousines. He walked on the other side of Hazel, looping his arm through hers.

"You know me and Francine are here for you," Butch said. "I know Jimmy would want somebody to look out for you and the kids. I owe him a lot."

"I just don't know how I'm supposed to go on with my life without him. He was always here and now he's gone. I can't believe I'm never gonna see him again. We had bad times but we sure had some good times, too. To tell you the truth, I ain't never even had to think for myself. It was all Jimmy. This is just so . . . final." Hazel stopped walking and covered her face with both hands. She couldn't stop her bottom lip from quivering. Butch hugged her and patted her back gently, telling her that everything would be okay. Hazel pulled away from him and tried to straighten herself up. The kids were walking slowly behind them.

"Look at me. What am I doing? I can't let the kids see me like this, I have to be strong for them." Hazel took Butch's hand and squeezed it. "Thank you for being there, Butch. I mean it. And you, too, Francine." Hazel rubbed Francine's arm. The two of them hugged.

A host of people returned to Hazel's house after the funeral. The house had never been so crowded. A few of the sisters from the church had stayed behind at the house to set up the food for everybody. Friends and neighbors brought over all kinds of dishes and flowers in Jimmy's name. Many of them stood around looking sad, while others stood around telling "Jimmy" stories.

Hazel's old friend Ethel Mae had driven all the way from Oklahoma City when she heard the news about Jimmy. Ethel Mae had big, wide eyes with the same dark circles around them that she had way back in high school. They used to call her Raccoon Face. She had the same high-pitched voice, too. She was the one who had voted Hazel and Jimmy most likely to get married when they were in school. As soon as she walked through the door she looked for Hazel.

"I'm so sorry, Hazel. I came as soon as I heard."

"Thank you, Ethel Mae. I'm glad you could make it."

"I want you to know that I feel your loss. Believe me, I know what you're going through. Remember, two years ago this time it was my Russell. It's like it was just yesterday. If you need to talk, call me."

"I'll do that," Hazel said, and they hugged.

Dolly stood behind Ethel Mae waiting for her turn to hug Hazel. Dolly was another friend from another lifetime that Hazel wrote to every now and again.

"You just pray, baby," Dolly said. "And remember that the good Lord will not put upon you any burdens that he don't feel you could handle. You just keep prayin' and he will give you all the strength that you need to cope. Everything is gonna be all right. I just know it is."

"Thank you, Dolly."

Hazel said and did all the things that were expected of her. She felt like she was moving in slow motion. Like she was in a vacuum looking out into a long, dark tunnel with not a flicker of light.

"Where should we put this food, baby?" Ethel Mae was holding on to a dish of shepherd's pie. "It's just a little somethin' to help you out in your time of need, 'cause I know you won't be thinkin' 'bout no cookin' no time soon. You gotta eat, though, Hazel; that's the main thing. You need your strength. If not for you, then for them kids."

"I know, Ethel Mae. I'll have a little somethin' after a while," Hazel said. "You can put the dish right over there on that counter."

"All right, baby," Ethel Mae said, setting the dish on the counter. "Let me say hello to ole Francine over there. I ain't seen that child in ages. Is that ole Bo Willy over there? Bo Willy who played on the football team at Manchester? I thought he was dead! You know it's a shame folks don't get to see each other until somebody dies. Um, um, um," Ethel Mae said, and headed across the room.

"That's the truth," Dolly said to Hazel when Ethel Mae walked away. "People don't realize that you never know when your final hour is near. You just never know when the Almighty Father is gonna call you home. We need to have more happy times while we're livin' so's we can all enjoy them together."

"That's the truth," Hazel said. "Tomorrow night we'll be doing the same thing for Frosty."

BUTCH LOOKED SOLEMNLY at each of the men standing in the corner of the room holding empty glasses. He took his time filling each glass with Dewar's White Label. As Butch started to speak, the group became silent.

"I'm sure none of us is ever gonna forget Big Man Jimmy. Jimmy was like the brother I never had. He ain't with us no more physically, but I know his spirit will always be here. And I know he would want to join us in this drink that we're about to have. I believe I speak for all of us when I say we're gonna miss you a hell of a lot, Jimmy. I know my life won't be the same without you. So, this one's for you. May you rest in peace and may God bless you." Butch poured an extra drink, then turned and poured it into the corner of the room. "Drink up, buddy." They all toasted.

———

UPSTAIRS, IN HAZEL'S bedroom, Franki and Bari sat on the bed watching Ricky, who was sitting on the trunk across the room holding a pair of Jimmy's shoes.

"I wish Daddy could come back," said Bari. "Why did he have to die?"

"I knew somebody was gonna die. I told you not to sing that stupid song. I told you so! Daddy is dead and buried. He ain't never comin' back." Ricky angrily tossed the shoes onto the floor. His chances of getting closer to his father were gone forever. He knew that. Franki and Bari looked at each other. They didn't know what to say or think.

"He's probably with God by now," Franki said.

"Or maybe he's with Granny. At least he'll have somebody to talk to." Bari looked down and slowly wrung her hands.

"Come on. Let's go see if Mommy needs help," Ricky said, and the two of them followed him downstairs.

"DID WE KILL Daddy?" Bari whispered to Franki on the way down the stairs.

"I hope not," Franki whispered back.

"What about Mr. Frosty?" Bari whispered again.

"We didn't kill nobody." That's what Franki told her but she didn't believe her. In Bari's heart and her mind she had killed her father. Whether Franki wanted to accept it or not and no matter what anybody said or how many times they tried to convince her otherwise, Bari was convinced that she was the cause of her father's death.

DOWNSTAIRS, HAZEL WAS saying good-bye to the last of the guests. Francine, Gracie, and Butch were just about to leave.

"Look, Hazel," said Francine. "I'll be more than happy to stay the night if you want me to. You shouldn't be alone."

"Thank you, Francine, but that's okay. I won't be alone. The kids are here. I'll be all right. You go home and spend time with your family. I'll call you soon." The women hugged.

"If you're sure," Francine said, pulling away.

"Hazel, you take it easy now, baby, you hear?" Gracie hugged her tightly. "I'll see you tomorrow at Frosty's funeral. But if you ain't up to it, I'll understand."

"I'll be up to it, Gracie. You know I'll be there for you. And I know it was hard on you to be here today, but I appreciate your comin'. Thanks so much for everything. I mean it." They hugged.

Butch stepped forward and held Hazel long and hard. His face was buried in her hair as he spoke. "You'll be all right, baby girl. I promise you. I'll look out for you. I'll be around." He turned to look at Hazel's children, who were standing behind him. "Y'all git over here and give ole Uncle Butch some sugar!"

Franki and Bari walked up to him. He hugged them tightly and then gave each one of them a big, wet suck on the cheek. The girls hated when he did that but Hazel had always told them to be polite. The minute Uncle Butch turned away to speak to Ricky, the girls wiped their cheeks with the backs of their sleeves.

"Come here, Ricky." Butch shook Ricky's hand and didn't let it go until he was done speaking to him. "You have to be the man around here now. You have to look out for your momma and your little sisters. Can you do that for me?"

"Yeah, I'm gonna look out for them."

Butch let go of his hand. "Good. And I want all of you to know that if something ain't right, I don't care what it is, you call me and I'll be right here. Hazel, are you sure you don't want Francine to stay the night?"

"I'm sure, Butch. Thank you."

"Well, to tell you the truth, I was kinda hopin' that I could get rid of her for a little while." Butch chuckled.

Francine gave him a playful hit on his head. Hazel managed a smile. Finally, they left and the family was alone for the first time since Jimmy died. For days, people had been coming and going, expressing their sympathy and hanging around the house eating and talking. Hazel looked all around the room at the half-empty food trays and the food spills on the table and on the floor. When the guests had offered to clean up, Hazel refused them. But now, looking at the mess, all of a sudden she felt overwhelmed.

"Don't worry, Mommy, we'll clean up for you. Do you wanna lay down?" Ricky asked.

"In a minute. Are y'all okay?" Hazel slumped down onto the couch and slipped back into her numb state.

"Yeah, Mommy, we're okay," Bari answered for all of them.

Hazel reached over and gathered her daughters into her arms. Ricky walked over to them and softly rubbed his mother's hair. Hazel stood up. She looked each one of her children in the eye. She could see all the questions that they had. Questions that would probably never be answered. She wanted to tell Ricky that Jimmy really did love him, but then she really wasn't so sure about that herself. All she knew was that she would miss her husband immensely and that she'd rather take the beatings that he gave her than not have him there with her raising their kids. From the very beginning he had directed her, commanded her. Now she was left to handle everything on her own. Where would she begin? She wanted to tell her children so many things.

"Do you think y'all can handle this mess?" That was all that Hazel could come up with to say to them.

"Of course we can. Don't worry."

"Okay, I won't worry. Thank you, my big man." Hazel touched Ricky's face. "I'll be in my room if you need me. Are y'all okay?" Hazel asked again. The children nodded in unison.

The stairs seemed to rise up at Hazel as she climbed them. She had to blink quickly several times to regain her focus. She thought it would be just a matter of time before she died from exhaustion.

INSIDE HER BEDROOM, Hazel closed the door and stood with her back against it. She reached up to the hook behind the door and took down Jimmy's house robe. She hugged the robe tightly to her and put it to her nose; then she put it on. As she tied the belt on the robe, she crossed the room and sat on the bed.

"Oh, God, Jimmy . . . what am I supposed to do now?" She clutched the robe tighter to her. "I'm so scared! Why, Lord?" Hazel lay back on the bed and slowly drew her legs up to meet her chest. Lying in fetal position, she hugged her knees tightly as the tears flowed down her face.

"Oh, God, it hurts so bad. It hurts so bad, Lord."

The kids could hear Hazel all the way downstairs. They stopped cleaning the kitchen and stood at the bottom of the steps and listened to their mother cry.

"Well, at least Daddy can't hit Mommy no more," said Bari.

four

1978

I T WAS A misty September morning. The rain had finally stopped
falling after three straight days, and now it was damp and chilly outside.

The duffel bag Ricky carried was just about the length of his body
and twice his width. Hazel watched Ricky walk before her as they entered the JFK check-in area. She couldn't get over how strong and
handsome he had become. He certainly looked like the Hunter men
now, she thought. When she looked at him from certain angles he was
the spitting image of Jimmy. Ricky had shot up to five-eight and was
lean but muscular. He didn't take on the build of the Hunter men, but
he was just as handsome and maybe just as smart.

It had been seven years since Jimmy died and ever since then Ricky
had taken charge of the family. Hazel had quit her job at the airport
cafeteria and was now only working at the Clean Towels Factory. Ricky
had helped her out by getting a part-time job. He had looked after
Hazel and his sisters just as he'd promised, and now he was moving on
to start his own life.

"I don't know what would make a handsome, young, talented man
go off and join the Navy, but I guess there's nothin' I can do about it."

"No, Ma. There's nothin' you or anybody else could do about it. I
gotta do this."

"I know. I'm just sorry that the girls couldn't see you off, too. They
were pretty upset that they couldn't come."

"I didn't expect them to miss school. Especially since it just started.

Anyway, I'm gonna see you all again sooner than you think. I'm plannin' on gettin' home as often as I can."

Hazel knew he was just trying to reassure her. She could even tell that he was trying to smile and look happy. The truth was that she knew that there was something missing in Ricky's life. She had watched him and she could feel it. It seemed like when Jimmy died, Ricky lost his foundation, whatever it was worth. Hazel never did understand the last encounter Ricky had had with his father before he died.

JIMMY HAD BEEN out at the Redwood for several hours. He was winning too much too fast, so he decided to take a break.

"I'm gonna have a smoke," he announced. He smoked only when he was hustling. He left the table and went to the back of the room, to the telephone booth. Jimmy dialed his house. He covered one ear so that he could hear over the noise. The phone rang twice before Hazel picked up.

"Hazel, it's me."

"Hi," Hazel said, clearing her throat.

"Were you sleepin'?"

"Yeah, I was sleepin', it's after eleven o'clock."

"Are the kids sleepin', too?" Jimmy asked.

"I don't know. Why? What do you want?" Hazel asked.

"What's the matter?" he asked, noting the annoyance in her voice. Hazel didn't answer him, so he continued to speak. "I need Ricky to come down here to get some of this money off me."

"What? Are you crazy? I ain't sendin' that boy outta here this time of night to meet you at some bar to get money from you. You must be drunk."

"Goddammit, woman! You baby that boy too much. That's why he acts like a goddamn sissy. He's almost thirteen years old. It's time he starts actin' like a man. Now, I need him to bring his ass down here to git this goddamm money off me, and I ain't gonna say it no more. I ain't askin' you, I'm tellin' you!"

Hazel sighed heavily. "Are you at the Redwood?"

"Yeah."

"I'll put him in a cab." Hazel said.

"That's more like it." Jimmy slammed down the phone.

"WHAT DO YOU want, son?" the bouncer asked Ricky when he showed up at front door of the Redwood.

"My dad told me to meet him down here." Ricky said.

"Looks to me like your dad should be seeing to it that your little young ass is in bed this time of night. Now do me a favor and take your little narrow ass home 'cause you can't come in here. Go home to your momma, boy." The bouncer attempted to shut the door, but Ricky pressed his shoulder up against it to keep it from shutting. The bouncer yanked the door wide open, then bent down to stand eye-to-eye with Ricky.

"Son, I done already told you to go home and I ain't about to tell you again. Now git going before I beat your little ass myself!"

"I told you my father wanted me to meet him down here! Don't make me have to tell him that you wouldn't let me come in," Ricky said, defiantly.

The bouncer laughed. "I don't give a damn who you tell. Who in the hell is your daddy anyway? Ha! Ha!"

"My daddy is Jimmy. Big Man, Jimmy Hunter, that's who!"

"Big Man, Jimmy Hunter?" The bouncer stopped laughing. "Well, why in the hell didn't you just say so from the git-go? Git yo' little ass in here, boy. Your daddy is downstairs in the cellar. Go on down."

When Ricky reached the bottom of the steps and stood there looking around nervously, Jimmy noticed Ricky's hesitance and motioned him over.

"Let me talk to my boy. Find me later." Jimmy said to Judy. Judy slid off the barstool and sauntered away.

"You got here fast. You took a cab?" Jimmy asked Ricky when the boy reached him.

"No, Pop, I caught the crosstown bus."

"I thought your mother was puttin' you in a cab."

"I didn't want to git in a cab. I wasn't worried about nothin'. I was just glad to be gettin' out. I wasn't doin' nothin' but watchin' television."

"I keep tellin' your mother to let you grow up. You stay underneath her too damned much. You need to git out of the house, away from her and those little girls," said Jimmy.

"There ain't nothin' else to do," Ricky said, looking down at his shoes.

"I'm sure you could find somethin' to do besides hangin' around them. Ain't you got a girl yet? That's what you need."

Ricky blushed. "No, Pop. I ain't got a girl yet."

"Let's get outta here." Jimmy led Ricky into a small dark room in the back of the club. He pulled the heavy red velvet curtain shut behind them and flicked on the light. The red lightbulb barely gave off enough light for them to see in front of them. Jimmy sat down on the wicker couch and took out a huge wad of money from his pocket. He carefully counted some of the bills and handed them to Ricky, then put the rest of the money back into his pocket. He would have to give Butch and Frosty their share later.

"Here, I want you to put this in your sock," Jimmy told him. Ricky's eyes widened at the size of the stack of money as he took it from Jimmy. He lifted his pant leg and stuffed the money into his sock, then pulled the sock up as high as he could then pulled his pant leg back down. Ricky and Jimmy both examined the leg to make sure that the money wasn't bulging out where it could be noticed.

"I don't have to tell you to go straight home, do I?" Jimmy asked.

"No, Pop."

"I mean, don't you stop for *nobody*, you hear me?"

"Yeah, Pop, I hear you."

"I'll put you in a cab." They went up the stairs and headed toward the front door of the bar.

The bouncer winked at Ricky as he followed Jimmy out onto the street. Ricky winked back. Jimmy put him in a cab right outside of the bar.

Ricky was six blocks away in the cab when he took the money out from his sock. He put the wad up to his nose and inhaled it. He flipped through each bill, smiling to himself. The cabby drove along Ogden Avenue, the busiest strip downtown. The night buzzed with life. The air was warm, thick, and still. When the car stopped at the red light, a woman in an extremely low-cut halter top, miniskirt that stopped at the top of her thighs, and fishnet stockings held up by a visible garter belt approached the cab. She stuck her face into the half-open back-seat window where Ricky was sitting.

"I'm Candy. How you doin' tonight, baby? You wanna have a good time?"

"Wha-what do you mean?" Ricky asked.

"I mean, I'll take you around the world and back for only twenty dollars. What do you say?"

"Wha-what do I have to do?" he asked.

"Just follow me and I'll take care of everything else." said Candy.

Ricky stuffed the money back into his sock. He hesitated at first. He thought about Jimmy for a moment. What would his father do in this situation? Would he go with the woman?

Ricky handed his fare to the driver and got out of the cab. He kept looking behind him as he followed the hooker across the street through an alley and up to a third-floor flat. They entered a very small room. The only furniture was a full-sized mattress on the floor in one corner of the room and a steel folding chair in the other corner with clothing draped over it. Considering how warm it was outside, the room was surprisingly cool.

The hooker started to take off her clothes right away. When she finished undressing, she turned to face Ricky. Ricky was standing with his back against the wall. He was scared to death of everything. He had no clue what to do.

"Now, I know you ain't gonna tell me that this is your first time, are you?" Candy asked him.

Ricky smiled nervously and started to pull at his belt buckle.

"Well, that's all right with me. Here, let me help you with that. Don't worry. You're about to learn one of the most valuable lessons that you'll ever have to learn in your life. And you're in luck 'cause it just so happens that I'm a good teacher and I get the feelin' that you're gonna be a fast learner."

Ricky smiled at her now. When the hooker unzipped his pants, he quickly stepped out of them, taking off his socks at the same time and rolling them up into his pants. He tucked them in the corner of the room where he could keep an eye on them.

The hooker reached down and squeezed Ricky's half-erect penis, then took a step back and watched his reaction.

Ricky's eyes rolled to the back of his head. She squeezed him again and felt his young, hard body tremble. Ricky would never forget her.

———

THE FOLLOWING MORNING when Hazel was done making breakfast, the smell of pork bacon, eggs, and hominy grits permeated the
whole house. Hazel was setting the table. Jimmy put down his news-
paper.

"Did Ricky make it home okay with that money I gave him last
night?" he asked.

"I guess he did." Hazel's voice sounded ice cold.

"You guess he did? I sent him home last night with fourteen hundred bucks. I just wanted to make sure he made it home okay."

"He made it home okay but you didn't send him home with no fourteen hundred. You sent him home with one thousand three hundred
and eighty dollars. I counted myself."

"Don't tell me what I sent. I sent fourteen hundred. Where is the
money?" he asked.

Hazel went to the cupboard and from the top shelf she took out the
empty hominy grits box that she used as a hiding place for the family
savings. She took the stack of money out of the box and put it on the
table in front of Jimmy. Jimmy counted it. He counted $1,380. He fig-
ured he made a mistake so he counted it again, this time putting the
money in individual stacks of one hundred. He had thirteen stacks
with eighty dollars left over.

"I counted this money before I gave it to that boy and I know for a
fact that it was fourteen hundred dollars. What the hell happened?
Where is that boy? I'll kill him!"

Jimmy knocked over his chair as he jumped up from the table. He
went over to the basement door and yelled down the stairs.

"Ricky! Get your ass up here right now!"

"Now take it easy, Jimmy. No need gittin' yourself all worked up
over nothin'," Hazel said.

"That little son of a bitch stole money from me and you could fix
your mouth to say I'm gittin' myself worked up over nothin'? Ricky!" he
yelled again.

Ricky came into the kitchen. "Yes, Pop?" Ricky's voice trembled.

"Come here, boy," Jimmy commanded. Ricky silently followed his
father into the den. He knew what this trip meant but he had no idea
what he did wrong this time.

Jimmy unhooked the thick, black leather belt from his waist and took it off as he walked. Ricky hated the den. It was where his father vented all of his anger, usually on him, right there in the den. He had grown to hate the very smell of the den. He hated his grandmother's and grandfather's accusing eyes that stared at him from the pictures on the wall. They were always there watching him as he took his licks. Were they mad at him, too? What had he ever done to them?

Ricky rubbed his hands on his pants to dry away the perspiration. His heart pounded so loudly inside his chest that he could hardly hear his father when he finally turned to speak to him. "Where is my money? I sent you home with fourteen hundred dollars to give to your mother. I just counted the money and I'm counting only thirteen eighty. You tell me what happened to the rest of the money. Did you steal from me?"

"N-no Pop. I-I didn't steal from you."

"Well, it didn't just disappear into thin air. Where is it?" Jimmy asked.

Ricky took a deep breath. He knew that this would be the day that he would die.

"S-see, Pop, what happened was . . . well, I know you said—"

"Spare me the bullshit, boy! What happened to my money?"

"See, there was this lady. She came up to the cab . . . and she said if I p-paid her, she would—"

"Are you tellin' me that you spent my money on a whore?"

"Y-yeah, Pop. I-I guess you could say that. . . ."

"You spent my money on a whore?" Jimmy asked again.

"Yeah." Ricky's hands dug deep into his pockets. His eyes stayed on the tips of his shoes. Jimmy slowly sprouted a smile. He playfully punched Ricky in the chest.

"That's my boy!" Jimmy said. Ricky was hesitant at first, but he smiled, too. Jimmy put his arm around Ricky's shoulder and they both walked back into the kitchen. Jimmy picked up his chair and sat back down at the table and went back to reading his paper. Ricky went back downstairs to the basement. Hazel stood at the stove with her hands on her hips facing Jimmy. Jimmy said nothing.

"Well?" she asked, finally, when she couldn't stand it anymore.

"Well, what?" Jimmy asked.

"Well, what happened to the money?"

"Oh, everything is fine. We worked it out. I probably miscounted."
Jimmy never looked up from his paper.

FOR THE FIRST time in his life, Ricky had felt like maybe Jimmy was
starting to see him as a man. For the first time, they had shared in
something. Now, Jimmy was gone, and he was leaving, too.

"All the men in my life are gone now," Hazel said.

"Don't say that, Mommy. You're making it sound like I'm dead or I
ain't never comin' back."

"I just wish you wouldn't go." Hazel avoided her son's eyes as she
tried to blink back her tears. "Who am I gonna talk to now?"

"I told you, I'll write every week. I promise. Besides, you still have
Franki and Bari to talk to."

"It won't be the same."

"C'mere, Ma." Ricky set his duffel bag on the ground and hugged
his mother. "Stop worryin'. Everything is gonna be all right." Ricky
slowly rubbed Hazel's hair while he held her. Hazel pulled herself out
of his embrace and started walking again. Ricky picked up his duffel
bag and followed her.

"I'll be making good money and I've already filled out the papers so
that a part of my salary goes to you every month," Ricky told her.

"Look, Ricky, you're nineteen years old and I know you wanna get
out there and see the world. And I want you to do that, too. It's just
that I'm your mother, and this is what mothers do; we worry. So you
just let me worry and I'll just let you go. Okay?" Hazel dabbed at the
corners of her eyes to wipe away the tears that had formed there.

"My plane should be boarding soon. I gotta get my bag checked.
Well, I guess this is good-bye for now."

Ricky put down his bag again and gathered his mother into his
arms. They held on to each other for as long as they could. Hazel
squeezed her son so tightly, her body trembled. She got in step with
him as he hurried toward the security checkpoint. Hazel's tears flowed
now. She didn't bother to wipe them away. She knew that they
wouldn't be stopping anytime soon.

Ricky walked through the scanner. He kept walking and looking
back every now and again waving to his mother. Finally, he was out of
her sight.

Hazel stood there even after Ricky was gone. Suddenly she felt ten years older than she actually was. She had noticed the new lines around her eyes and her mouth recently, and she was just plain old tired. The past few years hadn't been easy at all with Jimmy gone. She had grown used to the money that Jimmy was bringing in more than she realized. It was hard trying to live without it. Hazel had gone back to cutting corners on their meals and sewing her own clothes. Now Ricky was gone and she felt like she had just been stabbed in her heart.

BARI RUSHED HOME after school as she always did. She was sixteen years old, a junior and an honor student at Patterson High. She had emerged into a pretty, wholesome-looking girl. Her hair was long and thick just like Hazel's and the same flawless nut-brown skin. Her eyes sparkled when she smiled, and her dimples went deep. She carried a full workload and still managed to be involved in almost everything extracurricular. She was a smart girl and she looked even smarter when she wore her glasses. It didn't bother her that she wasn't considered one of the cool kids in school. Nor did she care how many nerd names Franki and her friends called her. Bari enjoyed her classes. She enjoyed studying and she liked being able to match wits against the other students in the school who were considered to be among the brightest.

Bari was excited because she had been picked to join the school debate team. She couldn't wait to get home to tell Hazel. Bari started trotting when she saw the city bus coming. She dug for her bus pass while she trotted. By the time she reached the corner, she still hadn't found the pass, and the bus pulled off. She stood at the bus stop right outside of Helene's coffee shop taking her belongings out of her book bag, one by one, looking for the pass. When Bari was convinced that the bus pass was lost she went inside the coffee shop to get change for the bus. Helene's coffee shop was crowded with students, the cool ones. It was where they gathered every day after school and sometimes during lunch when they were able to sneak off the school grounds. Anybody else who happened to be in the coffee shop was there simply because they loved Helene's famous cheeseburger with sautéed onions on a toasted sesame seed bun and vanilla egg cream deal.

Bari didn't notice Franki in the coffee shop until she called out to her. She could hardly see her sister's face for the cloud of cigarette smoke that circled her head. Franki had grown to be an attractive girl, too. She had wide almond-shaped eyes and olive-colored skin. Unlike Bari, Franki kept her hair cut close to her head. She had a thin frame with a nice figure.

Bari walked to the back of the restaurant where Franki was sitting. She barely spoke to Franki's friends. She leaned in very close to Franki so that nobody could hear her. "What are you doing smoking? I thought you said you were gonna stop," Bari said.

"I did stop. I'm just doing this right now just because." Franki let out a mouthful of smoke. She fanned it away from Bari's head.

Bari fanned the smoke, too. "Just because your friends are doing it? Is that why you're doing it? You know what smoking does to you and your lungs and your teeth. And it makes your whole body stink."

"All right, all right, I get your point." Franki crushed the cigarette into the aluminum ashtray. "Whose body is this anyway?" Franki sucked in as much wind as she could, then let it out, looking at her friends and rolling her eyes toward the ceiling.

"Franki, I'm only trying to help you." Bari was standing erect now. "Anyway, I'll see you at home," Bari said, turning to head toward the door.

"Wait for me, Miss Do Right; I'm goin' home, too." Franki picked up her belongings and followed Bari out of the coffee shop. They boarded the M14 eastbound city bus.

"Oh, my God, I never got my change for the bus," Bari said when the bus door closed.

"I'll pay for you." Franki showed the driver her pass, then dug in her pockets for change for Bari. "You owe me fifty cents."

"Yeah, yeah, yeah," Bari said as they walked to the back of the bus.

Franki's classmate Dominick was sitting in the very last seat on the bus, looking out the window when they came on.

"What's happenin', Dominick?" Franki asked. She and Bari took the two seats directly across from him.

"Hey, what's happenin'?" Dominick asked. He took a minute to look Bari over. Dominick sported a six-inch Afro and black-rimmed eyeglasses. Beyond the acne, he was a good-looking boy. A little overweight but good-looking.

"Who's your friend?" he asked.

"This is my sister: Bari."

"Hi, Bari. You're pretty."

"Thank you," Bari said, and looked away. She kept her ears cocked, though.

"Did you hear? The Breland twins are giving a hooky party to welcome in the new school year," Dominick told Franki.

"When? Where?" Franki asked, a little too excited. "The twins give the *best* hooky parties."

Bari shot Franki a look.

"At least I *heard* that they give the best parties," Franki corrected herself.

"Will I see you there?" Dominick asked Franki, but he was openly staring at Bari.

"Who, me? No, you won't see me there," Franki said, winking at him.

"Well, just in case you change your mind, it starts at ten tomorrow morning at the twins' house. And don't forget to bring your beautiful sister if you come." Dominick signaled for his stop; then he got off the bus. Bari decided that she hated Dominick.

"He likes you. I could tell," Franki said when Dominick was gone.

"I don't care if he likes me or not. You can tell him for me that I don't like rude, fat boys."

"Dominick's not fat; he's cuddly. Besides, you should be glad that somebody's paying you some attention. All you do is keep your head stuck in those books. Do you plan on doin' that for the rest of your days?"

"Speaking of plans, I hope that you're not planning on going to that hooky party," Bari said.

"I didn't say that I was goin' to any hooky party."

"You didn't say it, but I know you were thinking it."

"Oh, you read minds, too? I'm impressed," Franki said sarcastically.

"Come on, Franki; swear you're not going to that hooky party."

Franki crossed her heart. "I swear."

Bari was satisfied. "Did I tell you that I was selected for the debate team?"

"Whoop-de-do," Franki said in the most deadpan voice that she could conjure up.

HAZEL WAS JUST about done cooking dinner later on that night. She
had been at it for about an hour and a half.

"Have you seen the dictionary, Mommy?" Bari asked, poking her
head into the kitchen.

"No, I haven't seen it. But then again, I don't use it; you and Franki
do. Where did you put it last?"

"Mommy, if I knew that, I would know where it is, wouldn't I?"
Bari laughed.

"Don't get smart with me. Go ask Franki where it is. She keeps her
room cluttered with everything else. Maybe she has the dictionary in
there, too."

Bari walked down the hallway to Franki's room. She stopped short
just outside the door when she heard Franki laughing with somebody
on the telephone.

"Believe me, Regina, everybody who's anybody at our school and at
Wendel High is gonna be at this party. I can't wait!" Franki paused to
take a sip of her Coke. She broke out laughing from something that
Regina said. When Bari burst into the room, the Coke can fell over as
Franki was setting it on the dresser.

"Reg, I gotta go." Franki slammed down the receiver, then quickly
grabbed a T-shirt to wipe up the spilled soda.

"Don't you know how to knock on a door?" Franki asked, annoyed.

"I heard what you were saying. You were talking to Regina and
you're planning on goin' to that hooky party!"

"You don't know what you're talkin' about."

"I do know what I'm talking about."

"No, you don't."

"Then why don't you tell me?"

"Because it's none of your business."

"Well, I guess if that's not what you were talking about, then it
would be okay for me to yell out loud about the hooky party because
you don't have anything to hide from Mommy."

"If you feel like you need to do that, go right ahead."

Bari went to the door opening and spoke loudly so that Hazel could
hear her downstairs. "The hooky party should be a whole lot of fun!
Hooky party! Hooky party!" Bari yelled.

Franki leaped across the bed and pulled Bari into the room and shut the door. "All right, all right, I'll tell you."

"I'm listening." Bari sat at the edge of the bed with her arms folded across her chest, waiting patiently while Franki stalled.

"Well, what do you want to know?"

"I want to know everything; tell me everything."

"Okay, but first you have to tell me one thing."

"What?"

"Why do you want to know? Do you wanna go?"

"Why in the world would I want to go to a hooky party?"

"Hmmm, let me guess—because you're curious?" Franki smirked.

"I just think you're gonna get yourself into trouble."

"As far as I can see it, the only way that I can get into trouble is if Mommy finds out. And there's only one way she could find out." Franki eyed Bari.

Bari waved her off. "What about your classes?"

"What about 'em?"

"You're really gonna skip school and go to a party?"

Franki sighed. She threw herself down onto her bed with her arms stretched high above her head. "Yes, Bari. If the truth must be known, I'm gonna skip school and go to a party. Not just any party, a hooky party hosted by the Breland twins. That's my plan. Any more questions?"

"Well, what do you do at those parties?"

"We just have a whole bunch of fun."

"Really?" Bari had a wide grin on her face.

"Seriously, I kinda think that you do wanna go. Why don't you just admit it? Plus, I know you want to see Fat Boy again," Franki teased.

"Don't even joke like that."

"Look, Bari, if you feel you want to come then it's okay; you can come."

"I never said I wanted to come," Bari said defensively.

"Unless, of course, you think you might be just a little too nerdy to fit in. . . ."

"I don't think I'm nerdy at all, and I could fit in anywhere. I don't care what you say." Bari got up from the bed and walked over to the dresser and studied her face in the mirror.

Franki walked over and stood behind her. "Look, Bari, if you would just let down your hair once in a while." Franki removed the pins from Bari's hair that held her bun together. Bari's hair fell to her shoulders. "And take off these glasses." Franki removed Bari's glasses, picked up a comb from the dresser, and pulled it through her sister's hair a few times. "See? Look how much sexier you look already. Now you look like you could be related to me."

Bari smiled. "That does look kind of nice, doesn't it?"

"Of course it does. And hold on a minute." Franki went over to her closet and took down a short close-fitting rose-colored knit dress and handed it to Bari. "Put this on."

Bari put the dress on; then she put on the ruby red lipstick that Franki pressed into her hand.

"Oh, my goodness, who is this sexy lady?" Franki teased.

"Shut up."

"Okay, so will you come?"

"Will I come where?"

"Don't try to play dumb with me; you know what I mean. To the hooky party."

"All right, I'll come. But it's only so I can watch out for you."

"Yeah, right." Franki laughed.

"But wait. I can't let Mommy see me leaving the house dressed this way."

"Must I teach you everything?" Franki asked, rolling her eyes up to the ceiling. "Take off the dress." She impatiently held out her hand to Bari.

Bari took off the dress and gave it to her.

"Look, dummy, you take your books out of your school bag and you put your clothes in instead." Franki stuffed the dress into her school bag to demonstrate. "You close the bag, then you wave good-bye to your mother." Franki slung the school bag over her shoulder. "Then you head for the garage and you do what we call the 'quick change.' That's when you put on your little sexy number and your makeup. Then you go to your homeroom class to sign in. After that, we'll meet on the side street where we hook up with a few other people that are goin' to the party. It's all very simple."

"But aren't you afraid of getting caught?"

"Caught? No, never. Stick with me, kid. I'll get you places."

"Yeah. All the wrong places. I must be crazy."

THE NEXT MORNING Franki and Bari were all dressed for school. They sat at the breakfast table as usual before leaving the house. Bari found it hard to eat. She was a nervous wreck. She stared at her food for the most part and pushed it from one side of the plate to the other. What little she did eat may as well have been cardboard. Bari couldn't taste anything. She wouldn't have bothered to eat at all if it hadn't been for Franki convincing her that it was important for them to act normal.

Franki packed in her food as usual. "Do you want your bacon?" she asked Bari.

"Help yourself," Bari answered. She couldn't understand how Franki could be so calm.

When they were done eating, they picked up their book bags and headed for the door.

"Have a nice day, Ma." Bari's heart was beating so loudly in her chest that she could have sworn that her mother could hear it, too.

"Okay, y'all be good now," Hazel called behind them.

The girls walked out of the house. They kept looking back at the kitchen window when they got outside. They could see Hazel moving around by the sink just behind the curtains, inside the house. The moment Hazel closed the curtains and moved away from the window, the girls made a mad dash for the garage. They rushed inside and changed their clothes. When the garage door opened again, they came out fully dressed in their party gear.

Hazel thought she heard the garage door open and close, but she knew she had to be hearing things.

five

THE BRELAND TWINS' house was already crowded. Their house was located on a curvy street on what was known as the Hill. Many a location scout had found his or her way to the hill to use one house or another for the silver screen. The houses were huge inside and out, with twelve-foot cathedral ceilings, and had hard oak-finished floors and huge picture windows.

Malcolm and Maurice placed two large garbage pails full of ice and beer in the kitchen. The twins were identical. You could tell them apart, though, because Maurice had a shadow of a birthmark on his left cheek. They had filled bowls with potato chips and popcorn and placed them on tables and ledges and windowsills throughout the living room. Several couples were draped over the couch and standing along the walls hugging and kissing.

The twins were in the kitchen making the party punch. Maurice was adding the liquor to the punch bowl. He stopped pouring the liquor almost immediately after he started.

"What are you stoppin' for?" Malcolm asked.

"We don't wanna use all of Pop's liquor."

"Man, he won't even miss it. There's plenty more where that came from."

"Yeah, but we don't wanna be getting people drunk, do we?" Maurice asked, twisting the top back onto the bottle.

"I figure like this: If people don't wanna get drunk, then people shouldn't drink. Come on, man; pour some more liquor."

Maurice reopened the bottle and poured some more liquor but stopped again immediately after he started.

"Man, what's your problem?" Malcolm asked. He grabbed hold of the bottle while it was still in Maurice's hand and turned it upside down over the bowl, forcing Maurice to pour more.

"Come on, man; that's enough!"

"Gimme the goddamn bottle." Malcolm snatched the bottle and poured the liquor nonstop into the bowl. "You sure can't send a boy to do a man's job," he said when he was done. The liquor bottle was practically empty when Malcolm stopped pouring. Malcolm stirred the punch, then poured himself a sip to taste it. "Ah, now that's a party punch. A man's drink. Puts hairs on the chest." He beat his chest, then let out a loud belch.

"You are one crazy idiot." Maurice laughed.

"I'm gonna be one *drunk* idiot in a minute." They both laughed as Malcolm poured another drink for himself and one for his brother.

"Trust me," Malcolm said, as he punched on his chest to help ease the burning. "There ain't one female in here that's gonna be able to tell me no after she drinks this."

"Now wait a minute, man; I thought I knew you way better than that. Do you mean to tell me that that's what you need to do to pull a female? Get her drunk? My own flesh and blood?" asked Maurice.

"Bullshit. You know I've always been able to take my pick of the litter with my skills, and a hell of a lot quicker than you ever could. We may look the same but our game ain't the same."

"That sounds like a challenge to me," Maurice said, downing the rest of his drink.

"I'll tell you what, you and me are gonna go head-to-head. The next two females that walk through the door, we pull. We each have exactly one hour. We test the waters, see if they bite; then we pull 'em in. The first one who scores takes the female to the master bedroom, since we ain't lettin' nobody else use that room. That means that if you get there and you see that the door is locked, *I'm* in there and *I* win." Maurice smiled smugly.

"And if *you* get there and you see that the room is locked, then that means that *I'm* in there and *I* win." Malcolm laughed.

"Bet," said Maurice.

"What's the bet?" asked Malcolm.

"I just told you the bet. The bet is the next two females—"

"I know all of that. I mean how much are we bettin'?" Malcolm asked.

"We got an extra nine dollars left over from the money everybody paid to get in here."

"Then nine dollars it is," Malcolm said.

"I just had a scary thought," Maurice said, looking as if he had just seen a ghost.

"What's that?" asked Malcolm.

"What if one of the next two females that walk in here is Cheryl?"

"You mean fatal Cheryl?" Malcolm asked.

"Yeah, fatal Cheryl," Maurice said. "It took me ten months to finally get that crazy bitch to leave me alone. If I have to get with her for even one minute, it's gonna cost me at least another ten months of my life."

"That ain't my problem. The bet is on," said Malcolm.

FRANKI AND BARI walked up the narrow winding walkway that led to the front entrance of the Brelands' house. Bari nervously looked up and down the block to make sure that nobody was watching them.

They hurried up the steps and rang the bell. "Hurry, please," Bari said.

"Really, Bari, there's nothin' to be so nervous about. Calm down," Franki told her.

"How in the world can you be so calm? You do realize what we're doing, don't you?"

"We're cutting school."

"And it's okay with you?"

"I'm here, aren't I? And so are you, so let's just do this."

"Ring the bell again. Hurry up," Bari said, nervously tapping herself on the thigh.

Franki shook her head at her sister and rang the bell again. Malcolm opened the door. He looked the sisters up and down. A slow, wide grin appeared on his face and he turned around to look over his shoulder for his brother. When the twins' eyes met, they knew that they were both pleased and that their tasks were about to begin.

Regina, Franki's tall, slim best friend, appeared at the door beside

Malcolm. When Malcolm took too long to ask Franki and Bari in, Regina pushed him to the side and opened the door wider.

"I guess Malcolm is speechless. Come in," Regina said.

Franki and Bari stepped into the house and Regina whisked them away through the crowd. As they passed through the room, Bari took notice of the couples all along the walls and on the couches. She was surprised to see that they were openly kissing and groping one another right out in the open. She could tell that some of them had been drinking from their flushed faces and loud talking. The empty beer cans were a dead giveaway, too. Bari could hear her heartbeat well above the music. Her pulse raced and a sinking feeling dwelled in the pit of her stomach. Before she could complain, Karl, Franki's bucktoothed ex-boyfriend, stopped them in their tracks.

"Hello, Franki." He kissed her on the lips. He held on to her right arm, then used his left hand to run his hand down her back. He rested it on her behind.

"You still got that perfect ass, girl," Karl said, squeezing Franki's butt.

Franki moved his hand away. "Well, it's off-limits to you now. You lost your rights," she said.

"Oh, I see; it's like that, huh? Okay, I'm easy." Karl put up both his hands in surrender and walked away.

When he was out of earshot, Bari turned to Franki. "How in the world could you let him feel your behind like that?"

"It's no big deal, Bari. That's just how he is. He's harmless," said Franki.

"He disrespected you and you let him get away with it?"

"Bari, let's get things straight right now. Everybody here is pretty open, so you may as well get used to it."

"Why don't you tell me just how 'open' they are. Tell me what I'm in for."

"Let me put it to you this way: Don't be shocked by anything that you might see."

"Oh, God, now I'm really nervous. I must be crazy for coming here. I should have known better," Bari said.

"Just keep an open mind and you'll be all right," Franki told her.

"Okay, but just try not to leave me alone for too long," Bari said.

"So now you want me to babysit you?" asked Franki.

"No, no, I don't want you to babysit me. You're right." Bari sighed deeply. "I'm a big girl. I can handle this. Go ahead; have fun."

"Okay, I'll find you later. Do you want me to get you a drink?" Franki asked her before she walked away.

"No."

"It'll help you relax."

"I'm relaxed."

"If you say so. You're on your own, kid."

"Gee, thanks," Bari said, and Franki and Regina left her standing alone. Bari looked around the room again. It was becoming clear to her what these parties were all about, and she knew now that she didn't belong here at all. She also knew that she would probably have to live with the fact that perhaps she was a nerd after all, and that was okay with her. She realized that she preferred being in class, but it was too late for her to show up for class now. And she could never come up with a good enough excuse to tell Hazel if she went back home.

"Hi, I'm Maurice." He appeared from nowhere. Bari jumped at least a half inch off the floor.

"I'm sorry, I didn't mean to scare you," he said.

"It's okay." Bari giggled nervously. "I was in another world; I didn't see you walk up. I'm Bari." She extended her hand to him. They shook.

"So, where are you off to?"

"I was just going to find a quiet place to do some reading."

"To do some readin'? You mean now? Here? At the party?"

"Yeah, see I'm not supposed to be here. I mean . . . it's a long story."

"I can show you all the quiet spots; I live here," offered Maurice.

"Aren't your parents going to be upset with you about the house and all? I mean, look at all these people. Look at the mess they've made."

"Actually, no, they won't know anything about it. They're at least three thousand miles away. Everything will be back to normal by the time they get home."

"You're pretty brave."

"I guess. So, would you like me to show you around? We could talk, you know, spend some time. Can I get you some punch?"

"No. Thanks anyway."

"That doesn't mean that we can't spend time, does it?" Maurice asked her.

"You seem like a really nice guy, Maurice, but I really would like to be alone for a while. Maybe I'll catch up with you later on," said Bari.

"That's cool. I won't take it personal," Maurice said, and walked off.

Bari was alone again. Suddenly she was shoved from behind.

"What do you think you're doin', Bari?"

"Cheryl! What's your problem?" Bari spun around and looked at Cheryl through slitted eyes.

Cheryl was petite but she was strong. Her sandy brown hair looked red under the bright overhead light, and her fair skin was now red and blotchy since she was upset.

"You're a backstabbing bitch. That's what my problem is. And you're supposed to be my friend."

"I *am* your friend. What are you talking about?" Bari asked her.

Tears appeared in Cheryl's eyes. "Stay the hell away from Maurice, all right!"

"Cheryl, I swear I wasn't . . . I didn't know—"

"Save it!" Cheryl said, and stormed away.

Bari caught her breath and walked off looking for a place to sit and wait out the party. She walked up the stairs to the second level of the house. She had to weave her way through the people on the steps. Bari was surprised to see how many people were on the second floor. They were standing in the hallway seeming as if they were waiting their turn for the use of the bedrooms. Bari hung her head as she passed them. She was embarrassed for them. She really needed to get out of this house, but Franki was having fun, so she would have to bear with it. She worked her way through the crowd toward the back of the house on the second floor. Three bedrooms were back there.

Bari tried the door of the first bedroom that she came to on the left-hand side of the hall. The door was unlocked, so she pushed it open. An entangled couple jumped up when they heard the door open. Bari quickly closed it back. This was too much for her. She rushed down the hall to the next bedroom. This time she listened closely outside the door before she turned the knob. When she didn't hear anything, she tried to open the door. It was locked.

EARL JORDAN AND his friend Half were locked away in the last room on the third floor. They were both from Manchester High, the neighboring school, four blocks away from Dougan High. They had met Malcolm and Maurice on the city bus that they all took to get to their schools. The room Earl and Half were in was being used as the coatroom. Earl had too much to drink and Half needed to find a place for his friend to sleep it off, but Earl refused to sleep. Earl had deep brown expressive eyes that were captivating. On better days he was a charmer. He stood almost five-ten and had a stocky build, just right for his frame.

"If you think anybody gives a shit about you in this world, you got another think comin'. Nobody gives a shit about *nobody*," Earl said. His speech was slurred, his eyes unfocused.

"If you really believe that, that's really sad," Half said.

"It ain't sad, man. It's the truth, and the whole goddamned world may as well admit it. See, that's the problem with the world today. Nobody is willing to admit anything. Admit it if you did somethin' wrong. You know what I mean? Speak the truth!" Saliva sprayed from Earl's mouth when he spoke.

"You know, you can say some really bugged-out shit. But I understand. That's that punch talkin'."

"That ain't no punch talkin.' That's me talkin'! You don't recognize my voice, motherfucker?"

"I'll tell you what," Half said, "You need some rest, man. You need to sleep that shit off."

"I don't need no sleep; I'm all right. I'm just gonna lie down here for a minute."

"You do that, man, and I'm gonna check you in a few." Half walked out of the room, pulling the door shut behind him.

The bed in the room was piled high with coats. Earl made a bed on the ones that had fallen to the floor between the bed and the wall. He sat up on the pile of coats until he got his bearings. When he stood up, the light in the room seemed to fade to black, then back to full beam. He shook his head. Now he was focused. He needed another drink and he needed it now. He made his way across the room, damn near stumbling all the way. He opened the door to the room and stepped out into the hallway.

"Why in the hell is it so dark out here? Where in the hell is the kitchen? I saw it when I came in here. Now where the fuck did it go?" Earl stumbled ahead until he found the stairwell. He held on to the handrail and cautiously went down each step. When he reached the second level of the house, he weaved through all the students in the hallway and down to the first floor. Earl opened the door that he thought would lead to the kitchen. When he started down the stairs something told him that he wouldn't find the kitchen down the stairs. Earl went ahead anyway. He walked into the dark, damp room. He felt for the wall, then walked forward feeling the wall along the way to keep from tripping or bumping into something. Suddenly his hand went into a hole in the wall. When his hand was inside the hole, he thought he felt a bottle. Earl pulled the object out of the hole and saw that it *was* a bottle. He felt along the wall and realized that the whole wall had holes in it and each hole held a bottle.

"Bingo." Earl smiled and put one of the bottles into his back pocket and climbed back up the stairs to leave the basement the same way that he had come. When he returned to the last room on the third level of the house, he opened his bottle and took a long drink from it. Earl threw some more coats on the top of the ones that were already on the floor. He took another long drink, then settled down on his homemade bed and drifted off to sleep.

BARI HESITATED WHEN she came to the stairwell landing that led to the third level of the house. It was dark enough to make her a little nervous, but it seemed quiet enough to tempt her to go ahead. She went ahead up the steps and she walked past the first two rooms and went straight to the last room on the floor. She was glad to see that no one else was in there. A large pile of coats was on the bed, but Bari figured that she could just push them to the side and settle down there until the party was over. She pushed some of the coats to the farther side of the bed and sat down and dug for her writing pad and pen, then began making notes in her journal. She wanted to write about the party. She had a lot to say. Every now and again she would lift her eyes from her pad and look around the room. This time when Bari looked around the room she noticed the television remote control on the bed table. She picked it up and flicked on the television. She had gone through several channels when the sound of the television awakened Earl.

"Oh shit," Earl said.

Bari jumped when she saw Earl's body coming out from underneath the coats on the floor that he had been lying on.

"Oh, my God!" she said.

"You scared the shit out of me." Earl was scratching his head.

"I'm sorry. I didn't know that you were in here." Bari quickly stuffed her pad and pen back into her school bag, threw the bag over her shoulder, and headed toward the door.

"No, no. Please don't leave," Earl called behind her.

Bari stopped in her tracks.

"It's okay," Earl said, but Bari was still hesitant. "Look, I could use a friend right now. You know, somebody to talk to. Stay? Please?" He gave her a tired, drunk half smile.

"All right." Bari smiled. She put her bag on the floor and sat on the edge of the bed.

"I'm Bari." She extended her hand to him.

"I'm Earl. Earl Jordan."

"So, what is it that you would talk about with a friend?" she asked.

"We would talk about anything."

"Like what?"

"Like people."

"What about people?"

"Like why are they so fucked up? Like why nobody wants to be honest? And why don't people call a spade a spade? Do you believe that anybody's ever gonna really be one hundred percent honest with you? I don't think so," Earl slurred.

"I like to think that there are honest people in the world. I'm honest. Anyway, why do you feel that way? If you wanna talk about it, I'm a good listener. Try me."

"It's not that easy. I got somethin' to say that I've never spoken to anybody about. *Anybody*. See, I have this thing about talkin' to people about my fuckin' business because you spill your guts out to them and what? Either they think you're some kind of a fuckin' nut or they just plain ole don't give a flyin' fuck about you or your business anyway." Earl sprayed saliva again. He wiped his mouth with the back of his sleeve.

"Would you mind not cursing so much?" Bari asked.

"Oh shit. I'm sorry, I don't usually talk to a lady like that. I'm sorry." He picked up the liquor bottle and took a long swig from it. He swallowed the load and downed another one. Bari stared at him as he spoke.

"I like that. You set me straight. And you're right: I shouldn't speak to you that way." Earl took another long drink.

"And," Bari spoke hesitantly, "if you don't mind my saying so, I think that you're drinking a little too much."

Earl set the bottle on the floor. "You know somethin'? . . . I think you're very, very, very pretty." His speech slurred and now his eyes opened and closed very slowly. Slowly enough that one would think that he might have fallen asleep mid-sentence.

"I try not to judge people," he said. "You know why? Because you never know why people do what they do. Everybody has shit in their head that nobody else could ever know about. And the only way anybody could ever know about it is if that person tells you about it. If they don't tell you, you assume things and then you call the person stupid or crazy or some shit. I got shit that's been goin' on in my head since I was six years old! You hear that shit? Six years old!"

Before Earl spoke again, he picked up the bottle that was on the floor at his feet and took a quick swallow. "I ain't got no brothers or sisters. I don't even think I have any cousins. I ain't never met none of 'em if I do. Anyways, my mom started gettin' sick. They told us that she had somethin' called MS. That stands for 'Multiple Sclerosis.' We don't know where it came from. She got it just like that. She was okay for a while, though. She took care of me real good. But then slowly but surely the disease started gettin' worse and worse until finally she started gettin' kind of awkward when she walked around." Earl paused again. "Then she started usin' a walker, then a wheelchair."

"I'm so sorry, Earl," Bari said, walking around the bed to him. She sat next to him on the floor. She could feel his pain. She had her own sad stories to tell.

"My mother was the most beautiful woman in the world to me. She was like my fairy princess. It seemed to me like she knew everything." Even though it was obvious to Bari that Earl was drunk, she could see clearly how proud he was of his mother and how much he must have loved her.

"I was only six years old," Earl continued. "I think that my pops was kinda mad at my mother for gettin' sick. I remember they had started arguin' a lot. My father would throw chairs and all kinds of shit across the floor and he would just start breakin' things up. Then he would leave the house and we wouldn't see him again for a couple of days. He probably had a woman out there, now that I think about it."

"I'm sorry," Bari said. And she really was sorry.

"One day my moms must have pushed him a little too far, 'cause he went mad. He started yellin' at her at the top of his lungs. It seemed like he was havin' a hard time breathin', he was yellin' so loud, and he was trashin' the place. Then he slapped her in the face. I stood there and watched the whole thing." Tears filled Earl's eyes and rolled down his cheeks. He picked up the liquor bottle again and took a long drink from it before he spoke again.

"My moms kept yelling for my pops to get out, but he kept cussin' and screamin' at her. He was tellin' her what a bitch she was and how he wished he'd never married her. Mommy cussed him right back. She didn't take his shit, you know." Earl's eyes could hardly be seen now. They were half-closed. He slurred even more. "Then my father walked over to her and grabbed her by her nightgown; he held her up and slammed her into the marble fireplace. Mommy bumped her head and died instantly. I know Pops was mad as hell, but I don't think he meant to kill her." Earl shook his head like he was still trying to convince himself of that.

"Oh, my God. I am so, so sorry." The whole story tugged at Bari's heart. She took Earl's hand.

With his free hand, Earl drank the liquor straight from the bottle as he talked on. "When the cops came, Pops explained to them about my mother's MS. He told them that my mother was always so determined to walk. He said that she probably got up from the wheelchair and tried to walk and she fell and bumped her head."

Earl sniffled. After a moment he cried openly, still speaking through his tears and slurred speech. "That son of a bitch cried. He cried *real* tears. He acted like he was really hurt and just like that he was off the hook. There was no investigation, no nothin'. And you know what? She's mad at me."

"Who's mad at you?"

"Mommy."

"Why do you think she's mad at you?"

"Because she keeps comin' to me. I see her all the time. And don't tell me I'm dreamin' 'cause I'm not!"

Bari said nothing. Earl continued speaking.

"Every time she comes to me she's screamin' and yellin' and pointin' her finger at me. Yeah, she's mad. She's mad 'cause I didn't help her."

"I can't tell you how sorry I am that you've had to hold this in for so long. Have you thought about turning your father in to the police?"

Earl straightened himself up as best as he could. He wiped away the tears with the backs of his sleeves. "I thought about it plenty of times, but then I tell myself that that son of a bitch is the only family I got. If he goes to jail, I won't have no family at all. Every time I see him all happy and shit, I wonder how the fuck he could live with himself. You know? How he could sleep at night. Sometimes I wanna kill him. He took away my mother and then he was never really there for me. I mean he buys me clothes and shit and he makes sure that I eat and have a roof over my head, but we don't talk. We ain't got shit to talk about."

"Earl, if you ever feel like you want to talk, you could talk to me."

"Thank you. Now I don't know if that was me talkin' or if that was this bottle talkin', but I sure as hell feel a whole lot better. And you must be a real special lady, 'cause I ain't never told nobody that story. *Nobody.*"

Earl lay back on the bed. "I'm drunk," he said, and he closed his eyes.

FRANKI AND REGINA circulated through the house. Malcolm finally caught up with them. "Are you ladies enjoying yourselves?" he asked them.

"Yeah. The music sounds good," Franki said. They were playing the Jackson 5's "Dancing Machine." She gave Regina a wink. That was Franki's signal for Regina to leave her alone.

"So you're into music?" Malcolm asked.

"I like a good beat," said Franki.

"You're Franki, right?"

"Right."

"I'm Malcolm, one of the twins. It's a pleasure."

"I know who you are, and the pleasure is all mine," Franki said, openly flirting. They shared a lingering smile.

"Are you here with anybody?" Malcolm asked, staring at her bosom.

"Yes."

"I'm disappointed. I was kinda hopin' that you and me could . . ."

"Oh." Franki laughed. "You think that I'm here with somebody. No, I'm not with anybody. I mean, I'm here with my sister, Bari."

"Well, that's more like it. I like the sound of that better than the sound of this music. What do you say we find a quiet place to talk?"

"Okay."

Malcolm took Franki's hand and led her to the master bedroom on the second floor. He prayed that the door would be open and that he had beaten his brother to the room. The door opened easily when they got there. It was empty! They went inside and Malcolm locked the door behind them.

BARI SETTLED DOWN next to Earl on the bed while he slept. She watched him as he tossed and turned in his sleep. Every now and again his body jerked involuntarily. Finally, Bari nudged him until he opened his eyes.

"Earl, are you okay?" she asked.

"Hi, beautiful." Earl smiled lazily. His eyes rolled to the back of his head. Suddenly his body jerked again. Harder this time.

"Earl?" Bari stood over him now. His body jerked again. "Earl, you're scaring me. What's wrong?"

Earl groped around for the empty bottle next to him. Before he could get to it, Bari pushed it out of his reach. "You've had enough, Earl! Something is wrong with you!"

Earl's body began to twist and jerk violently. He rolled into fetal position as he gritted his teeth and clutched an armful of coats. Bari started to panic. Earl shivered and sweated at the same time.

"What should I do, Earl? I gotta get help!" Bari turned all around in circles in the middle of the floor as she ran back and forth, trying to figure out what she should do. Earl twisted and turned on the bed, tightening his arms around his body.

"Oh, my God, he's gonna die!" Bari said. She ran to the dresser and picked up the handset on the telephone and dialed 911. "Operator, I need an ambulance. My friend is sick. I don't know what's wrong. It's like convulsions. Please send help quick! I think he's dying! We're at 1400 Waverly Lane. . . . No, he can't talk. . . . No, he's not swallowing his tongue. Operator, please send an ambulance quick! He can't breathe and he's sweating a lot and his body keeps jerking and jerking and he's gagging. It's scary!" Bari slammed down the receiver and ran back over to Earl. "Earl, please hang on; I'm getting help. I gotta find my sister: Franki."

Bari ran from the room. She ran all the way down the first level of the, house, taking the steps two by two. When she reached the bottom of the steps, Cheryl was the first person she saw. "Cheryl, where's Franki?" Bari asked.

"I have no idea," she answered coldly. Bari could tell that Cheryl was still upset, but couldn't worry about her right now. Earl needed help.

"Has anybody seen Franki?" Bari yelled out.

"Sure. Everybody knows where Franki is. Didn't you hear? She's gittin' busy with Malcolm in the master bedroom," an unfamiliar voice informed Bari.

"Where's the master bedroom?" Bari asked.

"It's upstairs on the second floor, off toward the back of the house. Gold doorknob, you can't miss it," the same voice said.

"Thanks," Bari said, and she bolted back up the stairs.

"Franki! Franki!" she called out.

Bari ran around the corner and banged at the door with the gold doorknob. "Franki, are you in there? Please open the door; I need to speak to you. Hurry, please!"

Malcolm pulled open the door just enough to be able to peek out. "What's wrong?" he asked her, peeking through the slightly opened door.

"It's Earl. He's real sick and he needs help."

"I'm not sure who this Earl is but he had damn well better be *real* sick," Malcolm threatened. He pulled the door wide-open and he and Franki came out into the hall and followed Bari. Their hair was tousled, but they were fully dressed.

"He's having convulsions. I called an ambulance!" Bari said.

"You what?" Franki asked, stopping dead in her tracks.

"I called an ambulance!" Bari repeated. "I think he's dying!"

"Do you realize what you just did?" Franki asked. "The cops are gonna come here. In case you forgot, Bari, we're at a goddamn hooky party!" Franki said.

Bari covered her mouth in embarrassment, then fear. She had reacted so quickly that she never thought about the repercussions.

"I'll be damned," said Malcolm. "We have to find Maurice. I gotta let him know what's goin' on."

The three of them ran through the hall and up to the room where Earl was. They looked in on him, then ran down the stairs when they heard the bell ring. Before they reached the bottom of the stairs, the doorbell rang again. Regina opened the door. Two red-faced police officers and two ambulance attendants stood outside the door. The short, pudgy blond officer spoke first. "We're responding to a request for an ambulance at this address."

Regina was dumbfounded. "J-just a minute, Officers." She closed the door slightly while she looked through the crowd for Malcolm or Maurice. The music was still on full blast.

The blond officer pushed the door open wider and stepped inside the house. The second officer and the two attendants went in behind him.

"What's going on here?" the pudgy blond officer asked. "Hey! Hey! Stop the music!"

"Stop the music!" Maurice echoed the officer. He and Malcolm stood before the officers. The music stopped.

"Now, I'm gonna ask one more time, who called an ambulance?" the officer asked.

"Officer, sir, I have no idea who would have called an ambulance, because nobody here is sick. You must have the wrong house," said Maurice.

"Is there an adult in this house?" the officer asked.

"No, sir, our parents aren't home," Malcolm said.

"I see," the blond officer said. "So, youse are home alone, so youse decided to throw a party, and then youse called an ambulance as some kind of a joke."

"It was me, sir," Bari said, timidly stepping forward. The crowd gasped. All eyes in the room were on Bari. "My friend is sick! You gotta come now." Bari rushed toward the stairwell.

The blond officer instructed the ambulance attendants to follow her. The men ran behind Bari carrying a stretcher. Bari led them up the stairs to the third level of the house to Earl. As they went up the stairs, all of the students who were in the hallways upstairs quickly came running down the stairs, gathering with the rest of the students.

"These are school hours and youse should all be in school. In other words, everybody in this room is a truant. Are there any other people here? Who's upstairs?" the blond officer asked.

"No-no, this is it," Malcolm said, avoiding the officer's eyes.

"You wouldn't be lying to me now, would you, son?"

"No-no, Officer, I, I'm n-not—"

"I see you got yourself a speech impediment. You got a stuttering problem, son? Or are you lying? Why don't I just go up there and have a look-see for myself." He turned to the other officer, who was taller, with dark curly hair. "You keep an eye on them. I'm just gonna go up there and see what I see." The officer pulled out his nightstick and held it up before the crowd. "Don't anybody move. Don't scratch, sniff, or smell." The blond officer walked slowly and deliberately away from the crowd and headed up the stairs.

Upstairs, he walked from door to door, banging on each with his nightstick. One by one the doors opened and the wide-eyed, frightened students came out of the rooms zipping up their pants, fastening their bras, and straightening out their hair. The officer lined up the students to bring them downstairs. They all moved to the side when they saw the ambulance attendants come down from the top floor with Earl on the stretcher. Everybody looked on curiously, trying to figure out what was going on and who Earl was.

"Clear the way. Coming through," the attendant said, swiftly moving past the crowd. Bari walked alongside the stretcher down the stairs. Franki walked close behind her.

"What happened to him?" the officer with the dark hair asked.

"Looks like it could be a bad case of alcohol poisoning," one of the ambulance attendants said.

The rest of the students were directed down the stairs. The two

officers walked out of the house and down the curb with the attendants and helped them load the stretcher into the van. At least twenty
students made a mad dash out of the house. They ran in all directions.

"Hey, hey, get back here!" the blond officer yelled to them. They
didn't listen; they ran like mad and didn't look back. The rest of the
students remained in the doorway of the house and cheered their
friends on. The blond officer chased some of the students to the end
of the block. They had already gotten a head start on him, so they got
away. "Goddamned kids," he muttered as he rested his hands on his
knees and gasped for air.

By the time he returned to the house, the officer had composed
himself. "All right, that was pretty stupid of your friends," he lectured.
"I guarantee youse they won't get away with that. I don't want anybody
else makin' any stupid moves, 'cause I promise everybody will pay. Understand that?" His face was red and flushed. He looked like a wet
mop.

"Are we under arrest or what? We didn't break no laws," Malcolm
said.

"First of all, youse should all be in school. To make matters worse,
youse got alcohol on the premises with no adult supervision. Techni-
cally, we could haul youse all down to the station and book everybody . . . but I'll tell you what, we're gonna go down to the station and
we'll decide then what's gonna happen. Call for assistance, O'Brien,"
the blond-haired officer ordered.

"Requesting assistance." Officer O'Brien spoke into his walkie-
talkie. "We need two paddy wagons. We got approximately fifteen to
twenty truants engaging in a hooky party. We need to haul them down
to the station. Copy?"

"Copy, what's your position?" the reply came over the walkie-talkie.

"We're at 1400 Waverly Lane. On the Hill," said the officer.

"That's a copy."

"Transportation will be here soon. You kids cooperate with us and
we'll make this as painless as possible."

The faces in the crowd that were once defiant and menacing had
now softened. Some of the female students sniffled and cried.

"You mean we're gonna get arrested? Man, what kind of shit is
this? We ain't done nothin' wrong," Half complained.

"Pops is gonna kick our asses and it's all your fault," Malcolm said to Maurice.

"What do you mean, it's all my fault?" Maurice asked.

"Because if you had done what you were supposed to do, Bari would have been with you. But no, you couldn't score with her, so she ended up with some sick-ass idiot," said Malcolm.

"The only reason I didn't score with her is because she's uptight. She's nothing like her sister."

"Look," Bari said. "I thought Earl was dying, so I panicked. I was scared, okay?"

"You were scared? So do you feel better now? If it was up to me, that son of a bitch would have had to be sick somewhere else," said Malcolm.

"Aw, come on, man. We weren't havin' *that* much fun," Half said, defending Earl.

"I'm just sayin' that it don't make no sense for all of us to get into trouble. If she had told somebody that she needed help, we could've dragged his ass onto somebody else's lawn and let them get him help. Shit," Malcolm said.

BEFORE LONG, THE police vans pulled up in front of the twins' house. Some of the neighbors had been glued to their windows since the ambulance and the cops first came. They didn't usually get much excitement on the block.

The officers lined up the students and directed them into the waiting vans. Franki and Bari sat side by side. Once the van was in motion, Franki spoke to her sister in a low voice.

"I don't understand how you could cause all of this trouble over somebody you don't even know. I mean, what were you thinkin' about, if you were thinkin' at all. I mean, yeah, he was sick, but you should have told us first and maybe the cops didn't need to get involved."

Bari spoke in an equally low voice. "Franki, you don't understand. I know I don't really know him, but I felt close to him. He needed help and I was there."

"Gimme a break, Bari. How close could you have felt to him? You'd only known him for what . . . a minute? And whatever it is that you think you felt, I say it wasn't worth all the trouble you got us in. Now everybody is gonna be pissed off with me because I brought you to the party in the first place. I knew I shouldn't have told you about it."

"All you worry about is your friends," Bari said, speaking angrily in a loud whisper. "What if it was you who got sick? You heard them. Maybe it could have been you that they would have dragged onto somebody's lawn like garbage."

Franki didn't respond. Bari smiled and spoke more calmly.

"Anyway, I'm glad I came now, because if I hadn't come, Earl would probably be dead. I just pray to God that he's gonna be okay."

"You guys must have done much more than just talk," Franki said.

"Believe you me, all we did was talk. I'm not like you or any of your friends," said Bari.

"And what is that supposed to mean?"

"It means that I won't sleep with just anybody; I have morals. And, don't worry, after this I promise you that I will never want to hang around you or your friends ever again."

"Now that's the best news I've heard all day," said Franki.

"Well, good," Bari snapped.

"Well, good!" Franki snapped back.

Bari crossed her arms across her chest and turned to glare out the window. Franki glared straight ahead.

The police vans pulled up to the police station. The officers opened the doors and the students were led inside the station. They were instructed to line up against the wall. They moaned and groaned, but they cooperated. The blond officer came forth with his instructions.

"Okay, now listen up." He waited until he had everybody's attention. "Here's the drill. I want each and every one of youse to call your parents or guardians to come pick youse up. And I wanna make it clear right up front that it won't make any sense for any of youse to try to be slick and call anybody other than a parent or guardian, because youse will not be released until we have proof of guardianship." He pointed to the first kid in line. "Okay, let's start with you." The freckled, red-haired teen slowly approached the desk to make his phone call.

Several other students took their turn, and then it was Franki's and Bari's turn. They had explained to the officers that they were sisters and only needed to make one call. Franki convinced Bari that it was only fair that she should be the one to call. She couldn't argue with Franki. She stayed in place in the line while Bari called Hazel. Franki couldn't hear Bari's voice but could tell from Bari's face that she was upset. When she was done speaking to Hazel, Bari headed back to take her place in line. Dominick, big Afro, black-rimmed glasses, extra pounds, and all, had just finished making his call and caught up with Bari as she walked back.

"Hi again, Bari," Dominick said.

"Hi," Bari said dryly. "Dominick, right?"

"Yeah, that's right," he said. "It's okay to call me Fat Boy. That's what everybody else calls me. It doesn't bother me. I'm okay with it."

"Yeah, but that's not your name. Anyway, I like 'Dominick.' It has a nice ring to it. I guess you'll never forget my name now. I mean under the circumstances. I hear what everybody is saying about me." Bari had also noticed the dirty looks that they were giving her.

"I wouldn't forget your name anyway . . . but you gotta admit it is a fine mess you got us in. But don't worry, we'll forget about it soon enough." Dominick chuckled.

"I sure hope so. The funny thing is that I didn't really want to go to the party in the first place."

"You know what they say . . . always follow your instincts, you know, listen to that little voice inside you."

"I'll be sure to remember that the next time."

"Listen," Dominick said more seriously. "I told you before that I just wanted to be your friend. Well, I meant that. I guess what I want to say is that I heard you were in one of the rooms with that dude Earl. It's none of my business, but I thought I should tell you that you should stay away from him. I mean that's just my opinion and I know you don't really know me, but I just think he's kinda whacko. Everybody that knows him knows that about him."

"Well, thank you for sharing it with me. And you're right," Bari said.

"I'm right?" Dominick asked.

"Yeah. It isn't any of your business, and it is just your opinion. Well, my opinion is different than yours, so if it's all the same to you, I'll spend time with whomever I choose." Bari's tone was cold.

"Like I said, I'm just tryin' to be a friend, that's all. I guess I'll see you around."

"I guess." Bari sighed heavily as Dominick walked back to his place farther back in line.

"So, Bari, you and Fat Boy hittin' it off okay? What did he want?" Franki asked.

"His name is Dominick, and he wanted nothing. Absolutely nothing."

"What did Mommy say?"

"She had a fit. I think she was crying. She started reciting the Scriptures."

"Oh, God, we're dead," Franki said, backing up closer against the wall.

"Now *there's* somethin' we both agree on. She should be here soon. It's gonna be a long, hot summer."

"You can say that again."

"It's gonna be a long, hot summer." Bari sighed again.

Cheryl walked up behind Bari and tapped her on the shoulder. "I need to talk to you about Maurice."

"Cheryl, I really have nothing to say," Bari said, and turned her back to Cheryl.

"Well, you must like livin' dangerously, turning your back on me!" She grabbed Bari's arm but Bari snatched it away.

"Cheryl, don't you think that we're in enough trouble already? Look around you. We're in a police station."

"You were out-of-bounds messin' with Maurice!"

"I wasn't messin'. . . . Maurice isn't even . . ." Bari couldn't even get the words out.

"Get it straight, Bari . . . it's me and Maurice. I'm sick and tired of everybody goin' after him!" Cheryl went straight from zero to one hundred in a matter of seconds. Her voice was shrill and high-pitched. Irritating.

Franki wasn't about to listen to any more of her rantings. "Listen, Cheryl," Franki said. "Obviously, there is some kind of misunderstanding here. Maurice does not belong to you. Face it. If he did, he would have been with you today instead of trying to be with somebody else. If you're confused about the status of things, I suggest you speak to Maurice so he can clarify the situation for you."

Cheryl moved in closer to Franki. She pointed her finger into Franki's face as she spoke. "Oh, so you wanna put on a show for everybody? Okay, so let's put on a show." Cheryl lunged at Franki. Several students and a couple of officers had to restrain Cheryl. She was as strong as an ox, kicking her legs and swinging her arms wildly as they pulled her away from Franki.

HAZEL WALKED INTO the police station. She noticed the noise and the crowd of students yelling and jumping all about. When she approached the desk to ask about her girls, she noticed that Franki and Bari were dead center in the crowd, looking upset. Hazel pushed through the crowd until she reached them. She grabbed both Franki and Bari by the arm and pulled them to the side.

"I'll be damned! It's embarrassin' enough that I gotta come down here to a police station to pick up y'all's little wayward asses, and now I come down here and find you gettin' yourselves into a fight! What in the hell has gotten into y'all? Are you possessed or somethin'? I ain't raised no heathens. And what the hell are you doin' cuttin' school? I'm especially surprised at you, Bari! Your daddy must be turnin' in his grave right about now! Look at you. The two of you are dressed like streetwalkers." Hazel motioned to an officer that she was taking her girls home. The officer winked at her.

Hazel was still fussing at the girls as they walked out onto the street. "I know one damn thing, there ain't no way that y'all's fast little asses are gonna drive me crazy this summer. I should send y'all right down south to stay with Butch and Francine. Maybe *they* can teach you somethin'. Or better yet, I'll sign you up for summer school and I'll make sure your heads are so deep in those books, you won't be able to find your way out. That's it! You'll make up all of the time you probably missed cutting school."

Both Bari and Franki knew that tone. They knew that Hazel meant what she said. They were going to summer school.

THE LAST WEEK of school dragged by. While most students were looking forward to the summer vacation, Bari and Franki dreaded it. Bari dreaded it because she had just found a new friend in Earl and now she wouldn't be able to see him over the summer. She thought it was unfair since that was only her first time cutting school. Franki dreaded it because she was not looking forward to spending the summer in school and not being able to hang out with her friends.

Before their punishment kicked in, Bari had begged and pleaded with Hazel every day to let her go to the hospital to visit a "very sick" schoolmate until Hazel finally gave in and let her go. Bari surprised Earl the first time she went to visit him.

"Hey, beautiful," he said when she walked into the hospital room. He smiled at her, and Bari could have sworn she saw sparkles in his eyes.

"Surprise," Bari said, with a smile that would make him know that she was happy to see him.

"Yeah, I'm surprised all right. You're my second visitor; my father just left."

"I'm glad to see you're feeling better."

"Yeah, I'm feelin' a lot better. You saved my life."

"I guess I did." They were quiet for a minute. Bari picked at her nails and tried to think of what to say next.

"Truth is," Earl said, "I don't know if I should thank you or be mad at you."

"And I don't know if I should say, 'You're welcome,' or leave."

"Aw, come on, don't leave," Earl said. He took hold of the tail of her shirt and pulled her closer to him.

"I don't want to hear you talk that way."

"Okay, I'm sorry. I promise, nothin' depressin', okay?"

"Okay." Bari smiled.

Earl pulled a little harder on her shirt and forced her to sit down. Bari sat down but jumped right back up.

"Visitors aren't supposed to sit on the hospital bed," she said, like she was apologizing.

"I say it's okay for you to sit wherever I say you can sit. And I say I want you to sit on the bed."

Bari couldn't stop herself from beaming when he smiled at her so nice and soft in the way that he did. She had intended to surprise Earl with her visit but she was the one who got surprised when she found herself looking into his eyes and not being able to look away. Somehow he looked different to her under these new circumstances, not drunk. His whole face lit up when he smiled, and he even had dimples that she hadn't noticed before. Not even his almost perfect chalk white teeth did she pay attention to previously. This was the first boy whom she wanted to kiss. Bari stayed talking to Earl until visiting hours were over. They shared a lot of stories with each other and laughed a lot. It felt good to both of them, and when it was time for Bari to leave they were both sad.

"Can you come see me again tomorrow?" Earl asked.

"I'll try."

"Tryin' ain't nothin' but a failure. Promise me you'll come."

Bari smiled at Earl and she could feel her pulse racing. Her heart was beating double time. She knew that there was nothing that anybody could say or do to keep her from coming back to see him tomorrow.

"I promise," Bari said, and practically skipped out of the room.

six

SUMMER OF 1979. The heat wave was in full swing and it was only the first week in July. The temperature hadn't gone below 98 degrees for the sixth day in a row.

School was out for the summer and Hazel kept her word. Franki and Bari were all dressed and heading for summer classes. "You know, Mommy, we never really talked about this. You didn't even bother to ask us how we felt about goin' to summer school," Franki whined.

"The fact that I didn't bother to ask should tell you that I'm not interested in how y'all feel. The thing is, I ain't about to die before my time. I had a choice: Either I die tryin' to make respectable young ladies out of y'all or I send you away for the summer. And I sure ain't interested in spendin' the rest of my days in jail for committin' a double homicide, either."

"Since when did we get *that* bad? Mommy, you have to admit that you've never had a problem with me before this. I always get good grades and I always do the right thing," said Bari.

"That's true, Bari. You're fine until you start followin' behind Franki. Now this will show you where that gets you. There ain't no use in talkin' about it now 'cause it won't change nothin'. So go on and get out of here. And as soon as summer school is over, I'll be right outside to pick you up. So don't make no plans to be sidetracked."

"I'll be waiting for you, Mommy," Bari said happily. Unlike Franki, she decided to just go ahead and get through it. Franki gave her the evil eye so she'd calm down. Franki didn't want Hazel to think for one minute that they were happy about any of this.

"Look, Franki, you might as well just stop givin' your sister the eye and just go on out of here. Besides, it's only four weeks. You'll survive."

"I doubt it." Franki pouted. "Oh, God, Mommy, is there anything that we could do to change your mind? I swear I'll do just about anything. Can we talk about it, please?"

"Stop usin' the Lord's name in vain. I ain't got nothin' else to say. My mind is made up. Besides, I'm lookin' forward to a break, too. Y'all should have thought about what you did before you did it. You know what they say: You do the crime, you gotta do the time." Hazel laughed—a high, shrill laugh.

"That ain't funny, Mommy," Franki said. Defeat was in her voice.

"Come on now; get on out of here and go on to school," Hazel said.

"I guess you can't wait for us to go, huh, Ma?" Bari asked.

"No, I can't."

Bari walked over to her mother and hugged her. "I understand, Mommy . . . and I love you still."

"I love you, too."

Franki gave Bari the evil eye again. "Did I ever tell you that you make me sick?"

FRANKI AND BARI were on the city bus. Franki was tired of reading her magazine, so she leaned over closer to Bari and started to read over her shoulder. Bari covered her diary and looked up at Franki.

"You know what?" Franki asked her.

"What?"

"I have a confession to make," Franki said.

"What, pray tell, could that be? I'm almost afraid to ask," Bari said sarcastically.

"About the hooky party . . . you know when I was with Malcolm in the master bedroom?"

"Yeah, what about it?"

"We didn't do anything. I'm kind of embarrassed to say it, but I'm still a virgin."

Bari closed her diary. "You're kidding, right?" she asked, with her mouth hanging open.

"No, I'm not."

"Cross your heart and hope to die?"

"I cross my heart and hope to die."

"No, really. Cross your heart and hope to die."

"Aw, come on, Bari, grow up. We're not babies anymore," Franki protested.

"Then I don't believe you."

"You really make me sick sometimes." Franki crossed her finger across her chest. "I cross my heart and hope to die."

"Okay, I believe you now, but I don't get it. Why would you lead everybody to believe that you slept with Malcolm if you really didn't? He told *everybody* that, and you went along with it."

"I know. It didn't hurt anybody. I mean, as long as I know that I didn't really do it, it didn't matter to me what anybody else thought. The truth is that's all Malcolm wanted. And as much as I liked him, and in spite of what you think about me bein' easy and all, I do have a little respect for myself."

"Well, well, well, there is a God." Bari laughed.

"Oh, shut up, Mother Teresa."

"You can call me anything you want now. You're no different than me."

"Don't you ever let anybody hear you say that." They both laughed.

"Franki?"

"What?"

"I don't believe I ever said that I was sorry about any of this. I mean, about getting everybody in trouble. And I guess this whole summer school thing is my fault."

"It is."

"Well, how come you never said anything?" Bari asked.

"I guess that's because I'm partly to blame. I mean, I was the one who convinced you to come to the party. Of course I didn't realize how green you really were, and I guess I do need to be taught a lesson."

"Wait a minute," Bari said, briskly shaking her head as if to clear it. "Are you all right? Because you sure don't sound okay. What's going on?"

"Look, don't torture me. It's hard enough for me to say stuff like this." Franki slammed her back against her seat. "Oh, God, I can't believe I'm on my way to school."

"Oh, come on, Franki, I'm sure it won't be as bad as you think. I plan to make the most of it. And you should, too. We might just enjoy it."

Franki looked at her sister as if she had two heads. She couldn't think of strong enough words to express to Bari how crazy she thought she was, so she didn't say anything at all. Franki took out her magazine and started thumbing through it again. Bari went back to writing in her diary. They rode along for the next few stops with neither one of them speaking at all.

seven

T HE ONLY THING Franki and Bari were allowed to do when they returned home from summer school each day was run errands to the store for Hazel if she needed something. And even then, they had to go straight to the store and come straight back. The two of them moped around the house for the remainder of the summer. It passed pretty quickly, though. Before anybody knew it, it was time to return to school.

Bari decided that she would go back into her old pattern of staying focused on her schoolwork and staying as far away from Franki and her friends as possible. Even Franki had learned a lesson and didn't spend as much time away from her classes as she used to.

When Bari reported to her science class, she immediately noticed Dominick sitting in the back of the classroom. He smiled at her, but Bari pretended she didn't see him. She walked briskly to a vacant seat on the other side of the room. When Dominick changed his seat and moved over to Bari's side of the room to take a vacant seat right behind her, she thought she would scream.

"Hello, party pooper," Dominick said to her when he got settled.

Bari turned around in her seat to face him. She barely made eye contact with him. She gave him a quick "hello," then turned back around to face the blackboard.

"What's the matter, you don't remember me? Dominick? Fat Boy? How was your summer?" he asked.

"Awful," Bari answered without turning around. "How was yours?"

"Awful," Dominick said. They both laughed.

Later on during class, they found out that they were assigned to the same team for a science project. The class was broken up into groups to discuss how their project should be approached. Bari was impressed with how knowledgeable Dominick was about the earthquakes that the group discussed for their project and how he took charge of the discussion. At times while Dominick spoke, Bari would smile at him.

When the class was over, Bari walked out into the hall. Dominick walked quickly behind her. "Would you like to study with me later on this evening? We could talk some more about how we could attack our project," he said.

"I wouldn't mind that at all, Dominick. It's just that . . . well, I'm meeting Earl after school."

"Oh . . . I see," Dominick said.

Bari saw the crushed look on his face but she didn't think much of it. "We can study together tomorrow if you're free," Bari offered. That made Dominick smile.

As the two of them walked out of the school together, Earl was the first person that Bari saw. Her face lit up as she and Dominick approached him.

"Hi, Earl," Bari said, taking his hand into hers. "Do you remember Dominick?" Dominick and Earl grunted their hellos to each other.

"Okay, Dominick, I'll see you in class tomorrow," said Bari.

"Right," Dominick said.

Bari and Earl left, walking hand in hand. "I don't like him," Earl said after a while.

"Who?"

"Your friend Dominick."

"But you don't even know him. He's a nice guy," Bari told him.

"I don't care how nice he is, I don't like him."

"He's okay," Bari said.

"I said he's not okay, so that means he's not okay."

THE NEXT DAY after Bari's science class ended, she waited out in the hallway for Dominick. She smiled at him when she saw him, and he smiled back at her.

"Are you heading straight home?" she asked him.

"I planned on it. Why?"

"I just wondered," Bari answered.

"You just wondered what?" Dominick asked.

"I just wondered if you wanted to come over to my house so we could study together," Bari said.

"Oh yeah? And what about your boyfriend?"

"Earl has to work at his father's business tonight. Anyway, we're just studying. We're not doing anything wrong."

"You're right. We're not doing anything wrong. Okay, let's do it," said Dominick.

"Good. This way," Bari said, leading the way to her house. Bari insisted that they take the long walk instead of taking the city bus. It was a nice day and she wanted to take advantage of it.

"You know what?" Bari asked Dominick as they walked.

"What?"

"I think you're smart," Bari said.

"Who, me?"

"No, the man in the moon. Yeah, you."

"I'm not smart," Dominick responded.

"Yes, you are. How do you know so much about earthquakes and molten lava and just about everything?"

"I read a lot. I read just about everything I get my hands on. Especially anything concerning history and anything scientific."

"Wow. I'm impressed."

"Don't be."

"And you know what else?" she asked him.

"What else?"

"You're a cool guy."

"Am I?"

"You are."

"It's kinda funny, though." Bari giggled. "I have to be honest with you—"

"Don't tell me. I already know what you're gonna say."

"You'll never guess what I was gonna say."

"You were gonna tell me that you didn't like me when we first met but now you think I'm a cool guy."

"Wrong." She laughed.

"Yeah, right." Dominick laughed, too.

"I was gonna tell you that I hated your guts when we first met, but now I think you're a cool guy." The two of them laughed a hearty laugh together and silently they both knew that they were going to be good friends.

By the time they got to Bari's house, they had talked about so many things that they truly felt like they'd known each other for a long time. Bari had convinced Dominick to let her cut his six-inch Afro off. As soon as they walked into her house and she introduced him to Hazel, Bari took Dominick into the bathroom and sat him down on the toilet seat and proceeded to clip off his hair, section by section.

eight

ARI AND FRANKI were college women now, each with a job and
her own apartment. Franki watched Bari and Earl grow closer
and closer over the years in spite of her prodding and putting a
bug in Bari's ear against Earl every chance she got. Franki didn't know
exactly what it was about Earl that she didn't like, but there was something surly, dark, and sinister that she sensed about him.

No matter what Franki told Bari, she was too caught up in la-la
land to hear her. Bari couldn't see beyond her hand stretched out in
front of her when it came to Earl. If her head wasn't buried in her
books, it was buried in the sand.

BARI'S RELATIONSHIP WITH Earl was five years strong now, and the
two of them were very much in love. Earl was proud of Bari. He had
never seen anybody so dedicated to anything as Bari was to her stud-
ies. She had kept him up many a night after she got in from her classes
at Caton University talking on and on about her plans and her goals
for her career, and now she had graduated.

Earl never got the chance to go to college. Just as he graduated
from high school, his father told Earl that his help was needed full-
time at the business. His father changed the company name once Earl
joined him. Now he called it BJ & Son's Paper Mill. Sometimes Earl
wasn't sure whether he should consider himself lucky or not. A college
degree would have looked nice on his résumé, but here he was, twenty-
four years old, with only a high school diploma, earning thirty-two
thousand dollars a year and driving a company car that his father

leased for him to use to solicit business. All things considered, it wasn't a bad gig.

Earl wanted tonight to be special for Bari. He had been put on a two-month waiting list at the Water's Edge. He tried to book the date as close to Bari's graduation date as possible, but the best date that they could give him was six days after the graduation.

Tonight Earl intended to make Bari know how proud he was of her and just how special she was to him. The couple walked up the six wrought-iron steps leading to the restaurant's entrance. The murky water that surrounded the ship-turned-restaurant glistened under the setting sun. The soft, gentle music that the jazz band played found its way outside the door into the night air.

"I can't believe we're actually at the Water's Edge. I wonder if we'll see any celebrities tonight," Bari said, squeezing Earl's hand.

The maître d' greeted them once they were inside and escorted them to their table. Earl pulled out Bari's chair, then pushed it underneath her. When he sat down he looked across the table at her. In the pastel light that the peach-colored candle in the center of the table gave off Bari looked so feminine and pure to Earl. He didn't know how he would ever be able to articulate to anybody just how much he likened Bari to a flower. He knew that sounded as corny as hell, but it was true. Bari was so fresh, so vulnerable, to him. He would make it his duty to protect her from the cold, cruel world. He would never allow her to be soiled.

"You're staring at me," Bari said, smiling at him, showing her slight dimples.

"I can't help it. You're the most beautiful woman in this room."

Bari's smile deepened. She reached across the table and they held hands. Most of the guests at the restaurant were dressed in semiformal attire. It wasn't uncommon for the male guests to wear tuxedos or their finest dinner jackets. The ladies were dressed in shimmering fashions and wearing lots of jewelry and expensive perfume. Bari was wearing a soft gray ankle-length silk skirt with matching pumps and a baby pink sweater coming off her shoulders. Her hair was swept up to the top of her head, with tendrils hanging loosely at the nape of her neck and over her ears. Earl had on a navy blue suit and a gray silk shirt, with a gray silk polka-dot handkerchief tucked into his pocket. He was tieless.

The ambiance at the restaurant was unusually romantic. Crystal vases, each with a half-dozen peach roses, graced each table. As far as Earl was concerned, an artist couldn't have painted a more perfect setting.

"I love you, Earl. I love you very much."

"I love you, too."

"It feels so good being here on a hot summer night and being so near to the water. I feel so alive. So vibrant."

"Good. That's exactly the effect I wanted this night to have on you."

"Really? Am I to assume that you have plans for me, for this night?"

"Oh, but do I have plans for you, lady. . . ."

The waitress appeared from nowhere. "Good evening, my name is Maddie. I'll be your waitress for the evening."

Earl and Bari quickly let go of each other's hands to reach for the menus that Maddie handed to them.

"May I get you a cocktail?" Maddie asked.

"Yes, thank you. A bottle of Moët and Chandon," Earl said.

"Good choice. Take your time looking at the menus. I'll be right back." Maddie smiled, turned on her heels, and was gone.

Moments later, Earl called Maddie back over. "What are the specials?" he asked her.

"We have stuffed portabello mushrooms in a sherry cream sauce, veal medallions with scalloped potatoes. We have a very fine cut of filet mignon. . . ."

"I really can't decide . . . ," Bari said, looking up from her menu.

"We'll both have the filet mignon. Make 'em well done. We'll have vinaigrette dressing for the salads, and baked potatoes with butter on both. Oh, and give us the broccoli medley on the side," Earl told Maddie.

"Of course." Maddie jotted down the order and was gone again.

"I didn't want steak, Earl. What made you think I wanted steak?"

"After all of these years shouldn't I know what you like?"

"Well, I do like steak but—"

"Then that's all I need to know, right?" Earl playfully pinched Bari's cheek.

"I guess you're right." She giggled and reached across the table again to squeeze his hands.

"May I have this dance?"

"Earl, you know I have two left feet."

"That's okay. Just follow my lead."

"That's the hard part," Bari complained.

"Humor me."

Earl kept hold of Bari's hand while he pulled her up from her seat and led her to the dance floor. Some of the older patrons admired them as they walked by. Earl and Bari danced for two songs straight, resting their heads against one another. When they returned to their table, the champagne was set up in a silver ice bucket with two crystal goblets. The flame from the candlelight reflected off the ice bucket, and a soft blaze seemed to encompass them. Maddie popped the champagne cork and poured it in each goblet, then left them alone.

"I'd like to propose a toast," Earl said, raising his glass.

Bari raised hers, too.

"I want to wish you much success in all your future endeavors and I want to congratulate you on your graduation. Earning a college degree is quite an accomplishment. May you get everything you deserve. To the future!" They touched glasses, then sipped their champagne.

"Thank you, honey. That was as sweet as this champagne."

Earl ate quickly, glancing at Bari's plate from time to time to make sure that she was eating quickly enough. He even dug his fork into her plate several times to help her along. When they were done eating, Earl finished off another glass of champagne.

"Would you accompany me to the deck?" Earl asked.

The two of them walked out onto the deck and met a beautiful crystal night with a sky that was brilliant with stars. They chose a quiet spot on the balcony. Earl's trembling hands surprised him. He took hold of both of Bari's hands and looked deep into her eyes.

"Baby . . ." His voice cracked. He cleared his throat and continued. "I don't have to tell you how much I love you. I don't think that there is a man alive who will ever love you as much as me." Earl reached into his breast pocket and took out a small black velvet box. He opened the box and took out a pear-shaped 1-karat white gold diamond ring. He dropped to one knee. "I want you to be my wife . . . as soon as possible."

Both hands covered Bari's mouth while her eyes widened in disbelief. Her hands trembled; then the tears started falling. Earl placed the
ring on the third finger of her left hand and kissed it.

"I would like to spend the rest of my life with you," Earl continued.
"I love you, and I cherish you, and I want to grow old with you. Please
say yes."

Bari composed herself momentarily. A smile was stuck on her face.
"Yes . . . yes! Of course, yes, I'll marry you, Earl."

They held on to each other tightly.

Earl figured he had to be the happiest man in the world. He put his
mouth very close to Bari's ear. "I love you," he whispered.

Bari gasped lightly and weakened in his arms. Earl put his arm
around her shoulder and led her back inside the restaurant to their
table. When they sat down, Maddie suggested something from the
dessert cart. Bari asked Maddie if she could see the selections.

Earl interrupted. "Oh no. No, thank you." He patted his stomach.
"We're stuffed. Just give us the check, please."

Maddie looked at Bari. Bari quickly looked away. Earl signed off on
the credit card slip and they left the restaurant.

nine

BARI BURST INTO her apartment. She tossed her bags onto the dinette table just inside the door entrance. She couldn't wait to call Franki. Bari flicked on the light and held her hand out in front of her and admired her engagement ring for the hundredth time. She kicked off her shoes and dropped her jacket on the floor where her shoes landed. Bari grabbed the telephone handset and dialed Franki's number. The phone rang five times. Bari waited for the answering machine to come on so that she could leave a message, but for some reason it didn't come on. She hung up and dialed Hazel. Hazel's answering machine picked up.

"Hi, Mommy. You gotta call me as soon as possible. It's urgent." Hazel wouldn't miss the smile in her daughter's voice when she listened to the message.

Bari hung up and dialed Dominick's number. While she listened to his phone ringing, she flicked on the stereo. The mellow sound of Miles Davis flowed through the room. She held the phone between her head and her shoulder as she started to undress. Dominick's answering machine clicked.

"I'm tired of talking to answering machines—"

"Hello?"

"Oh, Dominick, I was just about to hang up."

"No, don't do that. What's going on?"

"Nothing much. I'm just calling—"

"You're up to something. What are you so happy about?"

"I guess you know me pretty well, huh?"

"You figure after so many years, if a person really cares about you, he gets to know these things about you."

"Dominick?"

"Yeah, babe?"

"I just wanted to let you know . . ." Bari paused.

"Let me know what?"

"Earl proposed to me tonight. He asked me to marry him." Bari grinned and plopped herself down on the couch. There was silence at the other end of the line.

"Dominick, are you there?" she asked.

"Uh, yeah. I'm here. Um . . . congratulations. I assume you said yes."

"Of course I said yes," Bari said, sounding as if she'd just been insulted.

"And you're sure that's really what you want to do?"

"I don't understand the question," Bari said. She was sounding a little more testy than she meant to.

"Relax. I'm just absorbing the news, that's all. Anyway, Bari, I never made it a secret about how I feel about Earl. I told you that a long time ago and ain't nothin' changed. Years ago you told me that my feelings were just my opinion, so let's just leave it at that. In the meantime, I do congratulate you and I will say that if you should need me for anything in the world, I'll be there for you. Good luck."

"Thank you, Dominick."

"And now you're just gonna dump me, right?" he teased.

"I would never dump you. You'll always be my boo." Bari pressed the telephone receiver closer to her ear and closed her eyes.

"Yeah, you say that now."

"I'm saying it now and I'll say it later, too, Fat Boy."

"Oh, so now it's Fat Boy?"

"Come on, Dommie. You know you're my main man." Bari put on her sweetest baby voice. "So, I can count on you to be at the wedding?"

"I'll be there with bells on. Did you set a date?"

"We did. Earl wants it to happen sooner rather than later, but we agreed on exactly one year from today. Anyway, I'm happy now that I know you're happy with it. If I were there, I'd kiss you. I'll see you soon."

"Yeah." Dominick sighed.

"Bye." Bari hung up.

ten

AZEL HAD BEEN awake since 6:30 A.M. She hadn't planned on getting up so early; it happened automatically. Even at times when she planned to sleep late, her eyes opened automatically at 6:30 A.M. whether it was Monday or Sunday. Most people would lie in bed for a while and stretch, yawn, and scratch first. But not Hazel. She got right up. She put on her robe, headed straight to the bathroom, washed her face in lukewarm water, and brushed her teeth. She ran the water for her bath, then went to the kitchen to brew her coffee. It was a ritual.

Hazel took out the homemade spoon bread that she had made just past midnight. She wanted it to be as fresh as possible when Bari got there. Hazel put the bread in the oven and set the dial to "hold warm." Hazel broke four eggs into a bowl and hand-beat them. When she was done, she stuck the bowl in the fridge, then went upstairs and took her bath.

Bari got to the house at exactly 10:30 A.M., just as Hazel had asked. The house hadn't changed much. The living room sofa and love seat were still in good condition. Hazel refused to get rid of them, even when Franki and Bari offered to buy her a new set. The only thing Hazel allowed them to do was rearrange the furniture for her one day when they were both visiting. Even though both girls had moved out, Hazel left their rooms in exactly the same order that they had left them in.

"Where is Miss Millie? I thought that you said that she was coming over this morning to have breakfast with you," Bari asked.

"Yes, I did say that. But then I changed my mind. I told her that I had to go and run errands instead," Hazel said.

"Why did you tell her that?"

"Because I knew that you were comin'. . . ."

"So?"

"So I wanted it to be just the two of us."

"But I thought Miss Millie was your good friend." Bari took off her jacket and tossed it on the living room couch as she walked past it. She followed Hazel into the kitchen and sat down at the table.

Hazel heated some butter in the skillet and started frying the eggs right away. She had already set out the coffee cups and breakfast plates on the table.

"Millie is my good friend, but isn't it okay if I want to spend some time alone with my daughter? Besides, you're gettin' married and I figured we should talk."

"You mean the mother/daughter talk? Do mothers and daughters still have those?" Bari laughed.

"Only mothers that care. I'm so happy for you, I don't know what to do. Y'all are just makin' me get old."

"You're not getting older, Mommy. You're getting better."

"Oh, is that what I'm doin'?"

"Yeah, that's what you're doing. If anything, Franki, Ricky, and me are the ones getting older."

Hazel put some scrambled eggs onto their plates; then she took the spoon bread out of the oven and set the pan on the table. Bari got up from the table and washed her hands in the kitchen sink. She ripped off a paper towel sheet to dry them. Bari came back to the table and sat down and blessed their food.

"Tell me somethin', Bari, you do love Earl, don't you?" Hazel asked after spooning in a mouthful of eggs.

"Of course I love him, Mommy. You have to know that I'm the happiest girl in the world."

"Well, I want you to be happy. Earl seems like a nice guy, but you know, sometimes you hear things or you see things . . . I just want you to be sure about what you're doin'."

"I'm very sure about what I'm doing."

"Good then." Hazel paused for a moment and reflected on what she would say next. "You know, baby, the main thing that you have to remember when you get married is that you have to take care of your house and your husband."

"I know that."

"'Cause if you don't take care of that, believe me, somebody else will be happy to."

"I plan to be the perfect wife to Earl."

"A good marriage is somethin' that you have to work at every day. I know it seems like it's easy, but I can't say it's easy at all. Especially when kids come along. I never told y'all this before, but your daddy and I had what we called back in our day a shotgun wedding. Oh, Jimmy and me loved each other all right, or at least we thought we did in the beginning, until I messed around and got myself pregnant."

"Mommy, how could you mess around and get yourself pregnant? It takes two to tango."

"Aw, you know what I mean. Anyway, that's when I realized that I wasn't as in love as I thought I was. Real love didn't come until later, much later. Your father and me had our problems, but we hung in there. It wasn't always easy hangin' in there, but it got easier over time. . . . Well, sometimes it felt like it got easier . . . or maybe I just convinced myself that it did. . . ." Hazel's voice trailed off.

Bari nodded her head and listened intently as her mother spoke.

"I'm just sayin' you're young, you're beautiful . . . and you don't *have* to get married right now. You have options. I didn't have any. It ain't like you're pregnant or anything, so you don't have to rush into this." Hazel thought about what she had just said. "You're not pregnant, are you?"

Bari laughed. "Of course I'm not pregnant, Mommy. Don't you think I would have told you? I tell you everything."

"Well, you can never be too sure. Anyway, you got your whole life ahead of you."

"Do you think I'm rushing into this? Are you kidding me? I've known Earl for five years now, and I've always been in love with him. I used to pray every night that he would ask me to marry him, and now that he has there's no way that I'm gonna let him get away from me."

"As long as you're happy. Lord knows life is too short to be miserable."

"I'm happy." They were silent for a few minutes while they continued eating.

"I can't wait to be able to say 'my husband.' That has a nice ring to it, doesn't it?" Bari giggled.

"Girl, you're just as silly." The two of them laughed heartily.

Bari clutched her arms to her chest. "Mommy, my man is so fine, if he wants me to have all ten of his babies, I'm willing!"

"You'll be another Francine, always barefoot and pregnant!" They laughed again.

"You know," Hazel said, "I have a little money that I've been puttin' away ever since your father died. I never really made any plans for it 'cause I've been savin' it for a special occasion. Now I figure you can't get any more special than this, now can you?"

"I can't think of anything more special," Bari kidded.

"I want you to have the most beautiful wedding gown ever. A beautiful white gown made of silk peau de soie, and a twenty-foot train. You can't find the dress I'm talking about in no store. No sir! I'm gonna have ole Miss Haley design it for me. You'll be the envy of all the brides past and present."

"Miss Haley? Oh, my God, Mommy, you would do that for me? It'll cost you a fortune!"

"Of course I would do that for you. And I don't care how much it costs. You're my daughter, and I don't want to spare any expense on this wedding. I want to help out as much as I possibly can."

Bari got up from her chair and walked over to her mother. She hugged Hazel. "Thank you, Mommy."

"You're welcome, baby." The tears that burned the corners of Hazel's eyes finally fell.

"Why in the world are you crying, Mommy?" Bari laughed. "Don't start getting all mushy on me."

"I'm cryin' 'cause I'm happy. And I'm cryin' 'cause I'm a little sad, too." Hazel sniffed.

"What are you sad about?"

"I'm sad because all of y'all is grown-up now and movin' on, so I decided to move on, too. I'm gonna sell this big ole house and buy me a little one down south somewhere."

"Are you serious?" Bari was shocked.

"Yeah, I'm serious. I don't need to be stayin' in this house all by myself."

"Wow," Bari said, still surprised. "We grew up in this house. I can't imagine it gone."

"I know. There are a lot of memories here, too. We're just gonna have to get used to it, though, 'cause I already made up my mind. I talked to a man about it just two days ago. He told me he's comin' by to see it soon."

"Wow," Bari said again. "Did you tell anybody else yet?"

"No, I knew I was gonna see you first, so I'm tellin' you about it. Franki is supposed to stop by later on tonight, so I'll tell her then. I have to write Ricky a letter."

"Well, let me know when you need to start packing up things and Franki and I will be right here to help you. All right?"

"All right."

"I love you, Mommy." Bari hugged Hazel again.

"I love you, too, baby."

eleven

BARI HAD ALREADY rung Franki's bell three times. She looked up at the window and couldn't tell whether the lights were on because the blinds were drawn.

"This doesn't make sense," she said, leaning on the bell this time. "Why would she ask me to come over and then not be here? Leave it to Franki to do something like this." Bari fumbled inside her pocketbook for the spare set of keys that Franki had given her to use in case of an emergency. She tried several keys in each lock but only managed to unlock one of the three locks at first.

"I'm planning a wedding, for God's sake. I don't have this kind of time to waste."

Bari got another lock opened. She fumbled with the last lock and was able to open the outside door. She pushed it open; then she walked inside the vestibule and opened the inner door. She walked up the long stairwell and unlocked the two locks on the apartment door. The apartment was pitch-black when she got inside. Bari felt around for the light switch. She found it and switched on the light.

"Surprise!" Franki and about eleven other women jumped out of their hiding places. Bari was startled. She stumbled back against the wall. Several pairs of hands grabbed at her and pulled her into the room. The music went on and the bachelorette party started.

EARL HAD EXPLAINED to his friends that it was cool if they didn't have a bachelor party for him. He could do without the fuss. They didn't listen, though. His best friend, Half, rented a suite at the Westbury

Inn to host it. For the right price he had arranged for the hotel to be at their service. The hotel provided hor d'oeuvre trays with lots of finger foods and a bottle of Dom Perignon that chilled in a top hat–shaped ice bucket. A half-dozen other brands of champagne filled a large pail that was packed with ice. The mini-bar was stocked and open. The men drank and talked loud—all but Earl. He drank, but he wasn't talking much. He sat at the end of the sofa, drink in hand, completely engrossed in his thoughts.

Peabo sat next to Earl. Peabo was an employee at Earl's father's company. They had befriended each other right away when Earl was only a student coming out of high school and had just started working there. Peabo was a Sammy Davis, Jr., look-alike, and for some reason women were crazy about him.

"What's up with that look on your face?" Peabo asked Earl.

"I was just thinkin'," Earl said.

"You wouldn't be gettin' cold feet on us, now would you?"

"Don't worry about him, Peabo." Half said. "My man is just havin' a moment of clarity. He's wonderin' what the fuck he done went and got himself into. Ha! Ha!" They all laughed.

"It's not like that, Half. I'm okay with this marriage thing. I can do this," Earl said.

"You sure about that, man? You better be sure, 'cause I'm gonna tell you right now what you're in for." Half said.

"What am I in for?" Earl asked, knowing he'd be sorry for asking.

"You see, shit is lookin' real good right now. You got that courtin' action goin' on, your rap is strong, but here's what happens next. Once you put that ring on her finger, the bitch's head is gonna start spinnin' all around like this here." Half was turning his body all around. "And then those eyes are gonna turn bloodred and that green shit is gonna come gushin' out of her mouth and flyin' all over the place and it's gonna scare the hell outta you. Only it's gonna be too late, 'cause she's gonna have your ass chained to the fuckin' radiator so you can't get away. Then your ass is gonna be doomed forever after."

"You little half-pint Negro, what do you know?" Earl asked him.

"I know a lot. I done seen that shit happen too many times. All brothers are doomed when they say, 'I do.' And that's why I don't!"

"See, that's why they call you 'Half.' It ain't got nothin' to do with your short little ass. It's because you only get *half* the shit right." They both laughed at Half.

"That's all right, man. Just don't come cryin' to me when Bari starts transformin' on your ass!" The laughter continued.

"I know one thing." Malcolm said. "There ain't no turning back after tomorrow."

"I can't believe tomorrow is the wedding already. Time sure as hell flies, huh?" Earl said.

"You see that? Reality is kickin' in right about now. Don't tell *me* my man ain't scared. Look how petrified he looks." Half pointed at Earl, laughing.

"Earl knows what he's doin'," Peabo said. "If he's smart, he won't let Bari get away." He nudged Half. "He ain't lettin' that go. She's ripe for the pickin'."

"Either that or it's really that love thang," Half responded.

"Hey, I ain't ashamed to say that I love my lady," Earl said.

"There ain't nothin' to be ashamed of. Bari is a beautiful and classy lady," said Peabo.

FRANKI'S APARTMENT WAS just the right size to host the bridal shower. She had moved into a two-bedroom brownstone apartment in the Clinton Hill section of Brooklyn just after graduating from NYU. One bedroom was converted into a den, which Franki also used as an office at times. Franki's assistant and good friend, Nell, had helped to plan the bridal shower. Since Barbara, another good friend, was completely unreliable, she was told just to show up. Franki had forced Cheryl and Bari to make up with each other years ago and they had stayed friendly ever since. Cheryl had insisted on being at Bari's shower no matter what.

Bari's bridal shower was in full swing. The women were dancing, laughing, and jumping around so much that they were hot and sweaty. Makeup dripped; hairdos fell. Nobody could remember the last time they had so much fun. Most of them were tired now or giddy from too much champagne. Bodies were flopped all over the room. Where there wasn't a space to sit, they made space. Bari threw herself down in what looked like a good-sized space between Nell and Franki at first, but she quickly realized once she hit the floor that the space was too small. She wiggled her body into place anyway.

"I can't believe that you guys gave me a bridal shower. I begged you not to. Everybody has already given me so much just by helping me with all my plans and putting up with my hysterics for the past few months."

"Come on, girl, there ain't nothin' like a party. Besides, where else would any of us rather be right now but here with you?" Cheryl asked.

"Damn. That's nice, Cheryl. But you sure weren't saying that back when we were in high school at that hooky party!" Bari teased.

"I know." Cheryl put on the fake English accent that she loved to put on so much. "We were young and dumb then. But now we're adults and you're getting married." She sniffled, pretending to cry.

"Don't cry, Cheryl." Bari playfully patted her back.

"Bari, I know you made us all promise that we wouldn't buy presents, you know, with the wedding being so close and all, but because you are the beautiful person that you are, we couldn't help but say to hell with you and we just went ahead and did what we had to do," said Barbara.

Barbara got up and left the room and went into the den. When she came back, she was pulling an old red wagon with chipped paint on one side that was piled high with colorful, beautifully wrapped presents.

"Oh, my God! You guys are relentless. Look at all those presents," said Bari. "And where in the world did you find your little red wagon, Franki?"

"Mommy still had it in the basement at the house after all these years. Since she's packin' up her things to move down south, I decided to take it. She has enough of her own junk to take with her."

"Mommy is a regular pack rat," Bari said, shaking her head and giggling. She stood up and looked around at all her friends. "Let me tell you guys something. I want you all to know that I feel so good today. I mean, I got all my closest friends with me, I'm getting married. My heart is smiling. You know what I mean?"

"Unfortunately, I, for one, can't relate. But if you really feel that way, Bari, that's a beautiful thing and I'm very happy for you," said Barbara.

"I intend to be happy with Earl. People talk about divorce statistics and all that, but that doesn't scare me. Earl and I are in it for the long haul. See, I have it all figured out. It's about communication. As long as two people communicate their true feelings to one another they really shouldn't have any problems. Besides, fate brought Earl and me together. Fate and God. We're perfect for each other. And it doesn't hurt that I still have my grandmother's posies. That's my lucky charm."

"So, this is all part of God's divine plan, huh? God, fate, and a lucky charm. Girl, you got it bad," Nell said, in her deep, deadpan voice, scratching her shaved head.

"Okay, so I have a question . . . ," Barbara announced. "What the hell are posies?"

"It's a long story," Bari started. "My grandmother used to tell me stories. She told me that when she was a girl a lot of people were plagued with the bubonic plague. She said that the nursery rhyme that we hear today—'Ring around the rosy, pocket full of posies, ashes, ashes . . . all fall down!'—actually was recited to ward off the plague. See, the 'rings' were the actual circles that would appear on the body from the plague. The 'pocket full of posies' was a flower that it was said would protect you from contracting the disease if you kept it in your pocket. 'Ashes, ashes' comes from the Book of Common Prayer, 'ashes to ashes, dust to dust.' They used to burn the clothing of the people with the disease to keep them from spreading it. Then the 'all fall down' means you die. So, thank you very much, I will hold on to my posy talisman as long as I can. Granny said it will bring me luck when I need it."

"That's pretty damn scary, if you ask me," Nell said. "That's not a nice song for kids to sing. Every parent in America needs to ban it."

"It's only a song. And it's a complete myth, too," said Franki. "I refuse to believe anything silly like that. It takes my mother to tell you about that crap. She swore my grandmother was nuts for believing it ever brought her luck. The things that happened to her were things that were probably gonna happen anyway."

"Nell is right, though; it's not a nice song at all," Bari said. "Trust me, it's not. I can tell you my own stories, but this is not the time or place. But please let's get back to having fun."

"I think it's a rare thing that Bari and Earl have. Very few people get to find their soul mate. I guess I'm like Bari. I like to think that there's that perfect person out there for me, that person that is the missing piece to my puzzle. Somebody who *jives* with me." Cheryl began to speak more rapidly. "I know he's out there and, goddammit, if it kills me I'm gonna find him!" Everybody broke out into raucous laughter.

"It sounds to me like you two have been reading too many of them Harlequin romance novels," said Nell when they quieted down. "And some of y'all, who shall remain nameless at the moment, are still livin' in a dreamworld. The 'perfect mate.' What a concept." Nell's face looked as if she'd tasted something bitter in her mouth.

Franki gave her opinion. "The way I see it is this. You find somebody that you're comfortable with and you teach him—yes, I said teach him—how you want to be treated. Period. So, as far as all this communication stuff . . . maybe, but I seriously doubt it. And good luck? Or lucky charms? Personally, I ain't never believed in nothin' unless I was able to see it, feel it, or experience it myself."

Now it was Barbara's turn. "I remember I was trying to do everything in my power to get close to this guy I was seein'. Y'all remember Chance?" she asked. "Tall, dark-skinned fella, goatee? Looked like Teddy Pendergrass? Now, deep down I knew Chance wasn't the right man for me. But I tried to force the issue. Chance was the finest brother that I had ever seen in my life, so when he asked me to move in with him after we had been seeing each other for a couple of months, what else could I say but yes. So, to make a long story short, once I moved in with him, things changed. I wanted to make the relationship work so I told him that we needed to communicate more, get to really know each other. I started opening up, telling him stories from my past, you know, trying to 'communicate.' The next thing I knew, every time he got angry or wanted an excuse to leave the apartment he would throw something up in my face that I told him. And that's how that went. Then he moved out on me. Since then, mum's the word. I keep my thoughts and feelings to myself." Barbara sighed.

"And the moral of the story is: Do not audition for marriage," Nell said. "It doesn't pay to play house. When you shack up with a guy all you're doing is giving him everything he wants right up front. It's like they say: Why buy the cow if you can get the milk for free?" Nell was looking at Barbara as if she really wanted an answer.

"That doesn't sound very nice." Barbara jokingly pouted.

"And what about Stephanie Lorde? Pretty Stephanie with the big house, big titties, two cars, and two cute little boys? She and her husband were so deeply in love," Cheryl recalled.

"Yeah. What ever happened to her?" Bari asked.

"Didn't you hear? Out of the blue, her man just decided he didn't want to be married to her anymore. He just packed his bags and told her to think of something to tell his boys 'cause he wasn't coming back. Stephanie nearly lost her mind. She still looks bothered up to today. I saw her just last month with that crazy look in her eyes. I guess he really didn't love her after all," Cheryl reported.

"That's just it," Nell said, banging on the coffee table. "It doesn't have anything at all to do with love. Think about it. Women operate from emotion. Men operate from reason."

"Pray tell, what the hell is *that* supposed to mean?" Cheryl asked.

"Oh, brother, now you're gonna get her started on her speeches about men," Barbara complained.

"*You* of all people, Barbara, should welcome my speeches about men," said Nell. "If you listened to me more often, you wouldn't have *half* the man problems that you have right now." Everybody laughed at Barbara's expense.

"Touché," Barbara said, looking sheepish.

"Now, as I was saying," Nell continued. "Before a woman leaves a man she will probably consider the time invested in the relationship, the kids and their need for a dad, the house, everything. And then she ends up gettin' all emotional about it and she may turn around and not leave the son of a bitch at all. A man, on the other hand, sees something that he wants, and he goes for it. That's his reason. Period. End of story."

Franki spoke up again. "We women tend to blame men for a lot of our problems, but a lot of times, if you think about it, we call a lot of things on ourselves."

"How so?" Barbara asked.

"Nell's right," said Franki. "You see how emotional we are? As women we have all these romantic thoughts and we're always in pursuit of that perfect relationship that everybody keeps talking about. So we tend to settle for somebody that we know will fall short of what we want. And then we think we can metamorphosize him. In the meantime, we never even discuss with the man what our plans or our expectations of him are. So, when he 'screws up' because he didn't follow the script that we wrote for him in our minds, we blame him for not being who we wanted him to be in the first place."

"Hey, whose side are you on?" Barbara asked.

"It's not a matter of being on anybody's side." Franki laughed. "I'm simply saying that we shouldn't overlook our own faults and shortcomings as women. See, I believe that once we recognize our own faults, and learn to love ourselves first, we can grow stronger and build better relationships. At least I can say it's worked for me and Darryl so far. And we don't get hung up on roles and we're not trying to force marriage. If it happens, fine, and if it doesn't, fine."

"Right on, Franki. That's pretty damned profound," Barbara said.

"You're stupid, Barbara," said Franki. Barbara waved her off.

"What are we gonna do about all these presents?" Cheryl asked.

"Oh yeah, open the presents," said Franki.

Franki handed each present to Bari and Bari opened them one by one, reading the cards and holding up the gifts for everyone to see.

A half hour later Franki picked up the last box from the wagon and handed it to Bari. "This is from me, Bari. In spite of how many other couples' relationships have fallen short, I want to wish you much happiness and joy in your marriage. You deserve the best, so I'm sure that's what you'll get. I couldn't begin to think of a gift that I could buy for you that would express my feelings and the fact that somehow I feel like I'm losin' you . . . ," Franki said, misty-eyed.

"You're not losing me, Franki," said Bari.

"Anyway, I decided to write you a poem. I hope you like it."

Bari had already removed the framed poem from the box. She handed it to Franki. "Please read it, Franki."

Franki cleared her throat and began to read.

We share the same memories
and for a lifetime we grew
together, forever
our bond just like glue

I remember so clearly
those camp songs we sang

I remember us jumping
and frolicking in rain

With dolls we told our stories
of how our lives would be
with you there by my side
many dreams have come to be

We still share the laughter
though the years have rushed on by
you're still right there to comfort me
when I feel the need to cry

Although we manage to talk
as the hours tick away
there still is always something
that we both forget to say

You know there isn't anything
I wouldn't do for you
you're my dearest sister
and that's why I love you.

Nobody spoke for about a minute when Franki was done reading but there was a lot of sniffling going on in the room. Franki handed the poem to Bari. Bari sat looking at it and rubbing the gold-speckled frame. She sniffed back tears. "That was beautiful. I can't believe you wrote that for me." Bari reached over and hugged Franki. The two of them untangled themselves and wiped the tears from their eyes.

"You guys are gonna make me cry again, and I'm so ugly when I cry," Cheryl said.

"All right, let's change the pace a bit," Franki said. She got up and walked over to the stereo and turned up the volume. "I want to show my sister how important it is for her to know exactly what to do to keep that *groove thang* goin' on in her marriage and how to show her man what she wants," Franki said. Then she yelled toward the den, "Come on out, Love Icon."

All of the women gasped and screamed and cackled at the same time when the Love Icon appeared in the doorway. All Bari could do was stand there with her mouth wide-open and her eyes bulging. The Icon was about six feet tall and about 220 pounds and was wearing a black muscle T-shirt. His eyes were as dark as coal and so was his skin, which looked nice and moist under the body oil that covered him. He was so perfectly toned that it looked like somebody had built him, piece by piece.

The atmosphere was charged. The Icon danced right up to Franki and the two of them started gyrating and grinding against one another to the music, all the way down to the floor. The Icon laid Franki on the floor and held his body over hers while he rose up on all fours and humped up and down in a lovemaking motion. When the music changed over to the next song, the Icon helped Franki up to her feet. The music got louder and the stripper went right into a new routine. He began to slowly remove articles of his clothing. The women went wild. The Icon danced his way through the room alternating routines with several of the women as they stuffed his G-string with dollar bills. He danced his way over to Bari, but each time he got anywhere near her she headed in the opposite direction. The Icon couldn't corner her. Franki made her way around the room so that she ended up standing just behind Bari. When the Icon got close enough to her, Franki pushed Bari straight into his arms. Bari tried to protest but he had her in his grip and she was powerless. Bari moved her head away from him as he made motions as if he was going to kiss her. The girls called out to her to go ahead and have some fun. Bari started to make small body movements at first. Little by little she increased her movements until finally she got completely into it. She ended up giving the Icon a run for his money. When the dance was over, the Icon disappeared back into the den.

"He was unbelievable!" Cheryl said. "Did you see the pecs on him!"

"And what about those abs? The man is a god. Put him in a bottle and pour him on me!" Barbara said.

Nell was out of breath. She spoke in between breaths. "Bari, you're gonna be too worn-out to get married tomorrow." She mopped the sweat from her brow with a wad of napkins.

"Wild horses couldn't keep me from getting married tomorrow," Bari said.

"I guess we should all get some rest. We have a long day ahead of us. How are you gonna look like the blushing bride with shopping bags under your eyes, Bari?"

"You're right. You know I need all forty of my winks."

"Yeah, we know." Franki laughed.

All the ladies got up and prepared to leave. They said their good nights at the door and left.

BACK AT THE Westbury Inn, Earl's bachelor party became more intense. Six female dancers joined the party. They pranced all around showing their wares and earning their dollars. One of the dancers was giving Earl her undivided attention. She stood in front of him slowly gyrating her body and rubbing his crotch. Earl looked a little stressed, so Half came to his rescue.

"Give me a minute with him, sugar." Half took out a ten-dollar bill from his pocket and slowly slipped it into her bra. He gave her breast a squeeze before he took his hand out. Half led Earl by the arm to join the group of men who had just gathered in the center of the room.

"So what do you want us to do, man? You want us to cut off your balls for you now or do you want to wait 'til later so Bari can cut 'em off for you?" Maurice asked when Earl joined them.

"Go to hell, man." Earl waved him off.

Half put his arm around Earl's shoulders and spoke into his ear. "Check this out."

"What's up?" Earl asked, his eyes half-closed. All the rum and champagne was starting to get to him.

"Did you like her?" Half asked, looking at the female's behind as she walked away.

"She was all right," Earl said.

"'Cause, check this out, we're givin' you the ultimate hookup." Half reached into his right breast pocket and took out a key. "I hooked it up so that you could take your pick of any one of these six girls and spend the night in the Executive Suite, room twenty-twenty. Is that cool or what? Compliments of me and the boys. It's your last hurrah as a single man. What do you say?"

Earl smiled but he looked skeptical. "Nah, I don't think I can do that."

"Of course you can do that."

"I don't know, man. . . ." Earl glanced across the room at the woman called Charity. He still wasn't sure if he was up for spending time with her. She returned his glance, smiling at him seductively.

Half nudged Earl on the arm and gave him a slight push in Charity's direction. "You see that? You got the green light. Go for it, man."

Earl walked hesitantly at first in her direction. When he reached her, he said a few words to her. With nothing more than a smile, Charity looped her arm through his, and they left the room. When they got into the elevator, Earl pressed the button for the twentieth floor. He fixed his eyes on the numeric display strip over the door. Charity said nothing.

The two of them walked down the hall in silence until they reached suite 2020. When Earl put the key into the door, he turned and looked over at the woman beside him. "I'm sorry, I have a bad memory, what did you say your name was?"

twelve

IT WAS A perfect day for a wedding. It was June and the sun was radiant. The church was artfully decorated with white and peach roses. White and peach silk scalloped ribbons adorned each pew. The altar exhibited a huge vase of peach-colored roses with fallen petals surrounding it. White carpet covered the aisle floor leading to the altar.

The church was already filled up and the ceremony was just about an hour behind schedule. Many of the guests were growing restless. They fidgeted in their seats and twisted and turned all about, looking for any sign that the ceremony was about to begin. The bridal party was tucked away in a room upstairs in the church where they were all helping each other make final adjustments to their gowns and tuxedos. They waited for the missing members of the bridal party to arrive. Earl and Half still had not shown up and Barbara was missing, too.

Bari paced back and forth nervously. "Where is he? How dare he be late. We're already almost an hour behind schedule. I am absolutely livid! He obviously doesn't know what an emotional wreck I am today. This is my wedding day and I'm supposed to be happy!" Bari complained.

"The bride is usually the one who is fashionably late, not the groom! This is bordering on ridiculous," Cheryl said.

"Everybody, please, calm down. They'll be here. I'm sure they're being held up for a good reason," said Hazel. "Let's not get excited for nothin'."

Suddenly Bari looked panicked. "You don't think that he's changed his mind, do you?" she asked.

"Of course not. Just relax. Please," Hazel said.

THE SUN'S RAYS found their way into suite 2020 at the Westbury Inn, where the window shades were only partially drawn. Clothing was strewn along the floor starting at the door and ending at the queen-sized bed. A drained champagne bottle and two empty glasses rested on the bed table. The sun shined in Earl's face.

"Oh shit!" Earl yelled as he jumped out of bed. He looked at the clock. It read 11:30 A.M. Charity woke up and sat up in bed with a smile on her face.

"What are you doin'?" Earl asked her. "Get the hell up! We gotta get outta here! I gotta go get married! Here, put on your shit!" Earl grabbed a handful of her clothing and threw it to her on the bed.

Charity slowly and sadly got dressed. When she was fully dressed, she headed toward the door. Earl rushed out of the room almost immediately after her and headed home to get dressed.

About forty-five minutes later, a loud knock at the door of the upstairs waiting room in the church startled everybody in the room. Bari rushed over to open the door. She pulled it open. It was Earl. He was looking sharper than ever in his white long-tailed tuxedo. Everybody gasped when they saw him standing there. Bari quickly tried to shut the door, but Earl stuck his foot in it to keep it from closing.

"Open the door, Bari. I need to see you."

"I'm glad you finally made it, Earl, but you can't see me before the wedding; it's bad luck."

"Come on, Bari, that's superstitious. You don't really believe that, do you?"

"I'm just not willing to take any chances." She moved closer to the door, still holding it tightly in place so that Earl couldn't see her. Earl didn't make any further attempts to come into the room.

"Why in the world are you so late?" Bari asked.

"Never mind why I'm so late. The important thing is that I'm here now. And the sooner we get this thing started, the better." Earl stuck his arm through the door opening and reached around for Bari's hand.

Bari took hold of his hand. She guided it to her mouth and kissed it. "Why did you come to see me?" she asked him, from behind the door.

"I just wanted to see you one more time before we went out there.

And I wanted to tell you that I love you to death. You're the only woman for me," Earl said, sounding completely convincing.

"I love you, too, honey." Bari squeezed his hand. "You'd better go now, so we can get started."

She let go of his hand and he left. Bari shut the door, then turned to face everybody. They were all staring at her. She giggled nervously. "I think Earl is more nervous than me."

"So it seems," Nell said, in her monotone.

Barbara came rushing into the room. "I'm so sorry I'm late," she said. "It was hell getting into this bridesmaid dress this morning and the traffic was torture coming in from Jersey."

"Yeah, yeah, yeah. Tell it to the marines, Barbara. I swear you're gonna be late for your own funeral!" said Cheryl.

"I sure hope so," Barbara said, throwing her bags down and digging for her makeup bag. She rushed over to the mirror and started dabbing at her face.

Half arrived five minutes later. "We can get started now that everybody's here. I'll tell Reverend John," Franki said, leaving the room. Hazel went with her and took her place in the first row of the church.

WHEN BARI ENTERED the church, a hush fell over the room. Then everybody started commenting on the beautiful bride, all at once. Bari was a stunning bride. Hazel had kept her promise and delivered a gown that would be talked about for a long time. It was a dramatic silk peau de soie gown with a ten-foot detachable train. The veil was a wide headband the same fabric as the gown, with falls of lace and beads. Somehow, Bari looked taller than she really was and elegant. She wore a smile that softened her entire face and she looked as pure as a ray of pristine light.

Ricky stood proudly by Bari's side. He had made arrangements immediately, the moment he heard his sister was getting married, a year ago.

The walk down the aisle seemed like an eternity to Bari. The whole act seemed surreal. Bari didn't mind, though. She wanted to savor every moment, to have each detail etched in her mind forever.

When she reached Earl, he removed her veil, took her hand, and they stood side by side facing Reverend John.

"Dearly beloved, we are gathered here today in the sight of God and in the face of this company to join together this man and this woman . . . ," the reverend began. The couple stood before him as he spoke, clinging to his every word. When the reverend asked if anyone saw any reason that the marriage should not take place, silence befell the church.

Bari stared deep into Earl's eyes. She made a silent and personal promise to God and to herself that she would do everything in her power to see to it that she made her husband happy. She would make sure that their love would be eternal.

". . . By the power vested in me by the State of New York, I now pronounce you man and wife. You may kiss your bride."

The words jarred Bari back to reality. She kissed her husband. The crowd cheered, and after three months of planning and emotions running rampant, about twenty minutes after it started the ceremony was over.

BARI AND EARL sat entwined in the back of the limousine. The driver sped toward the reception hall.

"I can't believe that you're my husband."

". . . and you're my wife."

"Finally." said Bari. "As much as I'm looking forward to enjoying our honeymoon, I can't wait to get back home."

"Why?" Earl looked puzzled.

"Because I can't wait to get settled into our new house and, you know, be husband and wife and live happily ever after."

"Like in fairy tales?"

"Just like in fairy tales." Bari smiled into her husband's face. "So, go ahead, call me by my new name. I wanna hear how it sounds."

"Congratulations, Mrs. Bari Jordan."

"Congratulations to you, Mr. Earl Jordan. I promise you, I'm gonna make you happy. You'll see." She snuggled closer to him.

Earl kissed her on her ear, then whispered to her, "I love you, lady."

Bari closed her eyes. The warmth from Earl's breath in her ear was intoxicating. It shortened her breath. She breathed in deeply and relished it. "Do you have any idea how much I love to hear you say that to me?" she asked him.

IN THE RECEPTION hall a huge crystal chandelier hung in the center
of the very high ceiling. The shimmering light made the room take on
a life of its own. The mirrored walls made the hall look huge. The tables were tastefully set. The tablecloths reflected colors of the bride's
choice, peach and white. The centerpieces were white china vases
with a mixture of white lilies, and peach roses.

The traditional wedding reception practices were carried out as the
night went on. Finally, Earl found himself alone, standing along the
sideline watching and smiling at the people who were dancing. Tommy,
a friend from Earl's old neighborhood, walked over and stood beside
him with his drink in hand.

"So, you're a married man now. I can't believe this shit," Tommy
said in a gruff voice that said he smoked a lot and drank plenty. He was
grinning and showing two side teeth missing. "I'm lookin' at a dead
man." He took out a cigarette and held it, unlit, between his lips.

"Don't say that shit, man," Earl told him.

"Listen, I haven't officially congratulated you yet, you know, on
your marriage and shit." Tommy reached into his inside breast pocket
and pulled out a small, clear plastic packet with white powder in it. He
handed it to Earl.

"What's this?"

"You could call it white cloud, or you could call it the white lady.
You could even call it nose candy. But most of us just call it blow."

"What am I supposed to do with this?"

"You're supposed to check it out and enjoy it. It's just a little somethin' for you to take with you and your lady to paradise. Go ahead,
check it out. Let me know how you like it. There's more where that
came from," Tommy told him.

Earl was still holding the packet in his hand when Tommy walked
away. He quickly shoved it into his pants pocket, then looked around
the room to make sure that nobody was watching him. Earl was no
stranger to the streets. He knew all about cocaine. He had been
around people indulging in it many times before, but for some reason
trying it never appealed to him. He had always found enjoyment in a
glass of rum and Coke. He may have overdone it every now and again,
but alcohol was his drug of choice.

After a few minutes, Earl made his way to the men's room. He kicked open the door to an empty stall, went inside, and locked the door behind him. He took the packet out of his pocket and carefully opened it. Earl leaned over and poured some of the cocaine out onto the flat top of the toilet paper dispenser. He stood there staring down at it like he was analyzing it under a microscope. Earl checked his pants pockets first, then his shirt pockets for something to use to get the coke into his nose. He looked all around the stall and saw nothing. Sighing heavily, Earl used his finger to sweep the cocaine back into the packet. He left the men's room and spotted Tommy right away. Earl went over to him.

"How in the hell am I supposed to get this shit up my nose?" Earl asked him.

"I'm sorry, my man. Here, use this to set up your lines." Tommy reached into his pants pocket and took out a plastic drinking straw that was cut to about the size of a pinky, with an angled tip.

"Thanks." Earl took the cut-off straw and went back to the men's room. He went back into the stall and poured the cocaine out again on the toilet paper dispenser and set up some lines. He used the packet itself to push the coke around. When Earl was done he sniffed a line into one nostril.

"Whoa!" The hit felt like it blasted a hole straight through to his brain. Earl wiped away the water that dripped from his eyes. He leaned his back against the door for a minute and then he leaned over again and took the second line into his other nostril. His nostril went numb and his eyes turned bloodred instantly.

"That's pretty good," Earl said. He closed the packet, tucked it back into his pant pocket, and left the stall.

Earl felt good. He felt strong. Powerful. And everything looked brighter, clearer. It was beautiful.

He went over to the sink and looked in the mirror at his glassy bloodshot eyes. "Damn!" Earl turned on the faucet and ran cold water over his face. When he raised his head to look into the mirror again, there his mother was, sitting in her wheelchair. Earl squinted his eyes to get a better look at her. Why wasn't she looking at him? What was wrong? Her image hadn't appeared to him for quite some time, but now there she was in living color. Earl instinctively reached his hand out and touched the mirror.

"Mom . . . ?"

His mother started to scream. She put both hands against her temples and screamed and screamed. "Mommy!" Earl yelled, but his mother's image was gone. He quickly looked around the men's room. He bent down and looked underneath the row of stalls to make sure that he was alone.

"She's mad at me again," Earl said, shaking his head and blinking real hard to clear it; then he left the men's room.

Earl went straight to the bar and ordered himself a rum and Coke. He noticed how good he felt. The nagging stress that was ever present in his head and always jumbling his thoughts was gone. He stood real still to see if the stress would come back, but he was right: It was gone. He was numb to it. *This is good,* he thought. He walked over and joined the group of people who had gathered around the dais.

"How's everybody doin'?" he asked. He knew they felt good. *He* sure as hell felt real good. He could take on the whole goddamned world right now. Everybody answered him in unison. They were fine.

"Oh, good, Earl's here," Barbara said. "I'd like to propose a toast." The bridal party and some of the people who were standing within earshot gathered around Barbara as she filled each of their empty glasses with champagne. "Here's to two of the most beautiful and most loving people that I know. Earl, Bari, may you both share eternal love and may your union be very long and very fruitful." Everybody touched glasses and sipped their champagne.

"I'll drink to that," Earl said, almost too loudly. He drained his glass in one gulp and held it out for a refill. Barbara filled it to the rim.

"I want to propose a toast, too," Half said. "I want to propose a toast to my best friend and his new wife. I want you both to enjoy love, peace, and happiness for all the years to come. Earl, I may be laughing right now, but to tell you the truth, I'm eatin' my heart out. You're a very lucky man. Good luck." They all touched glasses again.

"I'll drink to that!" Earl said again, and downed his champagne. He gestured to Barbara again for a refill.

"I want to propose a toast to my baby sister and her husband," said Franki. "I want to wish you much love and happiness always. Really, Sis. I want only the best for you. Here's to your delirious future!" Everybody touched glasses again.

"I'll drink to that!" Earl said, downing his champagne in two swallows. He grabbed Bari with his free arm into a bear hug and kissed her long and hard on the lips.

"Actually, I think he'll drink to anything," Nell whispered to Barbara.

"You're tellin' me," Barbara said.

"Excuse me," Earl said to Bari, and he was off to the men's room again.

BARI BEGAN TO make her rounds to greet her guests. There were many people to greet. There were her friends, aunts, uncles, and cousins twice removed to be seen. And then there was Dominick. Dominick was looking dapper in his black tuxedo and black bow tie. He had stopped wearing his black-rimmed glasses long ago and had switched to contact lenses. He never did grow back his Afro. His hair was cut so close to his head, he was almost bald. The look suited him well, especially since he had trimmed off some of his excess weight over the years.

Bari spent several minutes speaking with Dominick's parents, Mr. and Mrs. Howard. They had grown very fond of Bari over the years as they practically watched her grow up with Dominick. Bari had joined them several times on family trips and she had even dragged Hazel along with them a couple of times. They had all become extended family members of sorts. Bari's arms were wrapped around Dominick's neck when Earl came out of the men's room. Dominick handed her two envelopes. Bari tucked them into her money bag, then excused herself and walked over to the next table.

EARL CAME ACROSS the room to Dominick's table. He extended his hand to Dominick and they shook. "How're you doin', man?" Earl asked him.

"I'm all right. Congratulations, by the way. What's up?"

"Can I speak to you for a minute?" Earl asked; then he stepped back to give Dominick room to stand up. Earl led the way out of the room and into the hallway; then he turned to face Dominick. Earl's movements were quick. His eyes were shifting. Bloodshot.

"I just want to get some things cleared up right now, right up front," Earl said, wiping at his nose.

"Talk to me," said Dominick.

"I know you and Bari are friends. I never had a problem with that, you understand? But I'm a brother, and basically, I know how brothers are. Bari is my wife now, so I may as well let you know that I don't think it's a good idea for you to even think about maintainin' a friendship with her."

"Bari and me are friends for life. That's all we are. I'm not trying to be with her in any other way."

Earl wiped at his nose again. "I don't think you heard what I just said." Earl raised his voice and moved in closer to Dominick. "I'm tellin' you to stay away from my wife."

"You need to back up off me. This is your wedding reception, man." Dominick moved away from Earl and was about to turn and walk away.

"You just better not forget what I said." Earl poked his finger into Dominick's chest.

Dominick looked down at Earl's finger on his chest. Then he looked up at Earl and smiled, a half smile. "That's not your decision to make, my man. I think this is Bari's call," he said, then walked away.

Earl called behind him, "You've been warned!"

Earl went back into the reception hall and found Bari. He pulled her into his arms and gave her a squeeze.

"Okay, baby, that's enough. You're wrinkling my dress," Bari said, smiling.

"I can't help it, baby. You know how you make me feel." Earl looked over at Dominick's table to make sure that he was watching. He was. Dominick shook his head and looked away. "It's time to go," Earl whispered to Bari, and they quietly made their exit.

thirteen

THE HUMIDITY WAS stifling when Bari and Earl's flight landed in Cancún, Mexico. "This heat is unbelievable," Bari said, as she handed a begging kid who appeared to be about six years old an American dollar.

"*¡Gracias!*" The crooked-toothed child was overjoyed. He went running with the dollar bill, waving it high up in the air.

"*¿Un sombrero, señorita? Solamente cincuenta pesos para usted.*" "*¡Venga! ¡Venga!*" The street vendors called out to them. Sweat poured from their sun-drenched hair down to their brows and onto their faces to make them look slimy. Their shirts were glued to them by the moisture.

"I want to get to the hotel as quickly as possible, strip butt naked, and immerse myself in the pool," Bari said.

"Me, too," Earl said, pulling his wet shirt away from his chest and looking for a breeze that wouldn't come.

"*¡Hola!*" the cabby greeted them as they got into his cab.

"*Hola.* To the Cancún Plaza," Earl ordered the driver; then he settled back into his seat.

Bari looped her arm through his and rested her head against his shoulder. "I love you, baby," she said.

"I love you more," said Earl.

FINALLY, IN THE hotel room, Bari protested when Earl started to unbutton her blouse. They had checked into the hotel only ten minutes ago and Earl wanted to make love immediately. Bari knew that it was their honeymoon, but she wanted to take a shower first and put on one of the sexy negligees that she had taken her time picking out at Lola's specialty lingerie shop. Earl told Bari that he just wanted to have an appetizer and that when they were done they both would shower and make love some more. That sounded good to Bari but she wanted her first experience to be exactly the way she had pictured it. After all, it would be the story that she would tell for the rest of her life. Bari convinced Earl to wait. She promised him that since he had waited this long she would make sure that the few extra hours of waiting would be worth his while. In the meantime, she wanted to look around the hotel and familiarize herself with everything. They settled their bags in the hotel room; then they went back down to the hotel lobby and booked themselves on several tours for the next couple of days. When they were done, they decided to take a dip in the pool and hang out by the Tiki Bar, so they went back up to their room to change into their swimwear.

In the room, Earl remembered the packet of cocaine that Tommy had given him. While Bari was getting ready, he opened the packet and took a few hits. The drug hit him right away. Earl felt good now. He couldn't wait to get down to the pool, take a couple of strokes, have a few cocktails, and then soak up Mexico.

THE POOL WATER was as warm as a foaming bath. Bari sat on the side of the pool with her feet dangling in the water. They had just finished drinking the margaritas that Earl had ordered for them. Earl swam back and forth doing backstrokes and flips as Bari watched him.

"I'm gonna order us some more margaritas," Earl said, climbing out of the pool and drying off.

"Oh no. No more for me, please. I've had enough. My head is already spinning."

When Earl came back, he was carrying two margaritas and wearing a big smile.

"Honey, I told you that I didn't want another drink."

"Don't worry, these are mine. It's happy hour. You get two drinks for the price of one."

"I hope you can handle it. You've already had two," she said.

"Who's counting?" Earl downed the first drink immediately. He already felt good after the hits of cocaine that he took, but the drinks seemed to bring it all together for him.

Some of the other hotel guests who had been in the pool were starting to leave. One other couple lingered for a few minutes more, but they left, too, after a while. Earl and Bari were alone now. Bari wanted to cool off again, so she slid into the water while Earl sat on the ledge drinking his margarita.

"Hurry up and come back into the water, honey." Bari said. She did an upside-down flip in the water, then quickly swam away to the end of the pool. When she reached the end, she turned around and swam back to the other end. Earl finished his drink, and before Bari raised her head out of the water again for air he slid into the pool. He swam under the water and suddenly appeared in front of Bari and grabbed her into a bear hug.

"Whoa! Honey, I love you, too, but you're squeezing me a little too tight," she said playfully.

"Are you complainin'?"

"What if I am?" Bari laughed.

"And you're a smart-ass, too?"

"What if I am?" Bari laughed louder. She walked backward in the water, away from Earl as he walked toward her. He reached out to grab her, but she pulled away before he was able to get hold of her. Bari began to laugh as she turned to run away from him. The water kept her from running quickly enough, though. When Earl reached out to grab her again, he caught her. He held her wet body tightly against his and started to tickle her.

"Ha! Ha! Ha! Earl, stop it. Stop!" Bari laughed. "I'm gonna pee in the pool!"

"You wanna be a smart-ass, huh?" Earl asked, still tickling her.

"I am what I am." Bari laughed harder.

Suddenly Earl pushed her away from him. She stumbled forward with a splash. "Go to the bottom of the pool!" he ordered her.

Bari turned to face him. She wiped away the water from her face. "*You* go to the bottom of the pool!" she teased.

"I said go to the bottom of the pool!" Earl said, walking toward her.

"And I said *you* go to the bottom of the pool!" Bari laughed and moved away from him again.

When Earl reached her, he placed both palms on top of her head and dunked her under the water.

Bari was coughing when she resurfaced. "Okay, Earl, that's enough now!" Before she could compose herself, Earl dunked her again. She wasn't laughing anymore. She tried to catch her breath. "Earl, don't do that again. This isn't funny anymore."

"You don't think it's funny anymore, huh?" Earl palmed the top of Bari's head again and dunked her under the water. This time he held her down even longer than he did the last time. Earl looked around while he held Bari under the water. He noticed the poolside bartender looking at them. Earl let Bari up when he saw the bartender walk from behind the bar and head toward them.

Bari came up coughing and wiping the water out of her eyes. "What the hell is the matter with you?" she yelled.

"Shh, shh," Earl said. "It's okay, baby." He moved in very close to her and spoke into her ear. "It's okay." Earl hoisted Bari up around his waist.

Her legs wrapped around him. "I can't believe you did that!"

"Shh, shh." Earl kissed her on the lips to quiet her down. He glanced up to see if the bartender was still watching them. He was.

Bari caught on that Earl wanted to divert the bartender's attention, so she calmed down.

"Don't get all serious on me. I was just playin' with you." Earl kissed her on the lips, a slow, lingering kiss. When the bartender saw them kissing, he turned and walked back behind the bar.

"I can't believe you did that!" Bari said again, through teary eyes. "You scared me! What's the matter with you!"

"Aw, come on, baby. Lower your voice, he may hear you."

"I don't care if he hears me, Earl! That wasn't right. Were you trying to kill me? What the hell is wrong with you!"

Earl got serious. His eyes bored into Bari's. He spoked to her through clenched teeth. "I was only playing with you. This is our honeymoon; don't ruin it. You're still alive; nobody killed you." He softened his tone. "Come on, who loves you, baby?" He kissed her again.

Bari looked up at him. She was still angry, but Earl was right. It was their honeymoon and their first full day as husband and wife. She didn't want to ruin it. She thought about Hazel and Jimmy. Bari didn't remember ever seeing them being happy, laughing and playing with one another. She didn't want that kind of marriage. She would make her marriage work. She would give it her all, whatever it took.

"*You* do. And I love you, too. Let's start this over. Let's go up to the room," she said, taking Earl's hand and leading him out of the pool. As they walked toward the hotel elevator, Bari slapped Earl playfully on the behind. She ran off, giggling as he chased after her.

When they got to the room, Bari turned to face Earl. "You really scared me down there."

"Oh, come on, there was nothing to be scared of."

"I really thought you were trying to kill me."

"I thought we agreed to start over."

Bari didn't speak about it again. But she wondered about it.

BARI HAD JUST put on her peach-colored negligee and was brushing her hair in the mirror when Earl walked into the bedroom with the packet of cocaine in his hands. He took two hits of the drug directly out of the small plastic resealable package as he walked over to his wife.

Bari turned away from the mirror just in time to see Earl sniffing the drug up his nose. "What is that?"

"Here, I want you to try this," Earl said, holding the coke straw inches away from her nose.

Bari turned her head away. "What is it?"

Earl sniffed up the hit that he had held out to her, then dipped the cut-off straw back into the small plastic packet and filled the tip with some more of the drug. "C'mere," he said. Earl put the straw up to Bari's nostril.

Bari turned her head away again. "I don't want that."

"Come on, baby. It's called white lady. It ain't gonna hurt you. It ain't physically addicting or nothin' like that. I feel good and I want you to feel what I'm feelin'." He put the straw to her nose again.

"No, I don't want it, Earl. That's cocaine."

"Look, baby, it's all right. It ain't gonna hurt you. I promise." He stood very close to Bari and kissed her on the neck. Earl kissed her in her ear, then whispered to her, "I love you, baby. Do this for me, okay?" He knew the effect that his whispered words would have on her. Earl wanted Bari to experience getting high with him, and he would have done just about anything to make her do it.

"Would I give you anything that would hurt you? Would I?" he asked her.

"No." Bari's voice was barely audible.

"All right then. Here." Earl put the straw to her right nostril and told her to sniff the coke into her nose.

Bari did what Earl told her. She frowned when the drug slightly burned her nose. Earl scooped some more of the drug onto the straw and put it to her left nostril. Bari sniffed again. She stood very still all of a sudden as if she was waiting for something to happen. "Wait a minute," she said. "I have to sit down." Bari backed up and dropped herself down on the bed. "Wait a minute," she said again, and was back on her feet holding her head. "I don't like this, Earl. My heart is beating too fast. I'm scared."

"It's all right," Earl told her. "Just calm down and mellow out with it."

"No, no, Earl, I don't like this. Feel my heart." She took Earl's hand and put it to her chest. "Can you feel how fast my heart is beating? You can hear it, too. Do you hear how loud it is? Something's wrong." Bari ran from the room and went into the bathroom.

Earl ran behind her. Before he could catch up with her, she was inside the bathroom with the door locked. "Are you all right?" Earl asked from outside the door.

Bari didn't answer him. She slumped into the corner by the tub. "Oh, God, don't let me die like this. I promise I will never do drugs again. Father, please forgive me. I swear I won't ever do this again."

"Open the door, Bari."

"I'm scared, Earl," Bari called out to him.

"Open the door."

Bari got up from the floor and pulled open the door. She fell into Earl's arms, crying. "Earl, I don't like this. This isn't good at all." She sobbed. "Promise me you'll throw away those drugs and you won't ever do them again. Promise me!"

"Okay, okay, baby. Relax. I promise you, I won't ever do drugs again. C'mere," Earl said as he gathered Bari into his arms. "You're all right, baby. You're all right." Earl rubbed Bari's back while she buried her face in his chest. "Come sit down." He led the way over to the bed. "Here."

He lightly kissed her lips once they were sitting. "And here." Earl kissed her again. Finally, he parted her lips and stuck his tongue in her mouth. Bari kissed him back. Earl nudged her back onto the bed, kissing her deeply and sucking on her lips. He was breathless now.

"Wait, wait, Earl," Bari managed to say, in between his kisses.

"What for?" Earl asked, but he didn't stop sucking on her mouth.

"Just a minute. . . ." Bari tried to push him up off of her. Earl didn't budge. "I'm a little nervous. Just let me get a little more relaxed. . . ."

"What are you talkin'"—Earl kissed her again —"about? Huh? You're relaxed. . . ." He didn't wait for Bari to respond. He pulled both of her arms up over her head and pinned them down to the bed. He dipped his head down and sucked on her neck.

"Earl, please, I really want the first time to be special."

"It *is* special, baby. You're special. God, I want you." Earl started kissing Bari's breasts. He licked her nipples until they became hard. Bari's negligee was sopping wet around the breasts as Earl licked and sucked them all over, through the gown.

"What about the lights? Can we turn them off?" Bari's eyes pleaded with him.

Earl looked at Bari, but he was too excited to stop. He was breathing hard. Panting. All seven of the tiny buttons on the front of Bari's peach-colored negligee were fastened, stopping Earl from kissing her bare breasts. Earl used one hand to try to unbutton the first button but he couldn't pull it through the small elastic buttonhole. He tried the next one. His patience ran out when it wouldn't give. He let loose of Bari's arms and used both hands to grab hold of her negligee and rip it apart, tearing it right down the middle, breaking off the tiny little buttons.

"Earl."

"It's all right, baby. It's all right." Earl frantically sucked her breasts, leaving small red splotches in some spots.

Bari closed her eyes. She wouldn't fight him anymore. It was their honeymoon and they would enjoy it. She felt awkward at first and didn't know what to do with her hands. She remembered seeing a film once where a young girl was having sex for the first time. She remembered how nervous the girl was. Bari was just as nervous as the girl in the film. The young girl's lover had made it easy for her, though. He showed her what to do. Earl was too busy, too excited, to show Bari what to do. Maybe she had made him wait too long. Bari wanted him to be pleased, so she let him have his way with her.

Bari reached down and rubbed the back of his head at first. Then she rubbed his back. The licks that he was giving her were starting to feel good. They were starting to excite her. Earl made his way back up to Bari's mouth and kissed her. Bari kissed him back. She tried to match his fervor. They both began to softly moan together as they hungrily kissed each other. Earl reached his trembling hand down between Bari's legs and pulled the crotch of her panties to the side. He raised himself up slightly and used his other hand to plunge his penis into her vagina. Bari squeezed her eyes shut and clenched her teeth. She dug her nails into Earl's back to help her bear the pain.

"I'm sorry, baby. I'm sorry," Earl said. He didn't stop, though. Bari braced herself against Earl as he went harder and deeper into her. She numbed herself and willed her mind not to concentrate on the act. She was somewhere else now and the pain was gone. Bari was thinking about the white, sandy Mexican beaches, the bullfights, and the Mayan ruins that they would see on their tour the next day. She thought about the snorkeling that they would do for the first time. She was looking forward to the solitude of the underground with beautifully colored fishes swimming all around her. The coral reefs that she had read so much about . . . so beautiful she wanted to reach out and touch them.

Bari thought she was prepared for this act, but she wasn't. What she had imagined wasn't this. The tenderness, the caring . . . the exploring of each other's bodies, familiarity . . . where was it? Earl's body shuddered and collapsed on top of her. Bari felt his hot breath against her neck. She wrapped her arms around him and closed her eyes.

"That was unbelievable, baby." Earl still hadn't quite caught his breath. "Was it good for you? Did you come?"

"Yes." Bari kept her eyes closed and her arms tight around her husband, softly rubbing his back. The wetness between her legs made her feel uncomfortable but she lay there.

"I hope I didn't hurt you. I know I got excited. . . . I don't know what got into me. But as long as you enjoyed it, then everything is okay." He kissed Bari on the cheek and buried his face into her neck. "I promise you it's just gonna get better and better each time we do it. Okay, sweetheart?"

"Okay." Of course it would get better, she told herself. She just needed to learn her husband's ways. As long as he was pleased, then so was she.

Bari lay there listening to the even rhythm of Earl's breathing. Eventually, she drifted off to sleep, too.

fourteen

BARI WAS IN the basement of her house sorting the laundry when the call came in. It was only a week ago that she had gone on the interview, but she had pushed it out of her mind because she didn't want to get her hopes up too high. Even with Barbara putting in a word for her over lunch with David Martin and even with her carrying her posy kerchief in her pocket every day since the interview, she still wasn't too confident.

"Bari! Phone!" Earl called down to her.

"Okay!" she said. Bari ran up the steps two by two. She stopped at the undersink cabinet in the kitchen and took out a container of fabric softener and put it up on the counter so she wouldn't forget to take it back downstairs with her when she was done with her call. Bari picked up the telephone receiver, which Earl had left dangling from the base on the wall.

"Yeello!" she said, and waited for Franki to respond the same way she always did.

"Er, yes, er, Bari Jordan?" a voice at the other end asked.

"Oh, uh . . . yes, this is she," Bari said, straightening up and feeling embarrassed.

"This is Janet Buckley from the Human Resources Department of Choler-Raines. I'm calling to let you know that we enjoyed meeting with you last Thursday. We were very impressed with you and we would like to extend an offer of employment to you for the Account Manager position. Are you interested?"

"Oh yes, of course. Of course," Bari responded, her pulse racing and her palms sweating.

"Very good then. Would it be possible for you to come into our office on Thursday, November fourteen, at nine A.M.? We have some paperwork that you will need to complete, and we'll go over any questions or concerns that you may have. In the meantime, you can expect to receive an offer letter from us in the mail."

"Sounds good," Bari said.

"Okay then, so we'll see you on the fourteenth."

"Thanks. Thanks again," Bari said, and hung up. "Yes!" she yelled, squeezing at the posie kerchief through the fabric of her slacks. Then she slapped her palm against her forehead. "Oh, my God, I could die. I must've sounded like an idiot. Earl!" she yelled, running from the kitchen into the den where Earl was working.

"Earl!" she yelled again, just before she reached the room. "I got it! I got the job!" Bari ran into his arms just as he stood up.

"Congratulations," Earl said, kissing her lips. "I knew you would get it."

"I wasn't so sure," Bari said, withdrawing from his arms. "I mean, I sounded brain-dead on the phone just now. I didn't know what to say. The woman probably thinks I'm retarded."

"She probably knew you were nervous. It happens. Don't worry about it," Earl said, sitting back down.

"I can't believe I got my first real job. Oooh!" Bari grabbed hold of Earl again while he sat, and kissed him on the side of his head. "I have to tell Barbara," she said as she pulled herself away from Earl again and ran from the room. She stopped at the kitchen phone again and dialed Barbara's house.

"Barbara, it's me," Bari said when Barbara answered the phone. "I got it. I got the job!"

"Well, all right! Congratulations."

"Thank you, Barbara, thank you so much for everything."

"You don't have to thank me, because to tell you the truth, I don't think I had much to do with it."

"Of course you did; you put a word in with David for me."

"Yeah, but I don't think that mattered. I don't know what you said to those people but you blew their minds."

"You think?"

"Heck yeah. David can't stop talking about you."

BARI REPORTED TO work two weeks later and was surprised when she was shown into a small vacant office that would be hers. It was more than she had hoped for. Bari was grateful. She sat behind the desk when she was finally left alone and spun around in her chair, two full rotations. She couldn't believe it. A real job and her own office, too!

She opened the desk drawer and was surprised to see the small compartments in the drawer neatly stacked with paper clips, staples, and Post-it note pads. Several legal pads were in the tray on her desk, with pencils and pens beside them. She looked at the bare walls and decided she would buy some pictures to hang on them and some plants for the windowsills.

"Are you comfortable?" David asked her, appearing out of nowhere at her door.

"Oh yes. So far, so good," Bari said.

"Good. Come with me. Let's get a cup of coffee."

"Sure." Bari got up from behind the desk and walked to the kitchen with him. On the way there, David told Bari what he expected from the team and described for her what her role would be. He told her that he wanted to meet with her after lunch to talk about her first assignment.

WHEN BARI RETURNED to the office after lunch, she stopped in her office only to put down her pocketbook; then she went straight in to see David.

"Do you have a moment to speak with me?" she asked him.

"Absolutely. Come on in. Have a seat."

Bari had been trying to figure out the shifty-eyed man sitting in front of her since she first met him at her interview. She still wasn't quite sure what to make of him.

"I'm all prepared for you," he said, pulling out a manila folder stuffed with all kinds of documents. "First of all, let me explain to you how I work. I am here to help each and every member of my staff no matter what. That's my purpose. I'm never going to assign anything to you that is impossible to manage. It's to my advantage, to all of our advantage, to make the team strong, not to weaken it. If you look good, I certainly look good."

Bari nodded her head as David spoke. She kept her eyes locked into his and absorbed every word he said.

"I'm giving you a kind of a 'get your feet wet' type of assignment. It's a light load. I think you'll do good with it. It's called Katty Kids. You may have heard of them before; they've been around for a while. Get to know 'em, set up some meetings, and let's see how it goes."

"Great." Bari gave him a genuine smile. Her heart beat fast while reality kicked in. This wasn't school anymore, this was the real world, and she couldn't believe that she had gotten so lucky.

AT THE END of the day Bari and Barbara walked out of the building together. Bari had a smug, happy-go-lucky look on her face while Barbara looked stressed.

"So, how do you like it so far?" Barbara asked Bari.

"I *love* it so far. I got my first assignment. David gave me a small account. He said he wanted me to use it to get my feet wet."

"Cool. What did he give you?"

"He gave me the Katty Kids account."

Barbara stopped walking. "He did not give you Katty Kids."

"He did. Why? Is something wrong with that?" Bari asked hesitantly.

"Girlie, if David gave you Katty Kids, he didn't just want you to get your feet wet; he wanted you to drown." Barbara started walking again.

"What do you mean, drown?" Bari got back into step with Barbara.

"Listen to me. You don't want Katty Kids. It is completely unmanageable. The guy who runs the company, Mitch Howard, is a demon. He wants your blood. He already fired our company twice and rehired us twice. He hates the world. You can't please him."

"Then why does he keep coming back to us if we can't give him what he wants?"

"Good question. Our guess is that no other company is willing to put up with his crap like us. For the love of money Choler-Raines will put up with just about anything. We're good at kissing ass. Maybe that's why we're so successful."

"But I don't understand. Why would David give me such a tough account? And why would he lie to me?"

"Another good question. Maybe we're jumping the gun. Maybe he's just testing you to see what you're made of. In any case, my prayers are with you, because if you fail, especially being the new kid on the block, they'll form an opinion of you and it will stick. Believe you me, they can make your life real miserable."

"God," Bari said under her breath. "I knew this was too good to be true." She was feeling low by the time she reached home. Bari took off her clothes as soon as she got in and took a steaming hot shower. She replayed the conversations that she had had with David and Barbara over and over in her mind. She didn't know what to think or what to do. Suddenly she didn't feel so good. Bari didn't know how she would do it, but she decided that she wasn't going to fail. In fact, she promised herself that.

Bari took out last night's leftovers and prepared a plate for Earl. She placed it in the microwave, so all he would have to do was heat it up when he came in. She knew that he would be in any minute and he would be starving as usual. That done, she pulled out the Katty Kids file from her briefcase. She flipped through the stack of papers several times before she actually read anything. Bari wanted to get a feel for the client.

By the time she was done, she knew exactly what she had to do. She would give this project her best shot, and if that wasn't good enough, then so be it. The same way she got the job at Choler-Raines she would get a job somewhere else.

BARI WENT INTO the office bright and early the next morning. She got a cup of coffee and settled down to work. She set the Katty Kids account in front of her and studied it some more. Before noon, Bari had three meetings set up with the client contact, their sales team, and the production staff. She spent the rest of her day crunching numbers and writing her first proposal. Even though Bari told herself that it didn't matter to her if she didn't succeed with the account, she couldn't stop her stomach from churning. Even when she woke up the next morning, the churning wouldn't stop.

She had taken special care in choosing the suit that she would wear to her meetings that morning. She didn't have much to choose from. She planned to treat herself to one or two business suits once she got her first paycheck. In the meantime, she chose an olive green suit that Franki had given her six months before. The suit still had the tags on it. Franki gave it to her after she decided she hated it once she brought it home. It looked good on Bari and she felt comfortable in it. She even practiced her "power walk" in front of the mirror. Without even thinking about it, Bari opened her lingerie drawer and took out the posy kerchief.

Bari's legs were not her own as she stepped into the elevator at the Katty Kids offices. All of the confidence that she had felt earlier was gone. She tried to gather herself before she met Mitch Howard. She wanted to appear confident and experienced. But after sitting and waiting in the reception area for more than twenty minutes, Bari only felt annoyance and she wasn't sure if she would be able to hide it from him.

No one had briefed Bari on the client. Everything that she knew about the company and its owner she read about in the file. Mitch Howard was the president and CEO of Katty Kids. He was a self-made millionaire who started his company when he was twenty-six years old. Now he was sixty-six. No wonder he seemed so pompous, Bari thought. How dare he keep her waiting for so long. She was just about to ask the receptionist to call him again when he very casually walked out from behind the closed doors. He stopped short and motioned for Bari to come with him. Mitch Howard didn't smile, and he never said hello.

No amount of reading could have prepared Bari for the man who stood before her. At first glance, she saw the Devil. She had to blink her eyes twice to clear the image of his horn and his tail. His eyes were piercing underneath his deeply creased brow. His nose was bulbous and his lips were twisted into a snarl, with skin as white as baby powder.

When his gravelly voice finally grunted a hello, Bari stopped staring at him and shook his hand. She grimaced as his callused hand touched hers. Without another word, he turned and walked away. Bari followed him. When they reached his office he sat down behind his desk. Bari realized that he wasn't going to invite her to sit down, so she took it upon herself to do so. She immediately fingered the kerchief of posies in her pocket. If it had any power at all, she would be relying on it to work right now. She could already see that Mitch Howard was not going to be easy to deal with.

Mitch Howard didn't speak for several seconds, which seemed like an eternity to Bari. He looked directly into her eyes. His piercing eyes shook her to the core. It was as if he were looking through her. Bari timidly looked away. *What is his problem?* she wondered. Why was this man determined to make her miserable?

"Who are you again?" he asked.

Bari didn't answer him. She realized that he wasn't really speaking to her.

Mitch flipped a page from his daily planner to read her name. "Bari Jordan, Mrs. Bari Jordan. Yeah, from Choler-Raines," he said. He looked up from the paper and glued his eyes to hers again. "Let me tell you a little something about my company. This company is my blood. I'm very proud of it. I built it from the ground up. It's been around a lot longer than you've had breath in you. Trust me, I'm looking at you and I can tell you're still wet behind the ears. You got no fire. Tell your company not to waste any more of my time." He waved his hand, dismissing her.

Bari didn't know what to say—she only looked at him in disbelief. Just like that, she had lost her client before she ever had him. Her confidence was crushed. She didn't make a move to leave. She just sat there looking into his face. This time, Bari didn't take her eyes away from his—even when he stared back at her. She looked at his creased brow—she studied the thick lines that were permanently pressed there. Bari allowed herself to linger on the large bags under his eyes. Then she looked at his high cheekbones. For a fleeting moment, she saw a look of discomfort cross his face. She didn't care. She kept on looking at him. Her eyes roamed all over the pale, clammy skin on his face, while he looked on. This time, Mitch Howard lowered his eyes.

"Mr. Howard," Bari began, "even if I am wet behind the ears, that doesn't give you the right to be rude to me. Just like I'm not holding it against you because you're a mean, cold, miserable man."

Mitch Howard opened his mouth to protest, but Bari kept on speaking. "You don't have to tell me anything about your company because I know all about it. Yes, you've been strong in the industry since I was a little girl. But guess what? The industry has changed. Your numbers are falling rapidly. Do you want to know why?" She didn't wait for an answer. "Nobody wants your product anymore. That's right," Bari said when she noticed the question marks in his eyes. "Kids want toys that do things. They want video games, electronics. Now, if you care to look beyond my wet ears for a moment, I can show you a strategy that may keep you afloat for several more years, maybe even for the long run. This strategy will target a whole different market and even start collectors' editions for you."

Mitch Howard cleared his throat. His earlier, brazen look had become pained. He looked at Bari apologetically. "Perhaps . . . perhaps, I judged you wrong . . . ," he said.

"Perhaps."

"Please. Show me what you got."

WHEN BARI LEFT Katty Kids later that afternoon, she wanted to jump up and click her heels. She had done well. Very well, in fact, and Mitch Howard was eating out of her hands. His whole crew was.

With a new burst of energy, Bari returned to work and went straight to David's office. She was excited. She had to force her brain to slow down because her mouth was moving too slow to keep up while she spoke to David. Her words were tumbling out a mile a minute. David congratulated her, but there were no hoorahs. David simply knocked twice on the Katty Kids folder that she held in her hand and told her, "Good job." He walked away leaving her feeling perplexed.

Bari could only assume that David thought that she did good work, because he gave her more projects over the next few months. Complicated ones. And each time, she would secure the client for the firm. Soon enough, calls starting coming in with complimentary remarks for Bari. She had a way with the clients and they liked her. They trusted her.

Within three years, Bari was one of the best Account Managers that Choler-Raines had seen in a very long time. Bari's marriage was good, too. Earl was attentive and supportive. She found that out early on. On one of the many nights that Bari came in late from the office, she was too exhausted to even take her keys out of her bag. She dragged herself up the stairs to her house, and by the time she reached the top step the front door was pulled open. Earl opened the door for Bari and he was wearing the brightest smile for her.

"Wow!" Bari said. "How did you know that I was out here?"

"That's my duty. I'm *supposed* to know these things. Come on in, baby." He took her bags in one hand and held her hand with his free one. "I have something for you."

Bari just smiled. Every night it was something new. Earl was always doing something special for her. She didn't even try to guess what the "something" was. She just went along with him. Earl led her over to the couch and gently nudged her to take a seat. "Here, let me get these," he said, easing her shoes off her feet. "I'll take this, too," Earl said, as he unbuttoned her blouse and removed it. "And this. . . ." Earl opened the snaps down the front of her skirt. Bari stood up and let the skirt slip down to the floor. Earl, on his knees, gently pulled her slip down her long, sleek legs. He stood up and walked behind her. He kissed the small beads of sweat that had moistened her spinal column. Running his tongue down her back, he was on his knees again. Still licking her, he lingered at the small of her back. He slowly pulled her emerald green panties down her legs.

Bari stepped out of the clothing that lay at her feet. Earl stood up and reached for her hand and he walked her into the bathroom. Earl had unscrewed all seven of the lightbulbs from the lighting track over the sink. One bulb had been removed from the center of the track and replaced with a yellow one. The yellow bulb was the only one that was turned on. Two scented candles were placed at the head of the tub, and two were placed at the foot. Lavender-colored bubbles were piled high in the tub, their scent soft and sweet.

"This is for you, baby. I know you had a hard day."

She sighed deeply, then walked into Earl's arms. "You're so good to me."

"I love you," Earl whispered into her ear.

Bari's legs weakened. Feeling his breath in her ear excited her. There was a throbbing between her legs. Her breathing was rapid and deep. She would have let Earl make love to her right then and there, but Earl nibbled on her neck, then nudged her toward the tub. Bari soaked in the warm bath for twenty minutes. When she was done, she put on the yellow-colored satin pajamas that Earl had laid out for her.

Earl came into the bathroom just as she finished dressing, and guided her to the dining room, where their dinner was laid out on the table.

"How do you like this?" he asked her, showing the nicely set table with a wave of his hand. "It's a meal fit for a queen. *My* queen." Earl pulled out a chair for Bari. She sat down and looked at all of the dishes in front of her. Earl sat across from her. "That's stewed chicken with mushrooms." Earl pointing at the dish that was closest to Bari. "That's steamed cabbage; that's creamed corn, and I made some biscuits."

Everything smelled good, but when Bari tasted the chicken, it made her gag. The gravy was obviously made from ketchup, too much of it. She coughed to keep from spitting it out. She could see that Earl was proud, so she didn't want to disappoint him. The cabbage was overcooked and swimming in butter; the creamed corn was too salty and the canned buttermilk biscuits were burned on the bottom. Bari took little baby bites to get it all down. She smiled to herself. She couldn't help but think about the time when Earl baked her a birthday cake. He had forgotten to put the eggs in the batter, and the cake shrank up hard like rock candy. He was more disappointed than she was. He had driven around for over two hours after that, looking for a bakery that was open late. He wanted the cake to have a nice design on it with a special birthday message for her. The cake was beautiful. Bari knew that it must have cost him a dear penny. Earl had brought it to her grinning all the way.

"What are you smiling about?" Earl asked her.

"I'm just thinking about how happy I am. And how you take such good care of me." She reached her hand across the table and touched his. "I love you so much, Earl."

"I know." He got up from his seat and walked around the table to stand behind Bari. He started massaging her shoulders. "You're tense," he said.

"You have magic hands," Bari responded, purring under his touch.

"Why don't you go on upstairs and turn in. I'll take care of the dishes."

"Okay, honey." With that, Bari got up from the table and went upstairs to the bedroom. She was tired, but she wanted to show Earl some appreciation. She lay awake until he finished up in the kitchen and came upstairs to bed. She turned on her side to face him. She stroked his face as he lay beside her. Bari looked intently into Earl's eyes before she stuck her tongue into his mouth and kissed him long and deep. Bari moved her body closer to Earl's.

He put his arms around her and held on tight. "You'd better get some rest, honey, or you won't be any good to yourself tomorrow," he said.

Bari sighed deeply before she responded to him, "Okay, you're right." She sighed again, moving still closer to him and resting her face against his chest. They lay entwined until Bari's breathing became steady and deep and she drifted off to sleep.

fifteen

IT WAS INVENTORY week. That was when Earl and his father, Broderick, spent countless hours checking stock and making adjustments to their sales and inventory records. It wasn't something that either one of them enjoyed, but it came with the territory and was necessary. It was 8:00 P.M. and they had been at it for almost four hours. Earl's sleeves were rolled up and he was going from shelf to shelf physically counting reams of paper of every type and filling out order forms to restock any items that fell below count. Broderick was in his office reviewing the current sales report and checking out the trends from the previous quarters.

Earl was deep in thought when the sound of the click of a heel interrupted his flow. He turned around, but no one was there. He figured he was hearing things, so he continued to work, moving even quicker to try to hurry up and get through the night. Now, for sure, somebody cleared her throat. Earl turned around again.

"I miss you," Bari said, standing against the back wall of the room.

"I miss you, too," Earl said, smiling.

Bari's hair was parted in the middle of her head and hung long, black, and straight down her back. She was wearing a full-length mahogany mink coat and a pair of brown pumps. She wrapped the coat tight around her, crossing her arms over it to keep it closed. Earl had just bought the coat for her two days earlier, but he had only seen it on her in the store.

Earl walked toward Bari. Just before he reached her, Bari slowly opened her arms wide, still holding the coat with either hand, extending them back against the wall. She was completely naked underneath the coat.

Earl stopped in his tracks. It was like his breath was taken away, because he didn't say anything. He couldn't say anything. He only looked at her, shaking his head like he was in a trance. "You are truly beautiful," he said, finally walking toward her again. "So perfect." Earl touched her face first, like he needed to know that she was real. He looked deep into her eyes, saying nothing, and kissed her.

"I love you so much."

"And I love you so much more." Earl kissed her again.

Earl couldn't stop touching Bari. He caressed her breasts softly, then her belly. His hands touched the moistness between her legs while Bari moaned softly.

"I want you, Bari. Let's go into the room." Earl put both hands on Bari's waist and pulled her tightly to him and hugged her one more time. He whispered in her ear, "I love you."

The warmth of Earl's breath in her ear nearly made Bari collapse in his arms. Earl led her into one of the small side rooms in the warehouse where he and his father slept on cots if they worked through the night and couldn't make it home to sleep.

Inside the room, Earl removed Bari's mink and carefully laid it over a chair. He went back over to Bari and the two of them hungrily kissed, touched, and explored each other's body and made love until they both were full.

"I've kept you from your work long enough. I know you have a lot to do," Bari said as Earl helped her on with her coat, covering her nakedness.

"And you have to work in the morning."

"Don't remind me."

"I'll drop you home, then I'll come back here. Me and Pop will probably end up workin' through the night."

"I hate that I have to take you away from your work. I wish I wasn't too afraid to learn how to drive."

"Don't worry about it. Let's go."

"I'm gonna miss you." Bari touched Earl's cheek. "Anyway, let's hurry. I don't want to see your father like this."

Earl put on his coat and they hurried toward the door. Broderick came out of his office and stood at his door just as Earl reached for the doorknob.

"Hello, Bari," Broderick called out.

"Hello, Broderick."

"Nice coat," he said.

Bari smiled and waved, then hurried out the door.

sixteen

1988

IT WAS LATE in the afternoon when Bari decided she needed to take a break from her work. She rang Barbara's extension to see if she wanted to take a walk with her down to the company's cafeteria to get a cup of coffee. They got their coffee, then returned to Bari's office. Barbara sipped on her coffee as she sat in Bari's guest chair.

"Have you seen Larry today?" Barbara asked.

"No, I haven't. Anyway, I'm afraid to look in his face after what happened at the departmental luncheon yesterday."

"Well, thank God he has a sense of humor."

"Yeah, but did you see how red his face and neck got when that waitress said that to him?"

"That was hilarious! My girl took one look at him and she said, 'A Diet Coke, right?'" They both burst out laughing. Barbara's high, shrill laugh was so loud that Bari had to tell her to lower her voice. "She said that in front of everybody!" Tears rolled down Barbara's face. Her laughter was uncontrollable.

"I mean why did she assume he wanted a Diet Coke? Ha, ha," laughed Barbara.

"Because he's so overweight."

"Still, that doesn't make sense. The man ordered damn near a side of beef, a baked potato with sour cream, not to mention his fried clam strips appetizer. What the hell would he need a Diet Coke for?"

"True! True!" Bari laughed. The phone rang. "Good afternoon. Choler-Raines, Bari speaking."

"Hello, Bari speaking." It was Earl.

"Hi, baby."

"Hi yourself. What are you doing?"

"Taking a break. I'm talking with Barbara. *Crazy* Barbara, I should say." Barbara waved her hand at Bari.

"What are you wearing?"

"A beige pantsuit. Why?"

"You guys make me sick," Barbara said, getting up to leave.

"No, wait," Bari said, gesturing for her to sit back down. Barbara sat back down.

"I know it's last-minute, but we got an invitation to a dinner party tonight. It's kind of important to me because there's a person that's gonna be there—a Gary Whyte—who my father needs me to get next to. We need to try to get him to buy some more paper goods from us for some of those seminars that he hosts all around the city."

"Well, in that case, I don't see how I can say no."

"Good, now tell me somethin' else."

"What?"

"What are you wearin' underneath that beige pants suit?"

Bari's eyes softened; she blushed. "It's champagne pink and it's silk—"

"Underwear? Are you talking about underwear? That's it; I'm leaving!" Barbara said, standing up again to leave.

"Sit down before I kill you," Bari threatened her. Barbara sighed and sat back down again.

"Yes." Bari's eyes and voice softened again. "Of course you can. It's all yours. Okay . . . see you at seven." She hung up.

"I swear you two are sickening. I thought the honeymoon was over four years ago," Barbara complained.

"Well, you thought wrong. The honeymoon will never be over."

"If you could only see how goofy your face looks."

"Later for you," Bari said, waving Barbara off. "Anyway, I guess I'm working tonight until seven. I have to go to a dinner party with Earl."

"More power to you. I'm out of here when the bell rings at five."

"Oh, come on, work late. Keep me company?" Bari asked, her head tilted to the side, trying to look pitiful.

"Am I invited to the dinner party?" Barbara asked.

"No."

"Then there's your answer. I'm goin' home." Barbara got up and turned to leave. Bari playfully threw a paper clip at her, which hit her in the back.

EARL PULLED UP in front of Bari's office building at exactly seven o'clock. Bari was standing out in front waiting for him. Earl got out of the car and walked over to greet her. He kissed her on the cheek, then took her bags from her and put them into the backseat of the car. Traffic moved surprisingly steadily as they headed to Fifty-seventh Street where the dinner party was being held. Bari chatted on and on to Earl about her clients, her job, and her stress and Earl nodded from time to time as he listened.

"Listen to me. I'm talking a mile a minute about my job. You must be tired of listening to me."

"No, baby, I'm not tired of listenin' to you. I love to hear you talk shop. You know how proud of you I am." He reached over and rested his right hand on her thigh, giving it a squeeze. Earl looked at Bari briefly. He loved her completely, he thought. There was something clean and pure about Bari that had drawn him to her from the first day he met her. Her honesty was almost tangible. There was a warmth he got from her that he could never describe. It was the same feeling that he remembered as a boy. It was kind of a saintly thing. He knew it was crazy, but it was almost like maybe his mother had come back to him in Bari. God knows it had been hard for him to cope with everything and anything around him before he met Bari. He had always felt so alone. He walked around angry much of the time and there were many nights that he cried himself to sleep. But Bari gave him peace of mind. She comforted him.

Earl glanced over at Bari again. He made a silent promise to himself that he would protect her from the cold, cruel world and see to it that nothing tarnished her. He would make sure that he would never let their relationship get clouded with bullshit.

Earl was surprised when he pulled up in front of the building and got a parking spot from someone who was just pulling out. He and Bari walked into the building and took the elevator up to the third floor.

A short, blond, curly-haired woman, the hostess, answered the door when they rang the bell. "You must be Earl Jordan. I'm Wendy; we've been waiting for you."

"How are you?" Earl asked, smiling and shaking Wendy's hand. "This is my wife, Bari."

"How lovely," Wendy said. "Pleased to meet you, Bari."

"Likewise," Bari said.

Wendy shook Bari's hand, then led them inside the apartment. The apartment was wide, with high ceilings and hardwood floors that looked as if they had just been treated with a high-gloss finish. A spiral staircase was located right in the center of the room. It led to the upstairs bedrooms.

Two hired waiters in black suits and black bow ties had already started bringing in trays of meats, salads, and breads to the table. No one was seated yet. At least nineteen other guests were gathered around the spiral staircase sipping wine and munching on the crackers, imported cheeses, and grapes that were set about the room.

Earl was shocked when he saw his old friend Tommy standing in the circle of people. "I see an old friend of mine over there," Earl said to Bari, pointing in Tommy's direction. "You remember Tommy? He came to our wedding."

"He looks vaguely familiar," said Bari.

"I'm gonna go over and say hi to him. Do you mind if I leave you alone for a minute?"

"I'll be okay," Bari said, and Earl went over to Tommy.

"Tommy," Earl said, standing behind him.

Tommy turned around. "Earl. What's up, man?" They shook hands.

"You tell me what's up. I almost didn't recognize you in the monkey suit," said Earl.

"Oh, this," Tommy said, looking down at his navy blue pin-striped Pierre Cardin suit. "Yeah, every now and then I have to do this."

"You look like a true businessman. What the hell brings you here?"

"Business," Tommy replied.

"Don't tell me you're with corporate America now."

"Hell no, I ain't with corporate America. You know I ain't never gonna do no stupid shit like that."

"Well, in that case, I'm confused."

"Confused about what? Don't tell me you think all of these people in here are on the up-and-up."

"Well, I thought . . . I thought . . . ," Earl stammered.

"You thought wrong, my brother. Half of these mofos in here hit more shit than I can sell. I just made a little mint up here. I put on my suit and come up in here and do my thing; then I'm on to the next set."

"Sounds like a good gig."

"So, enough about me, let's talk about you. Had any good stuff lately?" Tommy asked.

"Good stuff like what?" Earl asked.

"You know, nose candy."

"Nah, man, I haven't as a matter of fact. I haven't had any of that since I last saw you—what, four years ago."

"You're kiddin' me, right?" Tommy asked.

"No, I'm dead serious," said Earl.

"Let's take a walk," Tommy told Earl, taking him by his elbow and leading him into the foyer, which was empty.

Earl looked over at Bari and put up one finger to let her know that he would be back in a minute. Bari had already worked her way into a conversation with a group of people who were standing nearby.

"So look here," Tommy said when he and Earl were alone in the foyer. "I'm gonna hook you up with a little somethin' for now. But when you're done with it, I want you to call me. I got a good price for you—whatever you want."

Tommy handed Earl a salmon-colored business card with his name and telephone number printed on it. Earl stuck the card in his jacket pocket. Tommy reached into his inner jacket pocket and took out a little plastic packet with small rocks of pure cocaine in it. He handed it to Earl.

"Thanks, man."

"No problem. Just let me know how you like that and we'll talk." Tommy left the room.

Earl walked out just behind him. He peeked over at Bari. She was deeply engrossed in the conversation in the circle now. He made a left turn into the hallway and went into the bathroom. Earl took out the cocaine packet and Tommy's business card. Earl placed the unopened packet on the sink. He took out a quarter from his pocket and ran it back and forth over the packet, crushing the rocks of coke. When the rocks became a fine powder, he bent Tommy's business card into a peak at the edge and poured some cocaine onto it and used it to put the drug into his nose. The first hit felt good to him. The second one was even better. Earl moaned softly. He remembered that feeling it had given him three years before. He remembered how it had numbed him. *This is good,* he thought. He took another hit, then put away the packet. He didn't want to overdo it before he was able to talk business with Gary Whyte. Earl leaned against the wall and stared straight ahead of him at the tiled wall. The small flowers that bordered the center of the wall irritated him. He forced himself to look away. Suddenly a scent, a potpourri scent coming from a dish beside the sink, made him feel queasy. He took out the cocaine packet again and took two more hits. He intended for that to last him for the rest of the evening. Finally, he left the bathroom and joined Bari.

"Are you okay, Earl?" Bari asked him.

"Am I okay? Why would you ask me that?"

"Your eyes look a little red, that's all."

"Oh, that, yeah, I'm a little tired. I just want to handle my business with Gary so we can leave."

"They have a delicious-looking dinner that they just finished setting up. I saw some baked ducks over there covered with hoisin sauce. I guess we should get ready to be seated."

"Yeah, well, I'm not hungry," Earl said, taking a glass of champagne from the tray that the waiter carried. "I'll just sip on this."

"This is a dinner party, Earl. You gotta eat something."

"I said I wasn't hungry."

When everybody was seated, the waiter came through and quickly placed a plate at every setting. Earl didn't get a chance to tell the waiter that he didn't want one, so he kept the plate in front of him and moved the food around it every now and again. The smell of the food nauseated him. He had ordered a glass of rum and Coke from one of the waiters and was working on his second one during dinner. When the meal was over, Earl excused himself and made a run to the bathroom again. Inside the bathroom, he took several more hits. This time when he was done he turned on the cold water, filled his cupped hands with the running water, and splashed it on his face. He dried himself off with a paper towel, then left the bathroom to find Gary Whyte. Earl recognized Gary right away. He had seen his face on Gary's company's brochure earlier that week. Gary was standing alone by the wall when Earl approached him.

"Hi, I-I'm E-Earl 'Ordan. . . ." Earl's hand was extended to Gary's.

"I'm sorry, what was that?" Gary asked, reaching to shake Earl's hand.

"I-I'm Earl Jo-Jordan," Earl said, his speech choppy, almost rubbery.

"How are you?" Gary asked.

Earl nodded his head, took a deep breath, and looked around the room. When he looked back at Gary, he was looking at Earl. He knew that Gary expected him to say something. He knew for himself that he should have said something, but the words, though they were in his head, would not come out of his mouth. Earl's throat constricted and his mouth felt slightly paralyzed. He stood there sharing a very awkward moment with Gary. Earl thought for a fleeting moment that Gary was looking at him disapprovingly. Then he could have sworn he saw a smirk on Gary's face. If he didn't walk away from the son of a bitch right then, he probably would have to kick Gary's ass right there in front of everybody. Earl didn't even say good-bye when he walked away from Gary. He stuck one hand in his pants pocket, looked down at the floor, and walked away.

"Are—are you ready to leave?" he asked Bari.

"I—we just—"

"Let's go."

Bari didn't ask any questions. She gathered her jacket and her pocketbook and they left. In the car, they drove along for a while in silence.

"You're awfully quiet," Bari said finally. "Are you okay?"

"Yeah. I-I just-don't—I got a-a lot on my mind."

"How did everything go with Gary?"

"Fine."

"Do you think you'll get his business?"

"I-I told you, I have a-a lot on my mind. I don't w-wanna talk 'bout it."

"Sorry." Sarcasm laced Bari's voice.

EARL HAD CAREFULLY filed Tommy's business card among his clients' business cards a week ago. When he got dressed that morning, he made sure that he put the card in his pocket. He had a very strong urge to contact Tommy. Earl's plan was to give Tommy a call and, he hoped, meet with him just after work.

THAT NIGHT, EARL met with Tommy and purchased a gram of cocaine. Four days later, Earl purchased another gram. He was in his office in the basement of his house, taking a break from his work and taking some hits of coke, when Bari came down the stairs. He quickly put the lines of coke that he had set up on a piece of cardboard into his drawer to hide it from her. Thank God she couldn't smell it, he told himself. He liked that. She didn't even have to know that he was using at all. That was the beauty of it. When Earl was high he worked smarter, faster. Hell, he could work all night long. As long as he took care of his wife and his home, he didn't give a shit what anybody thought.

"Are you coming to bed anytime soon?" Bari asked. She was dressed in a floral teddy with a white background and white fluffy slippers. "Should I wait up for you?" She gave him a suggestive look.

"Nah, don't—don't wait up for me. I-I'm gonna be a while."

"Well, if you're sure . . . ," Bari said, lingering.

"I-I'm sure." Earl's mouth slightly twisted. "Damn!" he said when Bari went back upstairs. Bari had blown his high. He decided that he needed to figure out a way to keep her from coming downstairs into his office.

After Earl's third trip to Tommy, he suggested that Earl buy something bigger so that he could save himself some trips. He agreed. Earl purchased his first eighth of cocaine. Tommy called it an eight ball, and he charged Earl only $150 for it.

seventeen

1993

"I NEED THOSE outfits, Bobby. I'm shooting a makeover show in less than three hours. If you don't get the dresses to me in an hour, don't bother calling this studio again, because we won't be needing your services." Franki slammed down the phone.

"Damn, Franki, cut the man some slack," Nell said. She sat on a storage box in the dressing room watching Franki slide around clothing from one side of the rack to the other.

"Cut the man some slack? The 'man' promised me nine outfits for today. If he knew he was just talking shit, he should have kept his mouth shut."

"But don't you think that a little honey goes a long way?" Nell asked.

"Please. Honey ain't nothin' but a temporary sweetener and I don't even like the taste of it," Franki said.

"Damn," said Nell.

"Look, Nell, we have a show to shoot. If that doesn't happen, it's your ass and mine. Okay? So spare me all of the nicey-nicey crap. That man has a job to do and he needs to do it."

"You're the producer," Nell said in her throaty, deadpan voice.

"You're damn right. And you're my assistant, so let's make this thing happen."

"Yes, boss." Nell stood her five-nine, 190-pound frame up from the box and saluted Franki. "Do you want me to take a ride over to Bobby's shop and see what's up?"

"That's your call," Franki said.

"Good. Then I'll hang around here a little while longer so I can follow up with some of the guests to make sure they know what time the limousines will be picking them up. You know how slow those out-of-towners can be. And I guess I need to make sure that the hotel reservations are tight."

"Yeah, you do that," Franki said. "And keep me up on what's happening."

Nell left the wardrobe room to make her calls. Franki continued looking through the outfits on the racks. She had to be prepared to go to Plan B if for some reason Bobby didn't come through. She knew she shouldn't doubt him. He had never let her down yet, but she still felt she needed to keep him on his toes just in case he slipped up.

Franki stopped at a velvet peach-colored gown with a simple neckline. It was plain yet elegant at the same time. She would be a knockout in that dress, she thought. She made a mental note to grab that dress the next time she needed something pretty to wear. She glimpsed the inside ticket and checked the size. It was a size 6. Perfect. She smiled to herself when she thought about how easy it would be for Hazel to make that dress. Franki considered taking a picture of it and sending it together with the fabric to Hazel so that she could make it for her.

"Franki." A mole-faced Freddie stuck his head in the door.

"What?" Franki asked. Annoyance was all over her face. She didn't try to hide it.

"Do you have the invoice from Stilene's?" he asked.

"No, I don't. I sent it to Accounting two days ago."

"Well, we don't have it. Do you have a copy of it?" he asked.

"Why in the hell would I have a copy of it? I sent it to you people to pay it. I had no clue that you would lose it. But that's not my problem now, is it?" she asked him.

"I—I guess not." Freddie all but cowered under her glare. He lowered his eyes and retreated out of the room.

"Does anybody know what the hell they're doing around here?" Franki asked herself out loud. "Shit," she said, and rushed out of the wardrobe room into her office. She dialed an extension.

"Yeah?" Ken Remos, the film editor, answered.

"Ken?"

"That's me."

"Did you still want to get together to review the edit of the *Teen Runaways* show?" asked Franki.

"Can we do it in fifteen?" he asked.

"You got it." Just as Franki hung up the phone, her second line rang. She picked it up on one ring.

"Hi, Franki, it's me: Bari."

"Hey, Bari, I'm glad you called. I needed to talk to somebody who sounds like they have a little bit of sense," said Franki.

"Thanks, but I have a lot more than a little bit of sense," Bari said.

"Shut up."

"Okay."

"So what's up?" Franki asked.

"What are you doing after work?"

"Running as far away from this hellhole as I can."

"Would you want to have a drink with me after work?"

"Sure."

"Oh, and Earl," said Bari.

"Earl's coming?"

"Yeah."

"Yeah, okay."

THAT EVENING THEY met at Crab Crackers. Bari and Franki got there first. They had already been seated when Earl arrived almost an hour later. When he got there, his eyes were glassy, bulging, and bloodshot.

"Hey, baby," Bari said, reaching for his hand and squeezing it.

"Hi, Earl," Franki said.

"What's up?" Earl responded, sliding into the vacant seat next to Bari. "Let me get a—a rum and Coke, honey." Earl told the waitress when she appeared at their table, "And-and give the ladies wha-whatever they want," he stuttered.

When the waitress walked away, Earl excused himself. He got up from the table and went into the men's room and took a few hits. A three-hundred-dollar-a-week habit had crept up on him without him even realizing it. Most of his waking moments were spent getting high now.

When Earl returned to the table, he was wired. His movements were quick and he sniffled a lot. His eyes darted around the room and at Bari and Franki.

"Are y'all okay?" he asked them.

"We're fine," Bari answered.

Earl was bopping his head to his own beat and drumming his fingers on the table while he continued to look around the room. "How many people do—do you think are in here?" he asked no one in particular.

"In where? This room?" Bari asked him.

"Yeah. How many people are in this restaurant?" Earl said.

"I don't know. Maybe a hundred, give or take," Bari said.

"Out of all of these people, how many of them do you think know themselves?"

"I have no idea," said Bari.

"I'm sure you'll tell us," Franki said.

"That's my point. Half of these people don't know who the hell they are." He sniffed.

The waitress returned to their table with their drinks. "Thank you, baby. That looks good," Earl said to her before she smiled curtly and walked away. Earl picked up where he had left off in his conversation. "You see, that's why p-people ain't for real. And that's why most of them are full of shit." Earl wiped at his nose.

"Well, I don't think that we need to be sittin' around here judgin' people," Franki stated.

"It ain't about judgin' nobody; I'm just sayin' it like it is," Earl said, taking a long sip from his drink.

"But who are you to decide how people are? You don't know anybody in here besides us. You don't know how these people live or what they've been through. If they're full of shit maybe they have the right to be."

"Look, Franki, you don't have to be so up-uptight. I'm just voicin' my opinion. Th-that's all," Earl said.

"And that's all I'm doin', Earl. I'm voicin' my opinion, too."

The waitress returned to the table to see if they were ready to order appetizers.

"No, sugar, we're not ready yet," Earl told her, giving her a sly smile. The waitress walked away again.

"Can we all just relax and have a good time?" Bari asked.

"You know what, Franki," Earl said. "I don't like your attitude. But lucky for me I don't have to put up with you." He got up and walked away from the table.

Franki sat there snickering and shaking her head as he walked away. "Your husband is trippin', Bari. What's up his ass?"

"Don't pay Earl any attention. He's just acting silly tonight."

"Oh yeah? Well, was he just acting silly when he was calling the waitress 'honey,' 'baby,' and 'sugar'?"

"What?" Bari asked.

"I mean the man was flirting with the waitress right in front of your face and you said nothing."

"Really, Franki, this isn't that deep. Earl used some terms of endearment with her. I don't see anything wrong with that."

"I'll tell you what, Bari, why don't I just leave you two lovebirds alone. Maybe I'll just make my exit."

Franki picked up her jacket and pocketbook and got up from the table. She laid a twenty-dollar bill on the table.

"I really wish you wouldn't leave, Franki," Bari said, looking down at her glass.

"I think it's best, Sis," Franki said, placing her hand briefly on Bari's shoulder before she left.

When the waitress returned again fifteen minutes later, Bari was sitting alone. "What happened to your party?" the waitress asked Bari.

"My sister left, but my husband should be right back," Bari told her.

Another half hour passed, and Earl still hadn't returned. Now Bari was squirming in her seat and constantly looking toward the men's room and the front door to the restaurant. After waiting another half hour for Earl to return, Bari paid the tab and left the restaurant.

"HOW COULD YOU do that to me?" Bari, on the brink of tears, asked Earl. She had walked into the house and found him sitting in the living room, remote control in hand, flipping through the channels on the television. Earl never looked up at her when she came in.

"You left me sitting in the restaurant by myself and you never even bothered to tell me that you were leaving," she said.

"I left you in the restaurant sittin' with your sister. She has a big mouth and I didn't want to deal with her."

"But you could have told me something. I just sat there like an idiot waiting for you."

Earl finally looked at Bari, deadpan. "I felt like leavin', so that's what I did."

Bari squinted her eyes at him. Earl stared at her for a moment, then turned off the television and got up and went downstairs to his office in the basement.

"Earl!" Bari yelled behind him. Earl didn't answer. He left Bari staring behind him, with her mouth hanging open.

THE FOLLOWING MORNING when Bari woke up, she looked over at her side and was surprised to see Earl still in bed. He was usually up before her, since he had to be in the office at 8:00 A.M. And even though he worked for his father, Earl was never late. She remembered that she hadn't felt him crawl into bed until after 3:00 A.M., so he was probably planning on taking the day off. Bari eased out of bed so that she wouldn't awaken him. She got showered and dressed and skipped her morning coffee because she needed to get into the office a little earlier to prepare for her 9:00 A.M. breakfast meeting.

The breakfast meeting was held only once a month, but it usually stressed Bari out. It was the time of month when all of the Account Managers tried to impress the executives. It was a dog-eat-dog session, and nobody wanted to get caught out there unprepared.

At 9:00 A.M. sharp everybody was present and seated in the conference room. Then, minutes later, the meeting was under way. Sheldon Mangrove, the company CEO, was speaking. Sheldon, with his thick, blond mane and ice blue eyes, had been the company's golden boy almost twenty years ago. He insisted on having the monthly breakfast meetings to try to keep that same spirit alive in all of the Account Managers. Everybody would get a chance to speak. A chance to update everyone on their project goals and their accomplishments.

Forty minutes into the meeting, Sidney, Bari's gay assistant, knocked on the conference room door before he stuck his head into the room. Sheldon Mangrove stopped speaking and the room went silent.

"I'm sorry for interrupting." Sidney said. "I have a phone call for you, Bari."

"I'm in a meeting, Sidney," Bari said.

"He said it's an emergency."

Bari sighed as she got up from her seat. "I'm sorry, everybody."

She walked over to the telephone that was on the credenza in the back of the room. "This is Bari," she said.

"Why the fuck didn't you wake me up?" the voice on the other end of the phone yelled.

"Oh, I-I thought—"

"You know damn well I had to work today. What the fuck . . . ?"

"No, sir," Bari said, quickly glancing over her shoulder. The room seemed so quiet to her that her voice seemed to vibrate off the walls. She could feel everybody's eyes on her back.

"Yes, yes," she said nervously. "I'll get back to you soon." She hung up.

Walking back to her seat, Bari grinned sheepishly. "I'm sorry," she said as she sat down.

Sheldon resumed speaking. Sidney knocked again. "I'm truly sorry, Bari," he said, sticking his head in the door again. "The caller is insisting on speaking to you again, immediately."

Bari looked pitifully around the room again. "I'm extremely sorry, everybody. I'd better take it in my office. My client seems to be a little upset." They excused her and Bari left the room and headed down the hall to her office. She rushed past Sidney's desk and went into her office and picked up the phone.

"Earl—"

"Why did you hang up the goddamn phone on me? Have you lost your fuckin' mind?"

"Didn't Sidney tell you that I was in a meeting? Earl, what's the matter with you? Why are you speaking to me like that?"

"Because I feel like I got the whole motherfuckin' world comin' down on me and I feel like you're turnin' your back on me, too."

"I don't understand where all of this is coming from. Are we having a problem that we need to talk about?"

"I ain't got time to talk about shit right now. I gotta get to work. But I'll tell you what—you need to stop spending so much time worryin' about those goddamned people at your job and worry about your husband."

"Look, Earl, I think we need to talk. If something is bothering you, we need to talk about it. But right now I need to get back into my meeting—"

Bari heard a click. The phone went dead in her ear. She looked at the handset for a few seconds, then hung up the phone. She shook her head, then walked out of her office. On the way out, Bari passed Sidney's desk, which was right outside her office.

"Sidney, I appreciate your not letting them know that was my husband," she said to him.

"No sweat, sweetie. I know how those sharks can be—just waiting to eat you up. Don't even mention it."

"Thanks," Bari said, reaching over and squeezing his arm before she hurried back down the hall to the conference room.

When the meeting was over, Bari and Barbara walked back to Bari's office together. Inside the office, Bari sat down behind her desk and Barbara plopped down in one of the guest chairs. Bari hadn't said much on the way back. She just half-listened to Barbara's chatter. Bari sat looking at Barbara, massaging her temples.

"You know," Barbara said, "I spend almost a month preparing for that meeting and when the time comes I have almost nothing to say. Isn't that funny? I figured out why, though; I think it's because deep down inside I just want to get through the day and collect my paycheck at the end of the week. I don't know how you do it, Bari. It's like you're one of them. You actually like this stuff."

Bari didn't respond to Barbara. She just kept on massaging her temples.

"They'll catch on to me soon enough, though," Barbara continued. "They have to see by now that I'm not turning out half the clients that I used to. Are you okay?" she asked Bari when she still didn't respond to her.

"I don't think so," said Bari.

"What's wrong?" Barbara asked.

"I'm not sure what it is, but something very wrong is happening to my marriage. Somehow, I have managed to screw things up. I think I'm giving Choler-Raines too much of my time."

"Why do you think that?" Barbara asked.

"Because Earl . . . I don't know . . . he's been acting kind of funny and drinking. . . . I don't know," Bari said, sighing heavily and shaking her head. She picked up a rubber stress ball from her desk that one of her clients had given her and started absentmindedly squeezing it.

"Barbara?"

"Yeah?"

"Don't think I'm crazy, but I was thinking . . . well, I was wondering . . . I think I'd like to talk to somebody."

"Er . . . yeah? . . ."

"You know, somebody that can help me. My grandmother Greta used to go to a lady who could tell her things. . . . She used to fix things. . . ."

"Oh, You mean like a reader? One of those spiritual readers?"

"Yeah, one of those."

"You don't want to deal with those people, girlie. They're scary."

"I don't see why I should be afraid of them. I'm just looking for them to help me."

"Help you how?"

"I was thinking . . . what if Earl doesn't love me anymore—for whatever reason? I was thinking maybe they could make him love me again," Bari said, scrunching up her face. "Sounds stupid, right?"

"I don't know, Bari. I mean, what if you're wrong about Earl and you go and get yourself all mixed up with those people? Besides, they're gonna have you doing all kinds of crazy things."

"Crazy things like what?"

"Let me put it to you this way: I know a story about this woman who wanted this man to love her and one of those spiritual people told her to wait until she got her period, then cook her man some stew. He told her to put some of her menstrual blood into the stew and her man would be drawn to her forever, no matter what."

"That's disgusting," Bari said, curling up her nose. "Did it work?"

"Well, I guess it did, 'cause the woman is my great-aunt Thea and the man is my great-uncle Eddie. And as ancient as he is, and as big a nag as she is, they're still together to this day."

"Wow."

"I know a lot of other stories like that," Barbara said. "As a matter of fact, my cousin Lottie goes to this woman and she ended up saving Lottie's boyfriend's life."

"How in the world did she do that?"

"The lady told Lottie her boyfriend was hanging out with people who were no good and that one of them was going to shoot him. She told Lottie to give her an article that belonged to her boyfriend, along with a few other things. The lady burned the articles that Lottie gave her; then she ran a silver charm through the ashes while she said a chant over it. She told Lottie to make her boyfriend wear the charm on a chain around his neck for protection. Now, of course Lottie didn't tell her boyfriend what the chain was for. She told him that it was just a gift. Well, he found out just how much of a gift it was when he was pumping gas one day and one of his boys wanted revenge on him for something and shot at him. The amazing thing was that the bullet just grazed the side of his head. It never hurt him. So even though that stuff scares the hell out of me, I have some faith," Barbara said.

"So, who is this woman?"

"Her name is Zuma. I hear she has a black tongue, too."

"A black tongue?"

"Yeah. When she talks you can see black spots all over it."

"And what does that mean?"

"That means that you had better believe what she says. People with black tongues know and speak the truth."

"Can you tell me how I can get in touch with her?"

"I'll see what I can do," Barbara said, as she got up to leave Bari's office.

eighteen

ARL GRABBED A suit and one of the crisp white shirts that were
ironed and hanging on the lower rack of his bedroom closet. He
placed them on a hook behind the door. He was pissed off that
he had overslept. He used to be able to pop right up when he first
started using cocaine, but now after so many months of doing so much
of it he figured that either he was getting old or the stuff was finally
catching up with him. Before Earl jumped into the shower he pulled
out the plastic Baggie that held his cocaine stash and spread some
lines inside a shoe-box top. He took the box top into the bathroom
with him and set it down on the toilet seat. Before he washed his face
and brushed his teeth, he sniffed up four lines, then spread two more
for when he came out of the shower.

Earl was out of the shower in no time. Just as he was putting on his
pants, the telephone rang. It rang three times before he started to answer it. By the fourth ring, he decided he didn't feel like talking to anybody. He didn't want to blow his high. The answering machine picked
up. Broderick Jordan's bass voice filled the room.

"It's me, Son, are you there?"

"Damn!" Earl said, standing very still listening to his father's message.

"I'm expectin' you to come in here. We got two trucks makin' deliv-
eries and it's real crazy today. Gino's out, Cynthia's out. I need you
here." Broderick hung up.

"Fuck!" Earl said, looking in the mirror and knotting his tie. "If
I didn't need that money from the office today I wouldn't be goin'
nowhere!"

When Earl was fully dressed he brought the box top with his lines on it into the bedroom. He sat down on the bed and sniffed the two lines that he had set up before.

"Ahhh . . . ," Earl said, closing his eyes and throwing back his head. "This shit is so fuckin' nice. Now maybe I can go in there and deal with those motherfuckers."

Earl took two more hits, wiped his running nose, and was set to leave the house. He looked in the mirror on the hall wall on the way out. His eyes were red and glassy. He made a mental note to pick up some Visine at some point during the day.

WHEN EARL WALKED into the office, it was chaotic just as Broderick had said. Nobody noticed Earl when he walked in. He intended to take care of his business first; then he would do whatever else needed to be done in the office. Earl went directly into the vault. It was his second trip there in two months. The six thousand dollars that he took two months ago had already run out. This time he would take a little more so that he wouldn't have to go in there again for a while. After leaving the vault, Earl went into his office. He put the money into his desk and locked it up. It wasn't that he didn't trust their employees; he just didn't want to tempt anybody.

"All right, all right, what's goin' on here?" Earl asked once he was out on the floor. "Tote that barge! Lift that bale!" Earl was grinning and clapping his hands. Somebody ran up to him with some papers that needed signing, and immediately after that he was called into another employee's office to look at an invoice. Earl didn't see his father's eyes blazing into his back.

FRANKI RENTED A Ford Taurus. She was providing the transportation for Thursday's girls' night out. She had made Bari promise that just because she was married didn't mean that she would stop hanging out with them once a week. Bari kept her promise and everybody had come to look forward to this night. Sometimes they made plans but most of the time they winged it. They would end up doing anything from seeing a movie to going out to dinner or clubbing. Sometimes they would even end up hanging out at one of their apartments or houses just talking, laughing, and playing music.

Franki decided to pick up Bari first. Not that Bari was the nearest to her, but Barbara wasn't ready yet, as usual.

Earl answered the door when Franki rang the bell. He pulled open the door and walked back into the room. He didn't bother to say hello. Franki walked in behind him.

"Hey, Bari," Franki said, as she walked into the foyer. She looked at Bari to see if she would notice her new, even shorter haircut.

"Hi, Franki. You're right on time," Bari said.

"Maybe you could answer this question, Franki, since Bari seems to be havin' such a hard time givin' me a straight answer." Earl addressed Franki before she could get a chance to get a reaction from Bari. "What is it that's so irresistable about this ladies' night business that would make a woman not want to spend the evening with her husband? I mean, what is it that you actually do out there?"

"Oh, Earl, leave Franki out of this." Bari laughed.

"No, seriously, Franki. Here it is, I'm practically beggin' my wife to stay home with me tonight, but she insists on goin' out with the girls. So, I'm askin' what could be so attractive out there."

"Well, it's not a matter of an attraction, it's just about us going out and letting our hair down after working so hard all week. That's all," Franki said.

"That's what I've been trying to tell him." Bari laughed.

"You two are obviously stickin' together. That means that somebody's got somethin' to hide."

"Don't be silly, Earl. Nobody's hiding anything." Bari waved him off.

"I'll tell you what then: If there's nothin' to hide, then that means that it won't be a problem if I came with y'all," Earl said.

"I know you're not serious," Franki said, looking at Earl with her nose and every other part of her face snarled up.

"I'm dead serious. If you say there's nothin' to hide, then what's the problem?" he asked.

"Nobody said it was a problem per se. It's just that this is a girl thing," Franki said. She noticed Bari's cute little smile but couldn't see anything to smile about.

"Well, if it's a problem for me to go, then Bari can't go, either."

"Don't be ridiculous, Earl." Bari laughed.

Franki looked at Bari like she was stupid. She wondered how Bari could think that this was funny. There was nothing cute or funny happening here.

"Who are you, the boss?" Franki asked.

"Yeah, I'm the boss and that's my decision," Earl answered.

"I don't mind him coming, Franki." Franki gave Bari a look. "Really, I don't mind. This way Earl will see that we're not doing anything wrong. Besides, this'll keep all the jerks from hitting on me."

"Yeah, all right, if you say so," Franki said, irritated. She couldn't believe what just happened. Earl was going a little too far right now, but there was nothing that she could do about it. For a fleeting moment she considered calling the whole night off, but she wouldn't dare give Earl that much power. She knew that he would have loved nothing better than to screw up their night.

"Earl controls you," Franki told Bari when Earl left the room to get dressed.

"Don't be ridiculous."

"He does. And you wanna know something else? He does it all the time."

"No, he doesn't."

nineteen

BARI KNEW WHAT kind of day she was going to have when she walked into the office twenty minutes late. The first person she bumped into was David, who was in a complete panic. Bari could always tell when he was working on something that was getting the best of him, because he would always scratch the top of his head and then he wouldn't bother to smooth the hair back down. Everybody called him Alfalfa behind his back.

"Come straight to my office when you put your things down, Bari," David said, and rushed right past her and ducked into a conference room. He picked up a folder, then made his way back down the corridor to his office.

Bari watched him the whole time. David made three stops along the way to his office before she even reached hers, which was only four doors down from his.

Bari spent about twenty minutes with David, and when she left his office she had instructions to rewrite the script for the Sashay clothes advertisement. She had already been working on it for over a month, and at this rate it would probably be another month and a half before David actually gave it his stamp of approval.

"It's just like David to want to make changes right at the deadline." Bari sat in her office, fuming. She thought that the last draft of her script was perfect and that David was just being anal. Things like this really pissed her off. It was definitely overkill. Three hours later, the copy was still blank.

———

EARL ENTERED THE building lobby and checked the directory for Choler-Raines. As many times as he'd been there before, he could never remember what floor his wife worked on. He noted the floor and the suite number on the building directory, then signed the visitors log. "How you doing, man?" he asked Sammy, the robust security guard, who was sitting at the desk.

"I'm good. Your wife is still up there. She hasn't left for lunch yet," Sammy answered.

"Thanks," Earl said. He wondered if Sammy made it a point to notice Bari's comings and goings or he just had an incredible memory and kept track of everybody. Earl took the elevator up to the fifth floor.

Annie, the receptionist, winked at Earl when the elevator doors opened. Annie was a sixty-three-year-old white woman who looked more like seventy-five but was as rambunctious as any twenty-year-old. She seemed to have a thing for black men and she flirted with them openly. She was harmless, though. Everybody knew that. The men usually laughed and played along with her.

"Hello, handsome," Annie said to Earl, looking him up and down.

"Hello, Annie," Earl said, flashing her a sly smile.

"Go on down. Bari is in her office."

"Thanks," Earl said, and walked down the long corridor to Bari's office.

Bari was surprised when she looked up from her paper mound and saw Earl standing there. Her heart fluttered. Earl still had that effect on her.

"Hey." She beamed.

"Hey yourself." Earl leaned over the desk and kissed her. "Put that stuff away, we're going out to lunch. I have a surprise for you."

"A surprise? Earl, you should have called me first. I can't go out to lunch today. I'm way too busy."

"Come on, everybody needs a break." Earl walked around the desk and pulled her up by the arms. "Let's go, I'm excited."

"I really can't, Earl. I have a five o'clock deadline to get this script done."

David walked into Bari's office looking a whole lot calmer. He had even combed his hair. He plopped himself down in one of Bari's guest chairs. "Earl. What's new?" David reached out and shook Earl's hand. Bari watched Earl slip his hand into his pocket and wipe away the moistness from David's hand. Earl had told Bari more than once how much he hated shaking David's hand, because it was always wet. Earl was right. David had touched her more than once and she couldn't stand his cold, clammy hands on hers.

"Nothin's new, David. I'm trying to convince my wife to have lunch with me," Earl said.

"What's the problem, Bari?" David asked.

"The problem is that I've just spent practically three hours trying to rewrite an already perfectly good script, and I keep coming up blank, and I have a five P.M deadline. Lunch is definitely out of the question."

"Oh yeah, that reminds me, that's why I'm here. We just got an extension. They've given us forty-eight hours to make the changes and complete the package. So take a break, take a nice long lunch, and come back to it later when you're fresh," David said.

"Yes!" Earl made a fist in midair.

"Gee, David, thanks for the stampede to tell me this," Bari said.

"You're welcome. So where are you guys heading for lunch?" David asked.

"We're taking a helicopter tour around the city," Earl said.

"A helicopter tour? Earl, that's so nice," Bari said, as she gathered her things to leave.

"What's so nice?" Annie asked, walking into Bari's office just in time to catch the tail end of their conversation. She dropped a few pieces of mail into Bari's in-box.

"We're going on a helicopter tour for lunch," Bari told her.

"How romantic. You're a man after my own heart, Earl Jordan. Do you have any younger brothers at home?"

"Sorry, Annie, I don't." Earl laughed. He led Bari out of the office.

They passed Sidney in the hall. Sidney smiled when he saw them, and when Earl's back was to him, he opened his mouth wide and bit at the open air. "Grrr," he said. Only Bari saw him. "Have fun, you lovebirds," he called behind them, his gray eyes sparkling. Bari's smile was wide and bright. She was relieved to see Earl in a good mood and seeming like himself again.

————

THE HELICOPTER TOUR lasted for forty-five minutes, and when it was over Bari felt completely rejuvenated. She thanked Earl for coming to take her out and she told him that she felt inspired and she was looking forward to going back to the drawing board to kick butt. The two of them held each other around the waist as they walked back to Bari's office. They hadn't eaten anything yet, so they stopped and ordered a personal pan pizza from Pizza Hut for Bari to eat while she worked.

"Hold me tight so that I can still feel you when you're gone," Bari said to Earl when he was about to leave her.

Earl squeezed her and kissed her nose and left. "See you at home, baby."

Bari sat in her office when Earl left. She thought about him while she worked and ate her pizza. He had become extremely moody. He was beginning to yell at her and even curse at her sometimes. She knew that he was under a lot of pressure at work, so she tried not to let it bother her. She wondered why he would walk through the house and barely speak to her at times, as though she were a stranger in the street. At first she thought that maybe he didn't love her anymore and that maybe the passion was gone, but their sex life hadn't waned. And Earl still made it a point to take her out and show her a good time every now and again. Maybe she was making something out of nothing. Maybe. Maybe even Earl's staying locked away for hours in the basement was nothing. All she knew was that she wanted her marriage to work. She knew that Earl needed her. He had no one else. She couldn't abandon him. She shuddered to think of what he would do or say if he knew that she knew that he wasn't that strong emotionally. He had no idea how many times she heard him crying behind closed doors or speaking out loud to himself. It pained her to think of what would happen to him if he were on his own with nobody looking after him.

Bari was so engrossed in her thoughts that she had probably erased more words than she actually wrote on the page that she was working on. She made a conscious decision that if ever she felt weak or doubtful, she would remind herself to think of some of the stories that Granny had told her and all of the praying that they used to do together and let that make her strong. She had to be strong for her and Earl. At least until Barbara set her up with her cousin's spiritualist.

twenty

BARI ORDERED LUNCH in for the second time that week. She was working on two client accounts simultaneously and was determined to make some serious progress on both of them. She was waiting for a return phone call from one of them and she didn't want to take a chance and miss it, since the call would be coming in from overseas.

When the phone rang, it startled her. Bari answered it on the first ring.

"You tell your little friend Dominick not to call my fucking house again!" Earl's voice roared. "You understand me?"

"Calm down, Earl. What is this all about?"

"All you need to know is that I don't appreciate that son of a bitch callin' my house. I'm not tellin' you again and I'm not tellin' him again."

"Wait a minute, honey, I know you don't care for him, but Dominick is my friend. He is one of the dearest friends that I have. And I don't think it's fair for you to tell him not to call my house to speak to me."

"Look, as long as I live at this address, I'll tell you who can and can't call my house, period!" Earl slammed down the telephone.

Bari kept the phone to her ear for a few seconds more; then she put it back on its base. She picked up the phone again and dialed Dominick's number.

"Hi, Dominick," Bari said when he answered the phone. She took a deep breath before she said anything else. "I just wanted to apologize."

"Forget about it, Bari. I expect that from your husband by now."

"There's no excuse for him being so rude. Anyway, it's my fault.

I told you that I was taking the day off, but then I decided to come into the office since I had so much to do."

"How are you, Bari?" Dominick asked her, changing the subject.

"I'm fine, Dominick. . . . I need a favor, though."

"Anything."

"I'm going to be working until around eight tonight. Do you think you could pick me up? I need to see somebody on the way home tonight."

"Sure thing, babe. I'll be waiting in front of your building at eight sharp."

Later that night, Bari came down from her office at twenty minutes past eight o'clock. She poked her head into the passenger-side window before she opened the car door to get in.

"I'm sorry I'm late, Dominick."

Dominick smiled at Bari. He leaned over and pushed open the passenger-side door. Bari got into the car, then turned around to throw her bags into the backseat.

"Every time I'm in a hurry, David comes to me with last-minute in-structions."

"No sweat, babe," Dominick said, as he pulled out into traffic.

Bari didn't want to put off seeing the spiritualist for another day. Earl was having his rampages far too often, and she believed it had a lot to do with his drinking. She told Dominick that she needed to stop to see an old friend who worked in a candy store. Bari promised him that she wouldn't be long. They pulled up to the store, and before Bari got out of the car she took out her posy kerchief and put it into her jacket pocket. She rolled it around and around in her hand as she walked into the candy store. She kept touching it when she walked up to the glass-topped counter. No one was behind the counter when she walked in. Bari stood still but her eyes roamed all around the room. She would have gladly brought a child into this candy land. There were four glass jars of gumballs in all colors on either side of the counter. Inside the case on display were all kinds of cream-filled cookies and some with jelly centers. A rack full of potato chips, popcorn, and all kinds of goodies stood by the store entrance. Then there was a shelf with stationery and steno pads. Bari glanced toward the window at Do-minick's car. She smiled at him when he looked at her. She reached down to touch one of the plastic bangles in a straw bin on the floor in front of the counter. A frail, elderly black man wearing wide, thick glasses appeared from behind the curtain in the back.

"May I help you?" he asked her.

Bari told herself that his voice sounded spooky only because she expected it to be. "Yes. I, er, I'm here to see Zuma."

"Ah, yes. Come this way," the old man told her.

Bari walked ahead of the man and passed through the dingy white curtain. It was dark back there. The only light was that given off by a single candle. The room was bare, except for the large area rug that Zuma sat on and the steel six-drawer cabinet that was set up behind her. A skeletal head sat on the edge of the area rug and a black velvet bag was set on the rug just in front of Zuma.

Once inside the room, the old man told Bari to remove her shoes; then he left Bari alone with Zuma. Bari was a little nervous now. She had never done anything like this before and she didn't know what to expect. The faint oil scent and the odor of burning incense that she had noticed when she first entered the store were stronger now. She held on to her posy kerchief as she stood looking down at Zuma. As Bari removed her shoes, she hesitantly sat down on the rug when Zuma gestured for her to do so. Not a word was uttered between them. Bari couldn't stand it when Zuma stared straight into her eyes, unblinking. She wanted to look away from the yellowed eyes that held her stare, but she couldn't. Zuma's hair looked like hundreds of small black, skinny snakes sticking from her head, and her nose was pierced, with a gold hoop hanging from it. Her lips were wide and full and her frame was wiry.

Bari slightly recoiled when Zuma picked up a handful of straight pins and filled her mouth with them. Then she spat them out onto the rug and stared up toward the ceiling for a moment before she said anything.

"You're sad; very, very sad," Zuma said, her voice sounding just as spooky as the old man's. "Affairs of the heart."

Bari slowly nodded.

"There are dark spirits surrounding your better half. We will destroy them and cast them back into the pit of hell." Zuma sounded like she was angry at the dark spirits—like she had seen them before. She knew their danger. She shifted herself and went into a crawling position, crouching very low to the floor. She was still. She glared at Bari. Bari braced herself. She was scared now. She had no idea what Zuma was about to do.

Slowly and very deliberately, Zuma crawled toward Bari. Bari held her breath. Her eyes were filled with fear. They were fixed on Zuma's hair, which was moving just as slowly as she was, like snakes winding to a quiet rhythm. Zuma reached Bari. She brought herself up and kneeled before her. *Slap!* Her palm went up against Bari's forehead. Bari was shocked. She almost wanted to hit Zuma back. Zuma held her palm in place against Bari's head. "The Devil is a liar!" Zuma yelled at the top of her lungs. "You have no rule here in this woman's heart. I command you to go back into the belly of the swine! I command you! You shall be replaced! You shall be replaced!"

Without another word, Zuma retreated back into her original position sitting across from Bari with her legs tucked up under her. She reached into her black velvet bag and pulled out a tiny green bottle and a small metal disk. She opened the bottle and allowed one drop of the green liquid to fall onto the metal disk. She lit a match to it. A small bright orange explosion was ignited and burned from the disk. Zuma was on her knees again. She tightly clasped her hands with her fingers entwined over the flame. Bari looked on. She couldn't believe that Zuma's hands weren't burning, being so close to the flame. "I am calling out to all of the ancestors of this child. Come forth and surround her. Make a fortress of peace for her. Carry her! Carry her!" she yelled like crazy, throwing her arms wide-open and up to the heavens. Then suddenly, with one breath, the flame extinguished. Zuma settled down again.

For the next fifteen minutes Zuma talked. Then Bari talked. When asked, Bari told Zuma exactly what she wanted in her relationship with Earl, and Zuma gave her everything she needed. When Bari left the store, she felt relieved. Somehow, she knew that everything was going to be all right. She smiled at Dominick as she got into the car.

"Is your friend okay?" he asked her.

"My friend is wonderful!" she replied.

EARL WASN'T AT home when Bari walked into the house at ten that night. She undressed and showered with more vigor than she had the previous weeks. She was energized. She had work to do. It was time to get her life—her married life—back on track.

After Bari had put on her nightclothes, she came back out into the living room. She took out the brown paper bag that Zuma had given to her. She followed Zuma's instructions very carefully. The first order of business was to get rid of any unclean spirits that were in the house. Bari laid out all her products from the bag, roots, weeds, small sticks, and powder, on the kitchen table. Then she went to the sink and filled up six eight-ounce glasses of water, one for each room in her house. Bari placed the glasses in an inconspicuous corner in every room. Next, she filled two ashtrays with an ashen mixture that contained skeletal scrapings that Zuma had mixed special for her. One ashtray was placed on a side table behind the lamp in the living room. The other was placed in the bedroom at the far end of the dresser. These were the two rooms in the house that were the most frequented by the two of them. That was all she could do for the time being. The other things would have to be worked directly on Earl little by little and without his knowledge. Her work done, Bari gave in to her exhaustion and went to bed.

She didn't feel Earl when he crawled into bed beside her an hour and a half later. She barely stirred when he pushed up close to her and rubbed his erect penis against her body.

The following morning when Bari awakened, Earl was already up as usual and out of the house before her. And, she knew now that he would not be home until well after her. It was the two-ships syndrome. "This has to stop," she said, sitting up in bed and wiping her eyes before she got out of bed. "Tonight's the night."

Bari knew that she had been spending a lot of time working late at her office and she was neglecting her house and her husband. Two big no-nos. It was Friday, and she promised herself that she wouldn't bring home any work. Tonight would be their time to spend time together and fall in love all over again.

BARI GOT THROUGH the workday and on the way home she stopped and picked up one of the two movies that she and Earl had talked about seeing when they were showing in the theater but never got a chance to see. She also picked up some microwave popcorn and hummed all the way home.

Bari decided that she would order takeout from Reno's Italian family restaurant when Earl got in. Earl liked his food nice and hot and Bari wanted to make sure that that's how he got it. She spent the first hour that she was home cleaning up the house. She went up to the bedroom and hung up all the clothes that never made it to the closet during the week and put pairs of both their shoes back on the shoe rack in the closet where they belonged. While she was at it, she decided to vacuum the floor, too.

Bari had finished her cleaning, so she decided to take a peek at the beginning of the video that she had rented to kill time until Earl came in.

EARL STOPPED BY Tommy's place, had a couple of drinks, and copped an eight ball. He was feeling real nice by the time he was ready to leave. Tommy saw to that. Earl sat talking to Tommy while the two of them worked on a dish of cocaine that Tommy had laid out like a platter of hor d'oeuvres being served at a party.

Earl was already high but he couldn't wait to get home to do his own stash. His urge for another hit was so strong that he took out one of the packages from his pocket while he walked toward his car and stood against a tree to shield the white powder from blowing away in the wind. He took a hit into each nostril and didn't bother to put the package away. When he got into the car, he took a few more hits, put the powder away, and then started the ignition.

When Earl walked into the house, both the kitchen and dining room lights were set on the lowest level on the dimmer switch. Earl didn't bother to turn up the lights. He went directly downstairs to his office in the basement. When he got downstairs, he quickly took off his jacket and took out one of the packages of coke and emptied it out onto the desk. He took out the spoon that he kept in the top drawer of the desk and started to crush the small pebbles of cocaine into a fine powder. When he was done, he took two more hits. He grunted at the potency.

Earl sat down at his desk and stared straight ahead. He sat there and stared at the wall and didn't move again for the next six minutes, when he took a few more hits. Then he got thirsty. He wasn't sure if he had any rum in the house, but he knew for sure that he had a six-pack in the refrigerator.

He looked down at the cocaine mound on his desk, and using his straw, he started to move the powder all around. Then he bunched it all back together again into a mound. Slowly and tenderly, he moved his hand like someone stroking the cheek of a lover about to depart. Finally, he got up from the desk and made his way upstairs to the kitchen. He took a beer from the refrigerator and went back downstairs.

THE VIDEO THAT Bari had been watching was just about to come to a climax when she thought she heard movement downstairs. She tiptoed to the top of the stairs. She stood still to see if she would hear it again. Another sound. Her heart quickened. She had definitely heard something.

Bari tiptoed back into the bedroom and shut off the television and the VCR. She picked up an old police club that Earl kept for protection in the house. She crept back out to the top of the stairs and listened some more. When she didn't hear anything else, she decided to creep downstairs and investigate further. She turned on the lights but saw nothing. Bari was convinced now that she was hearing things. She didn't know what could be keeping Earl, but she wished he would hurry up and come home. What if somebody really was in the house? What would she do?

Bari was starting to get hungry. She looked in the refrigerator for something to munch on but she closed the door and decided to wait it out. She eyed the laptop computer that was plugged in and pushed to the side on the kitchen table. That was usually where she worked. It was the only place where there was enough room for her to spread out and work comfortably. Bari had the Redman files stacked up beside the computer. She had left them there since the account was still in discussion and wouldn't be due for at least another couple of months. She worked on it every chance she got, though. Bari always liked to get a jump start on her projects. That was how she was able to give an immediate response for whatever was needed at the spur of a moment. She called it keeping her finger on the pulse at all times. Bari looked at the files and had a fleeting thought to do a little work to kill time, but she quickly decided against it because she had promised herself that she wouldn't do any work tonight. Within minutes Bari booted up the laptop computer, and it wasn't long before she was rhythmically banging at the keys and working on the Redman files. She needed to verify some numbers after a while, so she pulled out some more of the many files. Then she pulled out another file, and then another. Before long, the kitchen table was covered with notebooks, construction paper, stencils, and color pencils. Bari was perfecting one of the letters on her display board when Earl walked back upstairs from the basement to get another beer. Bari jumped. She knocked over a glue bottle.

"Oh, my God! Earl, when did you get here? I had no idea you were home. How long were you here? Why didn't you come upstairs to look for me?" Bari asked while she quickly wiped up the spilled glue before it made its way over to her papers.

Earl stared at her. He knew what he wanted to say, but his mouth was stuck. His eyes were glassy; his face was flushed. He was bare backed and shiny with sweat. "Why?" He barely got the word out for the slight paralysis in his throat.

"Why, because I waited for you all this time. And because whenever I come into this house the first thing I do is look for you. I actually look forward to seeing you when I come home. I'd like to think that the same thing goes for you."

Earl found his voice. "One day I would like to come home and not see all this shit all over my kitchen table. How about that? Waitin' for me? What are you doin' workin' if you're waitin' for me? What kind of bullshit is that?"

Bari looked helpless all of a sudden. She looked down at the table at all her work, then back up at Earl. "The thing is, all I want is to become an associate partner on my job. I know they're still testing me after all this time, so I have something to prove." Bari said. Her voice sounded whiny, like she was on the brink of tears. "David already told me that all I need to do at this point to become an associate is land a million-dollar contract. So, that's what I intend to do. That's why I work so hard. We're both gonna profit from it, you'll see." Bari forced her voice to sound a little more stable.

"Yeah, well. I don't recall askin' you for any of your money. And I didn't come up here to talk about you or your job. I came up here to get me a beer." Earl took his beer from the fridge. "You're a fool if you believe anything those people tell you."

"I'm not asking them for anything I don't deserve," said Bari.

"Whatever." Earl just wanted her to shut up. He just wanted an-other hit. "I'll tell you what, you go ahead and finish your work and I'll go ahead and do what I gotta do."

"I was going to order . . ."

Earl was already halfway down the basement stairs before Bari could say what she wanted to say. She stared behind Earl as he walked down the stairs. She knew that she should have put away her work right then. And that was exactly what she was going to do but she didn't want to leave the last letter on the display board undone. She decided to finish the letter and then she would tell Earl about the video that she had rented for them and find out what he wanted her to order from Reno's for dinner.

Bari was busy working on the board and didn't see Earl when he came back upstairs and walked past her and went upstairs to the bed-room.

The telephone rang. It was Franki.

"What are you doin', Bari?" Franki sounded out of breath.

"Hello, Franki, how are you? It's a pleasure speaking to you tonight."

"Spare me the small talk. Come with me to Splotches tonight. It's ladies' night. It's free before midnight."

"Are you kidding me? It's been a long week. I'm tired."

"Aw, come on, Bari. We don't do shit on Thursdays anymore. At least hang with me tonight. For old times' sake. Please."

"Actually, tonight I'm gonna be spending time with Earl. I feel like I've been neglecting him."

"You sound pathetic."

"Thank you."

"You're just old, tired, and married."

"I'm not complaining."

EARL HAD PUT on a shirt and some dress pants, washed his face, and brushed his teeth. He came down the stairs and headed toward the door. He didn't look back.

"Franki, let me call you back." Bari hung up the phone. "Why didn't you tell me you were going out, Earl?"

"So, now I have to report to you when I'm leavin' my house?" Earl asked her.

"No, you don't have to report to me, but I would like to go with you," Bari said, closing up her folders and shutting down the computer.

"You can't go with me. You go ahead and finish your little project there, and I'll be back later."

"Come on, give me a minute. I'll throw something on." Bari rushed toward the stairs while taking off her smock.

"Look." Earl grabbed Bari back by her arms, almost too tight, and held her in place. "You said you wanted this partnership thing, right? So go for it. We have plenty of time to go out, you and me. Okay? I'll be back later."

"All right." Bari sighed, staring him straight in his eyes. She paused at first, but then she kissed him on his lips. "I'll see you when you get back."

Earl left.

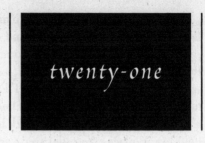

twenty-one

T HE DEN WAS Earl's choice spot for the night. It was located in lower Manhattan. The Den had the atmosphere that Earl liked to be in whenever he needed to forget that he had any responsibilities at all. No restrictions of a job, no goddamned high-ass mortgage. He knew that he was lucky to have a beautiful wife like Bari who loved him as much as she did, but that didn't matter to him right now. Right now he was not Earl the husband or Earl the Rock of Gibraltar or the decision maker. Tonight he would change his entire outlook. He would be Earl in name only.

Earl took a seat at the bar. Brenda, the head bartender at the club, approached Earl. She was an old friend of his. Brenda had grown up right next door to Earl's family. She used to run errands for Earl's mother when the multiple sclerosis first struck her. Brenda would push Earl's mother in her wheelchair around the block sometimes and sit on the front lawn talking to her for hours. Brenda had short jet-black hair, dark skin, and long, smooth legs that she loved to show off. Earl had lost touch with her after they grew up, but he rediscovered her at the club. Even though Brenda was older than Earl was, he always had a crush on her. The crush never amounted to anything because Brenda always made it clear to him that she wasn't interested in him in that way.

"What's up, Earl?" Brenda asked.

"Nothin' much, baby. You're looking good as usual," Earl said, leaning forward to kiss Brenda's lips. Earl had a bird's-eye view of her cleavage. He had already scoped the skintight spandex skirt she was wearing that barely covered her behind.

"Thank you. What can I get you?" Brenda asked.

"You know what I want." Earl smiled, looking her up and down, his eyes lingering between her legs.

Brenda smiled back, shook her head, and was off to get Earl's rum and Coke. Earl stared after her as she walked away. When Brenda returned with Earl's drink, she waved off the twenty-dollar bill that Earl offered her. "So what brings you down here tonight?" she asked him.

"The same thing that always brings me down here. I like the sights. When are you gonna give me some of your time, beautiful lady?"

"Come on, Earl, you know better than that. Besides, you're a married man, so leave it alone before you make me mad, and you won't like me when I'm mad." They both laughed.

"You can't blame me for trying. You're one very attractive woman."

"Well, I suggest that when things start looking attractive, you look the other way."

"I hear you; I hear you," Earl said.

Brenda touched Earl's shoulder and was off to serve other customers. Earl sipped on his drink. He looked up in time to meet eyes with Dominick. Dominick was halfway across the room, leaning against a pillar at the edge of the dance floor talking to two of his buddies. He and Earl locked eyes, then looked away from each other. Earl downed his drink, then headed for the men's room. He went into a stall and locked the door behind him. He pulled out the package that he had come to refer to as his "constant companion." He took several hits. Big ones. The coke was potent. Earl was in a zone after the first couple of hits. Just for the hell of it, he took two more hits before he put away the package. The world was his now and he didn't give a shit about no one and nothing in it.

He headed straight for the dance floor when he came out of the men's room. It wasn't hard for him to find a partner. Earl was a good dancer. The woman he chose to dance with kept up with him pretty well. When the music slowed down, Earl's dance partner started to walk off the floor.

Earl firmly held on to her hand and pulled her back to him. "Let's not stop now," he said to her. "What's your name?"

"Ebony."

"Ebony is a very pretty name."

"Thank you," Ebony gushed. "And what's your name?"

"I'm Earl."

"Hi, Earl."

"Hi, yourself. I've never seen you here before."

"That's because I've never been here before."

Earl moved in even closer to her. He wanted her to feel him. He was erect. He had no inhibitions tonight. Tonight he would enjoy the feel of another woman. See if he'd missed out on anything. Ebony's hips inched forward, meeting Earl's hardness. Earl whispered to her, then stuck his tongue in her ear as they danced slowly. He slowly and carefully ran his hand up and down her spine. Ebony's nipples hardened against his chest.

"I've never been to New York before. I'm visiting my cousins," Ebony said very softly. Her breaths were short and quick. Her eyes closed halfway and rolled to the back of her head.

"Do you think your cousins would mind if I showed you around?"

"I don't know about them, but I sure wouldn't mind."

Earl kissed her soft and long. When the song was over, the two of them left the Den.

WHEN EARL CREPT up to his bedroom the alarm clock on the bed table read 4:30 A.M. He shut off the television that Bari had had left on and quietly took off his shoes. Earl took off his clothes and threw them over the back of the chair, then walked around to Bari's side of the bed and kissed her on the cheek. He kissed her eyelids until she awakened.

Bari smiled up at him. "Hi, baby," she said, stretching. "I tried to wait up for you, but I guess I fell asleep."

"Well, I'm here now," Earl said, climbing under the covers next to her. He kissed Bari's eyelids again. Then he kissed her nose, then her lips. He parted Bari's lips with his tongue and kissed her deeply. He kissed his way down to her breasts. His tongue made small circles around her nipples, making them hard; then, one at a time, he took them into his mouth. When he could wait no longer, he mounted her.

LATER ON THAT morning, Bari was up and at it, while Earl stayed asleep. Bari always got up early on Saturdays, no matter what. She believed in making the most of every minute of her weekend. She was doing laundry in the basement and waxing the kitchen and dining room floors in between. She had been thinking about calling Franki when the phone rang.

"You're gonna live a long time, Franki. I just thought about calling you."

"We're in sync; what can I tell you? Do we still have our appointment at Saks Fifth Avenue at noon today?" Franki asked.

"Yeah, I need to get a gorgeous dress to wear." Bari sighed. "I hate freaking fund-raisers. And I hate that David is making me go."

"Yeah, well, this one may not be too bad. Besides, you never know who you're gonna meet at these things."

"Thank you for agreeing to come. You and Cheryl."

"Oh, please. You don't have to thank us."

"You guys don't mind that Earl is coming to the dinner, too, do you?"

"We expect Earl to come. Isn't he a permanent fixture every time we go anywhere?" Franki said.

"Oh, come on, it's not even like that."

"If you say so. It'll be twelve o'clock before you know it. Are you almost ready?"

"Are you kidding me? I still have a million things to do. I want the house to be nice and clean when Earl wakes up, and I wanted to make sure he had something to eat before I leave to go to Saks."

"Bari, I'm sure your son, er, excuse me, your husband, can fend for himself. We'll only be gone for a couple of hours. Gimme a break. Besides, we made the woman *squeeze* us into her schedule today; the least we can do is be on time."

"Don't worry, Franki; we'll be on time."

BARI AND FRANKI arrived at Saks at twelve o'clock sharp. They were greeted by a cheerful hostess, a very tall, regal-looking woman with salt-and-pepper hair that was pulled back tightly into a bun. The hostess handed them each a glass of wine and a small plate of pâté and thin wheat crackers. Then she whisked them into the showroom. The show started shortly after they were seated.

Several sleek models walked up and down the L-shaped platform wearing expensive designer evening dresses and gowns. Bari sat placidly while Franki studied every stitch, every cut, curve, and contour, on every outfit. Finally, a model appeared wearing a simple bronze-colored dress that clung to her like a second skin. The back of the dress plunged clear to the waist and the front had a sweetheart neckline that dipped just enough to reveal her cleavage.

"That's it, Bari! That's the dress!" Franki exclaimed.

"You think?"

"Absolutely. That's you! That's it!"

"Was there anything in particular that you ladies were interested in?" the hostess asked when the show was over.

Before Bari could answer, a very excited Franki responded. "Yes. Yes, actually, there was something that we liked. The bronze number. Could we see that again?"

"Certainly. Come with me," the hostess said.

They followed the woman into a very large fitting room with mauve-colored carpeting, mirrored walls, and one burgundy Gothic settee, which was in the middle of the room. She left them alone for a while, then returned shortly after, carrying the dress.

Bari took the dress and disappeared behind the double swinging doors. After a few minutes she came out wearing the dress. The dress hugged every single inch of her. Her waistline was tiny and her stomach was practically nonexistent. Bari could have been any one of the models on the runway.

"You look incredible," said Franki. "It looks like you actually have breasts."

"Shut up. Do you really like it?"

"Trust me, Bari, the dress is perfect."

"But do I really want to pay six hundred dollars for it?"

Bari pivoted in front of the mirror several more times.

"Look, you get what you pay for. It's worth every nickel."

"What the hell, you're right. I'll go for it," Bari said, sliding out of the dress. "Hey, what about you, Franki? Didn't you see anything that you liked?"

"Oh, you know me, I'll borrow something from the television studio wardrobe."

twenty-two

EARL WAS DRESSED in a gray pin-striped suit with a white shirt and charcoal gray silk tie. As usual, he was ready before Bari. He waited in the living room for her. He didn't mind waiting for her, though; he could take hits of his cocaine without being interrupted. Earl sipped on some rum and Coke and took hits of cocaine straight out of the small plastic package. The jazz music that he was bobbing his head to was sounding sweeter and sweeter. Before he took his hits, he would glance toward the stairwell to make sure that Bari wasn't coming down the stairs from the bedroom. Earl quickly closed up his package and stuffed it into his jacket pocket when he heard the creak at the top of the stairs. He wiped away the white residue from around his nose.

Bari glided down the stairs clutching her chest, with her head tilted toward the ceiling, as if she was the belle of the ball, making her grand entrance. "Excuse me, sir. Do you come here often?" she asked in a fake southern accent.

"Obviously, not often enough," Earl said. It was like a light was turned on in his face. He couldn't believe how beautiful his wife looked. The bronze-colored dress blended in perfectly with Bari's skin tone. Her smile reminded him of something fresh and sweet and good.

Earl grabbed Bari by the waist and pulled her to him. "Look, as far as I'm concerned we could just skip this whole deal and stay right here tonight," he said.

"Believe me, I'm tempted, but everybody is depending on us for a ride. We'd better go." Bari backed herself away from him.

Earl helped Bari on with her coat; then he put his on. He needed to take another hit and he wanted to take it before he left the house. He quickly tried to think of an excuse to turn back or even a reason to send Bari upstairs for something, but nothing came to mind. His mind was stuck on "off." The cocaine ruled.

Shit, he thought. *This is gonna be a long-ass ride with all those yapping women and I can't even take a goddamn hit. This is really fucked up.*

"Are you okay to drive?" Bari asked Earl, as they stepped out onto the porch. "I noticed you were drinking—"

"I'm fine," Earl snapped.

The rain started falling as soon as they walked out the door. Earl turned on the windshield wipers and pulled out of the driveway. He drove up to the corner and waited at the red light. "You should take this left and go up the ramp to Holland Street. It's quicker that way," Bari said.

"I was planning on taking this right and going up to Forty-fifth to avoid the construction on Billmore."

"Yeah, but with the rain—"

"All right, all right!" Earl took the left when the light turned green. His nerves were frazzled.

When they pulled up in front of the brownstone where Franki lived, she was standing underneath her umbrella, waiting at the top of the stairs. She ran down the steps when they pulled up, and jumped into the car.

"What's up, guys? Could you believe all this damn rain?" she asked.

"Yeah, it's gonna be a lousy night."

"Weather-wise, anyway. I hate the rain," Franki said.

"A little rain ain't never hurt nobody. And it's not like you're sugar or anything. You won't melt," said Earl.

"Go to hell, Earl," Franki said.

"Don't worry, I'll get there soon enough," he responded.

"I'm sure you're right," said Franki.

Franki and Bari turned their attention away from Earl and got involved in their own conversation. All Earl wanted to do was pull over and take a hit. He was getting irritable. Right now he just wanted everybody to shut the fuck up.

"The left, Earl, take this left," Bari said after they had already entered the intersection. Earl's left-turn indicator came on at the last minute as he swerved to the left.

"She lives at 1045 Collette Street," Bari reminded him.

"We've taken this trip many times before, Bari. I don't think I need a guide." Earl gritted his teeth. He tried very hard to keep himself calm. He was like a boiling teakettle.

They pulled up in front of Cheryl's apartment building. Earl nodded to the guys who were sitting on the steps. He blew the horn, and Cheryl came bouncing out of the building. Her breasts bounced up and down as she skipped past her neighbors on the steps. "Have a good night, lady," one of the men called behind her, as she climbed into the car.

The rain had subsided, but now it was starting to fall steadily again. Franki and Cheryl chatted on in the back of the car, while Bari concentrated on Earl's driving. Cheryl glanced into the rearview mirror and caught Earl looking at her bosom. She looked down at her breasts. The opening had widened when she sat down and her cleavage was showing big-time. She looked back up into the rearview mirror. This time she smiled. Cheryl sat more erectly so that her breasts would protrude even more. Earl smiled.

"Earl, what are you doing? You missed your turn," Bari complained.

Earl spun into a U-turn. The car screeched as it swerved around. The driver behind him laid on his horn as he sped to the right to avoid hitting Earl's car from behind. The oncoming driver facing Earl from the left lane stepped on his brake to avoid a head-on collision.

"What are you doing, Earl!" Bari yelled.

"What's the matter with you!" said Franki and Cheryl at the same time.

Earl punched the steering wheel and brought the car to a screeching halt. "Do you wanna drive?" He glared at Bari. "Goddammit, I'll turn this son of a bitch around right now and go the hell back home."

"All right, all right, Earl, calm down. I'm sorry," Bari said, looking down at her lap.

"I don't want you giving me any more directions. Okay? I don't want it," Earl said. He turned the car around and they continued their trip.

WHEN THE GROUP arrived at the hall, they looked for the table that displayed Choler-Raines' name. Barbara had arrived before them and was already seated. She waved them over to the table. Earl collected the ladies' coats and took them to be checked. He stood on the coat-check line and watched his wife as she walked across the room. He counted how many men looked at her ass when she walked by. He had thought that the dress was a little too revealing when he first saw her with it on, but he didn't say anything. Now, thinking back, he knew he shouldn't have let her wear it.

"Just look at this shit," Earl said, shaking his head. "Why in the hell is this line so long?" Earl was quickly losing his patience and getting irritable again. He definitely needed to take a hit. He could use a drink, too. After he checked the coats, he didn't go directly over to the table. He went to the men's room instead. His hands shook as he struggled to open the cocaine package inside the stall. The package dropped to the floor.

"Damn!" Earl quickly bent down to pick it up. "Thank God!" he said when he realized that the package was still sealed and nothing had spilled. Earl slowed himself down. He took a deep breath and took his time opening the packet. He finally took his hits.

Bari was the first person Earl saw when he walked out of the men's room. Kurt Russell, an employee at Choler-Raines' sister company based in Ohio, had joined the ladies at the table. Kurt stood over them as they spoke. Earl couldn't stand the way the women were all looking up and grinning up in the man's face. Bari should have known better. "If they only knew how stupid they look," he mumbled. He quickly walked toward the table.

"Well, ladies, it really is a pleasure to finally meet you all face-to-face," Kurt said, "especially you, Bari, we talk so much on the phone. At least now we all know who each other are, so when we start looking for allies out there—" Kurt stopped short as Earl furiously approached.

"What's up?" Earl asked. His eyes were glassy, his nostrils flared.

Bari's smile disappeared momentarily but quickly reappeared. "Oh, er, Earl, this is Kurt Russell, he's from our sister company. Kurt, this is my husband, Earl."

Kurt extended his hand to Earl. Earl didn't respond.

"Can you excuse us, please." Earl took Bari by the arm and helped her to her feet. He held her by her elbow and walked briskly away from the table. Bari's ankle twisted slightly as she tried to keep up with Earl.

"I've decided I don't want to be here anymore. I'm ready to go," Earl said when they were out of the ballroom in the corridor by the restrooms and telephones.

"You're ready to go? But we just got here. What's wrong?"

"I feel sick, that's what. I feel sick looking at all of the bullshit that's goin' on in here. Just go back in there and tell your sister and your friends that we're leavin'. If they wanna leave now, fine. If they don't want to leave now, fine. Either way, we're outta here. Give them these." He handed Bari their coat-check tickets.

"I don't understand this, Earl."

"Just do what I said! I'm in the car." Earl stormed out of the ballroom and out to the parking lot.

Bari went back inside the ballroom. "Earl and I are leaving," she told them.

"Why? What happened? Are you okay?" Franki asked.

"Yeah, I'm okay. Um . . . Earl wants to leave. He said something about feeling sick. Do you guys want to ride back with us, or are you gonna stay?" Bari asked.

"At two hundred dollars a plate, I think David would want us to stay. You go ahead, honey, I'll give them a ride home," Barbara offered.

"Call me tomorrow, Bari." Franki searched her sister's eyes looking for a clue that something was wrong. She got nothing.

WHEN BARI AND Earl got home, Earl headed directly to the kitchen and grabbed a beer from the refrigerator. Bari went upstairs to the bedroom. She didn't know what to think. She didn't know if this would be the start of another one of Earl's rages or what. She silently cursed herself for forgetting about putting the dust that she had gotten from Zuma in his pillowcase. Bari quickly took off her dress and carefully draped it across the back of the chair. She gathered up her nightgown and some toiletries and went into the bathroom.

Earl came up the stairs into the bedroom with his beer in hand, looking for Bari. When he didn't see her, he slammed the beer can down on the dresser. Through the dresser mirror he noticed Bari's dress on the chair. He pulled open the dresser drawer and took out a pair of scissors. Earl walked over to the chair and picked up the dress and started cutting it into small pieces.

Bari walked into the bedroom. Earl walked toward her pointing his finger and yelling, "You're gonna show yourself some respect and you're gonna show me a hell of a lot more respect than you showed me tonight!"

"What in the world are you talking about?" Bari asked.

Earl didn't bother to answer her. He raised his hand and slapped her across her face. Bari was stunned. Before she could get her bearings, Earl balled up his fist and punched her in her left eye. She stumbled backward, holding her eye and screaming.

"Earl, what's the matter with you? Why are you doing this?" she cried.

"I'm doing this because you disrespected me tonight. You understand? You disrespected *us* tonight by parading up and down that place half-naked. You think I didn't know what you were doin'?" His forefinger was pushing into her chin. "You wanna act like a slut, I'll treat you the way sluts get treated."

Bari stood as stiff as a board before Earl. She was afraid to move because she knew that he would hit her again. Her eye hurt like hell and she wasn't sure whether or not she could see out of it yet, because she couldn't open it. She could feel it starting to swell. It was throbbing to the beat of her heart. She tried to keep her voice even when she spoke. She didn't want to provoke Earl any further. She had never seen him so angry before and he had certainly never hit her before.

"I wasn't parading around half-naked. I really don't know what you're talking about." Bari's voice was shaky, almost a whisper.

"I'm talking about this!" Earl stormed over to the chair where Bari's dress was just a pile of swatches. "This shit right here. This garbage!" Earl picked up a handful of the dress remnants, then threw them back onto the chair.

"My dress," Bari whispered.

Earl stormed out of the room. He ran down the stairs and went out to the front porch.

Bari examined what was left of her dress. She picked up some of the pieces. She threw them to the floor and sat down in the chair on the rest of the pile. She put her head down into her lap and cried.

THE NEXT MORNING, Bari lifted her head to look at the clock on the side table. It was 9:30 A.M. She quickly dropped her head back down on top of the pillow when the pain in her eye reminded her that it was still there.

"Thank God it's still the weekend." She moaned.

Earl woke up when Bari stirred. "Hey, good morning." His voice was deep, still groggy. His eyes were puffy and red. Bari refused to look in his direction. She didn't respond to him.

"What's the matter? Cat got your tongue?" he asked.

Bari stared at the ceiling. She still didn't answer.

Earl turned on his side to face Bari. He propped himself up on his elbow.

"Listen, I know you're probably mad about what happened last night. I'm sorry about that. It's just that I saw something that I didn't like and I reacted. I'm really sorry. I should never have hit you. Okay? And that's something that I'll never do again." He rubbed Bari's face with the backs of two of his fingers, near her mouth. Bari didn't respond. "Oh, and about the dress, I'll buy you a new one. I promise." He kissed her lightly on the cheek. Then he kissed her swollen eye. He put his mouth to her ear. "I love you," he whispered.

Bari closed her eyes. She took a deep breath. The warmth flooded in. Earl sounded sincere. She would forgive him this time. Earl kissed her on the lips again.

"Can we stop fighting?" Bari asked softly.

"Of course we can. I told you before, I'm a lover, not a fighter."

Earl slipped his tongue into Bari's mouth, then climbed on top of her and made love to her.

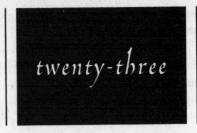

twenty-three

B Y MONDAY MORNING, most of the swelling in Bari's eye had gone down, but the eye was still discolored. Although she decided she wasn't going to work, Bari still got up early to help Earl along as he got ready for work.

Earl checked the contents of his briefcase while Bari emptied his unfinished cup of coffee into the sink and his breakfast plate into the trash.

"I don't see what the big deal is about your eye. You look fine to me. Nobody will even notice it."

"Easy for you to say. Trust me, Barbara will notice it. I will *not* go into that office until this eye is completely healed."

"Suit yourself. All right, I'm out." Earl kissed Bari on the lips, then headed toward the door. "Oh yeah," he said, turning back. "Since you're home today, could you do some shirts for me? I'm running low."

"No problem."

"Oh, and one more thing. . . ." He kissed her lips again. "Why don't we have a very special dinner tonight? Something on the romantic side, you know, the way I like it."

"Are you taking me out?" Bari smiled. It had been a while since they had been out together in a romantic setting.

"No. I figured we could make it home cooked. Like maybe you could make your delicious shrimp scampi."

"I could do that." Bari felt her pulse begin to race. "As a matter of fact, I'll go the whole nine yards. We'll do candlelight and everything. We haven't done anything like that in a long time." Suddenly Bari was feeling a lot better. She felt as if she could skip through the day. Yeah, she would see to it that the night was extra special.

"Have a nice day, baby. I love you," Bari said, as Earl left the house. As soon as she locked the door behind him, she dialed her office. Sidney picked up after two rings.

"Good morning. Choler-Raines, Sidney speaking."

"Good morning, Sidney," said Bari, twirling the phone cord around her fingers.

"Oh, hello, darling Bari. What's the matter, hon? You're not feeling well?" he asked.

"Actually, I'm not, Sidney. I'll be working from home for the next two days."

"Good for you. Do you need me to tell David anything?" Sidney asked.

"No. I'll leave him a voice mail." Bari pulled a slip of paper in front of her that contained the instructions that she needed to give to Sidney. "Listen, Sid, I need a favor."

"Anything, sweets."

"Look in my office in my Rolodex for the Paiseley account. Get the number of my contact person. I need to call them up. I have questions. I need to know what market they're targeting. I need to know if they've set up a proposed budget, you know, basic stuff," Bari said, glancing over her shoulder to see if the fresh pot of coffee she had put on was percolating.

"I'm already a step ahead of you, dear. Stewart Hassell called you from Seattle at eight-oh-five our time this morning. He sounds real good on the phone, by the way. You simply must tell me what he looks like in person."

"How am I supposed to know what he looks like? I've never met the man," Bari said.

"I'm getting to that. He wants you to fly to Seattle some time between this week and next to meet with him to discuss the things you mentioned."

"Fly to Seattle? Is he kidding? I'm not gonna be able to get them to approve a trip to Seattle when I'm not even sure if we're gonna get this account. Besides, I have too many other things going on right now," Bari said, sounding deflated.

"Don't get your pressure up on this, love. You know they'll give you whatever you need. They want this account . . . bad."

"You're probably right. Does David know they want me to do this?"

"He won't hear it from me. That's your baby."

"Okay. I'll give him a call."

"You do that, hon. I'll talk to you later. Feel better."

Bari emptied her portfolio onto the kitchen table. Just as she finished sorting out her drawings and cuttings, the telephone rang. It was Franki.

"What are you doing home?" Franki asked.

"If you didn't think I'd be home, why'd you call?" Bari asked.

"I just called your office about five minutes ago and Sidney told me that you weren't feeling well."

"Oh yeah, I'm feeling a little under the weather; I think I may be coming down with something." Bari faked a cough and cleared her throat for appearances.

"I was thinking about stopping by after work to pay back the money that you laid out for my shoes when we were shopping last week."

"Oh no, no. There's no hurry on that," Bari quickly answered.

"But I thought you said you needed the money," said Franki.

"Yeah, but it can wait until the weekend. Besides, Earl made a special dinner request for tonight. He wants shrimp scampi." Bari was glad that for once she was able to think quickly on her feet. She knew that Franki would never insist on coming over if she knew that Bari and Earl were having a private affair. The last thing she needed was for Franki to come over and see her eye discolored the way it was.

"Shrimp scampi? Are you sure you don't want to invite me?" Franki teased.

"Sorry. Can't do that. It's just for me and my guy."

"I guess you can't be that sick if you're cooking a special dinner."

"I could never be too sick to cook for my baby."

"I can't believe you'd do this to me. You know how I love your shrimp scampi. But hey, I understand." Franki laughed.

"Good, because I have to go. I have a lot of work to do." They hung up.

Bari tried to finish her work quickly. She spent the next three hours planning and forecasting the campaign for Paiseley. She needed to wrap things up so that she could start planning her and Earl's evening. Bari couldn't wait until tonight. She got excited just thinking about it. There was a lot to be done. She needed to clean the house to make it nice, fresh, and clean, the way Earl liked it, and she wanted to leave herself enough time for a long, leisurely bath. She made a mental note to stop at the Body Shop to pick up some body oils and foaming bubble bath when she went into town to pick up the shrimp.

Tonight Bari planned to really express to Earl how much she loved him. She wouldn't even mention anything about him hitting her. She would let it go. Since he had been so uptight lately, she figured that maybe he just needed some reassurance from her. Whatever the problem was, they would fix it tonight.

When Bari was done with her work, she threw on some old ratty jeans and a sweatshirt and jacket and caught the crosstown bus to the fish market.

Once in town, Bari zipped in and out of stores, made her purchases, and headed back home. She finished cleaning the house from top to bottom. It looked beautiful when she was done. She had picked up a dozen white tulips and arranged them in a ceramic vase in the center of the table. Two matching ceramic candleholders were placed on either side of the vase. Bari used the exquisite white lace tablecloth that her mother had given them for their third wedding anniversary. She had never used it before now. The tablecloth added the perfect finishing touch to her table. She would have to hustle to get the food cooked and still take her bath before Earl got home.

After her bath, Bari looked around to make sure everything was in place. She was satisfied. Then she remembered the gray dust that she had to put under Earl's pillow. She took out the powder from the small brown paper bag and sprinkled some of it onto a white paper napkin, then folded it into a neat square. Bari placed the squared napkin under Earl's pillow. She hoped, that after sleeping on it Earl would no longer have the desire to drink and fight. That done, Bari got dressed.

She opted to wear a soft, sexy look. She was wearing a simple short white satin slip dress and was showing plenty of cleavage. Bari's hair hung loosely down the back of her head onto her shoulders. Everything was perfect. Now, all she had to do was wait for Earl. He was already almost an hour late. Bari dimmed the light over the table, then walked into the living room and settled down on the couch to wait for him. She turned on the stereo to a jazz station and lay back on the couch and flipped through some magazines. Another hour passed. When she grew tired of the magazines, she poured herself a glass of wine, flipped on the television, and waited some more. Suddenly she had a terrible thought.

Earl would never be this late if he knew we had plans. He wouldn't be this late unless something was wrong.

Now that Bari thought about it, she could feel it in the pit of her stomach. Something was dead wrong. Her pulse raced, and suddenly she was feeling hot and feverish. Where would she even begin looking for him? The police wouldn't do anything until he was missing for twenty-four hours.

The telephone rang.

"Thank God," Bari said, picking up the receiver after only one ring.

"Bari. How are you doin'?" It was Dominick.

"Dominick, I'm glad you called but I can't talk right now. I have to keep the line clear." Bari's voice quivered.

"Are you all right?" he asked.

"Yeah, I'm okay. But I'm really gonna have to call you back."

"Okay," Dominick said, and hung up.

Bari paced the floor. "Oh, God, oh, God, please let him be okay. He probably ran off the road. Oh, Lord, I hope he wasn't drinking and driving. That's it! Hospitals! I'll call the local hospitals to see if they've admitted an Earl Jordan."

Bari ran across the room to the hallway and grabbed the yellow pages off the closet shelf and began dialing numbers. She called four local hospitals. Not one of them had any record of admission for an Earl Jordan. She dialed the hospitals in all the other boroughs. Still, no record.

Maybe he's hurt and they just haven't found him yet. Wherever Earl is in this world, I know he needs me, Bari thought.

"Lord, I know there are multitudes of people praying to you right now, but I'm asking you to hear my lone prayer. . . ."

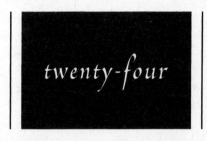

twenty-four

EARL WAS FEELING good. He had been to TJ's nightspot several times before. The last time Earl was there, he met Sandra. He liked her immediately. Sandra was a businesswoman and she was sexy as hell. Her big brown eyes and C-cup breasts had gotten Earl's attention immediately. They had arranged to meet again on this night. Earl had looked forward to it. He found Sandra to be quite interesting. She was very much into politics and she talked about it a lot. Earl didn't particularly care for that line of conversation, but it was too soon to let her know that. In fact, he found politics pretty boring. Soon enough, he wouldn't allow her to talk about it at all to him. In the meantime, tonight he was out to have a little fun. He had already invested enough money in drinks for her. He was hoping that he wouldn't have to delay things any further by having to take her out to dinner or anything. He was ready to get down to brass tacks. He had already figured out what motel they would go to when the time came. Earl hoped Sandra wouldn't try to play hard to get. He wasn't sure how he would handle that, but he did know for sure that he would be pretty pissed off.

Earl turned to Sandra, who was sitting on the bar stool next to him. "So, you're okay?" Earl asked her.

"I'm fine . . . but I would really like to powder my nose," Sandra said.

"That's fine with me. I'll be right here," said Earl.

"No, you don't understand. I'd *really* like to powder my nose." Sandra made a gesture toward her nose. "You do indulge, don't you?" she asked him.

"Oh sure, sure, I got you covered," Earl said. He reached into his pocket and took out the plastic cocaine package. He reached for Sandra's hand and pretended to caress it, slipping her the package. Sandra put the package into her pocketbook, then slid off the bar stool. She pursed her lips and told Earl that she would be back, then sauntered off to the ladies' room.

"This is gonna be easier than I thought," Earl said when Sandra walked away. When she came back, she snuggled up to Earl and slipped the package back to him. Now it was Earl's turn to make his trip to the men's room. When he returned to Sandra, he whispered in her ear. She giggled, then slid off the bar stool again. She handed Earl the trench coat that she had been sitting on and he helped her put it on. They left the club. It was 11:45 P.M.

BACK AT THE house, Bari had put away the food and started to clear up the kitchen. She wasn't worried about Earl anymore. Now she was mad. She figured if Earl wasn't dead, he could have called. Bari turned in at midnight. She took a stack of magazines with her upstairs to the bedroom and turned on the television and watched it until she fell asleep.

EARL CAME IN at 3:40 A.M. He eased through the door and slipped his shoes off. He moved through the house like a thief in the night. He got undressed, took the magazines off the bed, and switched off the television. Bari didn't stir.

WHEN BARI AWAKENED the next morning, Earl was sleeping next to her. "Wake up, Earl! You wake up right now!" Bari angrily nudged him.

"What's the matter with you?" Earl asked in a groggy voice, slightly lifting his head off the pillow.

"What the hell is the matter with you, not coming home last night? I was worried sick!" she told him.

Earl sat up. "Oh, that. Oh, baby, I'm so sorry about that. You know, Pop had me doing all that inventory shit. I thought I told you about that."

"No, you didn't tell me about that," Bari said in a sullen voice. "What you told me was that you wanted us to have a special dinner last night. You wanted shrimp scampi."

"Oh, man, I guess I forgot. I'm sorry."

"You guess you forgot? You're sorry? I called your office and I got no answer. I mean, you make this special request for dinner, and then you don't even bother to show up? You just forget about it?" Bari started to cry. "I thought something happened to you. I called every goddamned hospital in New York City to see if you were in there."

"Baby, I'm really sorry. We were working in the warehouse and . . ." Earl stopped mid-sentence. "Don't cuss, Bari; you know I don't like you cussin'."

"I'm upset, Earl!"

"Look, I started to call you, but I got diverted, and then I lost track of the time. I'll make it up to you. I promise."

"You don't understand. It's so upsetting to me when you leave me in the dark. It's almost like you do it on purpose. It's so inconsiderate."

"I said I'm sorry. What more can I say?"

"You can start by saying that you're gonna make sure that it doesn't happen again."

"All right, baby, you got it. It won't happen again."

"See that?" Bari smiled. "Most women probably would have thought that you were messing around on them, you not coming home like that. But I know you know better."

Bari reached under the covers and gave Earl's penis a firm squeeze, looking at him as if she dared him to even think about it.

"Now why would you wanna go and say some shit like that for? You always have to go and talk some shit!" Earl jumped out of bed, threw on his robe, and left the room in a huff.

Bari jumped up and ran up the hall behind him. "What?" she asked. "What's the matter? What did I say?" she asked, following him into the guest room.

"You know what you said! Shit!" Earl moved quickly from room to room. Bari had a hard time keeping up with him. Earl mumbled something under his breath about being accused.

"Earl, can you stand still for one minute and talk to me?"

"Look, just get out of my face, all right!" Earl rushed off again. He ended up in the bathroom.

Bari was still behind him. She went into the bathroom, too. "What the hell is wrong with you?" Bari asked, like she expected him to tell her.

"I told you before not to speak to me that way!"

"I'll speak to you any way I damn well please!"

"Look, shut the fuck up right now! I don't want to hear your voice anymore!"

"Don't tell me to shut up!"

"Back off!" Earl shoved her. Bari lost her footing and fell back against the tub ledge. She grabbed at the shower curtain to try to regain her balance, but she couldn't get hold of the curtain in time. She fell into the tub. Her shoulder caught the faucet fixture as she went down. Bari screamed out in pain. Her skin didn't break, but her shoulder was already starting to turn purple and blue.

"You see! I told you to back off. You see what you made me do? You see! Fuck!"

Bari was crying as she struggled to get out of the tub. Earl reached out his hand to her to help her.

"Leave me alone. I don't want your help. Just get the hell out of here!"

"Gladly." Earl left her in the bathroom without a backward glance. He threw on a pair of jeans, a shirt and jacket, and left the house.

EARL HAD BEEN gone for over five hours and hadn't called home yet. Bari thought that he would have cooled off by now.

"Come on, Earl, where are you?" she said aloud. Her stomach was starting to cramp from all of the Häagen-Dazs butter pecan ice cream that she had been eating straight from the container. Bari had been sitting in the living room watching television for the past few hours. *Where did I mess up?* she asked herself. She had always done the right thing. She lived right, didn't take drugs, wasn't a big drinker. She maintained a good job, had bought a nice house, paid her bills on time, and had good credit. Ever since she was nine years old, she never got out of bed and stepped with her left foot first. She always started walking with her right foot first. According to Granny, it was good luck to do that. So what happened? Where did she go wrong? All of a sudden she slammed the ice-cream container down onto the table and turned off the television.

"Enough of this." Bari started to strip off her clothing as she walked upstairs to the bathroom. She stepped into the shower. The bruise on her shoulder had risen and was now big and ugly. Bari

winced in pain when she washed it by mistake. When she came out of
the shower, she felt a whole lot better.

"Tonight, I'm outta here. Hell, all I do is work, work, and work.
When do *I* get to have any fun?" She squeezed into the tightest pair of
jeans that she could find. She chose the ones that she called her "yeast
infection" jeans. Anyone looking would swear that she sprayed them
on. She pulled out a wintergreen-colored silk midriff sweater and put
it on. It came just below her breasts and left her flat belly exposed.
Bari carefully put on her makeup and combed her hair straight down
her back. When she was done, she dug in the bottom of her closet and
found her high-heeled black lace-up boots. Now she was ready. She
looked closely in the mirror.

"Okay, now what? Who am I kidding? I have nowhere to go. How
pathetic am I? I need a life . . . bad," she said.

Bari picked up the telephone and dialed Dominick. She didn't care
if Earl came in and saw her or not. He owed her.

Dominick picked up on one ring. "Hello?"

"Hello yourself. I'm mad at you," Bari told him. She tried to sound
cheery.

"Hey, baby girl, what's up? What do you mean, you're mad at me?"

"Did you lose my number? I haven't heard from you in a while,"
Bari said.

"What are you trying to do, get me killed? You know your husband
doesn't want me calling you. He only told me that a dozen and a half
times," Dominick said.

"And I told you a dozen and a half times not to listen to him. You're
my best friend, and that's that," Bari said, one hand on her hip.

"You know I love you, girl, and like I told you before, I'd do anything
for you, but . . ."

"Good. Then come take me out tonight," Bari said, sounding sweet.

"I can't believe this. You finally call me to hang out, and you know
I would love nothin' more than to hang with you, but I already have
plans for tonight. You should have called me earlier," Dominick said,
disappointment in his voice.

"Now I'm really mad at you." Bari pouted.

"I'm sorry, Bari. I'll make it up to you. We'll hang out next weekend.
Okay?"

"We'd better."

"We will. I really gotta go, Bari. I'll talk to you."

They hung up. Bari didn't put the handset back on the cradle. She dialed Franki. Franki's telephone rang several times. Just as Bari was about to hang up, Franki picked up.

"Hi, Bari," Franki said.

"Hey, how did you know it was me?"

"E.S.P. What's up?"

"Nothing much. What are you doing? Let's hang." She held her breath and waited for Franki's response.

"You want to hang out? Miss 'married to her work'? Miss 'want to spend the evening with her husband'? Okay, talk to me; what's wrong?"

"Nothing's wrong. I'm ready to take a break from my work, that's all." Bari tried to sound convincing.

"I'm still nursing a hangover from last night. I simply can't do another club tonight," Franki whined.

"Okay, fine. So we don't have to go to a club. Just come over. We can hang out here."

"You got anything to eat?"

"As a matter of fact, I have plenty of shrimp scampi."

"Say no more. I'm there. I'll see you between seven and eight."

FRANKI GOT TO Bari's house at 7:45. She handed Bari a bottle of white wine and kissed her on the cheek.

"I'm so glad you came, Franki. I miss you," Bari said, smiling at her sister.

Franki stepped up into the house. "I miss you, too, Bari, but you're scaring me. Are you about to die or something?" Franki asked, taking off her jacket and laying it on the couch. She continued straight to the kitchen, walking behind Bari.

"No, I'm not about to die. It's just that it feels like we haven't hung out, you know, just you and me, in a long time. We used to be inseparable."

"Yeah, but now you have a Romeo in your life. And you know how women are. As soon as they get a man, they dump all their friends." Franki chuckled.

"That's not true," Bari protested. But then she had to laugh herself.

"Sure it's true." Franki washed her hands in the kitchen sink and ripped off a paper towel sheet from the dispenser and dried them. "I hope you don't mind, but I'm gonna heat the food up right now. I'm starving."

"Go right ahead. Pull out the big white casserole dish from the fridge. That's the shrimp. The smaller white dish is the pasta."

"Wait a minute," Franki said when she took out the casserole dishes and uncovered them. "You guys didn't even touch the food. What happened?"

"Could you believe Earl's father had him working all damn night, so when he finally came home, he was too tired to eat. We're saving it for tonight."

Franki looked at Bari curiously, but she didn't say anything. She spooned pasta and shrimp onto her plate, then stuck it into the microwave. "I live for this stuff," Franki said, as she settled down to eat. Bari sat across from her. "I must promise myself to work this food off tomorrow at the gym. Aren't you having any?" Franki asked Bari, her mouth already full.

"Not right now. I'm gonna wait for Earl."

"That's messed up, huh?" Franki asked, stuffing more shrimp and pasta into her mouth.

"What's messed up?"

"Earl having to work all night after all the hard work you did, and then not being able to enjoy your dinner the way you planned it. I mean, I could see you worked hard. The house looks really nice. You got fresh flowers. . . ." Franki's voice trailed off as she studied Bari's expression.

"Yeah, it's messed up," Bari said, brushing invisible crumbs off her lap. There was an awkward silence.

"Why didn't you call him? His father, I mean. Surely he would have understood it if you wanted Earl to come home to you, instead of working."

"I didn't think of that. Anyway, it doesn't matter now. Are you done?" Bari asked, reaching for her sister's empty plate. Bari went over to the sink and started to wash Franki's dish and the other dishes that were already in the sink.

"You're gonna get your silk sweater all wet and ruin it," Franki told her.

"I was just thinking the same thing. Let me go and put on a T-shirt." Bari pulled her sweater over her head as she walked up the stairs.

Franki watched her as she walked. "Bari! What the hell happened to your shoulder! Let me see that." Franki rushed up the steps behind Bari to get a closer look at the shoulder. The makeup that Bari had used to cover it had been wiped away. "My God, that's a terrible bruise. How'd you get that? And what happened to your eye?" Franki asked, touching it.

Bari winced. "Could you believe I bumped into the damn door? I fell backward. You know how spastic I can be."

"How could you bump into the door and get a bruise as nasty as this on the back of your shoulder and get your eye all discolored?"

"Apparently, very easily." Bari giggled.

There was that awkward silence again. Bari turned and went ahead up the stairs and changed her sweater. Neither one of them spoke for a while when Bari came back down the stairs. Bari went about wiping down the kitchen counter and putting away the casserole dishes that Franki had left out. Franki watched Bari as she worked.

"What?" Bari asked when she turned around and saw Franki staring at her.

"What, what?"

"Why are you staring at me?"

"Let me ask you a question, Bari," Franki said, squinting her eyes in deep contemplation.

"Go ahead."

"Are you and Earl okay?" Franki asked.

"Of course Earl and I are okay. Why do you ask?"

"Because, I hate to say it, but I think that Earl is out of control. I mean, you see him, he flies off the handle at the drop of a dime, he's got the worst attitude a person can have, and I don't like the way he treats you, Bari. He doesn't respect you."

"Of course Earl respects me. How could you even say something like that?" Bari asked, sounding indignant.

"It's what I see, Bari. It's what I've *been* seeing," Franki told her.

"I'm sorry, Franki, I don't know what you think you see, but even if there was something between Earl and me, it wouldn't be right for me to discuss it with anybody other than Earl. I mean, he's my husband, and you and I have to draw the line somewhere."

"I'm just concerned about you. That's all. I'm not trying to get into your business or interfere in your life. And, I'm sorry, but I just don't see it your way. I'm your sister and you should be able to talk to me if you're having a problem."

"I don't want to be put in a position where I have to defend my husband. And I already told you, we're not having any problems."

"Bari, this is me. We talk about everything. What do you think I'm gonna do with any information you might give me? I have never tried to hurt you. You know that. Besides, I know you, and I could always tell when you're not okay."

"I'm sure you didn't come all the way over here to discuss my marriage. And this certainly wasn't what I had in mind when I invited you over," Bari said.

"I know, but—," Franki started but was interrupted by the sound at the door. The key was in the lock, but the door wasn't opening. Earl fumbled with it for a few minutes. Whenever Earl couldn't open the door, Bari had come to know, it could mean only one thing. Earl had been drinking. His timing was off as usual. Of all times to come in drunk, he couldn't have chosen a worse one. Bari walked over and pulled open the door for him.

"Thank you, baby," Earl said, walking through the door. "I smell food. Hope you saved me some. Oh, I see we have company. Hello, Franki," Earl said. His words were loud and somewhat slurred.

"Franki was just leaving."

Franki looked at Bari questioningly.

"Good," said Earl. "'Cause I want to spend some time alone with my wife."

"You go right ahead and spend as much time as you want with your wife," said Franki, taking her sister's hint. Franki gathered her things to leave. Before she opened the door, she turned to look at Bari. "Call me," Franki said. It was more of a question. A plea.

"Yeah," Bari said, and Franki left.

"Come on, fire up somethin' for me to eat. I'm hungry," Earl said. A simple-looking smile was pasted on his face. He threw his jacket over the back of the chair and sat at the table.

Bari didn't speak a word as she took the casserole dishes from the refrigerator again and spooned out Earl's dinner. She sprinkled some of the crystallized powder that Zuma had given her onto Earl's food. Bari had left the powder in one of the kitchen cabinets for easy access. She stuck his plate into the microwave and set the timer for two minutes. Bari poured him a glass of soda and ice while she waited for the food to heat. When she turned around to look at Earl, he was asleep.

Bari gritted her teeth as she hit the "stop" button on the microwave, turned off the kitchen lights, and left Earl at the kitchen table. She went upstairs to her bedroom and turned in for the night.

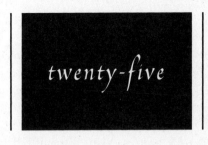

twenty-five

IT WAS WEDNESDAY morning and Bari was back at work. She had only been away from the office for two days, but it felt like it had been a lot longer. Bari's eye was completely healed and she didn't feel self-conscious about it anymore. In fact, today she felt good so she wanted to look good, too, on her return. She chose her outfit carefully. She decided on a conservative navy blue Jones New York business suit. It was double-breasted, with antique silver buttons and a suede collar. The skirt fell just below her calves, making her look a lot taller than she actually was. She was carrying a large shoulder bag, two portfolio cases, and a small shopping bag. As Bari approached the building where she worked, Sammy, the robust security guard, rushed over and opened the door for her before she could reach it.

"Good morning, Miss Bari," he said.

"Good morning, Sammy," Bari responded.

"Nice weather we're having," Sammy said.

Bari smiled and nodded. Bari didn't remember whom she had heard it from, but somebody told her that Sammy had a huge crush on her. She could actually see him trying to think of something clever to say to her. But he almost always seemed to lose the nerve and couldn't come up with anything.

"Let me help you with those bags, Miss Bari."

"Oh, thanks, Sammy. I appreciate it." She handed him the portfolios.

"I'm glad to see you back at work. I heard you were sick." Sammy was grinning like a Cheshire cat.

"Yes. I'm feeling a lot better now. Thank you, Sammy."

Sammy handed Bari's bags back to her when she got into the elevator.

"Thanks so much. You have a nice day, Sammy," Bari said, stepping far back into the elevator and leaning against the back rail on the wall.

Sammy flashed that Cheshire smile again. "God," he said aloud when the doors closed, "just one night."

WHEN BARI REACHED the fifth floor, she struggled her way down the corridor. Sidney looked up from his desk, and when he saw Bari he applauded. Everybody else in the office joined in.

"Well, well, look who decided to grace us with her presence," said Barbara.

"To what do we owe the pleasure?" they all teased.

Bari smiled and waved them off. She passed David's office on the way to hers.

"My star is back," David said, calling out to her.

"Your star is behind on her proposal," Bari said, stopping in front of his office. She rested her bags in front of her on the floor.

"I know that we're behind the eight ball on this project but I have every confidence that you'll get us ready. Got a minute? Come in, please, have a seat." David said to her.

Bari picked up her bags from the floor and went inside David's office and sat down.

"I have a deal for you, Bari. I'm putting a little something more on your plate. If you can pull this off, I will guarantee you an associate position with this firm because you will be responsible for putting Choler-Raines in a very steady position financially. I need you to land the Demeris account. But first you're going to have to go to Seattle to tie up Paiseley."

Bari didn't look enthused.

"Do you have a problem with that?" David asked.

"To tell you the truth, this is not the best time in the world for me to be traveling, but I guess I have to do what I have to do." Bari sighed.

"Bari, you can do this. Paiseley is gonna bite. All they need right now is to be able to put a face to the voice so that they can feel comfortable. They just want their hands held. We're talking about a two-million-dollar contract."

David's secretary buzzed in on the intercom. "David, pick up on line two. It's Mr. Peters."

"Not right now. Hold my calls."

"Right." She got off the line.

"What was I saying?" David asked. He was so forgetful at times. Bari found that annoying about him. "We were speaking about why it's so important for me to go to Seattle," she reminded him.

"Oh yeah. So like I was saying, Paiseley is in the bag. But you're gonna have to do your homework on Demeris. They're tough, but they're obtainable. And they're willing to talk to us. I'm giving them my best, Bari. I'm giving them you. I have complete confidence in you," said David.

Bari wasn't sure how Earl was going to react to her going to Seattle. She would have to figure out a way to make him understand that she had a lot riding on this trip. She would worry about the Demeris account when she returned.

"THAT'S FANTASTIC, BABY," Earl said when Bari told him about the trip as they sat down at dinner in the dining room that night.

"Well, aren't you gonna miss me?" She couldn't believe that he wasn't even a little bit upset. A part of her was a little disappointed about that.

"Yeah, I'm gonna miss you, but it's only for a few days, right?" Earl asked, gulping down the glass of rum and Coke that he had fixed for himself.

"It's only for four days. I'm gonna make you proud of me," Bari said, giving him a sweet smile.

"I'm already proud of you." Earl gave her a sweet smile of his own. Bari observed him smiling at her, and she saw a look on his face that she hadn't seen in a long time. Earl was calm for a change, and they had been having a normal, stress-free conversation before she told him about her trip. Suddenly she got excited on the inside. Zuma's powder was working, finally!

"Show me how proud of me you are. I only have two days left before I leave," Bari said, sensing a throbbing between her legs. Her eyes were quickly growing heavy with passion.

"Then every minute counts."

Inside their bedroom, they slowly explored one another's naked body. Bari and Earl looked at each other as if they were seeing each other for the first time, then they lapsed into uninhibited, unbridled lovemaking.

TWO DAYS LATER, Bari was at JFK Airport waiting for Flight Number 843, heading for Seattle. Earl had dropped Bari off, but he couldn't wait with her because he had set up a prior appointment. He had told Bari that he had to see a man about a dog. Bari smiled when she thought about Earl. She really hated leaving him now that their relationship seemed like it was just about to start heading in the right direction again. She had cooked up enough food to last him for four days, and she had made sure that his white shirts were cleaned, ironed, and laid out for him. Bari really hoped that she could wrap up this deal quickly so that she could hurry back home. She made sure that she packed her posy kerchief. She needed the Paiseley account.

After Earl dropped off Bari at the airport, he made it home in exactly twenty-five minutes. He had stopped to pick up Tommy on the way. Once Tommy was in the car, Earl did 65 miles per hour all the way home.

"Make yourself at home, man. *Mi casa es su casa,*" Earl said to Tommy as they walked into the house.

"What's that, Spanish or some shit?" Tommy asked.

"Don't matter. My home is yours," Earl said.

"Cool. Gimme somethin' to drink," Tommy said, taking off his jacket and throwing it on the couch, then sitting down beside it.

"I got some rum and a little vodka. I got some beers, too," Earl offered.

"Gimme a brewski," Tommy said.

"You got it."

Earl took two beers from the refrigerator. He handed one to Tommy, then popped open the other one for himself.

"All right, so what you wanna do, man?" Tommy asked, sipping his beer. He took a cigarette from a pack and stuck it behind his ear.

"What you got good?" Earl asked.

"I got whatever you want. You want small, I got small, or I can go as big as you want."

"Hook me up with an eight ball," Earl told him.

"Ain't nothing but a chicken wing." Tommy took a long swig of beer, then rested the can on the floor next to him and took out a large plastic bag filled with pure rock cocaine. He pulled out a scale, a grinder, and some other tools of the trade. "Check this out, man." Tommy scooped some of the white powder into a small gold spoon and handed it to Earl.

Earl took the hit. "That's some good shit."

"You're damned right that's some good shit. I don't deal with nothin' but the best," Tommy said, refilling the spoon and handing it to Earl again.

Earl took it into his other nostril. While Tommy was busy filling Earl's order, Earl took out his bankroll and peeled off two one-hundred-dollar bills and a fifty. He dropped the bills onto the table. Tommy downed the rest of his beer, then handed Earl a carefully measured one-eighth of cocaine.

"Put this away," Tommy said, as he handed Earl the bag that held the eight ball. "Get me a plate."

Earl put the bag of cocaine on one of the shelves on the wall unit, then left the room to get a plate from the kitchen for Tommy. When Earl returned, he gave the plate to Tommy. He poured a generous amount of the drug onto the plate and passed it to Earl.

"Sniff this. Save yours for later," Tommy told him.

"Look, man, help yourself to another beer." Earl told Tommy. "I already gave you the first one. You're on your own now."

"You don't have to tell me twice," said Tommy. He was up and in the fridge in the same breath. "Are your buddies still comin' over?" Tommy asked from the kitchen.

"Yeah. They'll be here," Earl answered.

"You know me, my time is money. I gotta make a move soon," Tommy told him, as he cracked open the beer can.

"They'll be here," Earl said again. He took another hit from the mound on the plate.

The doorbell rang. Earl looked through the blinds before he opened the door. It was Half and his cousin Ziggy. Earl let them into the house and offered them beers and some hits. They placed their orders with Tommy and he carefully ground and measured his product out into aluminum-foil packages for them. When their transactions were done, they all got up to leave. Earl took out three more beers from the refrigerator and handed one to each of them on the way out.

When they were gone, Earl stood for a minute, listening to the quiet in the house. "Damn, I'm gonna go nuts in here for four days by myself." He had a whole eight ball and nobody to share it with. Earl thought it would be a crime not to take advantage of the situation. He felt like doing something different. Something dangerous. "Cheryl," he said aloud. "That wild girl. I'll bet she'd come over."

Earl went upstairs and rummaged through Bari's underwear drawer for her telephone book. He had pulled the book out many times before when he needed to contact her when she was at a friend's house or if he just needed to verify Bari's whereabouts. He flipped through the book. He didn't know Cheryl's last name, but he knew her address. He would start at the letter A and work his way through until he saw the address. Earl found her on page 3. He dialed her number and was surprised to find her at home.

"Hello, Cheryl. It's Earl."

"Earl? Earl Jordan?" Cheryl asked, surprised.

"Yeah."

"What's up, Earl? Is something wrong with Bari?" Cheryl asked, sounding genuinely concerned.

"No, nothin's wrong with her. So, how are you doin'?" He tried to sound smooth.

"I'm fine. To what do I owe the pleasure of your call?"

"Actually, to tell you the truth, I was just thinkin' about you and I was wondering if we could hook up?" Earl didn't feel like playing games. He got right to the point.

"Hook up? I don't understand what you mean. I mean, where's Bari? What's goin' on, Earl?"

"Well . . . Bari's out of town, and I figured I'm here doin' nothin', and I was kind of hopin' that if you were there doin' nothin', then maybe we could hook up." Earl spoke clearly and concisely.

"Wow. I don't believe this. This is very funny. . . . Actually I am here doing nothing. What did you have in mind?" Cheryl's voice was bubbly, happy.

"Well, I figured you could come over here to my house and hang out with me for a while."

"Your house? Yours and Bari's house?"

"Yeah. Believe me, it's okay. Bari won't be home anytime soon. She's out of town for the next few days."

"Well, it's not just that. . . . I wouldn't feel—"

"Take a cab," Earl said, cutting her off. "I have something for you when you get here."

"Okay," Cheryl gushed.

CHERYL'S HEART RACED. She couldn't believe that Earl had called her out of the blue like that. He actually called her. She stood still for a moment and took in a slow, deep breath. In a trillion years she never would have thought that Earl would ever call her like that. She had always looked at him as not only good-looking but strong and sexy, too. Bari was a lucky woman. She had it all. If only Bari knew. If only Bari knew! Cheryl would not allow herself to feel guilty about any of this. Somehow, she felt that she owed it to Bari. Cheryl never did believe that Bari wasn't interested in Maurice way back in high school at that hooky party. She always felt that Bari planned to stab her in the back. It didn't matter that that was so many years ago. Bari was wrong. And wrong is wrong.

Besides that, Cheryl was lonely. She was sick and tired of standing by and watching all of her friends getting married, having babies . . . being happy. She always wondered when she would get her turn. Time wasn't standing still for her.

"What am I gonna put on?" she asked herself. "Oh, I know, I'll wear that yellow number that shows off my boobs. I'm sure he'll like that."

Cheryl rushed around her apartment getting herself together. Her "yellow number" was as bright as the sun, and it was plastic. Cheryl had tried very hard to find yellow boots to match her outfit but couldn't find them anywhere, so she had to settle for white ones instead.

"Well, whatever happens tonight happens, and I'm just gonna feel real adult about it tomorrow."

Cheryl got dressed. She took special care putting on her makeup.

As soon as she was done, she called a cab. She couldn't wait to get there. Cheryl tried to imagine what it was going to be like being with Earl. If he wanted to make love to her she could never tell him no. She couldn't fathom being able to do that.

EARL HELPED CHERYL off with her jacket when she got there. "Have a seat. Make yourself comfortable," he told her, smiling and looking her over.

"Make myself comfortable? I'll try. It's kind of weird being here without Bari," Cheryl said.

"Then, you need to put Bari out of your mind," Earl said.

Cheryl giggled. "So, I'm curious. What made you call me?" she asked, sitting down and crossing her legs.

"To tell you the truth, I've wanted to call you for a long time. But you know how that is. You seem like the kind of woman that I'd like to be with."

"Oh yeah? And what about Bari? What kind of woman is she?"

"Oh, man." Earl started laughing lightly and shaking his head. "Bari and me . . . we're not . . . Let's just say we're not that tight anymore. If you don't mind, I'd rather not talk about her right now. I'd rather talk about you and me."

Cheryl smiled big. She wanted to talk about them, too. She wasn't seeing anybody and she wouldn't mind seeing Earl whenever she could, as long as she could be with him.

"I have some champagne for us."

"That's nice," Cheryl gushed.

Earl reached up into the wall unit and took down two high fluted Toscany champagne glasses. The glasses were used only on what Bari considered very special occasions, and even then she would make a fuss over them. Earl filled the glasses with champagne. He handed a glass to Cheryl, then sat next to her on the couch with his glass in hand.

"Here's to the beginning of what I hope to be a long-lasting friendship," Earl toasted.

"Hear, hear."

Earl finished off his champagne, then rested his glass on the coffee table. "I told you that I have something for you."

"Yeah." Cheryl put her glass on the table, then smoothed out the wrinkles on her plastic skirt.

Earl got up and left the room.

"Oh, my God. Don't tell me this man done went and bought me a present. He really had this thing all planned out." Cheryl whispered the words.

When Earl returned, his hands were empty. Cheryl was puzzled. He sat back down beside her; then he reached into his shirt pocket and took out a small hand-painted ceramic pillbox. It was filled with cocaine.

"I want you to try this." Earl scooped some of the powder into a gold spoon.

"What is that, cocaine?"

"Yeah. Do you blow?"

"To tell you the truth, I can drink any man under the table, and I must admit that I've done a lot of things in my life, but I ain't never put no drugs in my body," she told him.

"Well, I certainly don't mean to be the one to corrupt you."

Cheryl could feel Earl's deep, soothing voice roll all over her body. She looked at him and she could feel his strength. Talk about smelling the testosterone!

"Here. Let me show you how it's done."

He put the spoon to Cheryl's nose. Cheryl didn't refuse. She wanted Earl to know that she was willing to do whatever he wanted her to do.

"Sniff it in."

Cheryl sniffed the drug into one nostril, then repeated it in the other when he gave the cocaine to her. Her eyes watered immediately. She wiped away the excess water, then cleared her throat.

"Nothing happened. I don't feel anything."

"Here. Do it again." Earl gave her another hit in both nostrils.

For the next hour Earl and Cheryl finished off the entire bottle of champagne and snorted an enormous amount of cocaine.

"Come on, Earl, let's dance. I wanna feel that hard body of yours next to me." Cheryl was standing in the middle of the floor with her eyes squeezed shut and her hand on her belly, grinding slowly to the soothing jazz music that was playing.

She pulled Earl close to her and they danced very slowly together. Cheryl rubbed Earl's back as they danced. Soon they started to kiss. Hungrily.

"What did you put in that stuff? I'm so horny." Cheryl laughed when they finally came up for air. She kissed Earl again. He began to unzip her skirt. Cheryl helped him when her zipper got stuck midway.

While Cheryl took down her skirt, Earl unbuttoned her blouse and took it off of her. They kissed again, and finally, when neither one of them could stand it any longer, they fell to the living room floor, tearing at each other's clothing. They made love several times, then lay side by side on the carpet when they were done.

"Will you stay the night with me?"

"I was hoping you'd ask. I brought some stuff, you know, a nightie, a toothbrush, just in case you wanted me to stay." Cheryl giggled.

"Good, then let's turn in. I'm not done with you yet."

Earl stood up, then reached down for Cheryl's hand to help her up.

"I need to freshen up first." Cheryl picked up her bag and headed toward the bathroom.

Earl pulled her close to him and hugged her. "Don't keep me waitin' too long."

"I don't plan to." Cheryl giggled as she pulled away from him.

While Cheryl was in the bathroom, Earl picked up the glasses off of the coffee table and put them into the sink. He went back over to the table and laid out some more lines for him and Cheryl. When she came out, she was wearing a red see-through teddy with matching crotchless panties. She struck a sexy pose for Earl. He motioned for her to come closer. Cheryl walked into his arms and they kissed some more before they went up to the bedroom and made love well into the night.

twenty-six

BRODERICK JORDAN SAT in his small, dimly lit office. His small, beady eyes and creased brow almost met each other as he frowned in concentration. The ashtray on his desk was full of cigarette butts from the pack and a half of cigarettes that he had smoked over the past four hours. He went over his books for the fourth time and he was aggravated now. Broderick was no accountant, but he knew enough to know that something was dead wrong. According to his inventory records, he was moving his merchandise, but those records didn't coincide with his cash records. If he didn't know any better, he would think that he was being robbed. But who in the hell would do that to him? The only people who were in a position to affect cash were he and his son. If Earl needed cash, Broderick was sure that he would have told him.

Broderick Jordan had been thinking over the situation for some time now, but the more he thought about it, the more convinced he became that it was very possible that Earl could have something to do with the cash shortage. He had to admit that he had noticed a definite change in Earl's attitude. Broderick had first observed Earl's mood swings a long time ago. There were many days when he had come in with glassy eyes and choppy speech. While Broderick took notice of this, he never spoke of it. He had his suspicions, though. And that's why he called Earl.

"I need you in here now!" Broderick yelled into the phone, waking Earl up at six that morning.

Broderick had meant to speak to Bari before she went to Seattle. He figured that maybe she could have given him some insight into whether or not there was a problem. But Bari wasn't due home for two days, and he certainly couldn't put this off for that long. He would just have to handle the situation the only way he knew how.

Earl came into the office an hour and a half later. "I'm sorry it took me so long to get here. I got hung up in traffic," Earl said as he made his way over to his side of the office. Earl's glassy, puffy, bloodshot eyes darted back and forth between the floor and the open space. He immediately started fumbling around with some papers on his desk, moving them from one side of the desk to the other to avoid looking at his father. Earl had only gotten two hours of sleep. Cheryl had been insatiable and that had excited him.

"So what's going on? You said you wanted to talk to me," Earl said, his eyes still focused on the papers on his desk.

His father had been silently watching Earl from the moment he walked in the door. Broderick stood up and walked to the front of his desk and sat on the edge of it, facing Earl.

"What can you tell me about this cash shortage?" Broderick asked, holding up the cash journal in front of Earl.

"What cash shortage are you talkin' about?"

"I just spent the past two and a half to four hours going over the inventory records, and I compared 'em to the cash totals in this book and I keep getting discrepancies. Now, I could clearly see that we're movin' merchandise, but we ain't got the cash to show for it. So, I'm asking you if you can explain what's happenin' here."

"If I can explain what?" Earl asked through squinted, red eyes.

Broderick was losing his patience. He could see that Earl wasn't all there and that he was wasting his breath on him. Broderick had been observing Earl's eyes opening and closing as if he was in and out of sleep.

"The missing cash. Explain the missing cash, Earl!"

"There's no missin' cash. It's not like the cash is missin'. As part owner, I borrowed some money."

Broderick threw the cash book across the room to Earl's desk. Earl moved his arm just in time so that the book didn't hit him.

"You borrow this much money from my company and you don't even bother to tell me! You've been working with me in this business for a long time. I think you know that it doesn't work that way. I feel robbed!" Broderick yelled. His voice exuded complete disgust.

Earl was on his feet now. "Robbed? It's not like I took *your* money. I took *my* money."

"Earl, you're a grown man. What's the matter with you? You don't understand this at all, do you? I gave you a title. That's all. It's not your money until I say it's your money! Now, I don't care what you do with your money, but I believe that you have a problem that's bigger than you would care to admit. I believe that you're messing around with them drugs," Broderick said, staring Earl straight in the eye.

"Whatever I do in my personal life has nothing to do with this company."

"What you do in your personal life has everything to do with this company when you're using my money to buy your shit!" Broderick yelled again, standing in the middle of the floor between the two desks.

"Since you feel that way about it, I'll pay you back every dime."

Broderick hung his head. He went over and sat down on the front edge of his desk again and clasped his hands in his lap. "Son, I don't want the money back. What I want is for you to get help."

"I don't need any help."

"Yeah, you do, Son. Yeah, you do. And I'm afraid that until you get yourself some help, you can't work here. You have to go and rehabilitate yourself." Broderick sounded solemn now.

"What exactly are you sayin' to me?" Earl asked, his red eyes squinted, the vein in the middle of his forehead protruding.

"What I'm sayin' is that I want the keys to the car and the keys to the office." There was no question in Broderick's voice.

"You can't do this!" Earl said. He started halfway across the room toward his father. Fire was in Earl's eyes. Broderick stood up as Earl approached him. The two men stood face-to-face.

"Don't make this hard. Hand over the keys," Broderick said calmly.

"Don't make it *hard*? You don't know *hard*. *Hard* is living with the fact of knowing that you killed my mother and not doing a damn thing about it. *That's hard*. You owe me!" Earl yelled into his father's face.

"I made peace with the Lord for that, Son."

"Oh, so you made peace with the Lord, and now it's supposed to be all washed away. Tell me how in the hell am I supposed to wash away the images of my mother in my head? How am I supposed to make her stop being mad at me? I was just a kid!"

Broderick and Earl held each other's stare for a full half minute. Finally Broderick spoke. "I'm givin' you enough money to get by for the next couple of months. I have nothin' more to say."

Earl slammed two sets of keys onto his father's desk. He stormed over to the door, kicked it open, and left.

BARI'S FLIGHT BACK to New York arrived at Kennedy Airport right on time. She was glad about that. She was tired and wanted to sleep in her own bed. When Bari left for her trip four days ago, she carried only a single shoulder bag. Now she had two more bags full of souvenirs. The leather strap on her shoulder bag was cutting into her neck and shoulder. The pain was excruciating, but there was nothing that she could do about it until she was able to put the bags down. Bari hailed a cab and was finally on her way home.

When the cab pulled up to the house the blinds were drawn.

"I guess Earl is out," Bari said aloud while she struggled up to the door with her bags. She dropped everything on the top step, then searched through her pocketbook for her keys. Finally, she opened the door and tossed her bags inside the vestibule. When Bari turned on the light, she jumped when she saw Earl sleeping on the couch. Then she saw the Bacardi bottle on the coffee table. She scanned the table for a glass, but Earl hadn't used one. Bari walked over to the couch and gently nudged him awake.

"Hey, baby. I'm home."

Earl opened his eyes and looked up at her. A faint smile appeared on his face. Earl's eyes were puffy and red, and stubble covered his chin.

"Hey, you," Earl said, his voice sounding like gravel had settled in the pit of his throat.

"Hey yourself." Bari lifted his head slightly up from the couch and slid her body underneath it. She bent over and kissed him on his lips. She could smell the liquor on his breath and through his pores. "Are you all right? Are you hungry?"

"Yeah. I guess I could eat a little somethin'."

"I'm hungry, too. I'm gonna make us some sandwiches."

Bari lifted Earl's head off her lap and got up from the couch. She went into the kitchen. The kitchen sink was full of dishes that had been there for at least two or three days. A loaf of bread was open on the table, and crumbs were on the countertop.

"My husband is such a slob." On automatic pilot, Bari started to clean the sticky juice glasses and crumbs off the counter. While she was tying up the bread, she walked over to the sink. "What the hell are my Toscany glasses doing in the sink? They could have gotten broken!" Bari carefully took out the first glass. She had to pull the second glass out from under other dishes in the sink. "Shit," she said. Bari held up the glass and examined it for cracks or chips. "What the hell is lipstick doing on my glass? I sure intend to find out . . . ," she said. She put the sandwiches on the table and went into the living room to tell Earl that his food was ready. When Bari walked back into the living room, Earl had drifted back off to sleep. "Wake up, Earl. Come to the table," she said.

Earl could hardly lift his head. And when he did, he sat on the couch for a minute before he actually stood up. He walked into the kitchen and stopped at the refrigerator and took out a container of orange juice, then sat down at the table with Bari. Bari knew that she had to approach Earl carefully. She had just gotten home and the last thing that she wanted to do was fight with him. She needed to know the truth, though. She needed to know who Earl had been entertaining while she was away. A part of her knew that he would never be unfaithful to her, but the lipstick on the glass was very real and she couldn't ignore it. Bari would feel Earl out first. She'd see what kind of mood he was in; then she would ask him about it. She watched him eat.

Bari looked for a sign. What if she was wrong? Would he ever forgive her for not trusting him?

"What was the special occasion?" she asked him. The words came out from nowhere, and it was too late to take them back. Bari held her breath.

"What?"

"What was the special occasion that made you use the Toscanys?"

Bari tried to smile and look pleasant while she waited for him to answer her.

"Look, before you start getting all suspicious about me, let me ask *you* a question. Where did you get that hickey on your neck?"

"I don't have a hickey on my neck," Bari answered defensively.

"I know what I see. You wanna know what I think? I think that whole Seattle trip was bullshit. Why don't you tell me where you really were and who the hell you were with?"

"I wasn't with anybody. And I did go to Seattle, that's where I called you from. It was a business trip—you know that."

"What I know is what I see. Do you think I'm stupid or somethin'? I should rip your fuckin' head off your shoulders!"

"I don't even know what you're talking about." She got up from the table and went over to the mirror on the door outside the small bathroom in the hallway. She looked closely at the two red marks on her neck. She couldn't figure out where they had come from. Then it hit her.

"Oh, my God, Earl, these aren't hickeys on my neck. These marks came from the shoulder strap on my bag. I remember it was hurting my neck and my shoulder." Bari was back at the table now. "I promise you, I wasn't with anybody. I went on my trip and that was it."

"You better hope you're telling me the fuckin' truth. Don't let me find out otherwise." He glared at her.

Bari looked back at him intently, hoping that somehow her eyes would convey to him what she felt in her heart. She needed him to know that she loved him absolutely and that he would never have to worry about her being unfaithful to him because he would always be the only man for her.

Earl looked away from Bari. He reached for the container of orange juice and poured himself a glass.

"So, tell me about the Toscanys," Bari said.

"Yeah, well, that's a long story. Pop and his girl, Ruby, came by. They wanted to have some dinner with me since they knew I was here all by myself."

"That was sweet of your father and his girlfriend."

"Yeah, well, my father and me had some beef about the business. He really pissed me the fuck off. Anyway, to make a long story short,

I ain't working for him no more. I left the company, and I gave back the car. I can't work with a man with his morals. I'm sorry, I just can't."

"I can't believe this. What happened?" Bari asked.

"It doesn't matter what happened. What is, is what is," Earl said.

"Well, what are you gonna do?" Bari asked.

"I'll find another job. I'm not worried about that," Earl said.

"Of course you'll find another job. Anyway, if things go as well as I expect them to you won't have to rush out to find one. If I get this account, I get a salary increase. I should be able to carry the both of us for a while. As a matter of fact, why don't you just take a break now? It's not like we're hurting for cash or anything. Take a month or two off and just kick back and relax. You deserve it. It'll be nice coming home to you after a hard day's work. Take a break; you look tired." Bari smiled as brightly as she could. She would have said anything to make Earl feel better right now. Her heart was heavy for him. She knew how his ego was, and she knew deep down that he must feel crushed.

Earl was quiet for a minute or two. "I'm not too crazy about the idea of my wife carrying me, but you're right. I'll take off a couple of months to get things straightened out. I'll do some things around the house and I'm definitely gonna relax some. It'll only be temporary; then I'll find a job," Earl said.

"Good," Bari said. She was starting to feel better. "I love you."

"I know."

Three weeks flew by and Bari was having a hard time getting into their new rhythm. It was hard enough gauging Earl's time when he was working. But now that he wasn't working, she never knew when or if he was coming or going. She didn't know what to make of him since he was out of sorts most times and he would blow a fuse in a heartbeat, for any reason.

Earl made love to her regularly and told her that he loved her, but then he would turn around in the same frame and treat her like a complete stranger in her own house. A lot of times his words would be brutal and condescending. Then he would become completely withdrawn. It was those times Bari learned that it was better to leave him alone. In the meantime, she would try to stay focused on her work.

twenty-seven

BARI WOKE UP with a smile on her face. She got up as soon as the alarm clock rang and stepped into the shower. When she got out of the shower, she rubbed her wet body down with sesame seed oil. There was something about the scent of the oil that made her feel happy. She knew it was crazy, but she needed to feel that way today.

Bari had done her homework, and now the time for her long-awaited in-house presentation was here. As many presentations as she had done, this would be the first one that David actually attended. In fact, Sheldon Mangrove and Carol Shaffer had been calling Bari frequently about this particular prospect because securing them as a client would allow Choler-Raines to tap into the automobile industry, which would be a first for them.

Bari had done enough number crunching and market research to take her well into the new millenium. Hell, she could probably write a book on the rise and fall of lucrative companies that failed to understand the needs of their customers. Not only did she plan to demonstrate to Herculon Motors the benefit of Choler-Raines' services, but she would convince them to pay double the usual fee. She was ready.

EARL CAME INTO the bathroom and interrupted the flow of her thoughts. "I didn't see any money under my cologne bottle on the dresser. Did you do what I asked you to do?"

"I went to the bank like you asked me to, but I was surprised when I saw how much the balance has dwindled down so quickly. I didn't realize how many withdrawals you already made for the month."

"Did you take out the money or not?"

"No, I didn't take it out, Earl. We really need to be a little more careful with our spending since I'm the only one working right now. What do you need so much money for anyway?"

"Since when do I have to explain my business to you!" Earl's voice boomed. "Don't think you can control me now just because I'm not workin'. Don't you ever think that!"

Bari didn't respond. She had learned that it was better to keep calm during Earl's tirades. She finished pulling up her panty hose, then walked past Earl, out of the bathroom and into the bedroom.

Earl followed her. "I don't know who's puttin' ideas into your head, but all of a sudden I'm sensin' attitude from you. You want out of this marriage? Is that it?"

"I never said I wanted out of this marriage and I'm not giving you attitude. I'm just a little worried, that's all." Bari said, turning to face him.

"Just give me the goddamned bank card. I'll take care of the shit myself."

"If it means that much to you, I'll do it," said Bari.

"No, you won't. I'll take care of it. You already fucked up. Where is your pocketbook?" Earl looked around the room and spotted Bari's pocketbook on the floor by the chair next to the window. He stormed across the room to get it.

Bari rushed behind him, trying to grab the bag from Earl as he picked it up. "I said I'll do it, Earl. You don't have to go into my bag like that."

"Oh no? What, you have somethin' to hide from me? Get the fuck away from me," Earl said, shoving Bari onto the bed. Bari sprang right back up. Earl unzipped the pocketbook.

"Give me my pocketbook, Earl!"

"Come any closer to me and you'll be sorry." Earl glared at Bari. She knew he meant what he said.

"This is ridiculous!" Bari yelled, and ran from the room into the bathroom, slamming the door behind her. She sat down on the toilet seat, crying and trying to figure out how the two of them got to this point.

Ten minutes later, Bari came out of the bathroom and went back into the bedroom. She saw her pocketbook on the dresser with all of its contents emptied out on the dresser and on the floor. Earl was gone. He had left the house without a word.

Bari slowly put all of her things back into her pocketbook. She pulled her suit out of the closet and continued getting dressed. Bari chose a burgundy-colored "power suit" to wear for her presentation. She knew that she would need more than a power suit to charge her up again.

SIDNEY USHERED THE team from Herculon Motors into the north conference room and pointed out the fresh bagels, muffins, juice, and coffee. As soon as the visitors were settled, he rushed into Bari's office.

"Are you feeling okay, hon? You don't look too good in the face to me. Are you nervous?" he asked Bari.

"You know me better than that, Sidney."

"I'm just making sure, babe, because I know you're gonna kick ass."

"You know it." Bari's smile seemed bright. Her spirits even seemed high. She was okay for the moment, but if Sidney stayed in her office for another minute she knew she would pull every hair from her body. All Bari wanted right now was to be left alone. She didn't want to hear anybody's voice or any laughter. As much time as she had spent preparing for this day and as much as she had looked forward to it, she resented that it was actually here now.

"Anyway," Sidney said, "I don't want to leave those vultures by themselves for too long, so let me go and entertain them until you guys are ready to rock and roll." Sidney sashayed out of Bari's office. Bari got up and shut the door behind him.

Before Bari sat down again, she opened her middle drawer and took out the Extra Strength Tylenol bottle. She hated taking pills. She didn't even know why she bothered taking them. She knew by now that they wouldn't stop her heart palpitations, and they hadn't been effective on her anxiety attacks up to now.

Bari popped the pills and sat back down behind her desk with her head between her hands. She took a few deep breaths, then stood again and left her office. She went down the corridor to David's office to pick him up so that they could greet their guests together. When they walked into the conference room, Sidney made polite introductions, then left the room, closing the door behind him.

David gave a brief summary of Choler-Raines' history as well as its track record in the industry. The group looked impressed when he was done. He had set them up well for Bari. Bari took the floor. She commanded their attention immediately. She had learned early on about the art of body language, and she was good at it. Her movements were sharp and swift and in between sentences she would pause for effect. Bari had them in the palm of her hand right from the start. Even David felt it. He gave Bari a discreet thumbs-up when she looked at him. Bari was ready to move in for the kill. She shut down the lights and turned on the overhead projector. A project plan appeared. Bari talked along as she pointed out the various aspects of the plan. Without warning, depression came down on her and her heart became heavy. Her voice quivered, and she was starting to stutter.

"H-Herculon could stand to Earl . . . er, earn at least . . . You could Earl-earn . . . I'm sorry." Bari breathed in slowly, looking down at the floor—anywhere but at the Herculon team.

Lines creased David's forehead. He waited for a sign from Bari to let him know that everything was okay.

Bari looked around the room. Under the glare of the projector light she could see all of their eyes on her. She thought about how smug their lives must be. Their wives were probably at home tending to their flower beds while they gave instructions to their housekeepers. And here she was tap-dancing and doing backflips for these men while she awaited their approval. Bari could see their cynical grins. She hyperventilated.

"Are you all right?" David asked. He got up from his seat and approached her.

Bari tried to speak, but no words formed. Slowly, she backed away from David. She covered her mouth and ran from the room in tears. Bari went into her office and shut the door. Inside the office, she plopped herself down on one of her guest chairs and put her head down on the desk, trembling and crying. Finally, she stopped crying and dug into her jacket pocket. Nothing. She dug into the other pocket and came up blank, too. Now she was up on her feet checking her coat pocket. She could have sworn she had put the posy kerchief in her pocket. She went over to her desk and opened her desk drawer. The kerchief wasn't in there, nor was it in her pocketbook. "Dammit!"

Bari said. She never even brought it with her into the office. This whole scene could have been avoided. "Shit!"

Since nobody had knocked on her door for at least an hour, Bari figured that word must have gotten out about her episode. She contemplated going home, but she knew she was in no frame of mind to deal with Earl. Besides, she would have to face David sooner or later, so she figured she might as well stick it out.

Soon enough there was a knock at the door. David came inside the office and shut the door behind him. His eyes stayed locked into Bari's until he sat down.

"How are you feeling, Bari?"

"I'm okay, David."

"Good." David paused before he spoke again. "I just spent an hour up on executive row speaking to Sheldon Mangrove about your future with Choler-Raines."

"What about my future with Choler-Raines?"

"I think I can be frank with you, Bari. I have to tell you that we're concerned. Granted, you are one of my best. I think you know that. I have given you some of the toughest assignments, and you always come through smelling like a sweet rose."

"So, what are you saying to me? My track record means nothing?"

"You made us lose a very important account today and I can't tell you how much revenue for the firm. I think you understand that business is business."

"Business is business." Bari repeated his words as if they were completely foreign to her. "You're telling me that I put my blood, sweat, and tears, my guts, into my work here and it means nothing? I put this company, my job, before everything in my life and it means nothing? And now I run into a few personal problems in my life and all of a sudden my job should be in jeopardy? I don't understand this, David. Please explain to me my position here, because I don't understand this." Bari was beginning to shake. Her voice was quivering again and her breathing was uneven.

"Calm down, Bari. Just calm down."

"I'm calm, David. Don't patronize me!" She banged on the desk.

"Look." David chose his words carefully. He didn't want to get her any more worked up than she was becoming. "It is clear to me that something is wrong. I know that this is not how you do things. Please, Bari, take a break. Maybe you need to take a leave for a while to work out whatever your problems are. I'll convince them upstairs that—"

"You'll convince them of nothing! I had a lapse. Period. I'm fine now. And you can tell that to Sheldon Mangrove and anybody else who cares to listen. *I'm fine*. Now, if you'll excuse me, I have work to do."

David got up from the chair. He opened his mouth to say something to Bari, but instead, he quietly turned and left her office.

twenty-eight

HAZEL HAD ADAPTED quickly to southern life. She had decided that her job of raising her children was done and now she only needed to worry about herself. She had sold her house in Brooklyn, retired from her job, and moved to Slothberg, South Carolina, not far from Butch and Francine. Hazel hadn't remarried or even dated since Jimmy died. Many of her friends tried to convince her that she was still attractive enough to date. They told her she shouldn't be alone, but Hazel just wasn't interested. She still had her figure, though she had become a little thicker around the middle. Her hair was still thick and long, with only a few gray hairs around the hairline. After being married for so many years and having raised three children, she had grown to like her privacy and her freedom. She missed her kids a lot, though, and now she was going back to New York to visit them for Christmas.

Franki sent Hazel the money to pay for her flight, but since she was petrified of flying, Hazel arranged to take the Greyhound bus instead. She knew that the trip would be a lot longer, but she didn't mind. She was prepared. She had packed magazines to read, crossword puzzles, word finds, and plenty of snacks.

Hazel had been up all night making trayfuls of pecan tarts. Ever since her kids were small, they had always looked forward to pecan tarts at Christmastime. She wanted this Christmas to be just like old times, so she made sure she had plenty of the tarts.

Hazel was sitting at her kitchen table sorting through her mail. She tossed the junk mail to the side and put the bills in one pile. Then she saw it, the military APO address. A smile quickly spread across her face. She knew that it was a letter from Ricky. In all the years that Ricky had been away, he wrote Hazel once a month without fail. Since she hadn't heard from him in almost four months, she had started to worry about him. As Hazel read the letter, she covered her mouth with her hand and she began to tremble. Her heart raced and tears welled up in her eyes. "Ricky is movin' back to New York," she said aloud.

That evening, when it was time for her to leave, Hazel gathered her suitcases and was about to leave the house. She stuffed Ricky's letter into her coat pocket, and all during the ride on the bus to New York she would take it out and read it over and over again.

IT WAS THURSDAY. Franki was waiting at the bus terminal when Hazel's bus pulled in. "Mommy!" Franki went rushing in Hazel's direction. She grabbed Hazel and gave her a bear hug.

"Oh, my God, Mommy, I'm so glad to see you!"

"Stop using the Lord's name in vain," Hazel said, squeezing her daughter equally tight.

"I'm sorry, Mommy, but you just don't know how happy I am to see you."

"I'm happy to see you, too, Franki," Hazel said, and they hugged again. Franki picked up her mother's bags and led the way to the taxi stand. As they drove along in the cab, the two of them took notice of the beautifully lit houses and colorful Christmas decorations and rated each one against the next. In the midst of all the holiday cheer, Hazel had to admit that she missed Christmas in New York.

"Your apartment is so nice and big and clean," Hazel said, as she walked inside Franki's brownstone apartment.

"Well, what exactly did you expect?" Franki asked, grinning.

"Look, I know how you kept house when you lived with me," Hazel told her.

"Come on now, I wasn't *that* bad."

"Believe me, you were *that* bad," Hazel said, and the two of them laughed.

Franki's apartment was artfully decorated with colorful pillows and throw rugs on the floor. Plenty of floor plants were placed all around the large living room. It was wide, with very high ceilings.

Franki showed Hazel around the apartment. There were four large

rooms in all. Each room was painted a different color. Franki had chosen earth tones and each one reflected a part of her personality. At
least that was her goal when she decorated. Franki gave Hazel her bedroom with the king-sized bed. She put a cot in the den for herself.
Hazel insisted on unpacking right away. She· said that she wouldn't
have been able to relax herself otherwise.

Franki was holding up one of Hazel's dresses that she was helping
to hang in the closet. The dress would come just to Hazel's knees. It
was fitted around the waist and would cling to her hips, showing off
her figure.

"Hey, sexy momma, have you developed sinful ways down south?"
Franki laughed, pointing out the deep V-neck on Hazel's dress.

"Girl, hand me that dress!" Hazel blushed. She snatched the dress
away from Franki. "My neighbor Lucille was out shoppin' with me one
day, and she insisted that I buy that dress. Now, you know I wouldn't
have bought this on my own, but I have to admit that I liked the way it
felt on me when I tried it on. The fabric is just as soft as cotton. And it
wasn't a bad price, neither," Hazel said with a slight drawl.

"Mommy, you're starting to sound just like those country people
down south."

"Child, please!" Hazel waved Franki off.

"See what I mean." Franki laughed.

Hazel threw a pair of folded-up sweat socks at Franki. They hit her
in the head. Franki fell across the bed, holding her head and chuckling
like she had been injected with laughing gas. Hazel stood over her with
her hands on her hips, shaking her head and laughing, too. When they
stopped laughing Franki sat up, fanning herself. She got up from the
bed and went over and opened the window slightly.

"I'm sorry, Mommy, but it is hot as I don't know what in here. It's
twenty-one degrees outside, so they blast all the heat in the world in
here. You know I never could take the heat unless I started breaking
out in a thousand little bumps."

Franki walked over to the bed and folded away Hazel's last shirt.
"So, how are you doin', Mommy?"

"I'm fine, Franki. I'm old, but I'm fine."

"You don't look a day over thirty."

Hazel sucked her teeth and waved Franki off again. Hazel finally sat down in the rocking chair next to the bed.

"Are you tired?"

"I guess I am. That long ride is startin' to catch up with me. I didn't sleep a wink 'cause I didn't trust that driver; he was driving a little too fast for me."

"Well, you could lay down as soon as I finish clearing up in here. So, how are you liking it in the South?"

"I wouldn't live anywhere else now. I don't know what took me so long to move down there in the first place. I find it right peaceful, nothing like New York. Did I ever tell you that I have a natural duck pond right in the back of my house?"

"Mommy, did you forget we moved you down there? Of course I saw your duck pond, so you don't have to show off."

"Child, you gotta admit it's the most beautiful thing you ever wanna see. Sometimes I just sit out back and watch the mother duck and her babies walkin' back and forth all day long, just quackin'." Hazel looked just as if she had launched herself into some spellbinding trance.

"Snap out of it, Mommy. I doubt that my little four-room brownstone apartment can compare to your house in the South, with a natural duck pond in the back. But I want you to make yourself at home just the same."

"Girl, you're just as silly," Hazel said, and the two of them laughed some more.

"I'm gonna make us some hot tea," Franki said, and without asking, Hazel got up from the chair and followed her into the kitchen.

"I thought Bari would have come with you to pick me up from the bus terminal."

"I thought that, too, but I told you about Bari, Mommy. Between Earl and her job, I don't know which one keeps her the most occupied."

"I haven't spoken to her in two weeks. Is she okay?"

"You'll just have to wait and judge that for yourself. I personally think that Bari is much too thin, and she's tired all the time. I also think that Earl is controlling her. Sometimes when I'm talking to her on the phone, it's almost like she can't talk if Earl is there. I noticed that a long time ago. I don't get to see much of her these days because I can't get her to come out to do anything. I'm not getting into her business, but I think there's definitely something up with her and her husband. I don't know what it is, but my sister is not looking like my sister."

"Get my child on the phone," Hazel said, looking down at the floor, shaking her head with her lips tightly pursed.

"She's not home yet. I left a message on her machine before I left to pick you up. Since she hasn't called me back yet, I assume she's still out. She's probably still at work."

"Well, I'll find out what's going on with her when I see her. She's comin' over here tonight, ain't she?"

"Yeah, she said that Dominick was giving her a ride over, after work."

"Good. I always did like that Dominick."

"Just take my advice: Be very careful when you speak to Bari. Anything that you ask her is a sensitive topic all of a sudden," Franki said. "As a matter of fact, don't even ask her anything until I give you a sign that it's okay. I've learned to read her. I think I know when she won't bite your head off. If I think it's okay to talk to her about it, I'll bring up the subject and you take it from there. Okay?"

"Okay," said Hazel, still looking disturbed.

The teakettle whistled and Franki got up and poured their tea. She had already set up their cups with sugar and milk for Hazel and sliced lemons and honey for herself. They were sipping and blowing on their tea for a good while before either one of them spoke again.

"I have some news that I been tryin' to save so I could tell you and Bari at the same time, but I don't know what time Bari is gonna get here and I'm just gonna burst if I have to wait another minute."

"What is it?" Franki asked.

Before the words were formed, emotion overtook Hazel once again. "Ricky's movin' back to New York! I haven't seen my child in so long." Hazel sniffled, and soon happy tears flowed down her face. She pulled Ricky's letter out of her purse and handed it to Franki.

"Ricky? Finally! When?" Franki asked, excited. She took the letter that Hazel had handed to her and started reading it. She walked over and hugged her mother before she finished reading it. Hazel pulled away and composed herself. Franki went back to reading the letter.

"He's comin' in on the eve of the eve, the day before Christmas Eve," Hazel said, wiping at the corners of her eyes with her fingers.

"I can't believe we're all gonna be together for Christmas." Franki left the room to get the box of tissues off the vanity in the bathroom. She handed it to Hazel.

"Did you read the part yet about him getting married?" Hazel took out a tissue and blew her nose.

"Yes, I'm shocked!"

"I can't believe my son done gone and got married. He's been married for about a month now, but you know how long it takes the mail to get here from Okinawa. He's bringin' his wife here with him. Said her name is Kim. Maybe I'll become a grandmother soon. Heaven knows, at the rate you and Bari are goin', I'll be in my grave before either one of you give' birth."

"Oh, Mommy, spare me. You are so melodramatic."

twenty-nine

ARI RUSHED AROUND inside her office, packing up to go home. She phoned home and left a message for Earl that she would be spending the night at Franki's place. Bari had asked Dominick to give her a ride over to Franki's apartment. She told him that she would be ready at 8:00 P.M. It was already twenty minutes past the hour, and if she knew Dominick, which she did, he probably got there at exactly 8:00 P.M.

When she was all packed up and ready to leave, Bari shut off her office lights and very quietly closed the door. She didn't want David to hear her leaving, in case he was still there. She walked down the corridor, then sped up when she got closer to David's office.

"Bari?" David called out to her.

"Damn," Bari said under her breath just past his office. She backed up and stood outside of his open door.

"You're leaving?" he asked.

Ten responses ran through Bari's mind before she actually answered him. All clad in her coat, scarf, gloves, and boots, carrying a pocketbook and two other bags, gave her the right to look at him as if he had just asked the dumbest question in the world.

"Yeah . . . ," Bari said. "Why?" she asked, knowing she was going to regret having asked that.

"I guess I should have asked you this a little earlier. I'm gonna be here for a little while longer, and I was hoping to get a chance to scope the contract for Demeris. If anything, I could always read it on the train on the way into Connecticut. Would you mind very much giving me the file before you leave?"

David didn't hear Bari when she sighed. The deep breath that she took gave her just enough calm to keep her from saying something sarcastic. She put down her bags and silently went back into her office and got the file.

"Did you get a chance to look at it at all?" David asked her, looking as if he was ready to discuss it.

"I did, David, but I really have to go right now. We'll talk about it first thing in the morning."

"Over coffee?"

"Over coffee."

She picked up her bags and barreled down the hall and out of the building.

"HI, DOMMIE," BARI said, throwing her bags into the backseat of the car, then climbing into the front seat. She kissed him on his cheek.

"How are you, babe?" Dominick asked her.

"I'm okay; sorry I'm so late. Whenever I try to rush, I just get all clumsy and nervous and things start falling; then David always waits until the last minute to want something."

"It's okay; it's okay, Bari. 'Tis the season to be jolly," Dominick told her, touching her arm.

"Thank you for giving me a ride to Franki's. I told you Mommy's in town for the holidays, right?"

"Yeah. Give her my regards. I'm sorry I won't be able to come inside to say hello to her. I'm running a little late now."

"Thanks to me. I'm sorry." Bari put on a cute smile.

"Don't worry about it. You're a busy lady; I understand that," Dominick said.

"I really have been pretty busy lately, and speaking of which, I know I probably won't get to see you again before Christmas, so I figured I'd give you your present now." Bari turned around and dug into one of her shopping bags in the backseat of the car and pulled out a beautifully wrapped box with shiny red paper and a big red satin bow on top. She had paid extra for the store to specially gift-wrap it for her. Bari would have paid anything. Dominick was the one true friend she had, and Christmas was the time of year that she chose to express her appreciation to him for his friendship. And when it came to whatever the gift was that she chose for him, money was never an object.

"What did you go and buy me a gift for?"

"I had to buy you a gift, Dominick; you know that. You say the same thing every year and I don't know why you even bother, because you know that I don't listen to a word you say. I don't know what in the world I'd do if I didn't have you for a friend. You lend me your shoulder when I need it—you give me good advice. You have patience with me. . . ."

"If you didn't have me you would talk to Franki even more," he said.

"Talking to my sister is not the same as talking to you. First of all, I know that you won't repeat anything that I tell you, and I know that you don't judge me and you don't ask questions. I really appreciate that."

Traffic was starting to slow down on the FDR Drive. The road was still damp and slick from the earlier snow shower. Two cars had collided and were still tangled alongside the ramp. Everybody driving by wanted to see what they could see of the accident.

"This is just what I need when I'm in a hurry," Dominick said. He wasn't riled up. He never got riled up. "So, should I open my present now, since traffic is crawling?"

"Of course not. Promise me you won't open it until Christmas."

"Okay, I promise, I promise."

Traffic was at a complete halt now. Bari could feel Dominick looking at her. She was watching the accident, too, but she could see him out of the corner of her eye. She turned to look at him, then smiled and went back to looking at the accident.

"You know, Bari, I was just curious about something."

Bari turned to look at him again.

"Let's say you had never met Earl and you had never gotten married . . . do you think that you and me could have gotten together?"

"Haven't we had this discussion before?"

"No."

"Oh."

"So?"

"So, the truth is I don't even want to think about that, because if we had gotten together in that way, then we wouldn't be the friends that we are now."

"I see."

"Why do you ask?"

"I guess because I care so much about you, and I guess because I know you so well. And I admire you a lot. It's like this: If somebody were to ask me to describe my ideal woman I would describe you. In my eyes you're the perfect woman. You're phenomenal."

"That's beautiful, Dominick. I'm truly flattered," Bari said, holding her hand to her chest.

"I wasn't trying to flatter you. That's really how I feel."

"I don't think we should be talking about this." Bari started digging into her pocketbook. She was looking for her lipstick. She didn't need it, but whenever she became uncomfortable when she was speaking to somebody she would put on lipstick. She blotted off the excess and put on some more.

Traffic started to pick up again. The two of them cringed when Dominick hit a pothole.

"Well, let me ask you this." Dominick pressed on. "Are you happy?"

"Of course I'm happy."

"I mean really happy?"

"Yes, I am really happy, Dominick. Why?"

Dominick turned off at the exit. "Well, because I think that you deserve a great deal more respect than your husband is giving you."

"What are you talking about?" Her smile disappeared completely.

"I mean, I sit here and I look at you and I know what you're all about. You're a good person, Bari. But Earl, he's no good. He's way out there. He doesn't deserve you."

"How dare you sit there and judge Earl. You don't even know him. You only know what I've told you about him. Please don't make me sorry that I ever confided in you. Is that why you're pouring your heart out to me tonight? You want me to leave my husband and get together with you. That's it, isn't it?"

"Come on, Bari. You know it's not that, and it's not the things that you've told me. It's what I've seen for myself. I see him out there. At this point I just think that you should know the truth."

"Whose truth, Dominick? Why should I trust anything that you tell me at this point?" Bari asked, sounding indignant.

"Look, Bari, forget it. I'm really sorry. I never should have spoken on this."

"You're absolutely right, you never should have spoken on it, because it's none of your business."

Bari could see the hurt look that crossed Dominick's face from the side of his head. She saw his jaw clench, and she could have sworn his temple throbbed.

"I'm sorry, Dominick. I shouldn't have said that."

"It's okay. You said what you wanted to say. And you're right: It's none of my business."

Bari wanted to squeeze Dominick's arm to make him know that she understood why he said what he said. She had a feeling that he wanted something more from their relationship and she truly was flattered, but that could never happen. But, instead, they rode the rest of the way to Franki's house in silence.

HAZEL AND BARI hugged and cried when they saw each other. And like old times, the three of them chatted on for hours as they sipped warm eggnog, munched on some of Hazel's pecan tarts, and trimmed Franki's Christmas tree. Hazel had forgotten about how tired she was, and they all stayed up half the night laughing and chatting, like adolescent girls. They got up early the following morning, and they got busy planning their menu and cooking for the homecoming dinner. They decided that even though Ricky wouldn't be there for several hours, it wasn't too soon to start preparing some of the dishes.

Hazel baked the ham and made a huge pot of collard greens; then she rolled out the dough for the peach cobbler. Franki made her socalled gourmet macaroni and cheese while Bari chopped up all the ingredients for a rice dish that she had been dying to try.

The smell of the food cooking, the seven-foot Scotch pine standing in the corner, and the soft blaze from the fireplace had a tranquilizing effect on all of them. Even Hazel didn't fight too hard when Franki and Bari insisted that she lead them in some Christmas carols.

The women had outdone themselves with the decorations. Franki had taken thick strands of angel hair and lined the windowsills of both windows with it to give the effect of snow. Then she had taken some sprayed white tree branches and strung them with tiny flickering white lights. She placed the lit branches just over the angel hair on the windowsills so that they looked like lit snow-covered trees standing in the snow. Franki called it her "winter wonderland." It was brilliant.

"Ouch!" Franki said when she missed the onion that she was slicing on the cutting board and cut her finger instead.

"Quick, run it under cold water," Hazel told her.

Franki put her finger under the running water. She wrapped the finger with a table napkin as best she could and went back to cutting the onion. "Could you believe that Mommy still makes me call her every time a show that I produced is going to air?"

"You're kidding me," said Bari.

"No, she's not kiddin' you," Hazel said. "I need her to tell me ahead of time so I can round up the girls and set my VCR. I have a tape of every single one of the shows that she produced. I don't let any of my friends leave my house until after they've seen my daughter's name in the credits. That's right. But we're all still waitin' for the autographed pictures of Sally Jessy Raphael. I told the girls you were gonna send 'em and we ain't seen 'em yet. I don't understand why it's so hard to get them. You see the woman every day."

"You're right, Mommy. I did promise them to you and I'm promisin' you again, I'll send them. It's just that it gets so hectic in the studio sometimes and I just don't remember."

"Don't make me have to come down there to that studio myself and stop the lady in her tracks to make her sign me some pictures," Hazel said, and they all laughed.

After a while, the three of them must have gone off into their own inner worlds, because nobody talked again for a while.

"I can't get over you buying Earl a brand-new car," Franki said, opening the oven to check on Hazel's bread.

"That's right. I'm buying him a 1993 Nissan Maxima. He needs it, and he deserves it."

Hazel was busy moving things around on the kitchen counter, looking for the dishrag. When she didn't find it, she looked toward the table. Franki had been trying to get Hazel's attention. When Hazel looked up, their eyes met. Franki opened her eyes wide and peered in Bari's direction. Hazel raised her eyebrows in question. Franki nodded toward Bari. Hazel still didn't get it. She had forgotten their plan.

Hazel missed her cue, so Franki decided to take charge. She figured Hazel could follow her lead and take the opportunity to ask Bari about her relationship with Earl.

"You're pretty brave," Franki said.

"Brave?"

"Yeah, I mean, Earl isn't working."

"No, he isn't, but I am. Excuse me," Bari said, slamming the potholder on the kitchen counter and leaving the kitchen. She went down the hall to the bathroom and sat on the side of the tub. *Not now, Franki,* Bari thought to herself. *Not now when I'm feeling so good.*

It had been a long time since Bari had a good hearty laugh and now it was about to come to an abrupt end. She could already see where Franki was heading, and as far as Bari was concerned, this was neither the time nor the place for this discussion. She stood up from the tub ledge and studied herself before the full-length mirror on the bathroom door. Bari studied her face in the mirror, then took a long look at her body. She noted how frail she was looking. She sighed deeply, then reluctantly went back into the kitchen.

Bari poured herself some more eggnog. She added rum to it this time. The rum burned her stomach when she drank it. At least, she thought it was the rum. It was the same burning sensation she got every time she thought about her situation at home. *Damn.* She wondered if she was getting an ulcer. She wondered why the hell Zuma's help wasn't working. Maybe Hazel and Franki were right about the stuff being crap. *What a waste,* Bari thought. All of a sudden she felt sad. She could have wrung tears from her heart. Bari had temporarily forgotten about her stress. Now it all came pouring back to her in a tidal wave after Franki's remark. Bari could already feel the tightness in her chest and the knots forming in her stomach. Franki had been questioning Bari a lot for the past couple of weeks, and she was starting to resent it more and more. And how could Franki pull this stunt in front of their mother, when Bari had gone to great lengths to paint a perfect picture of her marriage for Hazel? As far as she knew, Bari and Earl were as happy as the day they were married, and she intended to keep it that way.

"Wouldn't purchasing a new car be a lot of pressure on you, Bari?" Franki started all over again.

"I can handle it," Bari snapped.

"I can't wait to see the car when you get it," said Hazel, "and I can't wait to see that husband of yours, too. I have a couple of bones to pick with him."

"What bones do you have to pick with Earl?" Bari asked.

"Franki told me that—"

Franki shot Hazel a look, forcing Hazel to stop talking mid-sentence.

"Don't stop, Mommy. Franki told you what?" Bari put her cup down. She pushed it farther onto the counter, away from her so she wouldn't be tempted to slam it to the floor. Bari shifted her weight to one side of her body and stood with one hand on her hip. Her slitted eyes were charcoal black.

"I-I mean . . . I . . . ," Hazel struggled.

Franki came to her rescue. "I just told her that I was worried about you and that I don't think that Earl is doing the right thing by you. And that you look awful. There, I said it," Franki said, cocked for an argument.

"Franki, I'm glad to know that you're concerned about me, but how could you go around discussing my personal business behind my back? I would never do that to you."

"Now wait a minute, Bari; you make it sound like she talked about you to a stranger. I'm your mother, and since when did you start keepin' things from me?"

"Since I became a married woman, Mommy. There are many things in my life now that have nothing to do with you or anybody else."

"Well, those things have somethin' to do with me and everybody else if somebody is hurting you. We have the right to know if somethin' is wrong." Hazel's voice quivered.

"Who said that somebody is hurting me? I really don't understand why all of a sudden I'm in the spotlight. All of a sudden everybody's focus is on me. What did you do about it when Daddy was hurting you, Mommy? You don't even have a clue what it did to me all of those years when Daddy would beat on you. As soon as I would hear you scream, my belly would churn. For every bump against the wall my throat constricted, and I couldn't breathe. I always thought that Daddy was going to kill you, and I would be scared to death. Then I wanted to die because I didn't want to see *you* die. And I would cry all night long until

I finally cried myself to sleep. I don't remember you doing anything about that. What did you do to stop Daddy from hurting you? Or us? If Earl was hurting me, what would you do about it?"

"That's enough, Bari!" Hazel choked out the words. She sounded like a small animal that had just been wounded.

"There's no need for you to be so defensive, Bari," Franki intervened.

"I'm not being defensive. I'm just speaking the truth." Bari picked up her drink again and took an angry gulp. Her face was twisted into a frown.

"Look, Bari, I told you before, and I'm telling you now, if you ever wanna talk, I'm here, really." Franki looked at Bari as if she really expected her to break down and start talking.

"You know, you're unbelievable, Franki. I just stood here and told you that I don't have a problem. So why are you insisting that I do? I'm beginning to believe what they say. Misery *does* love company," Bari said, sounding seriously sarcastic. The rum was working on her.

"I can't believe you just said that," Franki said, glaring at Bari.

Bari returned the look. She was ready to fight now, if that's what Franki wanted.

"Why don't y'all just drop it now," Hazel interjected.

"Maybe if you used the same energy that you use worrying about Earl and me, and channeled it into you and Darryl, maybe you could get him to commit to you," Bari continued.

"First of all, Bari, I'm not miserable; I think you know that. Secondly, if you think for one minute that I'm jealous of your relationship, or anything negative like that, you're dead wrong. As God is my witness, the only thing that I *ever* wanted for you was good. And that's all Mommy wants for you, too," said Franki.

Bari's frown slowly erased from her face. She looked at Hazel, then at Franki. Bari bit down on her lower lip.

"Look at this," Bari said. "A few minutes ago we were in the holiday spirit. What happened? I'm so sorry, Mommy. I'm just so stressed and tired." Tears started flowing down Bari's face. She went over and hugged her mother. Bari's shoulders heaved as she clung to Hazel.

Hazel softly patted her daughter's back.

"I never should have spoken to you that way. I'm sorry, it's my job; it's starting to get to me." Bari sniffed.

"I know, baby," Hazel said while she and Franki exchanged a knowing look behind Bari's back.

thirty

EARL WAS GLAD when he got Bari's message telling him that she was going to Franki's apartment after work to spend the night. Bari had told him that she needed to help Franki and Hazel get Franki's place ready for the homecoming dinner for Ricky. Earl didn't give her a hard time. He didn't give a damn. And he didn't give a damn about the dinner that they were having, either. He wasn't interested in celebrating anybody's homecoming or anything else that Bari's family felt needed celebrating. Earl had other things on his mind. He was sitting on his living room couch with what was left of a small package of coke on the coffee table next to him. He was wearing a pair of jeans and no shirt. The television wasn't turned on, nor was the stereo. Earl sat staring straight ahead of him. He played with the small hairs under his chin while he was deeply engrossed in his thoughts.

It had been almost four months since he parted company with his father. Four long months and Earl hadn't gone on a single job interview. He knew that he had to get out there sooner or later, but in the meantime he didn't feel like worrying about it. Bari wasn't on his back about finding a job. There was no reason for her to be. Hell, he had worked hard for the past three years. The two of them had bought a house together, and he had given Bari everything that she wanted: brand-new kitchen appliances, beautiful, plush carpeting, expensive artwork. That had to count for something. It wasn't like he was free-loading or anything. Bari was supposed to kick in and help if he fell short. That was what marriage was all about.

Earl cursed himself for not having gone to college and for wasting so many years working for his father. Especially since he apparently hadn't appreciated anything that Earl had done for him. Anyway, Earl couldn't worry about that right now. Right now, he found comfort in the "white lady." She was the one who hugged him at the times that he needed to be hugged. The white lady talked to him and made him feel good about himself and the world around him. She numbed him from the pain he felt every day. She replaced Bari.

Sometimes he would leave the house and would stay away for hours. He didn't like being home when he was getting high. There was always the chance that Bari could come around and blow his high since he would have to pretend that he wasn't high.

Bari put up with his foul mouth and nasty temper and kept her mouth shut. She knew that whatever happened in their house stayed in their house. Earl made sure that she understood that. The more time Earl spent away from home, the better he felt. Every time he looked at his wife, she reminded him of everything that he wasn't. She was so damned good-natured and clean-cut. And she was smart as hell, too.

It was bad enough that he had to face Bari's mother, but now he had to deal with Bari's goddamned brother, too. He would probably play sick or something when the time came. All he knew right now was that he was running low on his shit. Once he took care of his business he would be able to think straight, figure things out.

It was Thursday night and Earl wasn't doing anything else, so he decided to take a trip across town to Tommy's place, cop, and hang out there for a while and get his high on. There was no way he could face Bari's family on a straight head, so he figured on copping an eight ball. That way, he would have enough blow to continue to get high tonight and have plenty left over for tomorrow night, too.

Earl picked up the package that he had beside him and took the last two hits from it. When he was done, he turned the small plastic packet inside out and licked it clean.

"I need to stop this shit; that's what I need to do," Earl said, looking in the mirror. He didn't like what he saw. His skin looked ashen. Dull. He needed a shave. He looked at his nose. Was the bridge really falling? He seemed to remember somebody saying that could happen after a while if you did too much shit. Earl looked at everything but his eyes. He couldn't stand doing that. He didn't like the person who looked back at him.

"All right, that's it. Today is gonna be my last trip to Tommy's. I'm gonna get fucked up today, and tomorrow, and then I'm never gonna touch this shit again." He picked up the drink that he had been nursing and finished it off in one gulp.

"This, too. I'm cutting this shit out, too." Earl slammed the drained glass of rum and Coke down on the table. He got up from the couch and went upstairs to his bedroom. He opened a dresser drawer and lifted a couple of pairs of jeans from his corner of the drawer. He pulled out his ceramic pillbox. He banged the opened box upside down on the dresser to empty it. Nothing came out.

"Aw, man. I know I had a little *somethin' somewhere.*"

Earl was hoping to take one last hit before he left his house. He reached up to the top ledge over the mirror on the dresser and pulled down some crunched-up aluminum foil. He opened the foil and licked it. There was nothing there.

"Damn!" He balled up the foil and tossed it into the wastebasket. Earl opened the drawer again and started to pull out several pairs of pants, checking the pockets on each. He came up blank every time. He quickly grabbed a shirt out of the closet. His coat was on in no time. He pulled a baseball cap off the hat rack on his way out the door.

Just as Earl walked to the corner of his block, Maurice Breland, one of the twins, was turning onto the block in his 1975 green Volvo.

"Yo, Earl!" Maurice called.

"Who's that?" asked Earl, squinting his eyes and looking toward the car.

"It's me, Maurice."

"What's up, boss?" Earl walked over to the car. They knocked fists. "I should've known it was you. I should have recognized the ride," said Earl.

The two of them thought that was funny. Maurice's car had been the brunt of many a joke ever since he bought it way back when.

"Where are you heading?"

"I'm headin' across town to see my man Tommy."

"Tommy the drug dealer Bridges?"

"Yeah. Tommy," Earl said matter-of-factly.

"You're still doin' that shit, man?" Maurice was surprised that Earl would still be indulging in something that had started out as a recreational thing so long ago. "You better cut that shit loose before it cuts you loose. I see too many people droppin' from that shit. That ain't no joke, man."

"Hey, how 'bout that?" Earl wanted to get off the subject right away. He sure as hell wasn't in the mood for any anti-drug lectures. The sooner he got to Tommy's place, the better off he'd be. He was starting to get irritable. "Are you gonna give me a ride or what?"

"Jump in," Maurice told him.

Earl walked around the car to the passenger side and got into the car. "It's not too far from here; go straight up and make a right at the next traffic light. I know a shortcut."

They rode for several blocks as Earl directed Maurice through the back streets that would save them time.

"Yo, where are you takin' me, man? It's dark as hell back here. Somebody could shoot our asses and nobody would ever find us," Maurice complained. "You know we're in the hood."

"It's all right, man. If it wasn't cool I wouldn't have brought you this way."

"Yeah, all right."

They rode for several more blocks. They talked and laughed about old times, and they talked about why Maurice refused to buy a new car.

"Call me paranoid, man, but there are too many ruthless sons of bitches out there for me. Motherfuckers are stealin' *air bags* now. Fuckin' *air bags*. I don't want nobody takin' nothin' from me 'cause I'll end up in Rikers fuckin' Island for shootin' somebody in the ass."

"I hear you, man, but what are you worried about? This piece of shit ain't got no air bags."

"Oh yeah," said Maurice, laughing. "Yo, what happened to your ride? Somebody stole it?" he asked, more seriously.

"Nah, nobody stole it. It's a long story." *Just hurry up and get me to where I have to go,* Earl thought. His jones was way down. They could barely see ahead of them on the dark street that they were on. They drove for several more blocks in silence.

"Yo, I saw you about a month ago, man. I was at Godfather's and I saw you. I was trying to make my way over to you, but it was so crowded that when I looked up again I didn't see you anymore. You were with a real cutie, though. I knew it wasn't your wife. How are you livin', man? You better be careful out there. Bari might just up and leave your ass just like my wife up and left my ass," Maurice said.

Suddenly Earl reached over and grabbed Maurice's shirt collar. Earl held Maurice's shirt collar so tight that the veins in his forehead and neck protruded and the pale skin on his face turned bright red. Maurice looked panic-stricken as he tried to keep his eyes on the road, steady the wheel, and watch Earl at the same time. The car swerved from one side of the road to the other.

"Yo, what's the matter with you, man?!" Maurice's voice hit all kinds of high notes.

Earl brought his face very close to Maurice's. "Don't you ever, ever joke about anything like that with me. You hear me? You keep my wife out of our conversation! Now, pull the fuck over!" Earl yelled.

The car screeched over to the side of the road.

Earl shoved Maurice hard against the driver's side door, releasing him. He pushed open the door on his side, got out, and slammed it shut.

"You're a crazy son of a bitch!" Maurice yelled after him.

"Yeah, you remember that!" Earl yelled back.

"You need to leave that shit alone! You're crazy! Leave those fuckin' drugs alone!" Maurice accelerated and was gone.

Earl rolled up the collar of his coat and continued the walk to Tommy's place.

thirty-one

"AREN'T YOU GONNA be late for work?" Earl asked Bari.

She smiled at him and shook her head no. She had changed her mind about going straight to work from Franki's. She got up very early in the morning and went home instead. "I'm going into the office late just to do a couple of things. It's Friday. Most of the people in the office have taken time off for the holidays. Hardly anybody's working but David." She had decided to have her coffee at home with Earl since she didn't have to rush. She was going back to the car dealer to sign a page on the contract that had been accidentally skipped over when she first made the deal to buy Earl's car. Earl had gotten up early, too. He sat across from Bari at the table, eating dry whole-wheat toast and chasing it down with black coffee. He looked tired to her. Drained. Bari wondered if the powder that she had been sprinkling in his food had anything to do with it. She didn't think it was really helping them. She was ready to try something else. Maybe even the menstrual blood thing that Barbara had told her about. She just needed to have her husband back.

Earl read the paper while Bari sipped her coffee and watched him. She longed to hold him, to be held by him. She wanted things to be back the way they were. Earl looked up when Bari pushed her chair out from under the table and stood up.

"I have to go see a man about a dog before I go into the office." She got a smile out of him when she said that. She didn't make a move to leave, though. She held Earl's eyes and hoped that he would make a move toward her.

"Come here." Earl's hands gestured.

Bari walked over to him. She put her arms around his neck and bent down to kiss him. Earl gave her a quick kiss on her lips.

"Have a nice day," he said.

"You, too." Bari put on her coat and left the house.

EARL LOCKED THE door behind Bari, and before he made it back into the kitchen the doorbell rang. "What the hell did she forget?" he said aloud. He walked back to the door and opened it. Cheryl quickly pushed Earl back into the house and walked in behind him. She kicked the door shut behind her. Her lips were planted on Earl's before he could speak. Cheryl pivoted him around and pushed him up against the wall. Her tongue frantically searched for his.

"What the hell are you doing here?" Earl asked, pulling his mouth away. "Bari just left. She could have seen you."

"I know. I took a chance. I waited outside for a while, and when I saw her leave, I rang the bell." Cheryl was breathing hard. She was pulling at Earl's shirt and kissing him again.

"You have to be more careful," Earl said, as Cheryl pulled his T-shirt over his head.

"Shut up. Don't talk. I waited all morning for this."

Cheryl was on her knees now, unzipping Earl's pants. She pulled his jeans down around his ankles and hungrily took him into her mouth. When Earl could stand it no more, he dropped to his knees and pushed Cheryl down onto the floor. He opened the snaps down the front of her blouse. He was glad to see that she wasn't wearing a bra. Earl kissed her on both breasts, then licked her nipples until they hardened. He removed Cheryl's skirt and smiled up at her. Cheryl smiled back. It drove him mad that she wasn't wearing underwear. She knew it would. Earl entered her, and they made love on the kitchen floor.

Cheryl called in sick and spent the next four hours with Earl.

"THANK GOD IT'S Friday." Bari sighed as she plopped down at her desk. She had just walked into the office at 11:30 A.M., and only a half hour later she was already on her second cup of coffee for the morning. It wasn't the work on her desk that overwhelmed her. She didn't plan to spend much time on that. It was her thoughts that weighed her down. The stack of papers in the middle of her desk seemed to swell before her. Bari fingered the diamond-shaped Lucite paperweight on top of the stack and tried to figure out where she would start first. She was distracted. Franki's words kept playing over and over in Bari's mind. She even thought about what Dominick had told her. Could everybody be wrong? She wasn't sure what everybody was looking at or what they thought they saw, but she certainly didn't intend to spend a whole lot of time trying to figure that out. She knew that Earl had his moments, but didn't everybody? Earl wasn't doing anything any different from what anybody else was doing in any other relationship. Nobody could know what it was that she and Earl had; therefore, she didn't expect them to understand it. Who could know how it felt to her when she was in the safety of her husband's arms? Or how it felt when he was making love to her? Nobody knew him like she did, so how could they understand his humor? His wit?

Bari grew up watching her mother and father fight like cats and dogs and she didn't remember hearing anybody complain. Even then, her parents had worked it out. They were together until Jimmy died. She and Earl would be just fine as soon as Earl got his business back in order. And as soon as Zuma's stuff did what it was supposed to do. Bari hoped that would be sometime soon. She was sure that the new car would definitely make Earl feel a lot better about things in the meantime.

She thought about Ricky's homecoming. She couldn't wait to see her brother. Ricky was always like her knight in shining armor. He was always so protective of her and Franki when they were kids. He took the blame for a lot of things that the girls had done wrong around the house in order to keep their father from beating them. Bari remembered feeling sorry for Ricky a lot as a kid. It seemed that even when he wasn't taking the blame for something that she and Franki had done, their father would find things to blame Ricky for. Jimmy would beat the boy unmercifully and would use whatever was nearest to him to get the job done. Whenever a toy was broken, it was Ricky who fixed it. Bari would never forget the beautiful playhouse that he had built for them. Thinking back, she realized it was still the best playhouse that she had ever seen. She wondered what ever happened to that house. For her, it was more than a playhouse. It was shelter. Shelter from hurt and pain. She would go inside of it and sit for hours at a time. Inside the house there was peace. There was no fighting between Hazel and Jimmy and no more beatings for Ricky. Maybe that's why Ricky had put so much into it.

Their father used to call Ricky a sissy a lot of times or would call him weak. Did Jimmy think that Ricky would grow up and not like girls? Bari's guess was that their father must be smiling now. Ricky had a wife!

David's voice over the intercom jolted Bari out of her thoughts.

"Bari?"

"Yes, David?"

"I need to see you." David's voice was expressionless.

"I'll be right there." Bari quickly dropped the call and ran a million thoughts through her mind, trying to figure out what was wrong. Why would David choose today of all days to talk about problems? It wasn't even a regular workday. What if she hadn't come into the office at all?

Bari left her office and headed down the corridor to David's office. She had knots in her stomach. Even though she had a pretty good working relationship with David, she couldn't forget his words "business is business." She knew that when it came down to business, David was definitely a no-nonsense kind of guy, and she wasn't sure whose side he would take in the end. It had been several weeks since Bari's trip to Seattle and the Herculon incident, and for weeks she hadn't been able to concentrate on anything else. No one had heard from Paiseley. Bari didn't want to call them because she didn't want to seem too pushy. Her plan had been to move on to another project and just hope for the best.

When she reached David's office, the devious look on his face said it all.

"Come in, close the door," David ordered.

Bari did what he said. The lump in her throat was so big that it made it difficult for her to swallow. She immediately remembered the mints that she had left on her desk. If she had popped one in her mouth before she made this trip, her mouth wouldn't be so dry now.

"How are you?" he asked.

He obviously wanted to make her squirm. Bari hated the smug look on his face. In fact, at this moment, she hated everything about him. *What a bastard*, she thought.

"I'm fine, David." Bari wondered why he didn't just get on with it.

"What have you been working on?" David asked. There was that menacing look again. She may as well come clean. At least that way she wouldn't have to see him gloat as much.

"To tell you the truth, David, I haven't been able to focus on my new project yet. I put so much into the Paiseley account and up to now we haven't gotten any response from them. Truth is, I'm really frustrated and stressed out. And at the rate of things around here, I'm afraid to even cough the wrong way. I have too many other things going on in my life right now." Bari was on a roll. Her head was starting to spin as the thoughts came flooding in. She couldn't stop herself. "I mean, I put my all into this job. I come in at the crack of dawn and I leave most nights after nine P.M. I'm putting in twelve- to fifteen-hour days. I have virtually no life! This job is causing me problems at home and then I have to come in here and be made to feel inadequate. I've had it, David. You know that? I've had it." Bari was on the brink of tears and she had no intention of holding them back. Slowly she was coming out of the tailspin that she had submerged herself in. She looked around the room. The walls were still standing. A calm came over the room. Bari set her eyes on the picture hanging on the wall behind David's head. She expected it to come crashing down. It didn't.

David looked puzzled. "Bari, I knew that something was wrong, but I had no idea that you were having problems at home. If you wanna talk about it . . ." When Bari averted her eyes, David said nothing more. He reached over to his telephone and activated his voice mail. He left the phone on speaker mode so that Bari could hear the message that he was about to play.

"Good morning, David. This is Chuck Winsell from Paiseley. I trust that all is well. I'm really sorry that it's taken so long for us to correspond with you. We were waiting for Werkman's blessing on this deal, but he's been traveling abroad for several months. So, up until yesterday, our hands were tied. We want to do business with you, but only if Ms. Jordan manages our account. We are particularly impressed with her vision and style. She understands where our company is heading, and with her help we believe we'll get there. I'll anticipate your callback so that we can work out the details and finalize this thing." The message ended.

Bari's defeated look slowly turned into a smile—a bright one. "That was . . . That was . . . ?" She didn't know what to say.

"Congratulations, Bari. You've done it again," David said.

As far as Bari was concerned, David had the sweetest smile that she had ever seen in her life. She could smell the scent of the eucalyptus plant on his windowsill flowing through the office now. Euphoria took over. Her life was about to change.

Bari reached across David's desk and grabbed his hand. "Oh, David, this is so wonderful. Thank you. Thank you so much for giving me the opportunity." Bari was holding on to David's hand and shaking it the whole time. She didn't care how clammy it was.

"And, David, please forgive me. . . . I freaked out on you, I didn't mean to."

"It's okay, Bari. I understand. . . ."

Bari let go of David's hand and rushed out of his office. She ran down the corridor to her own office to call Earl. The telephone rang seven times. There was no answer.

thirty-two

BARI RUSHED OUT of her office and was at the car dealership at exactly 4:00 P.M. Her heart raced as she slid behind the steering wheel of the new car—Earl's Christmas present. Bari had to force herself to breathe normally. She wiped her sweaty hands on her lap and gripped the steering wheel. After a few minutes Bari got out of the car and went back to talk to the salesman. She asked him to put a big red bow on the car and told him that she would be coming right back with her husband to pick it up.

Bari couldn't wait to see the look on Earl's face when he saw the car. It was exactly what he wanted. She had struck up a conversation with him earlier on and she tricked him into telling her the kind of car he would buy for himself. She could hardly control her breathing or the excitement in her chest as she hailed a cab and headed home.

The way Bari saw it, things would definitely start looking up. She was almost guaranteed to get the associate position, and she would almost double her salary. Then everything else would surely fall into place.

Bari's heart started to race again as the cab pulled up in front of her house. She wanted to take the steps two by two and burst into the house screaming out to Earl to come with her. But, instead, she was cool. She let herself into the house. The door to her bedroom was half-closed. Bari slowly pushed open the door and there Earl lay on his back with his hands propped behind his head, staring at the ceiling.

"I'm home, honey," Bari said, playfully poking her head through the door. She smiled and went all the way inside the room.

Earl looked over at her. "Hey," he said, and looked away, fixing his eyes back on the ceiling.

"How do you feel?" she asked him.

"I feel fine," Earl said, his face starting to twist into a frown.

"I'll bet I could make you feel even better," Bari said.

"Bari, I'm gonna tell you right now, I'm not in the mood for any of your little-girl games," said Earl.

"C'mere," she said, ignoring his remark. She pulled Earl up from the bed. Bari placed his arms around her waist and put hers high up on his shoulders and slowly moved her hips from side to side. She could feel his immediate erection grow against her. Bari pressed her lips to Earl's, then sucked on his lips until he sucked hers back. She slowly slipped her tongue into his mouth.

"I love you, Earl," she said in a throaty voice. "I love you so much. There's something I want to show you. But you'll need your jacket and you'll have to be patient, because I have to call a cab."

"What is this about, Bari?" Earl asked. He was starting to look aggravated again.

"Please, Earl, just this once, don't ask me any questions. Just trust me. I promise you it'll be worth your while," Bari said.

She called the car service and the cab was there almost twenty minutes later. Bari pulled Earl's leather bomber off the door hook and handed it to him on the way out of the house. When she opened the front door, they were met with brisk December weather. The earlier snow flurries had left a soft, white powdery blanket on the sidewalks, streets, and parked cars. Bari looped her arm through Earl's as they sat in the cab heading to the car dealership. Earl didn't say anything when the cab stopped in front of the car dealership. But he looked quizzical when they walked inside and went over to the black fully loaded Maxima with the big red ribbon on it. Bari flicked open the car door with the handheld automatic door opener. She turned to Earl and smiled. "Merry Christmas, baby." She kissed Earl's lips and handed him the keys.

"Are you serious?" Earl asked, looking like he just stuck his finger into an electrical outlet. "You bought me a car?"

Bari nodded. She opened the driver's side door for Earl and shut it when he got inside. Then she let herself in on the passenger's side.

Bari watched as Earl inhaled deeply, taking in the scent of the new leather. She smiled when he exhaled and slouched back against his seat. An excitement brewed in her.

"I can't believe you did this."

Bari put her hand over his, then looked deep into his eyes.

"Earl . . . I love you, with everything in me." Bari was shaking her head for emphasis, as if that would truly convince Earl of her words. "Now, I know we've been going through some changes. That happens. But I want you to know that whatever it takes to get us back on track, that's what I'll do. We can work it out. And I'm willing to take care of you, of us, for as long as I need to. I love you."

"I know that." Earl reached over and whispered into Bari's ear, "I love you, too."

The tingle always started at Bari's toes and worked its way up her legs. By the time it reached her chest, her breathing would become difficult and her body would weaken. Then she had no control over whatever would happen next.

"Let's take this baby for a spin," Earl said.

Earl stuck the key in the ignition. He started the car and they drove out of the car lot, down several blocks, and onto the freeway. Earl tested all the buttons that lit up the dashboard. He opened all four windows as he pressed on the gas pedal. They rode along at 45 miles per hour.

Bari was pleased. When her husband was happy, she was happy. The look on Earl's face made her know that she had done the right thing. Finally, they turned back. Once they were back at the house, Bari showered and got dressed to go back over to Franki's apartment. Earl dropped Bari off and told her that he would meet her there later. It was 5:30 P.M.

EARL HEADED BACK home again after he dropped off Bari. He planned to hang out at home for a while by himself. He still had at least three grams of coke left over from the eight ball he had gotten the day before. That was more than enough to do what he needed it to do. Earl pulled out his aluminum package and opened it onto the coffee table in the living room. He set up four neat lines, then went over to the bar on the cream-colored wall unit and poured himself a glass of straight rum. He took a sip of his drink, then took a hit of coke. The first hit was powerful. Earl's eyes and nose watered right away. He wiped at his eyes and nose with the sleeve of his shirt. He took another hit. This time, when he wiped at his nose blood got on his shirtsleeve. He went into the bathroom to get some tissue. Earl stuck the tissue up his nose to get the excess blood, then stuck the bloody tissue in his shirt pocket. He went back into the living room and took another hit. He would worry about his nose later. There was a quiet knock at the door.

"Damn! Who in the hell is that?" Earl wiped away the traces of cocaine from around his nose. He walked to the window and pulled back the curtain to see who it was. It was Cheryl. Earl pulled open the door. "What the . . . ?"

"Hi, Earl," Cheryl said, walking into the house and looking all around. Earl closed the door behind her. "Is Bari home?" she asked.

"No, she's not. Why? What if she was home, Cheryl? What if you came walking into my house, unannounced, while my wife was at home? What would you do then?" Annoyance laced Earl's voice.

"Then I would pretend that I came here to see her," she said, smiling triumphantly.

"That'll work." Earl smiled. He moved in to kiss Cheryl on her lips. He helped her off with her coat.

"Nice tree. Why don't you plug it in?" Cheryl asked as they walked into the living room.

Earl plugged in the Christmas tree. The brilliant-colored musical lights flickered off and on in time to the tune of "Jingle Bells."

"Is this a private party or can anybody join?" Cheryl asked when she saw Earl's drink and cocaine lines on the table.

"Join me, please," Earl said. He sat beside Cheryl on the couch.

Cheryl bent over the table and took some of the coke into both nostrils. "So," she said, "whose car is that in the driveway? I thought you had company."

"That's my car."

"Yeah, right." Cheryl giggled.

"Seriously. That's my car. It's my Christmas present from Bari."

"Your Christmas present from Bari? What is she doing buying you a car for a Christmas present?" Cheryl asked indignantly, "Haven't you told her anything?"

"I . . . I . . . ," Earl stammered.

"You didn't, did you?" Cheryl snarled.

"I did but . . ."

"You did but what? If you told her, I'm sure she wouldn't be buying you a car for Christmas!" Cheryl yelled.

"Well, what do you expect me to tell her?"

"Try telling her the truth for once. You tell her that you don't care for her anymore, that the marriage isn't working, it was a mistake. You tell her that you wanna be with me! That's what I expect you to tell her!" Cheryl yelled even louder than before.

Earl held Cheryl's face between both his hands. He kissed her chin. "Look, I told you that I'll take care of that. In the meantime, are we gonna let Bari ruin the time that we have right now?"

Cheryl smiled. "No."

Earl was glad that Cheryl fell for his game. He wasn't in the mood to tell her that as long as he was high he would tell her anything that she wanted to hear. He wasn't ready to tell her not to take their time together so seriously.

"Here, take another hit." He scooped some of the drug onto his small gold spoon and fed it to Cheryl. Then he fed himself.

"The last place on earth I want to be right now is at Franki's place with a bunch of people that I couldn't care less about," Earl said.

"I know what you mean, but we gotta do what we gotta do," said Cheryl. "Are you gonna be okay with me and Bari being in the same room?"

"I don't see why not," said Earl.

"I don't think anybody will look at us funny going in there together. After all, I got a legitimate invite," Cheryl said.

"Well, we don't want to raise anybody's eyebrows, so if anybody asks any questions, we'll tell them that I saw you two blocks down and I gave you a ride the rest of the way. If they don't believe us, then I figure fuck 'em," said Earl

The two of them spent the next few hours drinking, sniffing cocaine, and having sex. They climbed into the shower when they were done; then they got dressed and headed to Franki's apartment.

NELL WAS THE first one to arrive at Franki's place. She hollered Hazel's name when she saw her. Hazel stood up and stretched her arms out to Nell. They kissed and hugged each other.

"You look so good, Mrs. Hunter," Nell said.

"Thank you, baby," Hazel said. "You look good, too."

"Now don't look at this," Nell said, pointing to her wide hips. "This weight gain is only temporary." Nell's extremely short-cropped hair made her already big-boned body look bigger.

"Come on now. You better keep some meat on them bones," Hazel said, and they laughed.

Before Franki could lock the door behind Nell, Barbara pushed it back open again. "What's the matter, you didn't see me coming?" Barbara asked. She was breathing hard from running up the steps.

"Of course I saw you. Why do you think I was trying to lock the door?" Franki laughed.

After standing around for a while, everybody eventually gravitated over to the folding table against the wall and picked at the colorful, neatly arranged hor d'oeuvres.

"Where is Earl?" Barbara asked after they were all settled.

"He should be here very soon. He's out showing off his new car," Bari said.

"His new car?" asked Barbara.

"Yeah. His Christmas present . . . from me." Bari smiled and stuck her finger into her cheek, making a dimple.

"Wow, I'm impressed," said Barbara.

"Don't be. It's no big deal," Bari said.

"And what about our guests of honor?" Barbara asked.

"So far we haven't heard from Ricky yet. They should have been here already," said Hazel.

"Thank God they're not here yet," said Franki. "I asked Darryl to pick up the helium balloons for me, and I don't know what in the world is taking him so long. I mean it would be nice to have them floating all around the apartment before Ricky gets here, since they do say: 'Welcome Home, Ricky.'"

The doorbell rang at that moment. "Speak of the devil," Franki said, and she rushed over to open the door. When she pulled open the door, Earl and Cheryl stood there, glassy-eyed and grinning. "Well, how did you two meet up?" Franki asked, pulling the door open wider.

"He picked me—"

"I saw her—"

Earl and Cheryl spoke at the same time. "You tell her," Cheryl said. "I saw her two blocks from here, so I gave her a lift," said Earl.

"Oh, I see." Franki stepped aside and Earl and Cheryl came inside the apartment. Franki eyed them as they walked past her.

Earl said hello to everybody. He hugged Hazel, then went over to Bari. Cheryl took off her coat and held it across her arm.

"It's about time you got here, Earl. I wanted to show everybody the car." Bari got up from her seat when Earl approached her. She kissed him on the lips, then took him by the hand. "Come on, everybody, let's go see Earl's new car," Bari said.

Everybody put on their coats and jackets and followed Bari and Earl down the long steps of the brownstone building. They stood at the curb admiring and examining the car, interior and exterior.

"This is a beautiful car," Nell said.

"This is some serious stuff," said Barbara.

"Yeah, real nice," Cheryl said. "You're a good wife, Bari." The sarcasm in Cheryl's voice couldn't be missed.

"Thank you, Cheryl."

Franki was the only one who gave Cheryl a questioning look.

"It's a little too cold out here for me," Hazel said, and turned to walk back into the building. Everybody else slowly followed.

"Is that Darryl getting out of that car down there?" asked Nell.

Franki squinted her eyes in the direction that Nell pointed. "That can't be Darryl because he's not carrying helium balloons," Franki said, and they all continued into the house. Nell was the last person in, and she locked the door behind her.

Less than a minute later, the doorbell rang. It was Darryl. "I can't believe that not one of you saw me comin'," Darryl said.

Franki looked at him with an "I know you're not crazy" look. "Darryl . . . where are the helium balloons?" she asked.

"Oh, ha, ha, ha, you think I forgot 'em. Well, I fooled you; I got 'em. Ta da!" Darryl quickly snatched the bag of balloons out of his jacket pocket, as though he had just done an incredible magic trick.

"You're kidding, right?" Franki asked. Darkness slowly clouded over her otherwise deep brown eyes.

"Kidding about what?" he asked.

"You have the balloons outside in your car, right? This is not a good time to be funny, Darryl." Franki waited for Darryl to break out laughing like he usually did when he knew the gag was up. Darryl didn't laugh. He looked dumbfounded. Franki didn't say another word. She stormed away from Darryl and went into the kitchen.

Darryl quickly followed behind her. "What, Franki? What's the matter?" Darryl asked when the two of them were alone in the kitchen.

"You mean to tell me that you went to pick up helium balloons for me and you didn't make them put the helium in them?" Franki asked, glaring at him.

"I-I just . . ." Darryl stood shrugging his shoulders.

"I don't believe this! How do you think those balloons are gonna float in the air? They need helium, Darryl!" she yelled.

"All right, just calm down. I'm sorry, okay? Anyway, the lady should have told me."

"The lady should have told you?" Franki spat out the words. "You should have had sense enough to know . . . You know what, I am so angry right now that I wish that you would just leave!"

"Take it easy, Franki. It's not that bad. I made a mistake, that's all." Darryl held out his hands in front of him. He looked pathetic.

"You always make a mistake! I don't get it. I paid for the helium, Darryl. I *paid* for it!"

"No, you didn't; it's on me, all right? I'll give you back the money," Darryl said.

"Well, I hope you enjoy your balloons!" Franki said. She turned her back to Darryl and started checking on the food. She pulled open the oven to check on the dinner rolls. She slammed the oven door shut and started to bang pots and pans around on the stove as she checked on the remaining food. Darryl couldn't take the silent treatment anymore, so without another word of explanation, he turned and left the room.

Nell walked into the kitchen just as Darryl walked out. "Are you okay?" she asked Franki. "I don't know if you know it or not but we could hear you yelling all the way out into the other room."

"You know what, Nell? I don't even care. Men can be so damned stupid sometimes. They sure as hell don't think with their brains. Heaven forbid!"

"You were pretty hard on him," Nell told her.

"Look, as far as I'm concerned, Darryl can put an 'H' on his chest and 'Handle it,' or he can walk the hell away right now and I wouldn't care if he didn't look back."

"Come on, Franki, you don't mean that. Cut the brother some slack," Nell said.

IN THE LIVING room, Bari was engaged in conversation with Earl. Her hand was entwined with his. Cheryl sat directly across from them with her arms crossed, openly staring at them. "What does a person need to do to get a drink around here?" she asked, hoping that Earl would volunteer to fix her a drink and get away from Bari.

"The drinks are over there, Cheryl. Help yourself," Bari said, graciously pointing Cheryl to the rolling bar in the corner.

"Yeah." Cheryl sighed heavily and slowly got up to make her drink.

Darryl headed toward the bar, too. Earl stopped him before he reached it. "Yo, man, you okay?" he asked Darryl. "I mean Franki just blew up all over you in there and we could all hear her yellin' at you, you know? That ain't cool," Earl said smoothly.

"You know Franki, she likes to blow off steam sometimes. It's no big thing."

"Personally, I think it's a question of who's in charge," said Earl.

"Oh, is that what you think? Well, I think that we need to drop this conversation, 'cause I see where it's headin' and I don't want to go there."

"I'm just tryin' to look out for you, bro. Help you handle things," said Earl.

Bari could see Darryl biting the insides of his cheeks. Franki had told her several times that as much as Darryl liked to joke around, he could be like the Devil himself when he got upset. And if Darryl started to bite the insides of his cheeks, all hell was about to break loose.

"Just forget about it, Earl," Bari said, intervening.

"Yeah, yeah, yeah," Earl said, and he was on his feet heading to the bathroom.

FRANKI CAME BACK into the living room. She was a lot calmer now. She looked in Darryl's direction. The anger was gone. "I'm really concerned about Ricky. It's almost ten o'clock. They should have been here an hour ago," she said.

"I'm tryin' my hardest not to worry," Hazel said.

"They could be stuck in traffic," Darryl offered.

"That's true, what with the holiday weekend," said Franki.

Cheryl drained her wineglass. "I don't know about any of you guys, but something about the holidays always makes me feel depressed," she said.

"I know what you mean, Cheryl," said Bari. "Especially if you're alone."

"I didn't say anything about being alone. What I said was there is something about the holidays that makes me feel depressed." If Cheryl's voice were a knife, it would have cut.

"I-I wasn't speaking about you personally, and I certainly didn't mean to offend," said Bari.

"No offense taken, honey. I *know* I'm not alone." Cheryl got up to pour herself another drink. She was beginning to get edgy. She wondered what the hell was taking Earl so long in the bathroom. She needed a hit bad, and if she didn't get one soon, she was going to explode on everybody in the room if she had to spend another minute looking at Bari's smug little face.

"Earl had better pay me some attention," Cheryl mumbled under her breath as she went back to her seat on the couch.

Silence swept through the room when the doorbell rang. Franki went over to open the door. Hazel stood up slowly; her hands covered her mouth in anticipation. She slowly walked toward the door. Bari followed her. Franki opened the door.

Ricky stood there, looking mature and composed. He was extremely handsome in his uniform. When he walked into the room, the three women standing before him, Hazel, Franki, and Bari, rushed him all at once, hugging, squeezing, and kissing his face all over.

"I can't believe you're really here!" Hazel said. The tears started falling immediately.

"My brother is home!" Franki said, squeezing Ricky again.

Bari couldn't stop grinning. When they finally stopped fussing over Ricky, they all focused on the petite Japanese woman standing timidly behind him.

"Oh, hey, everybody, this is my wife, Kim." Ricky gently took Kim by the arm and pulled her forward. Kim smiled politely as Ricky introduced her to his family. Hazel hugged her and welcomed her into the family. Franki and Bari shook her hand.

Nell and Barbara came over and were introduced to Ricky and Kim. Franki motioned Darryl over, and he, too, was introduced. Cheryl remained sitting on the couch sipping on her wine. Earl finally came out from the bathroom. He was just about to approach the circle of people when Cheryl quickly walked up to him and grabbed him by the arm and pulled him away from the crowd.

"What's the matter?" Earl asked, his eyes glassy and bloodshot.

"Do you have something for me?" Cheryl asked him.

"You know I do, but do you expect me to hand it to you right in front of everybody?" Earl's voice was an angry whisper.

"No, I don't expect you to do that, but I do expect you to do *somethin'*," Cheryl said, whispering angrily, too.

"Well, give me a chance—"

"Just give it to me, Earl! When you try to hide somethin' is when you'll get attention," Cheryl said, holding her hand out for the package.

Franki looked across the room. She couldn't hear Earl and Cheryl but could tell that the two of them were in discussion about something and they looked upset. She saw Earl hand something to Cheryl, but it was too small for Franki to make out what it was. She turned her attention back to Ricky's story about his and Kim's flight back to the States.

Earl walked away from Cheryl and headed toward the circle of people around Ricky. Cheryl headed toward the bathroom.

"How are you doin', my brother? I'm Earl, your brother-in-law." Earl offered his hand to Ricky.

Ricky shook it. "Bari's husband, yeah, how are you doin'?" Ricky asked.

"I'm doin' all right, man."

"Taking care of my sister?" Ricky asked.

"You know that," said Earl.

Franki rolled her eyes and gritted her teeth. The crowd moved farther into the room. Earl managed to stay by Ricky's side.

Franki and Bari took Ricky's and Kim's luggage down the hall to the den. Franki dropped the two heavy suitcases onto the floor, then plopped down on top of them. "Are you as shocked as I am?" she asked Bari.

"About what?" Bari asked.

"Kim."

"What about her?" asked Bari.

"She's Japanese. Ricky married a Japanese woman!" Franki said.

"Shh! Franki, she'll hear you. She seems nice; what's the matter with her?"

"You mean to tell me he couldn't find one sister in Japan?" Franki asked.

Bari laughed. "Come on, let's get back out there. We have to heat up the food. I'm sure everybody's hungry by now."

"It's the end of the world! I just know it is." Franki threw her hands up in the air, feigning exasperation. She laughed at herself as she followed Bari out of the room.

Franki and Bari grabbed up some of the dishes off the table and went straight into the kitchen to reheat the food. After a while, Nell and Barbara joined them in the kitchen.

"We'll be happy to help you guys," Barbara said. "Between Ricky and Earl, I don't know who talks the most."

"Earl!" said Nell. "Definitely Earl. I'm sorry, Bari, but your husband doesn't come up for air. What drug is he on?"

"That's not funny," said Bari.

"Seriously, though. He's talked about sports; he's talked about Armageddon, the weather. People's psyches is obviously his favorite topic. He seems to think that he can read everybody. Nobody could get a word in edgewise," Nell told them.

"Earl must have had a drink." Bari giggled. "He talks a lot when he drinks."

"Wow." Nell shook her head.

Two hours later when everybody was done eating seconds and thirds, they settled back and relaxed in conversation. The leftover food in the serving dishes on the table had started to dry up around the sides of the bowls and on the table. Franki had told everybody not to worry about it, so they didn't.

EARL WORE A cynical half smile. His eyes roamed all around the room looking at everybody, long and hard. His half smile turned into a snarl as he took in what he believed was their phony laughter, their exaggerated stories, and their bullshit lies. He decided that he hated them, every single one of them. When he got sick of looking at them, he got up from the couch and went to the bathroom again. He figured this situation was nothing that a little hit couldn't fix.

CHERYL WAS A bundle of nerves, chain-smoking and seething. Earl hadn't so much as glanced in her direction in the past hour. She wondered who the hell he thought he was. She sat there with her legs tightly crossed and her arms folded across her chest. She was starting to feel the effects of the rum that she had been drinking, but it wasn't enough. She needed another hit, and so far Earl hadn't offered her another one. Cheryl made up her mind that she was going to explode if Earl didn't give her what she wanted. Right there in front of everybody she was going to let out Earl's dirty little secret. She glared in the direction of the closed bathroom door where Earl was.

EARL CAME OUT of the bathroom several minutes later. He had a wide stupid grin on his face. His glassy eyes bulged, but they looked brighter than they did before. He felt good now. Like he wanted to beat on his chest and show them who the man was. This time, he looked around the room to see which conversation he should get involved in. Since everybody was just talking boring bullshit, he decided to start his own conversation with anyone who cared to listen. "Could you imagine what life would be like if everybody was able to actually say what they felt?" he asked, in a loud, deep voice. Most of the conversations in the room stopped. Everybody looked at Earl. Now he had their attention. They listened but said nothing. "That shit would be so sweet," Earl continued. "You know what I think? People can't stand the truth. Let me give you a hypothetical situation. Say you're at somebody's house, because somehow you're obligated to be there. Meantime, you know nobody wants you there. And you sure as hell don't want to be there, but yet you have to sit there like an idiot tryin' to fit in, tryin' to be nice even though you're miserable. Why can't you just get up and tell everybody to kiss your ass and leave?"

Hazel shifted in her seat. Bari bit on her fingernails. Franki glared at Earl. Ricky's eyes rose in question.

"You know why you can't do that?" Earl asked. "Because everybody would think you're some kind of nut, or they may say you drank too much. . . ."

"So, you're saying that to say what?" Ricky asked. "I guess I missed your point."

"I guess my bottom line is that we go through life like robots, doing exactly what everybody else expects us to do. We victimize ourselves. That's what we do. Then on top of that, you can't really be honest with anybody 'cause people judge you, and weigh you if they get to know what you're really all about. So, ultimately, in the whole big scheme of things, everything is just plain ole bullshit!" Earl spat those last words out.

Hazel looked over at Bari.

"You need to watch your language, honey," Bari said, looking at Earl, then quickly looking around the room at everybody else. She had to say *something*. She knew everybody expected her to.

"I think we're all adults here," said Earl.

"That's not the point, Earl," Bari responded, attempting to be stern.

"Then make your point!" Earl snapped. His jaw clenched and large veins protruded from his neck and forehead.

"Relax, man; show the ladies some respect. Because hypothetically speaking, if a person is that uncomfortable, he can be shown the door. As a matter of fact, why don't we take a walk," Ricky said; his voice was calm but his eyes were calculating, glaring.

"Yeah, let's," Earl said. He got up and followed Ricky out the front door, carrying his drink with him. The two of them stood outside at the top of the steps.

"Look," Ricky started. "I don't know you. And since I just got here I haven't had a chance to speak to my sister yet, I don't know how things are with you two. But I'll tell you what, I don't like the vibe that I'm getting here. I'm not gonna stand for you disrespecting my mother or either one of my sisters. I'm just letting you know that right now."

"I'm cool. I'm not trying to disrespect anybody. Your sister is cool, too. I take care of mine, don't you worry about that." Earl guzzled down the rest of his drink. "I just wanted to make it clear to you that that's my family, period. And I'll do what I have to do to protect them and take care of them."

"I hear you, man, I would do the same thing for mine." Ricky said nothing more. He gave Earl a look like he really hoped he understood him. Earl avoided Ricky's eyes as they walked back inside.

FRANKI HAD STARTED clearing up the dishes in the kitchen. She excused herself when she couldn't bear to hear Earl's preaching anymore. After a while, Cheryl went into the kitchen behind Franki. Cheryl took out a cigarette from her cigarette case and lit it up. She leaned against the wall and watched Franki work. Cheryl's hands trembled as she smoked.

"You guys are very lucky to have such a close-knit family. I guess I miss having siblings . . . sometimes anyway."

"Yeah, I guess we are kind of lucky," Franki said. "That's a beautiful bracelet, Cheryl," Franki said when she caught a glimpse of the shiny gold.

"Thank you. It was a gift."

"A gift? Wow, somebody is trying to tell you something. That's really very pretty, and I can tell it's costly, too. Who gave it to you?" Franki asked.

"Earl."

"Earl?"

"Did I say 'Earl'?" Cheryl asked.

"Yes, you did."

"Oops." Cheryl turned on her heels and left the room.

Franki quickly walked behind her, but Cheryl was already well into the other room by the time Franki reached the door. Franki held the door open for a few seconds staring behind Cheryl. She told herself that Cheryl was drunk and didn't know what she was saying. Franki knew that Cheryl liked to stir the pot, but she would dismiss her for now.

Earl went into the bathroom again. He needed to get away from all the pressure in the living room. He had to mellow out. He brought his drink into the bathroom with him. He closed the lid on the toilet and sat down. Earl took out the ceramic pillbox from his pocket and laid out four neat lines on the edge of the sink. His heart pounded loudly in his chest at the sight of the coke. He took a long, slow hit from the first line; then he took another. He stood up and looked into the mirror.

"Yeah, that's nice," he said. Earl wiped away the excess powder from his nose. Earl's mother appeared in the mirror. She was sitting in her wheelchair stretching her arms out to him. He put his head closer to the mirror. He could see the stress in his mother's eyes. He blinked hard to try to erase the image. His mother sat there and started pointing her finger at him, scolding, and accusing. She was mad at him again. Earl knew it. He shook his head. His eyes were squeezed shut. When he opened them again, his mother was gone. She was replaced by the red-eyed devil. Earl smirked at his own image. He leaned back against the wall and slowly let the drug take over. He unbuttoned the top two buttons on his shirt, then leaned down close to the sink and took another hit.

"Whoa! This is some powerful shit," he said out loud. He looked into the mirror again, leaning in closer to it. Then, more quietly, he said, "I'm sorry, Mommy. I'm sorry—"

The bathroom door flew open. Darryl was rushing in to use the toilet. "What are you doin'?" Darryl asked, pissed, when he saw the cocaine on the sink.

"I-I was just leavin'.." Earl was scrambling, trying to scrape the cocaine off the sink and back into the pillbox.

"You're doing drugs in Franki's house? You know how she feels about that shit!" Darryl yelled.

"Yeah, yeah, I know, man. That's why she don't have to know about this. You know what I mean?" Earl's voice was hushed, and he had an almost pleading look in his eyes. "Ain't no need in startin' some shit and gettin' everybody all riled up for nothin', heh, heh. Besides, I don't plan on doin' this shit no more. I know this shit ain't no good for me," Earl said.

Darryl walked inside the bathroom and closed the door behind him. He stood very close to Earl, inches away from his face. "I'll tell you what, I really don't give a damn what you do, but don't you bring this shit around here. Nobody here has any use for it, and anybody that indulges in it. So, I suggest you clean this shit up and get the fuck out of here," Darryl said, slapping the pillbox out of Earl's hand.

Earl scrambled to keep it from falling. The open pillbox hit the floor and the cocaine that was inside of it was now a small circle on the floor. Earl jumped at Darryl and drew back his hand to strike.

"That's my money you just fucked with!" He withdrew his hand, then rushed down to the floor to salvage as much cocaine as he could. He took a business card out of his pocket and used his finger to sweep the cocaine onto the card. Earl worked quickly. He tried to get every drop. When he was done, he stood up to face Darryl again. He smeared the leftover cocaine dustings on the floor with his foot.

Earl's eyes stayed on Darryl's the whole time he did it. Earl's nose was snarled. "Motherfucker," Earl said, as he brushed past Darryl, leaving the bathroom. Earl walked back into the living room just in time to pick up on Franki's announcement.

"In case Bari hasn't told everybody yet, and I'm sure she hasn't because you know how modest Bari can be . . . she got the two-million-dollar Paiseley account that she was workin' so hard on like forever and ever," Franki said. "She's gonna be an associate partner at Choler-Raines."

"I knew she would get it," Hazel said, clapping. "I don't know why she was so worried."

"You know how your daughter is, Ms. Hunter. You should see her around the office, she's a worrywart," Barbara said.

"That's not true. It's just that I take my job very seriously," Bari explained, waving off Barbara.

"A little *too* seriously." Barbara laughed.

"Try taking your job a little *too seriously* once in a while, Barbara, and you, too, may land a two-million-dollar account." Now it was Bari's time to laugh.

"Touché!" Barbara laughed even harder, slapping her thigh and thumping her feet.

Earl was standing beside Bari now. "So, I guess you were keeping this a deep, dark secret," Earl said.

"What do you mean?" Bari asked.

"You got the account and you never even bothered to tell me?" Earl spoke loudly enough that anyone sitting nearby could hear him.

Bari looked around nervously. She spoke in a low voice. "No, Earl, it's no secret. I called home to tell you earlier today when I found out, but you weren't home. Then with all the excitement about the new car and Ricky's coming home, I guess I just forgot."

"You guess you just forgot?" Earl snarled. "You didn't 'just forget' to tell your sister. What do you think, you're too big for me now? Is that it?" he asked.

"Come on, Earl, you know it's nothing like that. I'm sorry. I wouldn't shut you out on purpose, you know that," Bari defended herself.

"Look, just get your shit and let's get out of here."

"But I told you I was staying here tonight with my family, remember? Are you okay to drive?" she asked.

Earl ignored her question. "Have a good night," he said. He left the apartment, slamming the door behind him. Earl stood outside the door on the top step of the stoop while he fished around for his car keys. Then he stormed down the steps and went down to his car. He thought of Bari's smiling face. He thought about the fact that she didn't even care that he was going to be home alone tonight. How could she even think about sleeping out knowing that? He knew what she was doing. She was trying to cut him out.

"I'm her goddamned husband. She'd better remember that shit." Earl got into the car. He didn't start it up, though; he sat there staring at Franki's building. He took out his ceramic pillbox. He opened it and took a couple of hits. "Damn!" He punched the steering wheel. He could use a drink. He drummed his fingers on the dashboard. Earl thought about Bari again. Laughing, not a care in the world. Ten minutes went by. Earl got out of the car and slammed the door shut. He pulled up the collar on his jacket and walked back to the building. He was cussing under his breath as he walked back up the steps and rang the bell. Before anyone could answer, he rang it again.

Franki opened the window and stuck out her head. "Who's that?" she asked. Earl's head was too far under the awning. Franki couldn't see him.

"It's me, Earl."

"Earl? I thought you went home," Franki said.

"Tell Bari to come downstairs!"

Franki left the window, and seconds later Bari stuck her head out the window.

"What are you doin' at the window? I told her to tell you to come downstairs! I'm not yelling up at the window. Come down here and bring your shit, you're leavin'."

BARI DIDN'T WANT Earl to make a scene. She quickly left the window and went over to the closet and grabbed her coat and picked up her pocketbook from behind the couch.

"I thought you were staying with the family tonight?" Franki asked when she saw Bari heading to the door with her coat and bag.

"Yeah, Sis, I thought you were staying. I haven't seen you in so long. I thought we were gonna spend some time," said Ricky.

"I know, I know, but I can't now." Bari was putting on her coat and still making her way toward the door. She wasn't sure what Earl would do if she took a minute longer. "I have to hurry up. I'll call you guys tomorrow. Mommy, I'll talk to you later." She blew a kiss in their direction. Bari saw the disappointment in their faces but she couldn't worry about them right now.

"Wait up, Sis, I'll walk you down." Ricky got up and walked Bari down the stairs.

Earl was standing at the bottom of the steps when Bari and Ricky came down. He straightened himself up when he saw Ricky. Ricky walked straight up to Earl. Ricky was so close to Earl's face that Earl could smell his breath.

"So what's up, man? Is there a problem down here? My sister was spending the night with the family. You have a problem with that?"

"Nah, man, no problem. I'm just takin' my wife home, that's all." Earl spoke smoothly, though he didn't back away.

"Is that what you want, Sis?"

"Yeah, Ricky. I'm gonna go home tonight but I'll be back first thing in the morning. We'll have our coffee together." Bari made herself smile real sweet so Ricky could relax himself. She wanted to assure him that everything was all right. "It's fine, Ricky, really," Bari said, gently tugging her brother's arm. She smiled that sweet smile again.

Ricky took a step back from Earl. "All right then. You take it easy, Sis. I'll see you tomorrow."

Bari stepped up and hugged Ricky. When Earl and Bari walked over to their car, Ricky stood at the bottom of the steps and watched them. Earl started the car as soon as he got inside and tore out of the parking spot.

Earl drove two blocks, then pulled over to the curb and jumped out of the car. He rushed over to Bari's side of the car and opened the door. He grabbed her by the arm and pulled her out of the car. Bari held on to her handbag as she got out of the car. She could feel the tension in his grip. Earl held her arm way too tight, but she wouldn't dare complain. She was afraid to speak. She waited for his next move. Earl threw Bari up against the gate of a closed store.

"Do you think I'm a sucker? Is that what you think?" he yelled.

"What are you talking about, Earl? What's wrong?" Bari asked.

Earl balled up his fist and punched her in the face. His fist landed on the corner of her mouth, opening a small gash. Bari was shocked. She put her hand to her face as she screamed out in pain. Earl drew back his fist to hit her again, but Bari put up her hand to block the punch. Her handbag fell to the ground. "Earl, stop it! Why are you doing this?"

A few cars drove by. The drivers slowed down as they passed. Some of them rolled down their windows to get a better look. Earl was oblivious to all of them.

"Did you forget who I am? I'm your husband! You remember that. Show me some respect!" he yelled.

"Earl, could you please stop for a minute and tell me what happened?" Tears streamed down Bari's face. Her mouth oozed blood. "I love you. Why can't you see that? I would never do anything to disrespect you. Can't we talk about this?" Bari pleaded.

"Love ain't got nothin' to do with this. Walk!" Earl yelled into her face.

"Get in the car. Goddammit, get in the car!" Earl shoved her ahead of him. He picked up her handbag and threw it into the car. "I'm sick and tired of fuckin' bullshit. I'm sick and tired of fuckin' people. Everybody wants to fuck with me. I'm tired of being fucked with!" Earl ranted as he got into the car.

Bari tried not to say much. She wasn't sure what to say. She knew that whatever she said would set him off even further.

EARL HEADED STRAIGHT to the liquor cabinet when they got inside their house. He pulled out a fifth of rum and drank straight from the bottle. Bari went quietly upstairs to the bathroom and locked the door behind her.

After a few swigs of rum, Earl looked around the room for her.

"Bari! Bari! Where are you?" He took another swig. "Bari!" Earl called out again. Bari didn't answer. Earl went up the steps and looked in the bedroom. He didn't see her.

Earl noticed an ashtray that was set on the dresser with strange-looking petals mixed with particles and dust in it. He picked it up and flung it across the room. He caught a glimpse of an eight-ounce glass of water that was set against the wall in a corner of the room on the floor. He picked it up. "And what's all this voodoo-lookin' shit I'm seeing all around my fuckin' house?" Earl flung that, too. Water and glass splashed all over the wall. "Bari, are you in there? Open the door; I wanna talk to you." Earl leaned his back against the bathroom door. He took out his ceramic pillbox from his shirt pocket and took another hit. Earl put the pillbox into his pocket. He turned around and banged on the door.

"Open the door, Bari! I just wanna talk to you. I won't hurt you, I promise." Earl banged on the door some more.

Bari slowly opened the door. Earl was calm. He took Bari by the hand and led her down the stairs to the living room. He motioned for her to sit down on the couch; then he sat beside her. "Do you really think it's okay to keep secrets from me, baby? Do you think that I'm not important?" Earl was beginning to get agitated again. He was taking short, quick breaths. "Don't you think that I should know what's goin' on in your life?" he asked emphatically.

"Of course you should know what's going on in my life. I don't keep secrets from you, Earl," Bari said.

Earl punched the coffee table so hard that the glasses in the wall unit rattled. Bari jumped. "Then why didn't I know about the account that you got before anybody else? I looked like a sucker in your sister's apartment." Earl got up from the couch. "Do you know what I could do to you?" He grabbed Bari up from the couch. "I could break your goddamned neck!" Earl turned Bari around so that her back was against him. He put his arm around her neck and squeezed.

Bari gasped for air while she struggled to pull his arm from around her neck. She started to cough. "Earl, stop it! Please!" Bari could barely talk for choking. "You're choking me!" Bari coughed some more. "Earl, stop! Please."

Suddenly Bari's eyes were panicked. Her body started to tremble.

She fell limp in Earl's arms. He helped her down to the floor. He waited. He knew it was a trick. Bari would jump up at any moment and laugh. When she didn't move for almost a minute, Earl got scared and started to pat her face.

"Bari, Bari, wake up," he said.

Bari's eyes opened. She was dazed and confused at first. Then the memory of what had just happened came flooding back to her. She slapped at Earl's chest.

"What are you trying to do? Kill me? Why don't you just go ahead and get it over with?" Bari cried.

Earl grabbed her arms. He pulled her close to him, holding her tightly by the arms. "I'm sorry, baby. I didn't mean to hurt you, I swear I didn't. I love you." He kissed her forehead. Then he kissed her eyelids, her cheeks. "Here, sit down." Earl helped her to the couch. "I'll be back," he said. He left the room and went into the kitchen and filled a hand towel with ice. He came back into the room and put the ice pack to Bari's bruised mouth, which was now swollen and discolored. Earl dabbed away the tears on her face. He put the ice pack aside and kissed her bruised mouth. Softly he kissed her nose, then her neck. He got up to her ear and whispered very softly into her ear, "I love you, Bari. I'm sorry. Please forgive me, please. I will never hurt you again." Earl kissed her ear, then made his way over to her lips. He kissed them very gently, then a little harder. He parted her lips with his tongue. Bari flinched from the pain, but Earl kissed her still. Bari kissed him back. Earl stopped kissing Bari long enough to take her hand and lead her upstairs to the bedroom. He held the back of her hand to his lips the whole time they walked. Once they were in bed, Earl hungrily kissed Bari all over, while Bari dug her hand inside his pillowcase to make sure that Zuma's powder was still in place.

thirty-three

*T*HE PHONE HAD already rung five times. "Get the telephone, Earl," Bari mumbled. The telephone rang two more times. Bari opened her eyes. She squinted at the sun glare while she felt around for the telephone. She picked up the receiver and got a dial tone. "Damn." Bari sat up in bed. "Earl!" she called. Then she put her hand to her face and winced in pain as she gently touched the swollen areas. She glanced over at the alarm clock. It was 10:45 A.M. She'd overslept. Bari's intention had been to get up early and go to church. She always went to church on Christmas Eve because it was Granny's birthday. And since Granny had been on Bari's mind a lot lately, she wanted to say a special prayer for her in church this morning.

Bari wondered why Earl hadn't awakened her. Where could he be off to so early in the morning?

The telephone rang again. Bari answered on the first ring.

"Hello?"

"We have to talk." Franki's voice was deadpan.

"About what?" Bari asked.

"Several things."

"Would you believe Earl and I were in a car accident on the way home last night?"

"No shit? A car accident, what happened?" Franki asked.

"Some jerk hit our car from behind."

"So, why in the hell didn't you call somebody? You did go to the hospital, didn't you?" Franki asked.

"No, we didn't bother. It wasn't that serious. I got a few bumps and bruises, that's all," Bari said.

"You should have gone to the hospital." Franki's voice was stern. "Did you file a police report? What about the car? Did the other driver have insurance?" Franki asked.

"Franki, we were too tired for all of that. The car is fine. It's really no big deal."

"Is Earl all right?" Franki asked.

"Yes."

"We have to talk, Bari. It's important."

"We'll talk, Franki, but right now I have so many things going on—"

"Look, I'm comin' over. I'll see you in a few." Franki hung up the phone before Bari could protest.

"Damn!" Bari said. She hung up the phone, went over to the mirror, and frowned at her reflection. She leaned in closer to examine her face. The bruises were still fresh. The side of her mouth was swollen. Dried-up blood sealed the wound. Red welt marks were still all around her neck.

"How in the world am I ever going to cover this? I look terrible." Bari pulled out her makeup bag from the bureau and set it out on the dresser. Then, she jumped into the shower. Bari stepped out of the shower, dried herself off, and combed her hair. She lotioned her body, then quickly threw on a pair of jeans and a shirt. She was just about to apply her makeup when the doorbell rang.

"Oh, God. How did she get here so fast? I haven't even gotten a chance to put on my makeup. Damn," Bari said. She hesitated at first, but she went downstairs and opened the door.

Franki stood there expressionless.

"You look terrible," Franki said, walking past Bari and stepping into the house. Franki looked all around inside the room as she took off her coat. "Where is your husband?" she asked.

"I don't know," Bari said.

"Your face is all bruised. You must have bounced all around in the car last night when you got hit. Look at your neck. Wow." Franki's voice showed no emotion.

"I sure did bounce all around," Bari said.

"You end up looking like that and you don't go to a hospital? Weren't you wearing a seat belt? What about the other driver? Was he okay?"

"The other driver was fine." Bari wished that Franki would change the subject.

"Earl was fine; the other driver was fine. So basically, you're the only one who got hurt."

"Basically." Bari avoided Franki's eyes. She knew Franki would know that she was lying if she looked into her eyes.

"Bari, tell me the truth. How did this happen to you? Did Earl do it?"

"Hell no!"

"Bullshit!"

"Earl didn't do this!"

"You're lying, Bari. I can tell. You're lying!"

"Okay, we got into it. I pissed him off and he hit me. Do you feel better now?" Bari flopped herself down onto the couch.

Franki went over and stood before Bari. She felt her blood pressure rising. It swelled at the base of her head and would explode any minute. "That son of a bitch should be locked up," Franki said, looking at Bari through slitted eyes. "You should press charges against him! Or kill him!"

"Then I would be locked up. Give me a break, Franki; he's my husband."

"So what? Look what he did to you. It makes me sick to hear women make stupid remarks like that. What in the world makes you think that because it's your husband that hurts you that makes it okay?"

"It's not like he really hurt me. Earl would never really hurt me."

"Because he loves you, right? Good Lord, Bari, you sound just like the people that come on our talk show."

"Well, of course because he loves me. That's not a question. And please do not compare me with any of those clowns that you have on your shows."

"Bari, if Earl loved you he wouldn't do this to you. Is this what you do to somebody that you love?"

"We talked about it. Everything's cool. It's never gonna happen again. Trust me."

"You know, for somebody so smart, you are so damned dumb."

Bari avoided her sister's eyes again. She got up from the couch, folded her arms across her chest, and paced in front of the wall unit.

Franki was close behind her. "I almost forgot the real reason why I came over. I don't even know how to tell you this. I'm not good at sugarcoating things; I think you know that."

"Just say what you have to say, Franki."

"Okay, Earl is a cocaine user." Franki's voice was flat.

"What in the world are you talking about?" Bari asked, shocked.

Franki tried to stay calm. She knew Bari well enough to know that she would clam up if the conversation got too heated, and today Franki needed Bari to listen to her.

"Bari, you have to believe me. This is the truth."

"Don't you think I would know it if my husband was on drugs?"

"I'm not sure if you would know or not, Bari. All I know is that Earl is definitely on cocaine."

"How would you possibly know this for sure?" Bari asked, sounding like she'd give anything not to believe it.

"Darryl told me."

"Darryl? Darryl doesn't even know Earl."

"Darryl caught him in the act in the bathroom last night at my apartment. Earl is doing cocaine. You might as well face it, Bari."

"I'll have to ask him about this." Bari walked back over to the couch and sat down.

Franki sat next to her. "And what if he lies? Then what? You can't stay with this man, Bari. You have to leave him."

"First of all, I don't even know if any of this is true. And furthermore, why should I leave him if he has a problem? Isn't it my job as his wife to get him help? What do you think happened to Mommy and Daddy? I don't want that to happen to Earl and me."

"Earl isn't going to change, Bari. Did you forget how you met this man? He was drunk at a hooky party, in high school. Don't you remember? They called it alcohol poisoning. He was messed up then and he's messed up now," Franki said.

"You don't understand the situation. I know why Earl is the way he is. Why he drinks so much. It's not his fault. I never told you this before, but when Earl was a little boy, he watched his father kill his mother. And now he's haunted by guilt every day of his life."

"Oh, my God." Franki covered her mouth and gasped in disbelief.

"He was only six years old when it happened and he never got over it. It tears him up because his father got away with it, and he blames himself for not going to the police all these years."

"That's a terrible burden for him to have to live with, but you know what? There's no excuse for what he did to you. Anyway, there's more."

"More?" Bari asked, looking defeated. "What more could there possibly be?"

"Earl is having an affair with Cheryl." There it was. Point-blank.

Bari looked at Franki with disbelief. Then Bari looked as if she were looking at the Devil himself. "I don't believe that! Earl would never do that to me! An affair!" she spat. "He doesn't even like Cheryl! She's not his type."

"He bought her a beautiful gold bracelet. She told me that. And she made it a point to tell Barbara that he was taking her Christmas shopping today. That's probably where he is right now."

"So Barbara knows about this, too?"

Franki's silence was her confirmation.

"How could it be that everybody seems to know all about my husband but me and I live with the man?"

"I'm sure that if you would allow yourself to open your eyes, you'd see the signs. They're all there, Bari."

Bari slouched farther back onto the couch. She crossed her arms over her stomach and squeezed herself like she was in pain. She spoke almost in a whisper. "I'm sorry. I just can't imagine Earl doing something like this to me. I'm a good wife to him. I take care of him, I pay all the bills since he's not working. I give him money. Why wouldn't that be enough?" Bari sat erect. "No, no, I won't believe this. Cheryl is my friend."

"And Earl is your husband. And what does it all mean? It means nothing. People are people first. Then they become your friends, your husbands, your sisters, and your brothers. And they'll always think of themselves and their needs first. I love you, Bari. You're my sister. I want to help you, but you have to believe what I'm telling you."

"It's hard, Franki. Would you mind leaving me alone for a while?"

"What I would like to do is help you pack your shit and help you get the hell out of here," said Franki.

"I really don't feel good right now, Franki. I need to think," Bari said, her eyes looking sunken and sad.

"Okay, Bari, I understand. But we have to deal with this. We have to. But, in the meantime, play it cool. Do not confront Earl about any of this; you don't know what he might do," said Franki.

Bari nodded her head. It was all she could do. She got up and slowly walked Franki to the door. After Bari let Franki out, she sat on the couch with her legs crossed underneath her. She stared straight ahead at the wall. The nausea was overwhelming. She wanted to die. Bari got up from the couch and went upstairs to the bedroom, lay down on the bed, and curled herself into a ball. She would have to get to the bottom of this. But how? Where would she start? She lay there in the same position until she drifted off to sleep. It was three hours later when she awakened. When she sat up, the memory of her conversation with Franki flooded back to her. Where was Earl anyway? Maybe he *was* with Cheryl. It was a crazy thought.

Bari picked up the telephone and dialed Cheryl's telephone number. Cheryl's answering machine picked up.

thirty-four

EARL HELD OPEN the front door to Cheryl's apartment building. Cheryl struggled through the vestibule, barely able to see over the bags that she held up in her arms. Earl had a bunch of bags in each of his hands, too. The two of them stumbled and laughed as they went up the steps to Cheryl's second-floor apartment. When they reached her front door, Cheryl searched through her pockets for her keys with one hand and tried to steady her bags with the other. A few of her bags fell to the floor outside of the door. When Earl quickly reached out to try to stop the bags from falling, he dropped some of his bags, too. They made a ruckus in the hallway, laughing even louder than before, throwing their bags into the apartment one by one, after Cheryl finally got the door open.

Cheryl was happy. She had a plan. She had spent enough time with Earl to know that she wanted to be with him—permanently. After all, Earl had spent enough time explaining to her how unhappy he was in his marriage. She had already hinted to him that she was interested in taking their relationship to another level. Tonight she wanted to know what his intentions were. Earl had told her that he loved being with her, so she knew he wouldn't have a problem moving in with her. She would suggest that. Her small apartment wasn't much, but with a man around to fix some of the things that needed fixing and to put a couple of coats of paint on the walls, they could be pretty comfortable. She knew Earl's job situation. She figured she could afford to handle the bills just as she always had until he got on his feet.

"Are you okay, Earlie?" Cheryl asked, as they settled down on the living room couch. They had just finished eating and she was planning to give Earl a massage to relax him and then she would pop the big question. But first she needed a boost.

"Do you have anything good for me, baby?" Cheryl asked in her tiniest voice.

"You know I do," Earl said, and reached into his pant pockets and pulled out his pillbox and handed it to her. He had just picked up another package earlier that day. Cheryl filled the small gold spoon and fed the coke to Earl first; then she fed herself.

Cheryl squeezed herself onto the edge of the couch to lie down next to Earl, who was stretched out with his arms behind his head, with his eyes closed. She lay beside Earl and made soft, small circles on his chest with her index finger.

"You know, Earlie, I like being with you. I know that I wouldn't be able to stand it if we couldn't be friends anymore. So, I was thinkin' that since we spend so much time together, I mean, hell, you're probably here more than you are at your own house . . . and I figured that since you're unhappy at home . . ."

Cheryl smiled, looking down at him. She thought he would have opened his eyes. She waited for a response, any response, from Earl. A small reaction. There was none. Cheryl was annoyed. That was the one thing that she didn't like about him. He was an enigma to her. Cheryl sighed and continued her pitch to him.

"I thought that you might want to seriously consider, well, you know, moving in with me." Cheryl stopped speaking and looked down at Earl again. He still didn't move, stir, nothing. Cheryl waited a few more seconds, and when she couldn't take it anymore she slammed her palm into his chest.

"What? What?" Earl asked, opening his eyes.

"You haven't heard one word that I said to you, have you?" Cheryl asked.

"I heard you," he said.

"Well, then what do you say?" Cheryl made her eyes appear soft. She propped herself up on her left elbow, as she looked Earl directly in his eyes. It seemed like an eternity to her before he answered. He looked pensive.

"Do you know that if I died today, I would die a happy man?" Earl sat up, forcing Cheryl to sit up, too. He took a hit of cocaine from the pillbox on the coffee table.

"That's really nice, sweetheart, but what does that have to do with what I'm askin' you?"

"I would die a happy man because I don't live for the future. I live for today. Tomorrow is not promised to nobody. Could you imagine how many people have died unexpectedly? I can guarantee you that those people didn't wake up on the day of their death and say, 'Hey, I'm gonna die today.' I'm sure they didn't have a clue about it. Then they die and their families and friends all sit around talking about 'oh, he was gonna do this, and he was gonna do that.' Well, now that person can't do shit 'cause he's dead, finished, kaput! Those people made plans . . . plans that will never happen. I won't do that. I say let things flow naturally and just roll with it." Earl picked up the pillbox and took another hit.

"So what exactly are you saying?" Cheryl asked.

"I'm simply saying that we make these plans to make a move like that and then *bam!* Something happens or maybe nothin' happens, 'cause it's like I said: Nobody's promised nothin'. But what I do know is that we definitely have 'now.' So why are we wastin' our time talkin' about tomorrow when we could be busy takin' advantage of our time today?" Earl pulled Cheryl closer to him and stroked her face. "Don't you think that's a good idea?" Earl softly kissed Cheryl on her lips. He pecked at her lips at first; then he kissed her deeper.

Cheryl looked up at him and smiled. She touched his face.

"Yes, Earlie. I think that's a very good idea." Her smile widened and she kissed him again.

"Take this off," Earl said, tugging at her shirt.

BARI COULDN'T THINK straight. She needed to get to the bottom of the situation. She was ready to talk to Franki now. Franki would help her sort things out. Before she could reach over to pick up the handset to dial Franki, the telephone rang. It was Franki.

"Bari, it's me: Franki. I just wanted to make sure that everything was okay. How are you feeling?"

"Numb. I still find it hard to believe that Earl would have an affair with Cheryl. And doing cocaine . . ."

"There's been plenty of signs if you think about it," Franki said.

"You don't understand, Franki. I take care of everything; there is no reason for him to go outside for anything," said Bari.

"The first thing I guess you'll need to do is see for yourself that something is really going on between Earl and Cheryl. Maybe once you've seen it for yourself, you'll know what you have to do. Right?"

Bari didn't answer.

"Right?" Franki asked again.

"Right," Bari said unconvincingly.

"Meaning, you'll have to leave him," Franki said.

"I know what it means," Bari said.

"Earl still isn't home yet, is he?" Franki asked.

"No," Bari said. The knots were slowly returning to her stomach, one at a time.

"Do you still need to get to the mall to pick up a gift for Kim? You know the mall closes early today. Remember it's Christmas Eve."

"Yeah," Bari answered.

"Okay, I'll pick you up in thirty minutes."

They hung up.

Bari's voice sounded strong enough, but deep inside she didn't have a clue how she would be able to shop and deal with the crowd at the mall in the state of mind that she was in. How would she prevent herself from puking her guts out when the nausea got the best of her?

WHEN BARI GOT home much later that afternoon, there was no sign that Earl had been there. She begged off from going to Franki's apartment to see Hazel and Ricky. Bari explained to Franki that she couldn't let them see her bruised face. Franki understood and she covered for Bari. Franki told Hazel and Ricky that Bari had a serious stomach virus. When they called her to check on her, she had no problem convincing them that she was sick because it wasn't a lie. She had never felt more ill than she felt right now. Bari had sent her family's Christmas presents home with Franki.

Imagine, Bari thought. *My family is finally in the same state at the same time for the first time in years and I can't see them.* That alone broke her heart. The whole Earl situation destroyed her. Bari spent the whole evening crying and throwing up. Throwing up and crying.

At 10:00 P.M. Earl still hadn't come home yet. The twinkling lights on the Christmas tree had lost their appeal, and the music that the lights made had become annoying. Bari unplugged the tree and the window lights. A part of her wished that the doorbell would ring and the police would be there telling her that Earl had been in a terrible accident. She could probably deal with that situation a lot better than finding out that her husband really was having an affair with Cheryl.

Bari tried everything to relax herself. The two cups of Sleepytime tea had no effect on her. She tried to read, but the words in the book were a blur. She listened so closely for Earl that her ears became accustomed to every sound in the house. Every creak. Each time a car passed the house, she would run to the window, hoping that she'd see the car pulling up in the driveway. Finally, she showered and turned in for the night. She lay still in bed unable to think of anything else but Earl. She couldn't stop the free-flowing images of Earl and Cheryl in the most compromising positions. And Bari couldn't help but wonder if Cheryl was the only one and if Earl used condoms. The thought made Bari even more sick to her stomach.

Bari sat up in bed and reached over and turned on the lamp. She got out of bed and walked over to Earl's closet. She opened the door. Bari stood there for at least a minute staring at the neat rows of shoes lined up on the floor of his closet. She smiled to herself when she realized that she was probably finally cracking up.

Bari needed to get a grip. She stepped back from the closet and closed the door. She crossed the room and got back into bed. Bari turned off the lamp and squeezed her eyes shut. Within a minute she was up again, turning on the lamp and standing in front of Earl's closet with the door pulled wide-open. She picked up a pair of brown Bally loafers. Bari placed the shoes on the floor in the form of a T and stooped down in front of them.

"If my love I wish to see, I place his shoes into a T."

She took a deep breath, and she slowly looked around the room. Somewhere deep down in her gut, she knew that Earl wasn't coming home. She climbed back into bed and finally fell into a restless slumber.

BARI THOUGHT SHE was dreaming when the doorbell rang. She looked at the clock on the bed table. It was 7:15 A.M. *I knew it!* she thought. Something had happened to Earl and in all the excitement he lost his keys. Bari jumped out of bed and ran into the bathroom. She looked at the puffiness under her eyes. Bari quickly grabbed a wash-cloth and ran it under ice-cold water and pressed it against her eyes. She splashed water in her mouth and spat it into the sink. She grabbed her robe off the door hook and pulled it on, then rushed down the stairs with her heart somewhere in her throat. Bari pulled open the door.

"Uncle Butch!" she said, surprised.

"Merry Christmas!" Butch grinned. He stepped forward and grabbed Bari into a bear hug.

"Merry Christmas to you, too," Bari said.

Butch's hair was a lot grayer than Bari remembered, but his skin was still smooth. He had developed crow's-feet around his eyes, but he still stood tall and handsome for a man who was pushing fifty.

"How you doin', little girl? What happened to you?" Butch asked, noting her bruised face.

"Oh, oh, this," Bari said, touching her face. "My husband and I were in a car accident the other night. It was nothing serious, though."

"Well, thank God for that. How are you doin' otherwise?" Butch asked.

"I'm fine. What in the world brings you to New York?" Bari asked.

"Well, I don't know if you remember my sister Alice, y'all were just itty-bitty little kids when she used to come around. Anyway, she ain't doin' too well. And since she's my last sister and it's Christmastime, I figured let me come on up here and see about her. And I figured I could try to stop by and see you and Franki if I could. How's Franki doin'?"

"Franki's fine. I'm sorry to hear about your sister, Uncle Butch. I hope she'll be okay. Are you hungry?" asked Bari.

"Well, I ain't had a chance to eat yet. But I don't want to put you to no trouble."

"Don't be silly. It's no trouble at all; come on in and make yourself comfortable. Just give me a minute to throw something on," Bari said. She ran up the stairs and took off her robe and searched through her drawers for some pants and a top to put on.

EARL SLIPPED HIS key into the door and eased himself into the house. "Who are you?" he asked Butch when he got inside. Earl didn't recognize the older man but could tell by looking at him that he was in good enough shape to still believe that he could have a chance with a young woman like Bari.

"I-I'm . . . You don't remember me?" Butch asked.

"I can't say that I do. Where is my wife?"

"Bari went upstairs to get dressed. I'm her uncle Butch." Butch reached out to Earl to shake his hand. Earl walked past Butch, ignoring his outstretched hand.

BARI WASN'T SURE if she heard Earl's voice, so she went to the top of the steps wearing a pair of jeans and a bra. She leaned over the banister to listen more closely. When Earl appeared at the bottom of the steps, Bari nearly jumped an inch off the floor. "Earl, you're home," she said, wiping her perspiring hands on her pants. Bari had spent hours the night before going over in her mind what she was going to say to him when he came home, and now she drew a complete blank.

"What did I just walk in on?" Earl asked, rushing up the stairs to her.

"What do you mean? Where have you been all night?" Bari asked.

"I walked in on you and a man in my house and you wanna ask *me* questions!"

"Earl, that man downstairs is my uncle Butch. Don't you remember he came to our wedding? Would you lower your voice so he doesn't hear you?"

"I don't give a damn if he hears me or not. You go downstairs and tell him to get the hell outta my house. And make sure you tell him that I don't want *any* man in my house when I'm not here."

"I won't do that!" Bari said.

"Well, if you won't, I will!" Earl stormed back down the stairs.

Bari followed closely behind him, pulling a sweater over her head. "Earl, don't!"

When they got downstairs, Butch was already standing at the door about to leave.

"My wife should have told you that I don't like anybody here when I'm not home."

Butch looked at Bari, his eyebrows raised in question. Then he looked back at Earl. "Let me tell you somethin'. I knew this young lady since she was just a little girl . . . ," Butch started.

Bari stood behind Earl with downcast eyes. She knew that she should give Butch an explanation. She wanted to tell him how sorry she was, but she couldn't. Her throat constricted and she couldn't speak.

"I really didn't mean to cause no trouble. I just wanted to say hello to Bari, since I was in the neighborhood. It's been such a long time," Butch said.

"Yeah, well . . ." Earl opened the door for Butch.

Bari looked up at Butch now. Tears burned the corners of her eyes. She opened her mouth to speak, but no words came. She wanted to tell Butch that Hazel and Ricky were in town for the holidays and that he could go by Franki's apartment to pay them a visit, but nothing came. Only sadness. Darkness and sadness overcame Bari and suddenly she wanted Uncle Butch to leave quickly before her tears fell.

thirty-five

BARI AND FRANKI had been on the telephone for two hours. Bari was feeling a little more at ease for the past few days. It was three days past Christmas and Earl hadn't disappeared once. He didn't seem to be drinking much and his temper was in check.

"I know what you're gonna think, Franki, but to be honest with you, I haven't really seen any sign of Earl using drugs. I've been watching him very closely and he seems just as normal as you or me. And I haven't caught him sneaking any phone calls and no one has called here out of the ordinary. Earl hasn't even left the house for any long period of time except for right now. He went out to his friend's house to have a belated Christmas drink."

"And why are you telling me all this?" Franki asked.

"I'm just saying, why can't we just leave it alone? At least until I see a definite sign." Bari pressed the phone closer to her ear. She waited for Franki to blast her. Franki was quiet, though—at first.

"Let me ask you a question, Bari. And please, don't answer me quickly. I want you to think about it before you answer me. What exactly is the reason that you want to hang on to Earl?"

"Well, I . . . er . . . ," Bari stammered.

"Wait," Franki said. "I'm not done yet. See, we produced a show back in February about women who love and the men who hate them. We had at least four extremely successful women on the panel, plus a pretty reputable relationship expert, and up to now I still don't have a clear understanding as to why women like you put up with men that hurt you."

"Can I speak now?" Bari asked.

"Sure," said Franki.

"I—Franki, I'm not like any one of those four women on your panel. I don't know what those women's stories were, but I don't believe for one minute that Earl hates me. All I know is that I have a husband who has issues just like everybody else and he very well may need my help. I think that it is my duty as his wife to do everything that I can to help him through whatever his problems are. I'm not saying it's an easy thing to do, ignoring everything that's happened, and I don't expect anybody to understand. And I certainly don't feel like I owe any apologies or explanations to anybody for what I do or don't do." Bari's gut told her to hang up the phone, but she didn't listen to it.

"What you need to do is be true to yourself, Bari. I think that you know that it isn't that simple. I think that you know that this is a lot deeper than you can handle," said Franki.

"I think I'll do okay."

"How?" Franki asked. "With the help of some witch doctor? Do you really think those people have special powers to help you?"

"I can't believe Barbara told you my business," Bari said, sucking her teeth. "Then again, I'm not surprised."

"Don't blame Barbara; I kind of pulled it out of her. But what were you thinking, going to those people? I mean I would have been scared out of my mind," Franki said.

"I don't know what I was thinking, Franki. I just felt like I was coming apart at the seams and I needed help fast."

Bari sighed loudly. Then she was quiet for a moment. Franki was, too.

"I just need to see a definite sign . . . ," Bari said.

"You may never see a definite sign, Bari. Earl is sick. He's good at pulling the wool over your eyes. I told you before that for somebody that's so smart you could be so damned dumb sometimes," said Franki.

"Thank you," Bari said in a monotone.

"Seriously. You only see what you want to see," Franki told her.

"You have it all figured out, don't you, Franki?"

"Pretty much. Are you still going with me to take Mommy to the airport?" Franki asked, changing the subject.

"To the airport? Mommy's flying?" Bari asked, surprised.

"My mistake. We both know that wild horses couldn't make that woman get on a plane. Barbara said that she'd give us a lift to the bus terminal."

"Yeah, okay. I'm coming," said Bari.

"And, Bari?"

"Yeah?"

"One more thing."

"What?"

"This may be a long shot, I mean, we could be wrong, but Barbara told me that she was talking to Cheryl earlier. Cheryl told her that she was having a candlelight dinner for her and her guy. Of course she never mentioned any names, but I have a feeling she's talking about Earl."

"Oh, Franki, you just don't quit, do you?" asked Bari.

"Follow me on this, Bari. I figure we could pick up Nell on the way back after we drop off mommy. We'll all dress in black. We'll wear black caps, and black shirts and pants. I figure it'll be harder for anybody to see us since it'll be dark," Franki explained.

"Don't forget the black sunglasses," Bari said sarcastically.

Franki ignored her. "After Mommy is on the bus we'll drive over to Cheryl's place and sit in the car and watch her apartment. Once you see Earl enter or leave, you'll have to be convinced."

Bari could hear Franki talking, but she was no longer listening. She heard Franki say something about pride and Bari's deserving better. Bari closed her eyes tightly and prayed silently. She was willing to make a deal with the Devil if she had to. She prayed for this whole situation to be put behind her and that everything would be like it was. If that couldn't happen, then she would have to face the situation head-on.

"Are you listening to me?" Franki asked.

"I'm listening," said Bari.

"So, are you okay with the plan?"

"I'm okay with it," Bari said quietly. And so it was set.

LATER THAT NIGHT at the bus terminal, Hazel was about to board the 6:59 P.M. Greyhound bus to Slothberg, South Carolina. "Y'all look so cute all dressed in black. Like a little singing group or somethin'." Hazel laughed as she stood with Bari, Franki, and Barbara. "I sure am sorry I have to leave you girls, but I don't want to stay away from my house too long. My neighbors might just drive up here to get me themselves if I take any longer to go back." Hazel laughed.

Passengers had already started boarding the southbound Greyhound bus.

"I hate to see you go, Mommy," Bari said, as she hugged her mother good-bye. "I'm gonna miss you. Why did you have to move so far away anyway?"

"Child, when the Lord told me to go, I didn't ask him where to. I just went," Hazel said.

"They're starting to board the bus, Mommy," said Franki. "You'd better hurry up and get on. You know how you hate sitting near the bathroom." Franki and Hazel embraced.

"You're right about that," Hazel said. "I need to sit near that darn driver so I can keep my eye on him."

"You don't need to watch the driver, Mommy. You need to get some rest. Try to sleep some of the way," Franki said.

"Of course," Hazel said, looking as if that was the last thing in the world that she intended to do.

Barbara stepped forward and hugged Hazel. "Have a wonderful and safe trip, Mrs. Hunter," Barbara told her.

"I will, baby," Hazel said, patting Barbara's back. "You take care of yourself."

"Call us as soon as they make the first rest stop, Mom," Bari said.

"I will," said Hazel.

Franki and Barbara picked up Hazel's luggage and headed toward the bus. Hazel and Bari walked arm in arm behind them.

"I'm worried about you, Bari," Hazel said in a whisper.

"You don't have to worry about me, Mommy. I'm a big girl." Bari tried to make her voice sound cheery.

"I don't like how you look. You're not eatin'; I can tell."

"I eat, Mommy. I'm fine. Really, don't worry," Bari said, releasing Hazel's arm and rubbing Hazel's back as they walked.

"Now, I don't wanna make you mad, but I'm gonna say this much: If Earl ain't treatin' you right, you better tell somebody. You got family and you know we'll be right here if you need us. You ain't by yourself."

"Okay, Mommy. I hear you. But I promise you everything is all right. I promise."

"Okay, Bari, I'm gonna take your word for it. But don't you forget what I said. And you call me as often as you can."

"Yes, Mother dearest." Bari smiled.

"I'm not jokin'," Hazel said.

"I know."

Hazel's large suitcases were loaded into the luggage compartment on the bus. She boarded the bus and was lucky enough to get a window seat three rows behind the driver.

BARI WAS SURPRISED at the empty feeling that she had when Hazel got on that bus to leave. Having her nearby to laugh with and talk about old times with took Bari back to a time when life was simple, comfortable. Now it was time to move forward and see where fate was leading her.

As she climbed into Barbara's car, Bari's heart sat somewhere in her lap. She took the backseat so that she could steal time to be quiet with her thoughts. Franki sat up front with Barbara. The car pulled out of the bus terminal parking lot and headed eastbound to Nell's place.

No one said much after Nell got into the car except for an occasional comment about a pedestrian. Nobody knew what to say. They sensed Bari's discomfort.

"Isn't it amazing how the people start to look different from one neighborhood to another?" Barbara asked no one in particular. It was her futile attempt to lessen the tension in the car. In Manhattan, the people had a pep in their step. They looked bright in the face and you could even hear their laughter. Closer to Cheryl's apartment, it seemed darker and gloomy outside and hard times were written on just about everybody's face that they saw.

"I've noticed the change in the people, too," Franki said.

The buildings in the city were tall and beautifully decorated for the holidays. The decorations were brilliant. In Cheryl's neighborhood, the scenery changed drastically. Fewer stores and homes reflected the holiday spirit. Some of the windows on some of the apartment buildings had been strung with flickering lights, but too many were without. Poverty was prominent.

"If people truly are a product of their environment, then this is pretty sad," said Nell.

"That's pretty much how I feel right now," Bari said. Nobody touched that.

It was quiet in the car again. The tension started building up all over again as they pulled onto Cheryl's block.

"Don't park too close to the building," Franki ordered.

"I know that," Barbara said.

The women scanned every parked car on the block, looking for Earl's Maxima. It was nowhere in sight.

"Are you okay, Bari?" Franki asked, turning to look at her.

"No," Bari said. She was sitting in the backseat quietly looking out the window.

Barbara drove along to the middle of the block where they would have a bird's-eye view of the front door of Cheryl's building. Nobody could go into or out of the building without being seen by them.

"Okay, this is a good spot," Franki said. "If he isn't already inside, we'll see him when he pulls up."

They sat in the car for an hour. Waiting. Cheryl's block was usually busy with people all over the place. But for some reason, tonight there were only a few people passing by here and there. The only real action was a stray cat ripping open a plastic bag from a garbage pail that was toppled over.

"That's probably about the most excitement that we're gonna get tonight. I mean, does anybody feel as stupid as I do?" Bari asked. "We should actually be ashamed of ourselves. Here we are, four grown women sitting outside of our girlfriend's apartment, expecting her to be screwing around with my husband. Doesn't that sound crazy to anybody else or is it just me?"

"It's just you," Franki answered very quietly.

"I'm kind of excited, to tell you the truth," Barbara said. "I feel like I'm in some kind of a movie and we're staking out the bad guy."

"Well, enjoy it," Nell said. "Because this is as close to being in a movie as you'll ever be."

"Was that an insult?" Barbara asked, sounding injured.

"We've been out here for over an hour and not a creature has stirred, not even a mouse. Except for the damn stray cat ripping open a garbage bag."

"Hey, that's actually pretty funny." Nell laughed.

"So, Barbara," Bari continued, "what do you say we turn this death trap of yours around and let's all go back to our corners?"

"There's a man!" Barbara said.

"Get down!" Franki told them. They all crouched down in their seats.

"Where is he?" asked Nell.

"Over there," Barbara said, pointing in the direction that she was looking in.

"Is it Earl?" Bari asked.

"I don't know," Barbara responded.

"Well, it doesn't look like Earl. That man seems too short to be him," said Franki, peeking up high enough to see through the window.

"And too fat," Bari added, peeking up through the window, too.

"Why in the hell are you getting us all excited for nothing?" Franki frowned. Everybody sat back up in their seats.

"I couldn't see him good. I'm not wearing my contact lenses," Barbara told her.

"You're not wearing your contact lenses and you just drove us all the hell the way from freaking Manhattan, you blind bat?" Nell asked.

"Well, I could see the street signs when I got up close, and I could see the car lights all around me; that helps."

"That's it, goddammit! I'm driving back," Nell said, slapping herself hard on the knee.

Suddenly a car entered the block with its high-beam lights on.

"Duck," Franki told them. Everybody bent down again in their seats.

"It's him! It's him!" Barbara said. They all panicked.

"That son of a bitch is coming! I can't believe this shit. That bastard!" said Franki.

The car was just pulling up to theirs now. Three sets of eyes peeked up just enough to see the approaching car. All eyes were on the car but Bari's. She stayed in her crouching position frozen with fear or anger. She wasn't quite sure which.

"Oh, God, he sees us!" Barbara said.

"He couldn't have seen us," said Franki.

Bari could feel the bile rising in her throat. She couldn't breathe, let alone speak. She wished the ground would open up and swallow her. Beads of perspiration slid down from her armpits. The approaching car slowed down as it passed.

"Oh, God, oh, God, oh, God. I'm scared," Barbara chanted.

Then the car passed. It never came to a full stop. It continued on its way until the taillights were out of sight.

"It's okay, everybody. It wasn't him," said Franki.

"It wasn't him? After all that drama it wasn't him? That's it! Take me home! I've had enough for one night. I have just wasted two hours of my life," Bari fumed.

"Come on, Bari. Let's just wait a little while longer. I'm sure he's coming. Just a few minutes more," Franki said.

"All right, but just for a few minutes more. But can we at least get out and stretch our legs?" Bari asked.

"Sure we can get out and stretch our legs but we can't do it here. What if Earl pulls up? He'll see us," Franki said.

"Don't forget, Earl could already be inside," said Barbara.

"Gee, thanks a lot, Barbara," said Bari.

"Sorry," Barbara said, covering her mouth, embarrassed.

"Just drive, Barbara." Franki hit her on the back of the head with her gloves.

"Oh no, you don't," Nell said. "On the count of three you run out of the car and take this backseat and I'm taking the driver's seat. One, two, three."

Barbara and Nell dashed out of the car from either side and switched places. Nell put the car in drive and slowly pulled out of their parking space. She drove to the corner, then around the block.

"Bari?" asked Franki.

"Yeah?"

"What is Earl's license number?"

"W44 OWX. Why?"

"Because there's Earl's car," Franki said.

"Are you sure, Franki?" Bari asked, craning her neck to see what Franki saw. Everybody else in the car moved closer to the windows to take a look, too.

"I'm pretty sure. License number W44 OWX," said Franki.

"Oh, God," Bari said when she saw the car. She felt like the bottom to her life just fell out. The car was parked just ahead of them. The headlights on Barbara's car illuminated the license plate. "That son of a bitch. How dare he do this to me! How dare he!" said Bari. Bari grabbed the Club that had been placed at her feet in the back of the car and she jumped out of the car before Nell came to a full stop.

"Where are you goin', Bari?" Franki asked. She jumped out of the car and ran behind her. Bari walked briskly toward the car with the Club in hand.

"Bari, wait! Where are you goin'?" Franki asked, trying to keep up with her.

"I'm going to kill that bastard and that tramp bitch!"

"Wait up, Bari. You can't do that. Wait a minute!" said Franki.

Barbara and Nell jumped out of the car and caught up with Franki and Bari.

"What are you doin', Bari? Calm down," Nell said, grabbing onto Bari's arm.

Bari yanked her arm away from Nell. "I'm gonna get that son of a bitch!" Bari yelled.

"Don't do this, Bari," Franki demanded.

"Like hell I won't. After everything I've done. After all that I've put up with! Oh no! Earl is as good as dead!"

Franki tried to pull the Club out of Bari's hand, but Bari snatched her hand back. She stormed away from them, heading toward Cheryl's building.

"It's not worth it, Bari." Barbara started to cry. "Please don't do this to yourself. Think about it."

"Well, if I can't kill his ass then I'll kill his car. I'll take my frustrations out on his fucking car. And I don't give a flying fuck!"

Bari walked up to Earl's car. She raised the Club high above her head and slammed it down onto the rear window. A loud crack sounded as the glass shattered. When Bari lifted the Club again, it landed on the trunk, leaving a two-inch dent. She moved around to the side of the car and slammed the Club against the side door, then down onto the hood.

"Bari, stop it!" Franki yelled.

"Please, Bari, stop this," Barbara cried.

The three women started toward Bari to stop her. Bari stopped hitting the car long enough to raise the Club up in the air threateningly at them. After that, they stood by and let her vent her anger, all of it, on the car.

When Bari was done, the car was extremely damaged and she was extremely exhausted. "Take me home," Bari said.

"Fine," Franki said. "Let's get the hell out of here." The four of them got into the car and they sped away.

"So, what now?" Barbara asked when they were several blocks away from the scene. "What are you planning on doing now, Bari?"

"I don't know. I really don't know," Bari said, anger still sizzling in the pit of her belly.

"Well, I know," Nell said. "You're gonna pack your shit and leave. You don't need Earl. If you stay with him, you're just gonna teach him that it's okay to treat you the way that he does and he'll never stop doing this to you. And you know damn well you don't deserve that. Show him that you won't tolerate his bullshit."

"Earl scares me," Barbara said. "He doesn't seem like he'll take very well to Bari leaving him."

"Who cares how he takes it?" Franki said. "Bari is outta there. Otherwise, I may end up killing him my damn self. I think you're right about him, though, Barbara. I don't trust Earl, either." Franki turned herself around in the front seat and faced Bari. "You have to be very careful, Bari. Don't show Earl your anger yet. We're gonna get you out of there, but right now just go through the motions with him as if you know nothing, until we figure out how to do it so he won't see it coming. That smug son of a bitch. You're way too good for him."

"That's for sure," said Barbara.

"Start packing your stuff right away," continued Franki. "Little by little start packing your stuff, whenever he's not around."

"Yeah. And we'll help you move everything out when you're ready," Nell offered.

"Well, whatever we do we'd better do it soon, because I don't know how long I'm gonna be able to keep up that charade. I may crack before it's over," Bari said.

LATER THAT EVENING when Bari had settled in for the night, like every other night, she found it hard to relax. She'd told herself over and over again that she would no longer concern herself about Earl.

That somehow she would have to erase him from her heart. But each time she heard a sound outside she would run to the window and look through the blinds to see if it was him. Bari lay in bed and willed her mind to drift. She didn't want to dwell on any problems that she was having, and she certainly wasn't searching for any answers. Not right now. She wanted her mind clear, for once, just for a moment.

Bari heard the key in the door. She rolled over onto her stomach and squeezed her eyes shut. She took in a deep breath, then slowly let it out. She pretended to be asleep when Earl opened the door to the bedroom. He walked into the room and shut the door behind him. He took off his clothes in the dark and tossed them across the chair in the corner of the room, then sat on the edge of the bed. Bari stirred. She yawned, stretched, then opened her eyes. "You're home," she said, observing Earl's hung head.

"Yeah . . . I'm home." Earl didn't turn around to look at her. Even though the light was off, Bari could see his clenched jaw from the side of his face. She could tell he was upset. "I was in an accident. The car was totaled."

thirty-six

BARI HAD IT all planned out. Every time Earl left the house, she would start her packing. She had gone to the supermarket the day before and bought four boxes of large lawn bags. She couldn't wait until Earl finished getting dressed that morning. He told Bari that he had a job interview. Even though it was Saturday, Bari didn't question him. She was glad to see him go. She had gotten up with him and had breakfast laid out for him by the time he was dressed. Bari sat and drank her coffee with Earl while he ate. She never would have guessed in a million years that one day she would sit across the table from her husband and look at him and not feel anything. No fluttering heart, no weakness in the knees, no adoration, nothing. She felt nothing now but anger and bitter disappointment. Bari just sat there and listened to him talk his talk. "You know, sometimes you get signs that you can't ignore," Earl said. "I got a sign when I crashed that car. I think somebody was tryin' to tell me somethin'. From now on, I have a whole new outlook. There are a lot of things that I've been neglectin' around here: the house, you. . . . I intend to correct that."

It was hard for Bari to sit there and look at Earl and listen to the nonsense that he was spewing out. She couldn't believe that he was sticking to his lie about crashing the car. Anyway, it really didn't matter to her at this point. She believed that her destroying the car in the way that she did may have saved her from killing him.

"I wanna spend more time with you. Get reacquainted, you know?" Earl continued.

Only a week ago, Bari would have soaked up his words. She had wanted nothing more than for the two of them to be head over heels in love again like it was when they first got married. But she knew that those days were long gone now and they weren't coming back. Ever.

"And I was thinkin'," Earl continued, "it's time we started a family. I need to work on gettin' you pregnant."

Bari couldn't believe her ears. Five thousand drums beat loudly in her head and a million pins penetrated her entire body at the same time. She had a hard time breathing and her mouth went bone-dry. Bari had to breathe in very slowly to regain her composure. She knew that she would probably pass out if she didn't calm down. When she spoke, her voice could well have been that of an angel. "I think it's time we have a child, too."

Earl smiled at her. He got up, walked around the table, and kissed her on the cheek, and then he was out the door.

Bari locked the door behind Earl. She peeked through the blinds and watched him as far as she could. She ran back into the kitchen and grabbed one of the boxes of lawn bags from underneath the sink, then ran up to her bedroom and opened up the silver trunk that was set before her bed. She took everything out of the trunk and filled one of the large bags. When the first bag was full, she filled a second one. She went up into the tops and bottoms of the closets, packing only those things of hers that she wouldn't need right away and throwing out things that she no longer wanted. When Bari was done, she had filled six lawn bags.

Bari slid each bag all the way downstairs to the basement and packed them into either of the closets. Earl hardly ever looked in the basement closets, and Bari knew that even if he did look in them he would never look inside the plastic bags.

Next, she went through the linen closet and pulled out sets and sets of beautiful linen, cotton, satin, and lace sheets. Some were still in the packaging waiting for that special night that would never come. Bari packed them into the lawn bags, too.

Three and a half hours went by, and she had just dragged the ninth bag down to the basement. She was on her way back upstairs to the bedroom when she heard Earl's key in the first door. She had left the closet doors in the basement standing wide-open. If she moved quickly enough, she could get back down to the basement before Earl came in through the second door.

Bari made a run for it. She dashed down the hall toward the basement door, which was facing the front door. Just as she turned into the
opening to go down the basement steps, Earl came through the door.
Bari froze.

"Hey," Earl said, shutting the door behind him.

"Hey, yourself," said Bari.

"Why do you look like the cat who just swallowed the canary?" Earl
asked.

"Believe me, the look on my face has nothing to do with any cats or
canaries," Bari said, looking at her husband seductively.

Earl caught it. He put his bag on the floor and moved in closer to
her. He took her into his arms and started to grind his body very slowly
against hers. Bari could smell the alcohol right away. She cringed, then
tensed up when he ground his body up against hers.

"So, why don't you break it down for me? What exactly is that look
sayin'?" Earl asked her.

"I'll tell you what, let me go downstairs and shut off the lights in
the basement and then I'll come back to translate it for you."

"I have an even better idea." Earl lifted Bari up off the floor. He
wrapped her legs around his waist. "Why don't I come downstairs with
you and we can start working on that little bambino down there?" He
had already started down the first step.

"Oh no, honey, I want to make it real nice for you. Put me down
and I'll go ahead and do what I have to do and I'll meet you in the bedroom."

"Sounds like a plan," Earl said. He put Bari down on the steps and
went upstairs to the bedroom.

Bari listened until she heard the bedroom door open and close. She
ran down the stairs. She had packed both closets too full, so she had
to take some of the bags out of one closet and put them into the other.
When she was done, she threw herself up against each door and forced
it shut.

Beads of perspiration were on Bari's brow. She ran up the stairs to
the bathroom and sat down on the toilet seat, conditioning herself for
what was coming. She needed to quickly figure out what she would do
before Earl came knocking on the door and rushing her out like he always did. She shuddered at the thought of him. Bari didn't even know

who he was anymore. All she knew was that she was shattered. Her whole world. Gone. Just like that. Earl had told her all of the things that she wanted to hear, and she had believed him. He had spent night after night making love to her like she was the answer to his question. She didn't know now if it was the drugs that had led him to do what he did or if it was his lust for Cheryl. Either way, Bari knew that she wasn't in the equation.

"I was about to come in there and get you," Earl said when Bari went into the bedroom.

"What's the matter, you can't wait for gratification?" Bari asked, managing a sweet smile. Her eyes even twinkled.

"Get over here," Earl said.

Bari was wearing a white terry-cloth robe with nothing underneath but white cotton panties. Earl was lying on the bed bare-backed in his boxers.

Bari walked slowly over to the bed, dropping her robe as she walked. She watched Earl's eyes devour her. He took her by the hand and pulled her down to him.

"I wanna *feel* you," Earl said, cupping her buttocks and softly squeezing them. Massaging. He kissed her neck as she lay on top of him. He rolled Bari over so that she was beneath him. Bari didn't resist as Earl spread her legs apart. Her mind raced. What could she do? How in the world could she keep this man, this stranger in her life, from touching her? She felt Earl's moist lips kissing the insides of her thighs. She felt his lips going up higher and higher. He kissed her hairy mound. Panic set in.

"Earl!" Bari cried out in pain. She sprang up.

"What's the matter?" Earl asked.

"Oh, my God. My stomach." Bari clutched her stomach. "My period is about to come and I keep getting these excruciating pains in my stomach."

"Is that so?" Earl asked.

"I don't know what's wrong," Bari said.

"Well, is there anything that I can do?" he asked.

Bari squeezed her eyes shut and winced. She grabbed Earl's hand with her free one and held it tightly. "I just need to wait this out for a few minutes. I'm sure it'll pass." Bari breathed slowly, in and out.

"Are you gonna be okay?" Earl asked.

"I think so. Would you mind making me a cup of tea? Maybe it's a bad case of gas." Bari was still holding her stomach.

"No problem. I'll be right back," Earl said. He got up from the bed and went downstairs to the kitchen.

Bari jumped up from the bed and went over to the door and listened at the steps to make sure that Earl was in the kitchen. She ran back into the room and went over to the chair by the window where Earl's clothes were thrown. Bari picked up his pants and went through the pockets. She pulled out some dollar bills, fanned them out, and then shoved the money back into the pocket. From his other pocket she pulled out a ceramic pillbox and a small gold coke spoon. Bari's heart sank. She twisted open the pillbox and saw the white powdery substance that covered the bottom. She thought she heard Earl coming up the stairs, so she closed the pillbox, shoved his things back into his pocket, and jumped back into the bed holding her stomach. Earl stuck his head in the room to tell her that the tea would be ready in a minute; then he went back down the stairs. Moments later, he came back into the room carrying her tea.

"Okay, baby, sit up. Here's your tea. You have to drink it while it's hot," he said.

Bari pulled herself up into a sitting position and sipped the tea. Earl lay next to her stroking her thigh as she drank. Bari set the teacup down and cuddled next to Earl.

"I'm so sorry, Earl. I really wanted to do this, but I'm really not feeling good right now."

"That's okay. It ain't your fault. You'll make it up to me." He was flashing that debonair smile of his.

"I just want to lie here for a while and hope that whatever this is passes. You're not upset, are you?" Bari asked.

"Nah, I'm not upset. Do you want to see a doctor?"

"No, that won't be necessary."

"Okay, if you say so."

They lay there entwined. Within the hour, Bari drifted off to sleep.

thirty-seven

*B*ARI HAD BEEN packing her things for one week now. Every chance she got, she would pack. She had been careful to pack all of her important papers and other things that she knew she would need. There was not much more that she could pack without Earl noticing.

Bari thought about the evening ahead while she and Earl were getting dressed. This was the night that Choler-Raines would announce her promotion to associate partner, and they planned to do it in style for her at the Breslin Grande Ballroom. Bari dreaded it, because she knew that she would have to put on the performance of her life. She would have to go before her coworkers and appear the deliriously happy wife and Earl, the debonair, doting, and faithful husband. She didn't need the pressure.

"Have you seen my striped gray tie?" Earl asked.

"Isn't it on the tie rack? I think you should wear the black bow tie."

Earl spun around the tie rack inside the closet door. He pulled out the black bow tie, then stood in front of the mirror holding it in place. "Yeah." He smiled. "You're right, baby. You see that? You know what you're talkin' about. That's why I keep you around." Earl was fully dressed in his black Armani tuxedo.

"Okay, how do I look?" Earl asked, his arms stretched out to his sides in front of Bari.

"You'll be the most handsome man there." Bari smiled.

Save for the bags under Earl's eyes and the worry lines that recently appeared on his forehead, Bari meant what she said. And his face, his face was a lot thinner these days.

"All right, so I'm gonna go ahead and take care of my business deal across town. I should be no more than a couple of hours. I'll meet you at the ballroom."

"Okay," Bari said, not looking away from the mirror while she tweezed her eyebrows.

"Wish me luck. This is the proposition of a lifetime for me," Earl said.

"Good luck," Bari told him.

Since Earl stretched his arms out to her for a hug, Bari hugged him. *Son of a bitch,* she thought. *A business deal. What kind of business deal could Earl possibly be involved in? The bastard is probably going over to lay that trifling no-good slut Cheryl. May they both drop dead during the act.*

"Okay, I'm outta here," Earl said, and he was gone.

WHEN BARI LOOKED at the clock, it was six thirty. She figured she had plenty of time to take a long, leisurely bath and still get ready. She wanted to look stunning tonight. She knew that she hadn't been herself lately and she had been looking like crap at work. Well, tonight was special. It was her night and she wanted to feel good for a change.

Bari thought about how Earl's face used to light up when she entered the room. He made her feel like the most beautiful woman in the world—the *only* woman in the world. Now it didn't matter to her what he liked or disliked. As far as she was concerned, their whole marriage was a lie. A horrible, terrible lie.

Bari went into the bathroom, sprinkled floral-scented Calgon into the tub, then ran her bathwater as hot as she could stand it. She immersed herself into the water and slid as far down into the tub as she could without wetting her hair.

Since Earl needed the rental car for his meeting, Bari had arranged to be picked up by the company car service. The driver was right on time at 7:45 P.M. When Bari stepped out onto her porch, she was wearing a red Tahari silk dress with spaghetti straps and a matching bolero jacket. The tiny pleats at the hemline of the dainty dress danced happily with every step she took. She wore her 24-karat gold diamond pendant necklace and matching diamond earrings that Earl had bought her from Tiffany's on their first wedding anniversary. Her hair was swept up away from her face and long, loose curls hung from the top of her head. Soft tendrils dropped down her face and at the nape of her neck. She put on a long black velvet cape to top off her outfit.

As Bari approached the car, the driver got out to open the door for her. When Bari looked up at him she saw the most handsome man that she had seen in a long time. His smile revealed the whitest teeth that she had ever seen on a person, and his skin was dark and smooth. He got into the car and shifted into drive. Bari was embarrassed when he looked into his rearview mirror and caught her looking at him. She quickly shifted her eyes. She didn't want to give him the wrong impression.

"Excuse me, miss," the driver said. His voice was as smooth as his skin. "I really don't mean to be rude, but you are so beautiful. Why in the world would such an obviously classy woman like yourself be going out unescorted?" He seemed genuinely concerned.

Bari smiled shyly. Then she saw his wedding band. Her blood started to boil. She couldn't respond to him at first because a huge lump welled up in her throat. She looked at him and thought what a lousy bastard he was. She wondered if his wife even suspected that he flirted with women while he worked. This could be *her* husband. "I'll tell you what, I would thank you to keep your eyes on the road and just do your job. That is, make sure that I reach my destination safely and in a timely fashion. I don't think that you should concern yourself with anything other than that."

"I-I'm sorry if I was out of line," the driver said.

Bari didn't respond. She turned her head and glared out the window.

THE TEMPERATURE WAS mild for January. Many of Bari's coworkers took to the outdoors to smoke and get some cool air. Everybody watched to see who was getting out of the car that was pulling up. The driver got out of the car and walked around to the passenger side and opened the door. Bari stepped out of the car.

"Have yourself a good evening, miss," the driver said.

"I certainly will," Bari said coldly, and walked off to join her coworkers on the curb.

"You look gorgeous as usual, Bari," Sidney said.

"Thank you, Sidney, you look hot yourself," Bari said, checking out his purple silk tuxedo with a purple leather cummerbund and purple leather bow tie. His shoes were purple, too.

"Where is that beautiful specimen of a husband of yours?" Annie, the old receptionist, asked.

"He was called away on business. He's meeting me here later on," Bari said.

"You know," Annie went on, "Earl is the only one I care to dance with. He's the only one who can probably keep up with me. All of these other fellows are too old." Annie threw her head back in raucous laughter.

"You're something else, Annie. I'll make sure Earl saves a dance for you. Why is everybody outside?" Bari asked.

"Because it's hot as hell inside. And because David is giving the Choler-Raines history speech. We've all heard it a thousand times before, so I don't have any idea as to why in the world he'd think we'd want to hear it again tonight. He's gotta be stopped," Annie whined.

"Come, Bari love." Sidney took Bari by the arm. "Let's get you inside so that David can see you and remember why we're here tonight."

The two of them walked arm in arm into the ballroom and everybody else followed.

"There she is . . . ," David said, cutting his speech short.

All heads turned to the entrance as Bari walked in. The room filled with applause. "For she's a jolly good fellow . . . ," they sang.

Bari blushed. She put her finger to her mouth and playfully shushed the crowd as she made her way over to her reserved table.

Sheldon Mangrove, Richard King, Mickey Davis, and Carol Shaffer, all from executive row, were present and seated at Bari's table. One by one they all stood and shook Bari's hand before she sat down. The table was set dead center in the room.

While the tablecloths on all of the other tables were cream colored, the one on Bari's table was gold. Long-stemmed crystal goblets were set on each table, and fine china dishes and sterling silver graced every setting. At the center of each table was a pot of white gardenias. Two large floral displays were set on either side of the podium where David stood.

All of the smiles in the room were genuine. Everybody knew that these occasions marked a growth sign for the company. The company recognized talent when they saw it and they understood fully that it was the creativity, hard work, and dedication of the young, fresh new talent entering the firm that was responsible for the level of success that they all enjoyed. This is why the executives thought it important to acknowledge their staff and show their appreciation through pro-motion. It encouraged firm commitment. They stood solidly by their guiding principle, and so far so good.

"When I first interviewed Bari for the job, somehow I knew in my gut that she would be a star," David said, proudly singing Bari's praises while he made subtle hints that it was his taking her under his wing and his direction that led her to becoming the advertising maven that she had become. Bari didn't mind that he was sharing in her credit. She figured that for whatever reason, David felt he needed to impress this group. She knew for herself all the hard work, the blood, sweat, and tears, that she had put into her performance. She knew her stuff and she knew that she required very little help from management. That was all that she needed to know. She would accept this promotion knowing that she earned it the old-fashioned way.

The evening had been in full swing for a while. Bari made her rounds and mingled with her coworkers. Each time somebody greeted her they would ask about Earl's whereabouts. Earl was blatantly late. Once again, he had no regard for her or what was important to her. Every now and again, she would glance at the door to see if he had come in. He hadn't.

Son of a bitch, Bari thought.

thirty-eight

TOMMY'S PLACE WAS busy as usual. Traffic was flowing steadily, with customers coming and going. Others had come to make their usual purchases and to hang out. Tommy had put out a dish of cocaine that was constantly being passed around. The drugs and the laughter were plentiful. His friends had gotten comfortable. A lot of them walked barefoot and others were just sprawled around the place.

Cheryl sat next to Earl on the couch. One of her legs was draped over his. She put her cup of rum and Coke to Earl's lips for him to take a sip. Earl had already had too much to drink. He was inebriated. His eyes were glassy, bulging, and bloodshot. His tuxedo was wrinkled and disheveled now. Cheryl had reminded him earlier to leave to go and meet Bari, but he told her that he would leave when he was good and ready to leave. Earl knew that he should have left, too, but the conversations in the room had been so stimulating to him that he'd lost track of the time.

It was 2:00 A.M when Earl was ready to leave.

"Baby, you look catatonic. Why don't we just go to my place so you can sleep it off? Okay, Earlie?"

"Are you okay to drive?" Tommy asked him.

"Hell yeah, I can drive. I'm all right." Earl staggered when he stood up.

Tommy looked to Cheryl for reassurance.

"Believe me," Cheryl said. "If he says he's okay to drive, he's okay. I've seen him drive in much worse condition."

"And you let him drive?" Tommy asked.

"You know Earlie; you can't stop him from doin' nothin' that he wants to do," she said.

"Yeah, but if he's drunk . . ." Tommy didn't press the issue.

"Come on, Cheryl, I'll drop you off," Earl slurred.

"That's all right, Earlie. It doesn't make sense for me to go home to my empty apartment. I'll just hang around here for a little while longer. You don't mind, do you, baby?" she asked.

"No," Earl said. He was too high to care. He left.

Earl stood outside the apartment in the vestibule of Tommy's building. He leaned back against the wall and closed his eyes. Earl patted both his pant pockets and found the keys. They fell to the floor when he pulled them out of his pocket. He picked them up, then stumbled out the front door and onto the stoop. He used the handrail to support himself down the stairs. His car was parked in front of the building. Earl bent over to unlock the door and lost his footing. He fell to the ground, his legs sliding underneath the car. After a struggle, he managed to pull himself from under the car and back up on his feet. Earl got into the car and started the engine. He flicked on the headlights and activated his left-turn indicator. Earl pulled halfway out of his parking spot. He stopped for a moment and put his head back on the headrest. Earl shut his eyes. Three minutes went by before he opened them again.

Earl finally pulled out onto the street, driving a lot slower than usual. The car went in and out of the lane as he drove along. For a fleeting moment, his eyesight was blurred. He blinked several times to refocus.

THE AFFAIR AT the Breslin ballroom had been winding down for the past half hour. Bari was now officially an associate partner at Choler-Raines. She was elated. She had only dreamt of becoming a partner in a firm, any firm, on any level, and now, from her own hard work and perseverance, she had earned it. That felt real good.

The management team and some of Bari's coworkers came over to her table one last time before they made their exit from the ballroom. They congratulated her and wished her continued success. She wondered where the hell Earl was. He had humiliated her for the last time.

Annie approached Bari. "I hope your husband is okay. I see he never showed up."

Sidney was next. "Hey, love, what ever happened to Earl? I was looking forward to seeing him."

"I'm sure he's okay, Sidney. He told me that this might happen," Bari lied.

"If you need a ride home, I'll be happy to give you a lift," said David.

"Thanks, David, but Barbara is giving me a ride," Bari said.

Bari and Barbara said good night and headed toward the door. When they reached the parking lot, they noticed Sheldon Mangrove and Carol Shaffer peering into the window of a dark blue Honda. They walked away from the car shaking their heads. Another coworker went by and seemed to find interest in the car.

Bari and Barbara chatted on about the events of the evening as they walked through the lot. When they were closer to the car that everybody seemed so interested in, Bari thought to herself that the car was the same as Earl's rental car.

As she thought it, Barbara said it. "Hey, wait a minute, Bari. Doesn't that look exactly like the car you guys rented?" she asked.

"I was just thinking the same thing, but it couldn't be Earl's car because why would he be sitting outside in the parking lot?"

"I have no idea," Barbara said. "But I'm curious. I wanna take a closer look."

Without a word, Bari followed Barbara over to the car. Before they reached the car, two more people walked by the car, looked inside, and laughed pretty loudly as they passed.

Bari couldn't believe her eyes when she saw Earl sleeping in the car. His head was way back on the headrest, and his mouth was hanging open. Desperation gripped her and she felt faint. "My God!" she said. "I can't believe this son of a bitch! What am I gonna do, Barbara?" Bari was desperately looking all around to see if anyone was watching them.

"Calm down, Bari; that's the first thing." Barbara's voice was as soothing as it always was. "We're just gonna walk out of here and leave this bastard sitting right where he is. Then we're going to your house; we're gonna call those movers, and get you the hell out of there. Just be cool and let's go."

"My God, but everybody must have seen him sitting out here," Bari said.

"Forget about them; forget about him. Let's go." Barbara took charge. She took Bari by the arm and hustled her into the car. Barbara started up the car and sped out of the parking lot.

"Do you still have that business card for the movers?" Barbara asked.

"Yeah." Bari sounded weak.

"Do me a favor: Reach into my pocketbook and take out my cell phone. Get them on the line and tell them to meet us at your house posthaste. Then call up Franki and Nell and tell them that we're on our way to get them. Tell them the deal."

Bari made the phone calls. Franki and Nell were ready when they got there. When the women walked into Bari's house, they wasted no time getting started. Franki and Nell went downstairs to the basement and pulled open the closet doors and started pulling out all the plastic bags that Bari had stacked up in there. The women dragged the bags upstairs and set them at the front door. Bari stayed upstairs. She was pulling out some of the boxes that she had put into the living room closets and putting them in the center of the floor. She was crying the whole time. Barbara was helping Bari move the boxes and pull furniture from the walls.

"Come on, Bari, please stop crying. I know this is hard for you, but haven't you shed enough tears for Earl already? The crying is over. Those tears are just slowing us down. We need to get you out of here in one piece. We don't know when Earl is gonna get here, and personally, I'm already scared out of my mind."

"Okay." Bari sniffed. She wiped her tears and took a deep breath. "Yeah, okay. I can do this."

"Of course you can do this. All right then, let's get busy."

Bari wiped her eyes with the backs of her hands. She took a deep breath and put some pep in her step.

Bari went upstairs to her bedroom. She quickly changed into a pair of blue jeans and a gray hooded sweatshirt. She took out a T-shirt and some jeans for Barbara to change into. "Barbara!" Bari called down the stairs. "Grab these!" Bari said, then threw the clothes down the stairs. In the bedroom, she removed the handmade powder packet that she had gotten from Zuma from underneath Earl's pillow. Bari pushed a chair up against the door and climbed up on it and reached up to the ledge over the door and removed Zuma's words—the printed words of

Zuma's ritual. The words that were supposed to prevent all evil spirits from entering the room and to chase all the ones that were already in there away.

Bari almost laughed out loud as she climbed down from the chair, crumbling the paper with both hands and throwing it into the wastebasket. She reached into the small porcelain vase on her dresser and took out a little brown paper bag that held the herbal mixture that she mixed into Earl's food and drinks. The herbs were to decrease his desire for alcohol and drugs. Another joke. Bari tossed that, too.

DOWNSTAIRS, FRANKI, BARBARA, and Nell pulled furniture out from the walls, and they went through the kitchen, the living room, and all the upstairs bedrooms, tying up all the wires from the electronic appliances.

Barbara ran to the window and peeked through the blinds.

"Are the movers here yet?" Nell asked.

"I don't see any movers, but I don't care about them right now. I'm making sure that Earl is not out there."

"Very good," said Nell.

The women gathered all of the appliances in the center of the living room floor for the movers. When Bari came downstairs she looked around the room. Her eyes lingered on her plants. Her dried-out, droopy, sad plants. The plants looked just like her, she thought. "I guess they really do pick up your vibes," she said aloud. Bari went over to the windowsill, dragging a large box with her. She picked out the plants that didn't look so bad and the ones that she thought she could save, and she set them in the box.

Soon the movers were ringing the doorbell. Four big, burly men walked through the door. The men moved quickly. All they needed to know was who was in charge, in case they had any questions. They were told to direct all of their questions to Bari. The movers had seen this situation many times before. They understood that time was of the essence. The last thing anybody wanted was for the husband or boyfriend to walk in on them while they were moving out the wife or girlfriend.

thirty-nine

T HE PARKING LOT at the Breslin ballroom was empty with the exception of Earl's car. It was 3:40 A.M., and the old white-haired attendant wanted to go home. It had been a long night and he was tired. The attendant waited at least twenty minutes for the car to pull out on its own, but he couldn't wait any longer. It was already ten minutes past sign-off. He thought that he saw somebody sitting in the car but couldn't be sure. Why would anybody just be sitting in the parking lot for so long? If somebody was in the car, he would have to tell them that they had to leave. It was that simple.

The parking attendant walked toward the car very cautiously. The closer he got to the vehicle, the clearer it became to him that someone was, in fact, in the car. He took out his nightstick and tapped on the driver's side window.

Earl was startled awake. He opened his eyes and pushed the car door open in one swift motion. Earl shoved the door so hard against the attendant's legs that he lost his balance and fell to the ground. Before the man could compose himself, Earl bent over him with a gun to his head.

"You wanna fuck with me? Huh? You wanna fuck with me?"

The action played out in Earl's mind in slow motion. He felt powerful. He had just bought a gun from Tommy earlier that evening. Earl liked the feeling that it gave him. He was proud of himself. He had drawn the gun as if it was second nature to him. He figured he could learn to like it.

"Take it easy, man. I ain't gonna hurt ya," the attendant said.

"You ain't gonna hurt me? Ha! Ha! Ha! You ain't gonna hurt me.

Ha! Ha! Ha! I got a gun pointin' to your motherfuckin' head and you . . . ha, ha!"

"I'm just a parking attendant tryin' to do my job, man. I'm just three months away from retirement. Please," the old man said, holding both hands up in front of him.

"I thought you were some punk tryin' to jack me. Man, get your ass up," Earl told him. Earl put the gun back in his waistband, then smoothed out his clothing. He extended his hand to the old man and helped him up. "You gotta be careful who you walk up on, man," Earl said. "And you gotta excuse me; I'm a little jumpy. There's a lot of crazy people around here." He offered his hand to the man again for a handshake. "You have yourself a good evening," Earl said. He looked all around at the deserted parking lot. He glanced at his watch. It was 4:00 A.M. "Oh shit, I blew it," he said.

Earl got into his car and took off like a lightning bolt. He would think of a plausible excuse to tell Bari when he got there.

forty

BARI'S NERVES WERE on high. She didn't think that the movers were moving quickly enough.

"What's going on? Am I not paying you guys enough money?" She reached into her pocket and pulled out a roll of cash. She peeled off two fifty-dollar bills and slapped them into the head mover's hand. "Now do you think you can move any faster?" She peeled off another bill. "Here! Give this to your buddies. Maybe now they can get the lead out."

"Oh, er, come on, guys, you heard the lady. Let's move it; hurry up!" the head mover said, as he shoved the bills into his pocket.

Bari put her palm to her head. She felt like it was about to explode.

"Calm down, Bari." Franki spoke in a low, even tone. "The house is almost empty. See? Everything is movin' right along." Franki rubbed Bari's arm to comfort her.

The moving men hustled. They operated like a well-oiled machine. The four men wrapped up the last few large furniture items and loaded them onto the truck.

"I guess that's about it, ma'am," the head mover said when they were done.

"Could you inspect the house to make sure everything is out? I don't imagine you'll be wantin' to come back here anytime soon." He smiled, showing chipped coffee-stained teeth.

Bari couldn't smile back. "Sure," she said, and she and the other women went from room to room, from upstairs to downstairs, opening and closing closet doors, making sure they hadn't missed anything.

"Leave him nothing!" Franki yelled. "That's just what he deserves. Nothing!"

Franki had even urged Bari to take the telephones, but Bari didn't listen. She knew deep down that Earl would need to contact her when he realized that she was gone. The only remaining items were Earl's clothing and the telephones on the kitchen wall and the living room floor.

"Okay, we're done here. Let's go," Bari said, and they left the house. Bari locked the doors, then tossed the keys back into the house through the mail slot. The women piled into Barbara's car and the movers got into their truck.

The head mover leaned into the car window. "Where to, ma'am?" he asked.

"Oh, my God, I wasn't prepared for this tonight. I haven't found an apartment yet. I was looking for one, but I . . ."

"May I suggest you store your stuff with us? We're not only movers; we do storage, too. Store your stuff with us and I'll give you the first month free," the mover said.

"It's hardly free," Franki said. "Surely she greased your palm enough already to cover the first month or so."

The mover smiled sheepishly. "All right, where to?"

"Storage," Bari conceded.

Very slowly the moving truck rolled up the driveway ramp. The driver was being careful not to shake up the truck's contents. Bari was turning all about in the car as the women sat there in the driveway behind the moving truck waiting for it to pull out of the driveway. She knew that she couldn't even think about relaxing until her house was well out of her sight.

EARL WAS DOING 65 miles per hour in the residential zones. He cursed every red light that caught him. He punched the steering wheel as hard as he could. This time it was a stop sign that caught him. A few oncoming cars prevented him from making a quick left turn. He was two blocks away from home.

THE MOVING TRUCK came to a standstill just as they pulled out onto the street. The driver got out of the truck.

"What the hell is he doing?" Bari yelled.

"I have no idea," Franki said. "And we're not stickin' around here to find out, either. Go around him, Barbara!"

Barbara swerved around the truck and went ahead to the corner of the block. They all turned around and looked back at the driver as if he'd lost his mind as they waited at the red light.

He walked around to the back of the truck where a long chain was still hanging from the truck onto the ground. He opened the back of the truck and threw in the chain. On the way back into the truck, the driver stopped to stuff his pant legs into his boots, and then he loosened his scarf around his neck.

"He's crazy!" Bari said, punching the backseat. "What the hell is his problem? Get in the truck, goddammit!" she yelled, as if the mover could hear her.

Barbara shot out into the intersection when the light turned green. A huge cloud of exhaust followed them as they sped off.

The driver finally climbed back into the truck and pulled off. The truck reached the corner of the block and stopped at the red light.

EARL PULLED ONTO the block from the other direction. Just as the moving truck pulled off at the corner, Earl pulled into his driveway. He got out of the car and looked up at the house to see if any lights were on. He figured if he was lucky, Bari would be asleep and he could deal with her later. He carefully climbed the stairs up to his front door. Earl didn't notice the small series of pictures that usually hung on the vestibule walls missing when he went inside. When he walked into the living room, his mouth fell open. The room was empty. Every piece of furniture, every vase, every picture that had hung on the wall, was gone.

"What the fuck?! We were robbed! Bari! Bari, please be okay. . . ." Earl went running into the dining room. It was empty, too. He ran upstairs to the bedroom.

"Bari! Bari, where are you?" Earl went into the guest room. The guest room was empty. "Is this a fuckin' joke?" He barreled downstairs to the basement. Empty. Then it hit him like a ton of bricks. Earl went back upstairs to the living room and dropped to his knees.

"Oh shit . . . aw, man. Where the fuck is she?" Earl asked. "Bari, where the fuck are you?" He noticed the telephone on the floor. Earl stood up and stumbled over to the phone. He dialed Franki's apartment. The phone rang four times before the answering machine clicked on. Earl slammed the phone down onto its cradle and leaned back up against the wall. "Damn, damn, damn," he said. "Oh shit." Earl's eyes filled with tears. He put both of his hands over his eyes and cried out loud. When he calmed himself down he tore through the front door and got into his car. He headed to Franki's house. He did 65 miles per hour all the way. He was at Franki's house in twelve minutes.

Earl jumped out of his car, leaving the door standing wide-open. He took the steps two by two. He rang the bell two times and waited for a response. He rang two more times. No answer. Earl leaned on the bell for a good thirty seconds. He slammed his fist into the door, then turned and ran down the stairs and got back into his car. He sat there for several minutes contemplating his next move. A hit. He could think better once he had a hit. Earl took out his ceramic pillbox and took several hits of cocaine. He put away his package and sped off of Franki's block. *Damn.* The hits felt good to him. Earl slowed down his pace after a few miles. He had nowhere to rush to. He tried to think of what could have gone wrong. What would make Bari leave him so abruptly? It must have been the celebration dinner, he thought. He knew he should have been there, but fuck. Was it that big a deal that she had to leave him? She didn't tell him that anything was wrong. Everything seemed fine. What the fuck was her problem?

It became obvious to Earl that somebody had been talking to Bari and putting ideas into her head. Probably her bitch sister, Franki. Bari would never have left him on her own.

Earl decided to go home and figure out what to do. He needed to contact Bari. If he was able to speak to her, he knew that he could make the situation right again.

forty-one

ARI AND HER friends sat in the car and watched the moving men unload the big white graffiti-ridden truck. They watched as Bari's world, every piece of it, was being neatly stored away at the Rapid Moving and Storage Warehouse. As Bari watched the men work, she felt sad. She realized at that moment what it was to be truly sad. She couldn't help but wonder about Earl and how he would react when he discovered that she was gone. Bari leaned forward on the seat in front of her and rested her chin in her hands.

"You know, Franki, I didn't plan for this to happen tonight. I didn't get a chance to make any real plans. I was supposed to start looking at apartments, but I've been so busy. I have nowhere to stay."

"Of course you have somewhere to stay. You'll stay with me," Franki said.

"I can't stay with you. That's the first place Earl will come looking for me. And to be honest with you, I'm petrified," Bari said.

"He doesn't have to know that you're with me. I'll tell him you're not there. And I'll certainly make him aware that he's no longer welcome in my home," Franki said.

Bari's heart ached. *Imagine,* she thought. *Earl no longer welcome.* "I guess I could stay temporarily. Thanks, Sis," said Bari.

"You're welcome," Franki said.

"What do you think Mommy's gonna say when I tell her I left Earl?" Bari asked.

"She'll say, 'Hallelujah!'" said Franki.

"Just for the record, I want you to know that I'm sorry I doubted you about Earl," Bari said.

"Would you two like to be alone to talk about this?" Barbara asked.

"No, no," Bari answered quickly. "Actually, I want to tell you all at one time how much I thank you. I'm sure that at different times every one of you tried to warn me about my situation. Anyway, I know who my true friends are. I know it's gonna take me some time getting used to being alone. I mean, I've been with Earl for so long, I feel out of sorts. You know, like I'm standing on a tall mountain and if I look down I'll lose my footing."

"Time," said Nell. "Time's gonna fix that. Believe it or not, in time this will be a vague memory and soon enough we will be sitting around laughing our asses off about this. And about how Earl probably fell to his knees when he came home to that big, empty house. And how you packed all your shit and hauled ass . . ."

Barbara and Franki laughed and nodded in agreement.

"See, we're laughing already," Nell said.

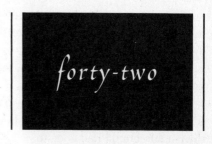

forty-two

FRANKI SIPPED THE last drop of her mint tea and placed the cup back on the matching porcelain saucer. She closed the *Essence* magazine that she had been leafing through and stood up, stretching.

"I'm gonna brush my teeth and turn in. Do you want my bedroom tonight?"

"No, the den is fine," said Bari.

"Good night, Bari." Franki walked slowly down the long corridor to the bathroom, turning the hall light off behind her. Her heart felt heavy for her sister. Franki knew that this was hard for Bari, but it was for her own good. It was good for her sanity and her physical well-being. All Franki could do right now was give Bari support and encourage her to move on.

BARI TOOK THE seven unused vacation days that she had carried over from the previous year. Her plan was to return to work after her seven days and then she would be off on a business trip to Chicago for five days following that. She was happy with the arrangement. The more time she spent away from the office, the less of a chance there was for Earl to catch up with her. Franki took a day off, too, to stay home and help Bari get her business in order.

Franki prepared a hefty breakfast for them. They both loved beef bacon, so she fried an entire package and made scrambled eggs with plenty of cheese. Franki even attempted Hazel's recipe for spoon bread. She squeezed a whole bag of Florida oranges by hand for what she considered to be the best orange juice in the world.

Franki was a little disappointed when Bari told her that she didn't have an appetite. Especially since the spoon bread came out looking and tasting so good.

"Come on, Bari. Why did you let me cook all of this food if you knew you didn't want any?"

"I thought I told you that I wasn't really hungry. I'm sorry, Franki. All right, I'll have just a little bit," Bari said when she thought about all the trouble Franki had gone to.

Franki was usually very conscious of what she ate. But not today. Today she ate until she couldn't eat any more. What Bari didn't eat Franki ate. Bari sat across from Franki and picked at her food.

"Your spoon bread tastes a lot like Mommy's, Franki," Bari said.

"Oh yeah? Who can tell from looking at you? You're eating the food like it's a burden."

"I know; I'm sorry."

"That's okay. There's more for me. Believe me, I'll be spending my evening at the gym working off all of these extra calories," said Franki.

Franki sat with glassy eyes, moaning and rubbing her belly, when she was done. "I swear, I look like I'm at least three months pregnant," Franki said, smoothing her shirt over her stomach to accentuate the mound that once was her flat belly.

"You look more like you're six months," Bari said. "It's a good thing you're wearing that oversized shirt."

"That's right. I knew exactly what I was doing." Franki laughed. Suddenly she stopped laughing. Her eyes bulged as she clutched her stomach. "Oh, my God! I'm in labor!"

This time Bari laughed, too. The telephone rang.

"I'm sure it's Earl. This is his fourth time calling. When is he going to stop?" asked Bari.

"He obviously likes talking to my answering machine," Franki said.

The phone rang two more times before Earl's voice filled the room. He sounded angry.

"Franki, if you're there, could you please pick up the phone? I need to contact Bari. Is she there? Bari, if you're there, could you please call me. I just want to talk to you, that's all. Look, somebody call me back!" The message ended.

Bari shook her head from side to side as she spoke. "The only way that I'm going to be able to make him stop calling here is if I meet with him and talk to him and explain to him that it's over between us, that he may as well move on with his life."

"Promise me you won't do that. Come on, Bari, we talk about women who do stupid shit like that. He could hurt you."

"What are you saying? You think Earl is one of those men?" Bari said.

"Of course he is, Bari. How many times has he hit you for real? Earl does drugs, remember?"

Bari hung her head. She got up from the table and started to scrape all the leftovers into one dish and clean up the breakfast dishes.

EARL SAT ON the floor in the living room, his back locked against the wall. He meant to be cool on the phone, but the thought of Bari staying away from him like this really pissed him off. He needed a drink, bad.

Fuck, his cash was running out. He would do whatever it took to get Bari back. He looked around the house. Empty. His eyes scrolled along the walls from top to bottom. Bare. The warmth was gone, no hustle, no bustle, nothing. For now he'd head over to Cheryl's apartment. He was hungry. She would be good for a hot meal. She loved to feed him. Cheryl was starting to bug him, though. Ever since she found out that Bari had left him, Cheryl kept insisting that he move in with her. Earl had another plan, though.

Earl took the drive to Cheryl's house. He hated her neighborhood. "A tired, played-out scene," Earl would say whenever he saw some of the dudes who lived there hanging out on the corners toting forty-ounce bottles of beer, talking loud and saying nothing. Cheryl knew all the guys who hung out around there. She said they "looked out" for her. Earl was sure that they did.

He parked the overdue rental car and made his way into the building and up to Cheryl's third-floor walk-up apartment.

Earl couldn't believe it when he got up to the top of the stairs and saw Cheryl standing on the landing wearing a sky-blue-colored teddy. He figured she'd lost her mind. Anybody could have walked outside their door and seen her. They were all probably looking through their peepholes at her. She loved attention.

"What are you doin'?" Earl asked, reaching the top step and standing face-to-face with Cheryl. "Are you crazy?"

"Crazy for you." Cheryl threw both her arms up around Earl's neck
as she moved in closer to him and started grinding slowly against him.
Earl removed her arms from around his neck. "Come on inside. I got
something for you," Cheryl said.

Cheryl walked quickly ahead of him into her apartment. By the
time she turned to face Earl again, the two snaps on her teddy were
undone. She stood there before him with her swollen breasts pointing
at him and looked at him provocatively. "Do you still want to eat?" she
asked him.

"I'm not hungry anymore," Earl answered, almost too gruffly.

"But I thought—"

"I need to make a phone call," Earl said, cutting her off.

"You know where the phone is." Cheryl crossed her arms in front
of her. "And who do you wanna call anyway? Bari? Bari's not even with
you anymore. Are you gonna let her ruin our night?"

Earl looked at her, expressionless, as he held the receiver to his ear,
waiting for an answer at the other end of the phone.

"What are you callin' her for? Bari is nothing but a dumb bitch.
She doesn't want you, leave her alone. I told you I'll take care of you!"
Cheryl said.

Earl got the answering machine, so he hung up the phone. A calm-
ness came over him and he stared blankly at Cheryl for at least twenty
seconds. He moved his eyes away from her and looked down at the
floor. He looked up at her again, then slowly moved toward her.

Cheryl smiled. "I knew you'd see things my way."

Earl moved very close up to Cheryl. She smiled up into his face.
Still expressionless, Earl pressed his body up to hers and edged her
back against the wall. Seductively Cheryl put her arms up around
Earl's neck again. Earl's hand cupped her chin and pressed her head
hard upward against the wall. He put his face very close to hers. He
spoke clearly and concisely.

"Let me tell you one goddamned thing. Don't you *ever, ever* call my
wife a dumb bitch. You're the only dumb bitch that I know. And as far
as I'm concerned, you're not worth much more than a wooden fuckin'

nickel, you tramp junkie bitch! You're not in my wife's league. How she even had you as a friend is a mystery to me."

Cheryl didn't speak. Her bottom lip trembled and tears formed at the corners of her eyes.

"Now what did you wanna do?" Earl continued. "You wanna fuck? Huh? You wanna fuck?" Earl held Cheryl's chin steady. His fingers pressed harder into her skin. He used his free hand to unbuckle his belt. He unsnapped his pants and they fell halfway down his legs. He used the same hand to rip off Cheryl's thong. Earl flipped Cheryl around to make her back face him. He rammed his hardened penis into her vagina from behind. Cheryl screamed out in pain. Earl continued to jam her. Harder and harder. The harder he pushed into her, the louder she screamed.

"Is this what you wanted? Isn't this what you wanted?" Earl asked; then he was done. He backed away from Cheryl in disgust. He pulled up his pants and buckled his belt.

Cheryl turned around to face him; her back stayed against the wall. She slowly slid down the wall to the floor and watched Earl as he turned away from her and walked toward the door. Earl never looked back at her. He opened the door and walked straight out. Cheryl called behind him, "Are you comin' back?"

The door slammed shut behind Earl.

WHEN EARL WALKED through his front door, he couldn't help but notice the draft that filled the room. The room felt damp and dank. The musty odor was unmistakable. He picked up the handset from the cradle and dialed Franki's number. He walked through the room checking all five windows to see where the draft was coming from while he waited for an answer at the other end of the phone.

BARI DIDN'T THINK twice about answering the phone since she had just dialed Barbara, who had been on another call and had told Bari that she would ring her right back. Bari was lying back, relaxing on the couch, when the phone rang.

"Hello?"

"Bari, how are you doin'? Earl's voice was calm.

"I'm fine," Bari answered. Her heart beat loudly in her chest as if it was drumming out some danger warning. Her hands trembled. She made a fist to steady her free hand and tightly clutched the receiver to steady the other one. Bari inhaled deeply so that her voice wouldn't shake when she spoke. She intended to sound cold and distant. It worked. She sat up on the couch now.

"Bari, I want to see you. I need to see you," Earl said.

"Why?"

"Because I love you. You know I love you. Why did you leave me? Don't answer that yet. Can I see you? Can we talk about this in person?"

"There is nothing to talk about, Earl. You wanted to be able to have your cake and eat it, too. Well, now you have your cake and you do whatever the hell you want with it."

"Bari, I need you with me. Why don't you come home?"

"That is no longer my home. Look, I don't have time for this. I have to go," she said.

"No! No, please don't go. Don't hang up. I'm comin' over there," said Earl.

"I don't want to see you, Earl, and I have nothing more to say to you," Bari said.

Earl ignored her protests. "I'll be there in ten minutes."

Bari hung up the phone. She turned to look at Franki. Franki had been sitting there with her arms crossed over her chest listening to Bari's conversation.

"Don't talk to him anymore," Franki said.

"I have to get out of here. I think he's coming here," Bari told her.

"Go, hurry, get dressed. Get out of here," Franki said.

Bari ran into the den and put on a sweater, a pair of jeans, and her boots. She ran to the front hall closet and grabbed her jacket.

"I'm gone, Franki," she yelled back toward the kitchen. "I'm gonna get a cab and go over to Dominick's for a while."

Shortly after Bari left Franki's apartment, Earl sped onto the block. He screeched into a catty-corner parking position and jumped out of the car. He ran up the stairs and eagerly rang the bell.

Franki took a deep breath and went down the stairs to open the door. "Yes, Earl. What can I do for you?" She braced herself in case he tried to rush past her.

"I want to see my wife. Could you please call her for me?"

"I can't do that. She's not here," said Franki.

"I just spoke to her, not even ten minutes ago."

"Well, she left here not even ten minutes ago. Let me give you some advice. Leave Bari alone. She doesn't want to see you. She doesn't want to speak to you. If you have a problem understanding any of this, I'll be happy to break it down further for you," Franki told him.

"I don't need your sarcasm. Tell Bari that I was here and I'll be back." Earl turned and started back down the stairs.

"Don't bother comin' back, because you're not welcome here. Besides, Bari won't be here."

"Bitch," Earl said under his breath. "I'd like to snap her fucking neck in two. I'd like that a lot."

Earl got into the rental car and headed toward Tommy's place. He knew that he didn't have enough money on him to make a buy, but as much money as he'd spent with Tommy, Earl was sure that Tommy would give him a little something on the house.

BARI WAVED TO Dominick as she approached his building. She knew that he would be watching for her from his window just as he always did when he knew she was coming. Dominick left the window and rushed down the stairs to open the door for her.

"Hey, girl," Dominick said, hugging Bari.

"Hi, Dommie. I'm sorry for intruding on you again."

"You could intrude on me anytime you want to. You know that," Dominick said. He nudged Bari toward the stairwell. The two of them went up the stairs to Dominick's apartment.

"I'm interrupting your video," Bari said, as Dominick helped her off with her jacket. She noticed the movie playing with the volume muted.

"That's okay. Actually, you came in on the good part. Come on, watch it with me. You'll like it. It's an old Jack Nicholson film."

"Okay." Bari sat down on the couch, kicking off her shoes.

Thirty minutes into the movie, Dominick noticed Bari staring into her lap, picking at her nails.

"Are you okay?"

"I'm fine," she said, still looking down.

"Could I get you somethin' to drink?" Dominick asked.

"No, thank you."

"Are you sure?"

Bari sniffled at first. When she looked up at Dominick, her eyes were filled with tears. "Hold me, Dominick," Bari cried.

Dominick put his arms around her as Bari cried against his chest. He held on to her until the tears stopped.

Bari looked up into his face. "Make love to me."

"What?"

"Please, make love to me," she repeated.

Dominick sat with his head back against the couch. He took in a deep breath before he spoke. "Bari, I think you know that I would like nothing more in this world than to make love to you, but I could never take advantage of your vulnerability."

Bari stood up. She reached out for Dominick's hands and pulled him up, too. "I want to do this, Dominick," Bari said, kissing him on his lips. She looked into his eyes. "I want to do this," she said again. "Come on. . . ." Bari kept hold of Dominick's hand while she led him into his bedroom. They stopped at the foot of his bed.

Dominick pulled Bari to him and kissed her.

"You're absolutely okay with this?" Dominick asked, one last time.

Bari smiled. "Just don't make me regret this."

"Never," Dominick said. He pulled Bari's sweater over her head, then kissed her on the neck. He held on to her as she stepped out of her jeans. Bari climbed into the bed, pulling the covers over her. She lay back against the pillow and watched Dominick as he undressed. When Dominick was done, he got into bed beside her. He reached over and kissed Bari, long and sweet. He kissed her from her forehead down to her navel.

Dominick raised his head long enough to unsnap the front catch of her bra. He licked Bari's bare breasts, then reached down to remove her panties. Bari clutched her hand over his. Dominick hesitated. He looked up into Bari's face.

"Dominick, I-I-I'm so sorry. I can't do this . . . ," she whispered.

Dominick breathed in deeply, then quickly rolled over on his back with his hands squeezing the back of his head. "It's okay," he said quietly.

"I'm sorry, Dominick," Bari said.

"It's okay . . . it's okay. . . . Don't worry about it," he said. "Get dressed; I'll take you back to Franki's."

Quietly, very quietly, they both got dressed and left the apartment.

EARL MADE IT to Tommy's place in just a few minutes. When Earl got there, as usual Tommy had people all over the place. *Damn*, Earl thought to himself. If he had to put his tail between his legs to ask for a freebie, he wanted to do it in private.

Tommy took Earl into his office when Earl told him that he wanted to speak to him alone. "I don't mind helpin' a brother out, but you don't need to be askin' for handouts," Tommy said, as they sat across the room from each other on the adjacent couches.

"Well, er, I'm not exactly askin' for a handout . . . ," Earl said.

"Let me put it to you this way," Tommy said. "A little birdie told me that your lady left you. Now, we talked about this before, so I'm comin' at you one more time."

"Look, man—," Earl began.

"Wait a minute, my brother; hear me out. You need an income and I need a distributor, right? So we have a match made in heaven. It's called supply and demand. It's simple. The demand for the drug is there. You're the supplier. It's a win-win situation."

"Man, I don't know," Earl said

"You don't know what? You don't know if you want the finer things in life? You don't know if you want more money than you can count? What?" Tommy asked.

Earl sat farther back on the couch. His mouth was actually watering over the thought. The money sounded good, and the drug always being available . . . that was even more appealing. Earl didn't want to seem too eager, but Tommy had a point. He needed an income. And if he could avoid all of the bureaucratic bullshit working for the Man in his bullshit establishment, then it was a damn good proposition.

"I'll tell you what," Earl said. "Let's talk turkey."

"We can talk, but there's just one little issue we need to deal with first. Straight up, you know I ain't no fool. I really need a dude over on the south side 'cause I got untouched territory over there and that's just money out the door every day if I don't tap into it. So why am I talking to you when you're one of my biggest customers? You're a cokehead,

Earl. I know that. But see, I'm a businessman. I know you're smart. You've done distribution with a legitimate product before, so this will be a walk in the park for you—there's no red tape here. I know you'll take just enough off the top to take care of your nasty little habit, and I'm okay with that. But if you fuck up, I know how to handle it. I killed my own brother, so you know I don't give a fuck about you. As long as you understand that, we're good to go."

"We're good to go," Earl said confidently.

The two men shook hands. They spent the next forty-five minutes discussing the mechanics of the business. When they were done talking, Tommy gave Earl a package on the house. Earl's hands trembled as he struggled to unlock the fast-grip edges on the small plastic packet. He made a few lines on Tommy's side table. Earl took several hits, then helped himself to a glass of straight rum and chased it with a Heineken from Tommy's mini-refrigerator. Earl mellowed out real quick. Tommy left Earl to his thoughts while he reached into his desk drawer and took out a large unopened package of pure rock cocaine and mixed and measured out enough coke to get Earl going for a couple of weeks. He sat there quietly and waited for Tommy to finish. Earl couldn't stop thinking about Bari. He needed to touch her. To smell her. She was his *wife*. She had no right to stay away from him.

When Tommy was done, he handed Earl a black canvas bag. "I know you have good business sense, man, otherwise, I wouldn't deal with you," Tommy said. "I'm givin' you twenty-five hundred dollars' worth of my product. All you have to do is move it, then see me again. That's how we'll do this. You get your rhythm goin' and I'll be right there to back you."

"This is cool, man. I could unload this," Earl said, as he accepted the bag.

"Oh yeah. Take this," Tommy said, handing Earl a cellular phone. "We're gonna need to stay in touch."

Earl took the phone from Tommy and tucked it inside his jacket pocket.

Tommy flicked on the big-screen television that sat in the far corner of the room. He scanned several channels, then settled on the music videos.

Earl's mind was somewhere else. Suddenly he was up on his feet.

He made a decision. Tonight would be the night that he would get Bari back.

"I'll be in touch, man. I'm makin' a move," Earl said, as he walked briskly toward the door.

"Later," Tommy said.

EARL WAS IN his car and on his way back to Franki's. When he got there he contemplated ringing the bell, but then he decided against it. He wasn't sure how he'd react if Bari didn't want to see him. He decided to sit in the car and wait to see if he could catch up with her on her way in or out. In the meantime, he would make himself comfortable.

Earl parked several cars away from the building. He turned on the radio and reclined in his seat. He pulled out a silver flask from one of the pockets of his down jacket. He sipped rum, then dug into the black canvas bag and dipped into the cocaine that Tommy had just given him and took some hits while he waited and waited. The street was dark and silent. Cars drove by occasionally. When one stopped in front of Franki's building, he braced himself. He hoped that it wasn't Bari and another man. That could be ugly. The thought of Bari being with another man made Earl feel sick. No, it made him crazy.

When the door of the double-parked car opened, it was Darryl. As he locked his car door and walked up the building steps. Darryl had Earl's full attention. Darryl looked up and down the block as he walked. Earl slid lower down into his seat so that Darryl wouldn't see him.

Wouldn't it be nice to see that son of a bitch laid out on his ass? Earl thought to himself. He pulled out his gun from his pant waist. He twirled it around his index finger. He never took his eyes off Darryl. Earl rolled his car window halfway down. He cocked the gun and pointed it through the window at Darryl. Earl aimed it at his head.

Click, Earl mouthed the word. He put the gun to his lips and blew away the invisible smoke. Then he returned the gun to his pant waist. Earl sat for another forty-five minutes and still he saw no sign of Bari.

"Shit," Earl said, looking all around him for any movement whatsoever. He took out his cocaine stash again and took some hits. He didn't bother putting it away. He figured he could be in for a long wait. He took a long, deep swig from his flask. "Where in the hell could she be?" Earl asked out loud. "Shit. She might already be inside."

He turned up the volume on the radio and adjusted his seat even farther back. The music was pumping. Earl closed his eyes and concentrated on the saxophone playing in the background of the sweet song that was playing. He held his hands out in front of his mouth and fingered the keys on the invisible saxophone that he played. When the bass kicked in, Earl played the invisible bass guitar right along with the music.

"Yeah . . . that's nice," Earl said, turning the volume up even higher. He let the music seep into his body, every pore. He was thinking about how he and Bari used to lie there against one another on the couch, grooving to the music. He thought about the time when he first introduced her to jazz music and taught her how to listen to it the right way. She had loved it right from the start. Damn. He missed that.

"Oh, fuck, this music sounds good." Earl sighed heavily, took another look around, then took another hit of his cocaine. He leaned back into his seat with arms folded behind his head. Eyes shut tight, he bobbed to the music.

When Bari and Dominick pulled onto the block and Dominick walked Bari up the stairs and hugged her good night before he left, Earl never saw them. Even when Dominick revved up his engine before he left, Earl never looked up.

forty-three

I T WAS A lazy Sunday morning. Franki was buried in the Business section of *The New York Times,* while Bari studied the Real Estate section. The breakfast dishes were pushed to the center of the table. Neither one of them rushed to clean up the table.

"I had a weird dream last night," Bari said.

"What about?" Franki asked, turning the page and only half-listening as she scanned the articles on the next page of the paper.

"I was standing in the most beautiful, tranquil garden that I had ever seen in my life. I remember taking note of the bright colors of the birds and the butterflies and how sweet the chirping sounds were that the birds made. Then I remember being particularly aware of the scent from all the pine trees," Bari said.

"Is this gonna be another one of your long, crazy, abstract dreams that mean absolutely nothing?" asked Franki.

"No," Bari said, and continued. "Then all of a sudden water started coming up through the grass. It started getting higher and higher until it was thigh deep, like a swimming pool. All of the people that were walking around couldn't walk anymore. It was like the water was too thick or something and nobody had the strength to move. Then all of a sudden one of the trees in the garden started growing right before my eyes. It had a mean face. And it frowned down at me, and of all the people in the garden, it reached downward and grabbed and squeezed me. I was so scared that I passed out. And that's when I panicked and woke up."

"That doesn't sound like a good dream at all," Franki said, looking up from her paper. "I could tell you right now that from what I read in my dream book floods are *never* a good thing. And that tree in the garden sounds a little too much like somebody that we both know. I'm telling you, Bari, be very careful. I do not trust Earl Jordan. Not even for a minute."

Bari hated when Franki talked that way, but she knew that Franki usually knew what she was talking about. Lord knows she spent enough time reading her trusted dream books and analyzing every dream that anybody told her.

The telephone rang. The two women looked at each other, smiling. Neither one of them moved.

"It's Darryl. Get it for me, please," Franki said.

"What if it's not Darryl?" Bari asked.

"It had better be him; he always calls me like clockwork at this time every Sunday."

"Well, you're closer to the phone than I am," Bari complained.

"Come on, Bari, you know how I get after I eat. I can't move."

Bari sucked her teeth as she pushed her chair back from the table. She ran across the room and answered the telephone. She stomped loudly two times on the floor to get Franki's attention. It was Earl.

"Hello, Earl. What can I do for you?" Bari's voice was deadpan.

"You could do a lot for me, baby. I want to see you, that's all. I just want to see you," Earl said.

"Please don't do this. I told you that I don't want to see you. You're free now to see Cheryl or anybody else that you want to see. Just leave me out of it. Please forget about me," Bari said.

"I can't forget about you, Bari. You're the only woman that I want. I know what you're thinking. I'm gettin' help for the drinkin'. I go to this group thing. It's helping. As a matter of fact, they're gonna help me through all of my problems," Earl told her.

"Oh, really?"

"Yeah. And here's a surprise for you. I went to church today. And I plan on goin' every Sunday."

"That *is* a surprise."

"Yeah, well. I've learned that if you don't have God in your life, you don't have nothin'. I go to the First Calvary Baptist Church, uptown. That's where I'm just comin' from. I was kinda hopin' that you would come with me next Sunday."

"I don't think that's a good idea, Earl."

"Just give me another chance, Bari. I don't want to push you. Why don't I come over right now so we could maybe go for a drive and talk about things?" he asked.

"No, Earl, don't come here. Don't even bother."

"It's no bother. I promise, I'll be right there." Earl hung up the phone before Bari could protest.

BEFORE EARL GRABBED his jacket, he settled down on the floor where he had set up shop in what used to be his and Bari's master bedroom. He had to finish sorting the many packets of cocaine that he had made up for sale. He sorted them out by the value of the package.

The only items in the room were two cardboard boxes. One box was used for him to store his product, and the other was used to store the cash. Earl worked quickly. When he was done he pulled out his personal cocaine stash and took a few hits. Now he was ready. He left the house to head for Franki's apartment.

BARI HEARD THE dead air on the phone. She figured that since Earl had hung up so quickly he was more than likely on his way to her. Apparently, he wasn't taking no for an answer. Bari slowly put the handset back on the switch hook.

"That was Earl."

"I know," said Franki. "What did he want?"

"He said that he wants to see me."

"And . . . ?"

"And he said that he was getting help for the drinking," Bari said.

"How did he sound?"

"He sounded okay. I mean if he says that he's getting help, then I'm sure that he's getting help. He also said that he went to church today." Bari smiled.

"Earl?" Franki asked, surprised.

"Yeah. Can you imagine?" Bari asked

"Well, I certainly wouldn't believe a word he says. Don't trust him," said Franki.

"I'm not defending Earl, but I do believe that everybody deserves a chance to make corrections. Who knows? Maybe he's learned his lesson."

"Bari, don't do this to yourself. Don't look back. There ain't nothin' back there," Franki said.

"All I know is that he's on his way over here right now, so I'm just gonna throw some clothes on and leave the apartment for a while. I really hope I find an apartment soon, Franki. I can't keep this up much longer," Bari said.

"Hurry up, Bari. Get out of here," Franki urged her.

Bari rushed into the den to get changed. She knew that the way Earl drove it would only be a matter of minutes before he would be there.

"Be careful, Bari!" Franki called behind her as she left the apartment.

When the doorbell rang ten minutes later, Franki's heart stood still. Although Earl had been to the apartment a couple of times before looking for Bari, Franki still felt uneasy dealing with him.

"Hello, Franki." Earl's expression was twisted into what could have been taken for a half smile, except that it looked demonic, snarling. His eyes were glassy and bloodshot.

"What do you want, Earl?" Franki asked coldly.

"I'm looking for Bari," he said.

"Well, you won't find her here." Franki attempted to close the door but Earl stuck his foot in it to prevent it from closing.

Earl stuck his head in the door, looking past Franki. His eyes scanned the room behind her. "I just spoke to her; I know she's here," he said.

"I told you she isn't here," said Franki.

"Well, then you give her a message for me; tell her that I need to see her. And soon!" Earl pulled his foot from the door.

"I wouldn't hold my breath if I were you," Franki said, slamming the door shut.

EARL RAN DOWN the steps and got into his car. "Damn!" He pounded the steering wheel. The vein in the middle of his forehead protruded. He clenched his teeth. "I have to figure out exactly how I'm gonna handle this shit. *Nobody* fucks with me! *Nobody!*"

When he walked into his front door, the stale air rushed out at him. The sound of the closing door echoed through the room. "Shit,"

Earl said aloud. That echo was his constant reminder of Bari's absence. He was tired, hungry, and too high.

Earl needed to think. He paced back and forth in the living room like an animal, caged. Things were out of control. He didn't like it when he lost control. He went into the kitchen and looked into the overhead kitchen cabinets. They were bare, except for the lone bottle of rum that was set in the middle of the shelf. He grabbed the bottle, opened it up and took two long swigs from it, then slammed the bottle down onto the counter.

"What the fuck am I gonna do?" He stood in the middle of the room squeezing his head as if that would make him think better. "I know what I'm gonna do. I'm just gonna bring her back home. Period."

Earl ran up the stairs to his bedroom. He took down his gun from the top of the empty closet and stuck it in his pant waist. This was a natural move for him now. He pulled a few bills from an envelope that he kept in the top of the closet. Earl clipped his cellular phone to his waist and headed down the stairs. When he reached the front door, he yanked it open.

"Hi, Earl," Cheryl said in her sweetest voice. She was wearing a leopard-colored catsuit with brown suede cowboy boots and a leather bomber. The faint sun illuminated her auburn-dyed hair. A huge duffel bag was slung over her shoulder. She was standing just outside the door and was about to ring the bell when Earl opened the door.

"Well, don't just stand there; invite me in. This bag is heavy," she said.

"What are you doing here?" Earl asked her.

Cheryl stepped up into the house. She dumped the bag on the floor when she crossed the threshold. "I'm here because I *know* you. You're probably hungry and you won't take a minute out to feed yourself. Wow, she's really gone," Cheryl said, taking note of the empty house. "I brought some Chinese food."

"I'm not hungry, Cheryl. As a matter of fact, I was on my way out the door. I have some things to take care of." Earl picked up Cheryl's bag and nudged her toward the door.

Cheryl slightly resisted. "I figured you and me could hang out tonight. You know, eat some food, drink some wine, do a little blow—"

"Maybe another time, Cheryl. I don't have the time right now." Earl took her arm again and nudged her a little harder toward the door.

Cheryl jerked her arm away from him. "I'm not leavin', Earl! You've been puttin' me off for too long now. At least tell me what's wrong."

"It's nothin' personal. Look, I gotta go. I'll give you a call later," he told her. Earl was already losing his patience. He had seen Cheryl's hysterics many times before, so he could tell by the way her voice trembled that she was about to get started.

"No, not this time, Earl. I'm not leavin'," she said.

Earl opened the door wider and looked at Cheryl, inviting her to go out the door first. Cheryl walked toward the door as if she were going to leave, but when she reached it she grabbed hold of it and slammed it shut. She planted her body in front of it so that Earl wouldn't be able to open it and put her out.

"Please don't do this to me, Earl. Look at me! I love you. All I want you to do is love me back. What's the matter with me that you can't love me?" Cheryl asked.

Earl took a deep breath and he put her bag down on the floor. He knew that he would have to be calm so that he wouldn't end up slapping the shit out of her. "It's just that I have things to do. That's all," he said.

Earl stepped forward and reached for the doorknob. He firmly took hold of Cheryl's waist and pulled her forward off the door. Cheryl immediately slammed herself back against the door. Earl pulled again, harder this time. It was a tug-of-war.

"Stop it, Earl! Don't do this! I just wanna help you; let me help you!" Tears were streaming down Cheryl's face. Black mascara ran from both eyes. "I swear to God if you throw me out I'll kill myself!" she screamed. She threw her arms around Earl's neck. "Please love me, Earl. I just want you to love me." She held her eyes to his. "I love you," she said softly, kissing his neck. Both sides. Then she kissed his ears. Cheryl opened the buttons on Earl's shirt and kissed his chest. She worked her way back up to his lips, pecking at them until he parted them and kissed her back. While Cheryl was kissing Earl, she unzipped his pants. She dropped to her knees as she pulled his pants down around his legs. Earl changed his mind about leaving.

forty-four

IT WAS MONDAY morning and Bari had no choice but to return to work. She dreaded it because one of her biggest fears was that Earl would try to contact her at her office. As Bari approached her building, she noticed Sammy, the security guard, watching her. She smiled to herself as she watched him. *Poor Sammy,* she thought. Several people had told her that Sammy was always asking about her when she was out of the office. Bari could see that Cheshire cat smile of his a mile away. She didn't think he could control it.

"Welcome back, Miss Bari," he said when she reached him. "Could I carry your bags for you?"

"You're sweet, Sammy. I'm okay, thanks. You have a good day."

"You, too, Miss Bari." Sammy couldn't lose the grin.

Bari walked into her office, put down her things, and sat behind her desk. She looked at all of the mail that was stacked in her in-box, some on her desk. All of the unread memos and other correspondence waited for her. File folders—new clients—were everywhere. She took a deep breath, then noticed the steady red message light on her telephone. Her heart quickened. Bari took her pumps out of one of her bags and changed from her walking shoes into the pumps. When she was done, she pressed the message button. She had twenty-two messages. Not bad, considering she had been out for the past week and never checked them. Bari spent the next sixteen minutes listening to her messages and jotting down names, numbers, and notes. Eleven of the twenty-two messages were from Earl. All of the messages said the same thing, so Bari stopped listening. She hit the "delete" button on each one of them. She was relieved to know that the last message was left four days ago.

"Thank God," Bari said aloud. "Maybe he thinks I quit my job."

No one at the office knew about Bari's split-up with Earl except Barbara, and Bari had asked her not to tell anybody. Bari figured it was none of their business.

Bari was uneasy during the first half of the day. Her heart stood still every time the phone rang. By noon, she felt like she was catching her balance and felt like she had never been away from the office at all. Earl hadn't called at all and she felt good about that. Bari was crunching numbers and setting up client strategies like a champ.

Bari was just about ready to deal with the three neat stacks of paper on her credenza with "see me" Post-it notes from David, but she knew that if she went in to see him now, she would never get out to lunch. She quickly gathered her jacket and handbag and tried to make a quick getaway before she bumped into him.

David appeared at her door just as she was about to leave. "Are you heading out?" he asked her.

"I am. Why?" Bari asked.

"I just wanted to run something by you and I wanted to talk to you about a few ideas. Plus your new office . . ." David smiled.

"Okay, so I'll see you after—"

"This'll just take a couple of minutes." David brushed past Bari and walked into her office. He grabbed one of the stacks of paper from her credenza, then seated himself in one of her guest chairs. "First, let me tell you that your new bigger and brighter office is being painted."

"Great," said Bari.

"Also, I've been thinking a lot about the Jorgi account. Where is their file?" David asked.

Bari put down her jacket and pocketbook and dug into her desk drawer. She took out the Jorgi file and handed it to David. David opened the file and flipped through the many pieces of paper. He pulled out the company's financial statement. "Here it is," he said finally, pulling out one of the pages from the file. "Do you see these numbers on this financial statement?"

Bari looked over his shoulder at the document that he held. "Yes." Bari sat down.

"I have an idea that goes totally against what the client says they want, but if we could sell them on it, I believe it would almost triple their sales and they'd love us forever. It would take you to convince them to look at it, though."

Now Bari was interested. She loved a challenge. The Jorgi account was the other reason she had taken the week off. It was her toughest assignment yet, so she was open to *anybody's* ideas at this point.

"So what are you thinking?" Bari asked.

"I was thinking you could change their slogan altogether. 'Jorgi, the perfect fit' is so . . . boring, to say the least," David said.

"You're right, but that's what the public knows. You think 'Jorgi,' you think 'the perfect fit.' Not even I could convince them to change that. I have a thought, though. I've been looking at their file, and I think that we need to take a more realistic approach with their product," Bari said.

"More realistic? How so?" David asked.

"We need to seriously consider the market that they're targeting. It's all wrong. The ads we've done in the past appeal mostly to Caucasian women and men in their late twenties, early thirties. The fact is, the people that actually buy their jeans are mostly African-American teenagers. It wouldn't hurt to make the ads a little more colorful," said Bari.

"That's a thought," David said, digesting what Bari had told him.

The two of them tossed ideas back and forth for the next hour. After the first ten minutes, Barbara had stuck her head into Bari's office for lunch, but Bari motioned for her to go without her. Bari was back on track again, and she didn't want to mess up her rhythm. She and David were in and out of each other's offices for the rest of the afternoon, and before they knew it the day had come to an end.

"Is it going to be a late night for you, Bari?" Barbara asked, standing at Bari's door again, all buttoned up and ready to go home at 5:00 P.M. on the nose.

"It looks that way. I'm looking forward to the quiet so that I can really get busy. I'm kind of excited about this project now."

"Better you than me. Get home safe," Barbara said, and left.

David stopped by Bari's office, too, to say good night. "Don't stay too late, Bari," he told her.

"I won't. Have a good night, David."

———

EARL SAT ACROSS the street from the office building where Bari worked. He had been sitting and waiting there every night at the same time for almost a week hoping to be able to catch up with Bari. Since he hadn't seen her up to now he figured that she was probably on vacation or she had quit her job. He made up his mind that tonight would be the last time that he made this trip. He needed to be convinced either way of what Bari's status was. He needed to get up to her office so that he could see if her office had been cleaned out. A couple of times he thought about calling her and hanging up, but he figured that Bari might have known that it was him.

Earl sat there and watched most of Bari's coworkers leave. Luckily, he knew the people she worked with, and he counted them down one by one as they left the building. Earl wanted to be absolutely sure that everybody was gone, so he sat for another half hour and waited. If she was there, she would be there alone. All he needed to do now was get by the security guard. Earl decided to entertain himself while he waited. He opened up his small black canvas bag and took out one of the aluminum-foil packets that he had packaged for sale. He opened the package and took a hit.

"Goddamn, this is some good shit." He took another hit and put the package away. "Yeah." He was mellow now. Now he was ready. It seemed that nobody else was coming out of the building, so Earl decided to make his move. He wasn't sure how to play it. If Bari didn't work there anymore they would be on to him right away. He needed to think some more. Earl wanted to see Bari so badly that he couldn't afford to blow this. He stepped out of the car. He smoothed out the wrinkles on his clothing, then looked up and down the street before he crossed over to the building. When he got closer to the revolving door, he strained to see if he recognized the security guard. He did. It was Sammy. Sammy was working a double shift.

Earl walked into the lobby. "Hey, man, how are you doin'?" He stretched out his hand to Sammy.

"I'm fine. How have you been?" They shook hands.

"I'm good. I'm good. I gotta pick up the wife. She never knows when to quit." Earl was cool. He flashed his debonair smile.

"Just sign the register for me, man," Sammy said.

When Earl finished signing his name, he took the elevator up to the last floor. When the elevator door opened, he quietly got off. He stood perfectly still. He listened for movement. The cleaning lady was busy cleaning the offices. Earl waited until she moved on to the next office before he made his way down the hall to Bari's office. When he got to Bari's office, she wasn't there. He quickly slipped inside. He saw her jacket hanging on the coatrack. The desk lamp was on, and papers were strewn all over her desk.

"She's here," Earl said aloud. His pulse raced. He was finally going to see her. He would finally get his wife back. He stood behind the door for what seemed like forever. Finally, Bari came into the office. She walked in and stood in front of her desk reading the papers in her hand.

Earl pushed the door shut. When Bari turned around and saw him, she gasped, stumbled backward, and fell into her chair. She couldn't speak. Earl quickly made his way over to her before she composed herself. He took her by the arm and helped her back to her feet. He covered her mouth. Panic filled Bari's eyes.

"Shhh. Look at yourself. Look at you. Why are you so afraid of me?" Earl asked. "You don't have to fear me. Look, I'm gonna move my hand. Don't scream. I'm not gonna hurt you. I only want to talk. Okay?" Earl removed his hand from her mouth.

Bari made no sound. No movement.

"Good," Earl said. "Now, I told you that I wanted to talk to you, but you refused to see me. Why? Why, Bari? I want an answer!" Earl slammed his fist down on the wooden desk.

Bari jumped. "Be-because there was nothing to discuss, Earl."

"There was nothin' to discuss? You just up and remove everything that we own together from my house and then you disappear without a word or even a note, and you can stand there and tell me that we have nothin' to discuss?" All of Earl's suppressed anger surfaced.

"You left me no choice, Earl."

"Why didn't you talk to me?"

"Because you were never home. You were out having fun with your friends or doing whatever it was that you were doing."

"You *left* me! That was not your decision to make. Goddammit, I'm your husband! We're supposed to decide together where our relationship goes, and I say I'm not ready to give you up. We belong together, Bari."

"You have to let it go, Earl. There are too many things wrong now. I just want to be alone."

Earl picked up the diamond-shaped Lucite paperweight off of her desk and flung it against the wall. "You don't get it, do you? You *can't* be alone. We made a promise to God that we would be together until death do us part. You remember that? This thing is bigger than the both of us. I love you, Bari. Why can't you see that?"

"You're making this more difficult than it has to be." Bari looked away from him.

"It's not difficult at all. Yes, we have our differences but we can start over. Give me a chance."

"What about the drinking, Earl? What about the drugs?"

"I already told you I'm gettin' help for that." He calmed himself down. He decided to reason with her. "Look here, I want you to come home with me tonight."

"That's not my home anymore. I can't go there," Bari told him.

"You know what, baby?" Earl asked. Bari looked at him questioningly. "I have to be honest with you," he said.

Earl pulled his gun out from his pants waist. Bari gasped and backed away from him.

"You don't have a choice." Earl pulled her back to him by her arm. "You see, if you don't come with me, I will hurt you. Period."

"But . . . but if you love me . . . ," Bari stammered.

Earl was worked up again. He put the gun to her throat. "*If I love you? If I love you?* Do you question that? If I didn't love you, do you think I would be goin' through all of these changes? I'm makin' an effort to make things right. I'm doin' this for *us.*" Earl backed down for the moment, but he kept the gun handy. He pointed it all around as he directed her, "All right, now pack your shit. We're goin' home."

"I GOTTA MAKE a stop," Earl said almost fifteen minutes later as he pulled the car over.

Bari welcomed the diversion. They were very near to the house and she wasn't looking forward to whatever it was that lay ahead.

"Come on." Earl motioned for Bari to get out of the car. He met her as she walked around the car to him, keeping his hand in his pocket on the gun with his finger on the trigger. Earl took Bari by the arm and led her into Reno's Italian family restaurant. Earl felt like pasta. He took the liberty of ordering shrimp Parmesan for both of them. They made one more stop on the way, and once again Bari found herself being hustled out of the car and into Stingray's grocery store, the only grocery store that was within a radius of fifteen blocks of the house. Earl wanted candles. Lots of them. He wanted the night to be special. Tonight he would have to teach his wife how to love him all over again, and he would prove to her how much he loved her. The thought of seeing Bari's body in the glow of the candlelight excited him. He looked over at her. Bari was beautiful to him. He was a very lucky man, he told himself. "Let's go," he said. Bari followed him and they climbed back into the car. Earl pressed hard on the gas pedal as they sped off.

Bari clutched the door handle tighter and braced herself. She felt Earl's eyes on her, so she looked straight ahead. She couldn't believe that the very man that she had loved so deeply, the very man that she had cherished, would turn out to be the man that she feared the most. Even with all the arguments and fighting, Bari never imagined that it would ever come to this. She was numb. She could feel her bottom lip tremble. Breathing was difficult. A small whimper escaped from her mouth. Bari cleared her throat to camouflage the sound. She didn't want Earl to know how afraid she was. She needed to think. Quickly. There had to be a way out of this. Maybe if she sweet-talked him. No. Earl would know that she was pretending. *Think. Think.* If this were a movie, Bari could predict exactly how the film should end. But this was real life and help wasn't waiting at the other end. She closed her eyes and prayed silently. Profusely. She thought about all of Granny's wise words. Words that were wasted on the ears of a seven-year-old. Bari was a hell of a lot older now and suddenly wiser. Now she understood exactly what Granny wanted her to know. Granny always said that the biggest snake in the grass was the man in the bed lying next to you. *She was right,* Bari thought. And Granny told Bari to be true to herself and the Lord above. Now she thought about all of the days and nights that she had spent working so hard, putting her career and her marriage ahead of herself. Neglecting herself. Because somehow now, under the circumstances, none of those things seemed important at all.

When Bari opened her eyes, they were pulling into the driveway. She wanted to protest before she got out of the car, but the words wouldn't come. Earl got out of the car and walked around to the passenger's side and opened the door for her.

Bari cringed when three little girls two houses down were holding hands and going around and around in their formed circle singing, "*Ring around the rosy, pocket full of posies.*" She willed herself to tune them out. She willed away Grandma Greta's sweet face.

"Don't forget the food," Earl said to Bari.

Bari gathered her pocketbook, her portfolio, and her tote bag into one hand. She picked up the two brown paper bags that held their food in the other. When her portfolio fell to the ground, Earl took the food bags from her. When they walked into the house, the dampness enveloped Bari right away. The house that was once her sanctuary, her peaceful corner in the world, was no longer receptive. It was cold and foreboding.

Bari stood at the doorway as if she were a stranger waiting to be asked in. She looked around at the dried-up plants that she had left behind. Earl had never even bothered to throw them away.

"Come on in," Earl said. "This is your home. Put your stuff down. Let's get comfortable." Earl gestured to her to put her things against the wall.

Bari did what he said. She walked back over to the comforter that Earl had spread out in the center of the floor and sat down. Earl sat beside her and unpacked the paper plates and forks that were in the bag with the food. He removed the lids from the small foil pans and spooned out the shrimp Parmesan and spaghetti onto their plates.

"Take off your shoes. Relax," he said to her.

Bari got up and took off her shoes. She set them against the wall with the rest of her things.

"I'm not hungry," Bari said when she came back to the comforter.

"I want you to eat," said Earl.

Bari knew that it was pointless to argue with him. "I'll need to wash my hands first," she said.

"Okay," Earl said, as he stood up. He waited for her to stand as well; then he followed her to the bathroom. Bari didn't know that Earl was walking behind her until she turned to close the door. Earl quickly stuck his foot into the door to stop it from closing. "You don't need to close the door," he said.

Bari bit her bottom lip, but she remained silent as she washed her hands. When she was done, she brushed past Earl on the way out.

"Just a minute," Earl said. Bari stopped. "I have to use the bathroom."

"I'll be outside," Bari said.

"I want you to stand right there." Earl pointed to the spot where he wanted her to stand. Bari stood where he said. It was going to be a long night. When Earl was done, he guided Bari back to the comforter, where he wolfed down his food and she picked at hers.

"Are you done?" Earl asked, standing up to clear away their aluminum dishes and paper plates. Earl was anxious to get the evening started.

"Come with me," Earl ordered Bari, as he stood up with the dishes in one hand. He reached out his other hand to Bari and helped her to her feet. She followed him into the kitchen. Earl discarded the uneaten food. When he was done, he walked back into the living room. Bari obediently followed him.

Earl took out the candles. He placed all thirteen of them in a circle around the comforter, then lit them all one by one. Earl stood back to admire his work. He walked across the room and picked up the handset on the telephone and held it out to Bari. She looked puzzled.

"Call your sister. Tell her that you're with me and that you came here because you wanna work things out with me."

Bari shot him an angry look. She didn't take the telephone.

"Do it!" Earl yelled. He moved his shirt to the side so that she could see his gun in his pant waist. It was her reminder that he was in control.

Bari took the phone and slowly punched in Franki's number. Earl backed out of the room and went into the kitchen and picked up the receiver on the other phone on the wall. He stretched the long cord on the phone and walked back into the living room. He stood in front of Bari. Bari prayed that Franki wouldn't be home. The phone rang six times. When Franki picked up she sounded like the last thing in the world she wanted to do was talk on the phone.

"Hello?"

"Hi, Franki. It's me, Bari."

"Where are you?" Franki asked. "I'm worried about you."

"I'm calling to let you know that I'm with Earl."

"With Earl? Why?" Franki asked, pissed.

"I want to try to work things out." Bari spoke carefully. She tried to make her voice sound unnaturally calm, hoping that maybe Franki would realize that something was wrong.

"Have you lost your mind? What about all the things we talked about? How could you ever think about going back to him? I don't understand this, Bari. You know that Earl is nothing but a goddamn loser."

"That's not true, Franki."

"You must be sniffin' what he's sniffin'. Can we talk, Bari? Can you just come home so we can talk about this?"

Earl gave Bari a sign to cut the conversation short.

"We'll talk about it later. I love you, Franki. I have to go. He's waiting for me."

Earl quickly pressed the switch hook on the base and disconnected the call. "What the hell was that supposed to mean? 'He's waiting for me.' Is that supposed to be funny? Bari, don't fuck with me, okay?"

"I was only trying to get her off the phone," Bari said.

Earl grabbed Bari by the arm and pulled her into the kitchen. He reached up in the overhead cabinet and pulled down his fifth of rum. Without a word he pulled her back through the living room and up the stairs. Bari stumbled as she tried to keep up with him. When they reached the top of the stairs, Earl instructed her to wait just outside the door. He didn't want her to see his makeshift office setup. She didn't need to know how he was making his money. Not yet, anyway. He went inside the room and opened up his product box and took out one of the tinfoil packets and stuck it into his front shirt pocket.

"Let's go," Earl said, taking Bari by the arm and leading her back down the stairs. Bari sat down on the comforter. He sstood over her. He opened his bottle of rum and took a long sip, then held the bottle out to Bari.

"No, thank you," she said.

"I want you to have a sip. It'll help you relax."

"I'm fine, Earl."

"Have it anyway. For me," Earl said. He put the bottle to her mouth.

Bari held her breath and took a small sip. She squeezed her eyes tightly. The bitter taste of the liquor made her face twitch.

"Have another."

"I don't like this stuff, Earl. Please."

"Have another," was all he said.

Bari didn't protest any further. She took another sip. The excess rum in her mouth ran down the front of her white silk blouse. Since she was only an occasional drinker, the alcohol went straight to her head.

Earl got up from the comforter and went and stood across the room from her. He stood there and stared at her. His eyes were heavy with passion. A twisted smile was pasted on his face. "You are so beautiful. I want you to take your clothes off," Earl said.

Bari looked up at him in complete surprise.

"What's the matter? I've seen your body a thousand times. This is me, Earl. Stand up."

Bari slowly rose to her feet. Earl walked over to her and put both hands on her waist and looked her straight in the eye.

Bari's mind was working overtime trying to think of a way to change his mind. "Listen, Earl, don't get me wrong. I do want to be here with you. I just figured that this would be a good time for us to talk, to really iron out our problems. But that doesn't mean—"

"I've waited too long for this night. Are you gonna do what I asked, or are you gonna piss me off?"

"I don't want to upset you, Earl. I'm trying to work with you. I want to do this the right way."

"Come on, baby, you and me, we could *only* do it the right way. Take off your clothes." He kissed her on the cheek; then he was about to kiss her lips. Bari turned her head to the side so that Earl would miss her lips and kiss her cheek.

"What's wrong? You don't want to kiss me?" he asked.

"I don't have a problem kissing you, Earl. It's just that the food has my stomach a little upset. That's all."

"Take off your clothes," he whispered. His voice was husky with passion. He walked over to the opposite side of the room again and leaned against the wall and watched her.

Bari was scared. She felt self-conscious knowing that he was openly staring at her. She slowly unbuttoned her blouse, looking away from him. Earl never took his eyes off her even as he took out the tinfoil packet from his pocket and opened it up to take a hit. Bari couldn't believe her eyes when she saw him take a hit.

"My God, you're still doing that. You lied to me."

"What I told you is that I was getting help for this. In the meantime, a little hit ain't gonna hurt nobody."

Earl took another hit. His eyes immediately became watery and glassy. He picked up the bottle of rum from the floor and took a drink from the bottle. The liquid was hot going down his throat. He unbuttoned the two top buttons of his shirt.

"You're still as beautiful as you were the first day that I saw you," Earl said.

Bari looked away from him. Her mind raced. She had to find a way out of the house. She knew now what made Earl turn into the beast that she had seen him turn into so many times before, and now seeing him in action petrified her. Would he kill her if she didn't do what he said?

Bari visualized the small window in the bathroom. She was sure she could squeeze through it. The drop from the window to the ground was only about six feet. As woozy as she felt from the alcohol that Earl had given her, she figured she wouldn't feel a thing when she jumped. She would let the water run full blast so that Earl wouldn't hear the window open. Then she'd climb through and jump down to make her escape.

Bari slowly looked up at Earl. "Earl, I was thinking . . . why don't I go in and take a nice hot bubble bath. You know how that relaxes me. Then I'll make it good for both of us." She tried to smile, but it ended up looking more like a lopsided half-moon. Bari held her breath and waited for Earl's response.

Earl took a hit before he answered her. "I can't wait for you that long. I want you right now, baby." He closed up the foil packet and put it down on the floor next to his rum bottle. He walked over to her.

All of Bari's clothes had been removed except for her bra and panties. Earl was touching her now. His hands slowly ran up and down her belly, then around to the small of her back. She could smell the alcohol on his breath. He moved closer to her ear and whispered, "I love you, Bari." And nothing. No weak knees. No heart fluttering. No breath

quickening or loss of control like there used to be. All of those feelings
were replaced by fear, anger, and disgust. Bari's body tensed under his
touch. She wanted to lash out at him. To scream at the top of her lungs.

"Earl, please. Let's take it slow."

"Don't worry, I won't hurt you, baby." He guided her down onto the
floor. He kissed her eyes, her nose, her lips. "Here. Let me get this
outta the way." He opened the front snap on her bra. It fell open, ex-
posing her full, rounded breasts. "They're so beautiful," Earl said. He
kissed each of Bari's breasts, then tugged at her panties.

Bari held on to them, keeping them in place. "Wait . . . if you really
want to show me that you've changed, then use a condom. Please," she
said.

"A condom? I don't wanna use no—"

"Please."

"All right. All right, fine," Earl said, getting up from the floor. "If
my baby wants me to wear a condom, then I'll wear a condom."

Bari smiled at him. "Thank you." She sighed, relieved to know that
he actually did use condoms.

Earl reached down to help Bari up from the comforter. "Get up.
Come with me." He led her up the stairs again. When they got to the
top of the stairs he made Bari stand outside of the bedroom door
again. Earl searched through the pocket of a suit jacket that hung in
his closet. He kept his eyes on Bari the whole time. He led her back
down the stairs and back to the comforter on the floor. He hungrily
started kissing her all over. When Earl spread Bari's legs apart and entered her, she didn't flinch. He thrust, kissed, rubbed, and panted. But
still, Bari did not respond. She lay there on the comforter as stiff as a
board. Lifeless. Two streams of tears rolled down the sides of her face.
When Earl was done he rolled over on his back. He folded his arms behind his head and looked at the ceiling, wearing a satisfied smile. Bari
quietly got up to go into the shower. Earl got up and followed her. He
sat down on the floor outside the bathroom. The door was left slightly
open. Earl took some hits of cocaine and drank rum from the bottle
while he waited for Bari to finish.

"You know, I'm really glad you're back, Bari." Earl spoke to Bari
over the running water. He got no response. "I know that we have
some problems to work out, but I know we'll work 'em out." Silence.

Earl took another hit. "I really love you, baby. You know that? I love you more than I love myself."

Bari stepped out of the shower and dried herself off.

"Let's go to bed," Earl said when she was done. He closed up his package and held it in his hands. He handed Bari a shirt he had worn the day before that was hanging on the banister. Earl went into the hall closet and pulled down two pillows that he had bought right after Bari moved out of the house. He put the pillows down on the comforter, then blew out all thirteen of the candles. Bari lay quietly on her side facing Earl, while he sat against the wall across from her and watched her. Earl had his bottle of rum set before him on the floor and he reopened his foil packet of cocaine. He took intermittent hits of coke and rum straight from the bottle. In between hits, he played with his gun, twirling it around his fingers and shining it with his shirttail.

BARI WAS EXHAUSTED but she didn't dare close her eyes. She couldn't sleep as long as she knew that Earl was watching her and as long as he had his gun in hand. When Bari couldn't keep her eyes open anymore, finally she fell into a choppy sleep. Earl paced back and forth all night.

At 7:45 A.M. Bari was awakened by Earl's telephone conversation.

"What do you mean you don't serve beef bacon! Do you think everybody wants to be eatin' swine?! Gimme beef sausage then. . . . Then what *do* you have? . . . Just give me two orders of hotcakes and scrambled eggs with cheese. . . . No! I ain't comin' to get it. You deliver, right? . . . Well, all right then! I already gave you my address!" He slammed down the phone. He looked over at Bari and noticed that she was awake. "Did I wake you? I'm sorry. You know how those assholes are at Marty's. I have a good mind to go over there and blow another asshole into that idiot that answered the phone."

Bari looked up at Earl. She could tell from his glassy, bulging, bloodshot eyes that he hadn't slept.

"I ordered us breakfast."

Bari didn't respond. She got up from the floor and went into the bathroom to wash her face. Earl was right behind her. She wondered how long he planned to keep her there. She was afraid to ask. She needed to be at work. She needed to see Franki.

"I didn't get to tell you about my good news yet. I was kinda waitin' for the right time to tell you," Earl said. "I'm workin' again. Actually, I'm runnin' my own business." Earl paused and waited for a response from Bari. When she didn't respond, he continued. "I'm making good money. I figured on us buying all new stuff. I'll let you pick out everything. Cost won't matter. Hell, if you want to hire a decorator that's cool, too. I know you're busy with your work, but we need to hurry up and get some furniture in here. I'm just about tired of sleepin' on the floor." He waited again for a response from Bari. Silence. "So what do you think? Do you like that idea?"

Bari quickly gathered her thoughts. She knew what she wanted to say, but she also knew that she would have to choose her words carefully. Bari cleared her throat. Her heart rate must have increased, because suddenly her palms became moist and her breaths became short and rapid. She fidgeted with a hangnail.

"You know, Earl," she began slowly, "I really don't think that our marriage was all bad. I remember the good times. . . ." She trailed off. She waited for Earl's response.

"Yeah?" He was listening. "And?"

Bari stammered on. "And I miss those times."

Earl stood in front of her now with his arms across his chest. He looked at her intently, waiting to hear what she had to say.

Bari spoke more rapidly now. "Now, you told me that if I spent the night with you and I still felt like I wanted to leave in the morning you would let me go. Well, I decided that I don't want to be here. . . ." Even as Bari spoke she could feel the blood leave her head. The room started spinning slowly. She held her breath and waited for the fallout.

Earl glared at her. He squinted his eyes when he spoke. "I know what I said! Is that what you want? You wanna walk out of this relationship?"

"I wouldn't say that I'm walking out—"

"That's exactly what you're sayin'! You're walkin' out!"

Bari didn't respond. Earl was getting riled up and she didn't want to make matters any worse. And she remembered his gun.

Earl glared at her. His jaw was clenched, but when he finally spoke, his voice was calm. "So? So, what's the problem?"

Bari looked at him, puzzled.

"What are you waitin' for? You wanna go, go! And don't expect a ride from me. You wanna walk out, you walk out on your own!"

Bari hesitated at first but then she quickly started to put on her clothes.

The doorbell rang. Earl pulled open the door. It was his food delivery. "It took you long enough!" he yelled at the deliveryman. "I don't want this shit now. Cancel the order. Cancel it!" He slammed the door before the man could respond.

Bari was fully dressed now. She had already gathered her things and stood facing Earl. When Earl turned around and saw her standing there he yanked the door open again. He gestured for Bari to walk through the door. Bari quickly walked toward the door. She slowed down when she reached Earl. She stood silently before him, saying nothing. She knew that if she were any closer to him he would surely hear her heart beat. Bari was almost paralyzed with fear. She didn't know what Earl had up his sleeve. She didn't know what his next move would be.

Earl looked at her. He let go of the door but stuck his foot in front of it so that it wouldn't shut. He put up both his hands to let her know that he had nothing more to say. Bari walked past him now. She went out the door and shuddered as she walked down the four short steps and down the walkway to the street. Bari had half-expected Earl to grab her from behind, figuring he would change his mind about letting her go, but he didn't.

When she and Earl had first bought their house she was happy that they had chosen this isolated village of houses that were far enough away from all the hustle and bustle. But now she longed for the noise, people, taxicabs. She was miles away from Franki's apartment, and cabs didn't frequent this neighborhood. They only came when they were called.

Bari walked quickly at first, and then without even thinking about it, she started running. She ran as fast as she could. She looked back every now and again as she ran and stumbled and walked until she reached the main road.

EARL SLAMMED THE door when Bari left. He went to the window and practically ripped down the curtains looking out to see which direction Bari went in. He moved from the window and picked up his empty liquor bottle. He flung it clear across the room. The bottle shattered as it hit the wall. The sound of breaking glass echoed through the room. Glass was everywhere. Earl grabbed up the comforter from the floor and threw it. He stormed into the kitchen and kicked the garbage can up against the wall, sending it on its side, spewing trash and food all over the floor. He punched the kitchen wall. Earl's knuckles were covered with blood when he pulled back his hand. Bari was gone.

forty-five

BARI HAD WALKED and run twenty or more blocks before she was able to get a cab. She was sweaty and distraught as she climbed the steps to Franki's apartment. Bari banged frantically on the door. When Franki pulled open the door, Bari dropped her things and fell into her sister's arms crying.

"Bari, thank God. I was worried to death about you. I couldn't even go into the studio today because I was up all night."

Bari's tears flowed nonstop as she told Franki what had happened.

"That's it! I'm calling the police. That bastard needs to be in a cage like the fucking animal that he is! How _dare_ he do that to you! How _dare_ he hold you there against your will. Thank God he didn't hurt you!" Franki stormed toward the telephone.

"No, Franki, don't call the cops. It's okay. We talked. Earl understands where we stand. He knows that it's over between us. I really don't want to get him in trouble with the law."

Franki looked at Bari like she was crazy. She hesitated to put down the receiver.

"Please, Franki, hang up the phone." Franki hung up the phone. Bari walked over to the couch and pulled herself into a fetal position. "Franki?" she said in a small voice.

"Yes?"

"Could you run me a bath?"

"Of course. Are you okay?"

"Yeah. I'm okay. And Franki . . ."

"Yeah?"

"Could you please call my job? Tell David something, tell him any-thing, but tell him I'll make it in tomorrow."

"No problem."

Franki went into the bathroom and started running Bari's bath. Be-fore the tub was even full, Bari drifted off to sleep.

An hour and a half later, Bari woke up in a panic. She calmed down when she saw Franki standing over her. Bari got up from the couch and went into the bathroom to take her bath. She didn't say much as she ran more hot water into the tub to reheat the water. When she got into the tub she left the door partially open so that she wouldn't feel closed in. Every now and again Franki would speak to her through the half-open door while she cleaned the apartment, but for the most part she left Bari to her thoughts.

Bari couldn't help but think about how foolish she must look to Franki and to everybody else who tried to warn her about Earl. She thought about how lucky she was to have a sister like Franki. A sister who was always there for her, no matter what. Bari finished her bath and changed into a pair of stretch shorts and an oversized T-shirt. She sat on the couch talking to Franki and before long, drifted off to sleep again. This time Bari slept for three hours straight. When she woke up again, Franki was still cleaning the apartment. Bari wondered where Franki got her energy.

"I left your dinner on the stove. I figured you'd be starving when you woke up," Franki said.

"To tell you the truth, I have no desire for food. I have no desire for *anything*."

Franki finally rested her broom and dust rag and she and Bari set-tled down at the kitchen table. Bari was distracted, though. She stared into space a lot and only half-listened when Franki talked.

"You're not missing him, are you?" Franki asked.

"The truth? A little. It's just habit, I guess. It's amazing how things turn out. The very things that you find so attractive in a person in the beginning are the same things that you end up loathing in the end. But now even his good isn't good enough for me."

Franki just shook her head and continued reading the *New York Times* article that was opened before her.

"Talk about bad luck in my life," Bari continued. "I know that there has to be some truth in those old wives' tales and superstitions. You know, like I'm sure there was something to Granny telling us not to play 'ring around the rosy' in the house. We used to sing it all the time: 'Ring around the rosy, pocket full of posies.' I mean, aren't posies supposed to ward off death or something like that? That song *has* to be bad luck. And remember when Ricky told us that we would have bad luck for the rest of our lives when we kept singing it in the house? And what about Daddy and Mr. Frosty? I still wonder about that. It sure gives me a lot to think about. Then on top of all of that, I turn around and I go and talk to a spiritualist named Zuma. Zuma! Should I have taken somebody with a name like that seriously? No wonder my life is in this state. I probably just made matters worse."

"Look, Bari, don't try to rationalize Earl's behavior. You know and I know why what happened, happened, so you might as well face the truth. Earl needed help years ago. His problems have nothing to do with you or a nursery rhyme we sang as kids or anybody named Zuma! You told me that you heard those little girls singing 'ring around the rosy' last night. Well, look around you. Nobody died."

Bari didn't respond. She just looked straight at Franki.

"So, what are you gonna do now?" Franki asked her.

"I'm going to see an attorney, file for divorce. Start over. . . ."

"Startin' over is good. At least you're still young and pretty. You can meet a nice guy, who deserves you. You know, like Dominick. I think he really cares about you. Earl didn't appreciate you. You were a good wife, Bari. Better than I will ever be."

"You really think I was a good wife?" Bari asked.

"You're damn right you were. A lot of women would never have put up with half the stuff Earl did."

"Yeah, but somewhere along the line I went wrong. Maybe I neglected something, overlooked something—"

"Don't blame yourself for any of this. Earl was just a jerk," Franki said.

"How stupid was I?" Bari asked.

"You weren't stupid at all. I think maybe you just loved him too much, if that's possible."

"I guess I did. I just thought that our relationship would be different from everybody else's. I thought it would be perfect. I really did. I never ever wanted to have a divorce on my record."

"Yeah, well, sometimes shit happens."

"Anyway, thank you," Bari said.

"For what?"

"For my life. I never would have found the strength or the nerve to leave Earl if it weren't for you, your encouragement."

"Just don't blame me when you're havin' one of those long, cold, lonely nights." Franki laughed.

Bari managed a slight smile. "Anyway," Bari said, "I think I've learned a lot now. I think I could probably help prevent a lot of other women from making the same mistakes that I made."

"Not for nothin', Bari, but what are you gonna do to help these women, hand out posies to every woman you meet?"

"I won't even dignify that with an answer," Bari responded, annoyed.

"I'm sorry, Bari; I shouldn't have said that." The telephone rang. Franki looked at the clock. It was 9:30 A.M. "That's Darryl. He said he'd call at nine thirty. You see, you have to train them Bari, *train* them. Take a lesson."

The two of them laughed as Franki answered the telephone. Her smile faded and her jaw dropped when she heard the voice at the other end. "No!" she yelled into the receiver. "No, you can't speak to my sister! And you have a lot of goddamn nerve calling my house! I should call the police on your ass!"

Bari went over to Franki. "I'll take it," Bari said quietly, calmly.

Franki held the receiver down by her side. "What?" she asked.

"I'll take it," Bari said again.

"Why do you want to talk to him?"

Bari didn't answer. She just held out her hand for the telephone. Franki sighed and gave it to her.

"I thought you said that you weren't gonna call me again. I thought we agreed that it was over. What do you want?" Bari asked him.

"I know what I said. Look here, I was thinking that before we call it quits, we should make sure that we've done everything that we could to work out our problems. Why don't we go for counseling?"

"Counseling? *We* don't need counseling, Earl; *you* do. And you need rehab, too."

"This is not about you or me. It's about both of us. Don't you think we owe it to ourselves to do whatever it takes to get us back on the right track?"

"No, Earl, I don't think that. I think that it's too late for us."

"How could you say that? Don't you know that God put us together? And he put us together for a reason. He has plans for us, Bari."

Franki motioned for Bari to hang up. Bari put up her hand to let Franki know that she would hang up in a minute.

"We shouldn't be discussing this over the phone, Bari. You're my wife. This is our life. Why don't we talk about this over dinner?" said Earl.

"No, Earl. I don't want to *eat* with you. I don't want to *be* with you. I just want you to leave me alone," Bari said.

"I'll come pick you up right now. Come on, baby, let's do this for us."

HE HELD THE cellular phone between his head and shoulders while he changed his clothes. He quickly put on his shoes and was out the door and into his car. He kept Bari talking on the cell while he drove. "So, where do you think we went wrong?" Earl asked, pressing hard on the gas pedal. "What happened to us?"

"I think that there were some problems that should have been worked out long before we got married."

"Like what?" Earl asked, still pressing hard on the pedal, the phone glued to his ear.

"Like the problem with you and your father for example. You should have gotten therapy years ago. I think you're having a problem dealing with the fact that your mother died at your father's hands. You should have confronted him years ago. That's probably why you're doing what you're doing."

"I'm gettin' help for that. I told you that."

"That's not my point, Earl."

Earl's cellular phone started temporarily breaking up. "What's wrong with your phone?"

"Nothin'. I think it's the cord."

"Oh," she said.

"Hang up the phone," Franki told Bari.

Bari covered the receiver and whispered to Franki, "Would you let me handle this?" then got back on the line with Earl.

"Have you been drinking? You sound like you've been drinking. Are you high?"

"No, I haven't been drinking and I'm not high." He moved the phone away from his ear quickly enough to bring the silver flask of rum to his mouth. He took a gulp of the liquor and put the phone back to his ear. Earl was drunk. He had been hitting cocaine and drinking rum from the flask, and he hadn't slept since Bari left earlier that morning.

Earl was driving like a madman. He needed to reach Bari before she caught on to him and got a chance to leave Franki's apartment. He was almost there.

"You see that?"

"What?"

"You still care."

"Well, of course I care. I do want you to take care of yourself. You have to do it, because nobody else is gonna do it for you."

The two of them talked for a while longer. Earl was careful to keep the conversation going at a nice easy pace so that Bari wouldn't get upset and hang up on him.

Earl pulled onto Franki's block. He stopped a few doors away from the building and parked. Now he would just sit and wait.

"So, what do you say? I'm comin' over. We'll talk then," he said.

"No, Earl. Don't—" The line went dead.

"Shit! He's coming over. This really pisses me off," Bari said as she stomped through the room, pulling on a sweatshirt over her T-shirt and putting on a pair of jeans.

"Well, what did you expect him to do? Why did you talk to him for so freakin' long? I told you to hang up. Don't you see what he's doin'? He's trying to get on your soft side. He wants you to feel sorry for him so he can break you down."

"Well, his plan didn't work. I haven't changed my mind for one minute. I don't know what I'm gonna do, Franki, but I know that I can't continue to live this way, running in and out whenever he calls. I gotta get out of here. He's probably already on his way. I'm going over to Barnes and Noble in the mall or maybe to the coffee shop in the Circle. I don't know where I'm going, but I'll be gone for a little while." Bari threw on a three-quarter-length down jacket and was at the door. "I'll call you when I get to wherever," Bari said.

"Okay," Franki answered. "And I'm telling you right now if Earl comes ringin' my doorbell, he's a dead man. I will put him out of his misery. Do you hear me?"

Bari smiled at her sister and left the apartment. Bari rushed down the front steps and headed toward the avenue to hail a cab at the short end of the block.

RICKY HAD SPOKEN to Hazel earlier. He told Hazel that he and Kim were visiting some friends but they were going to surprise Bari and Franki and bring lunch for them when they were done. They had ordered six types of different-flavored chicken wings with all the available sides and a strawberry cheesecake. Ricky knew his sisters always loved that. He also brought two bottles of wine that he had picked up when he was in Japan. Ricky had waited until his football game ended; then they had set out on the road as soon as the food was delivered to him. They had been driving for forty minutes.

EARL SAT UP when he saw Bari. He looked up and down the street to see if anybody was coming onto the block. The street was clear. He slowly pulled out of his parking spot and drove up the street behind her. Earl double-parked the car and got out when he was close enough to her. He walked behind Bari for a few steps.

"Bari," he called out.

She turned around. "Earl," she gasped. "What are you doing here?" She backed up to the high wooden fence near her.

"I told you I was comin', didn't I?" Earl moved closer to her. Bari backed up farther. Earl touched the gun in his pants waist. With his free hand he gripped Bari by the throat. "Don't scream. You understand me?"

Bari nodded her head.

"Why don't you wanna see me? Huh? All I wanna do is talk to you. Is that why you were runnin' out? 'Cause you don't wanna see me? Let me ask you a question. Do you really think that you could just walk out on me and I'm supposed to just smile and let you go? Do you want me to beg you to stay? Is that it?" He dug his fingers into her throat.

Bari started to cough. "Earl, please . . ."

"Please? Oh yeah, that's what I want. I want you to beg me like you want me to beg you! Get on your fuckin' knees!" Earl pushed Bari down toward the ground still holding her by the throat. He reached for his gun and pulled it out from his pants waist. "Do you think I need a bitch like you! Bitches like you are a dime a dozen! Beg me! Beg me for your life, 'cause I'm about to put a bullet hole right through your fuckin' head!" Earl put the gun to Bari's temple.

Bari started to whimper. Her eyes were squeezed tight and her body trembled. "Earl, please don't. I'm begging you. Please don't do this."

"You'll do anything I want you to do now, won't you? You wanna run away from me? All right, then, run!" Earl moved the gun away from her head and stood erect.

Bari opened her eyes and looked at Earl. She looked at him questioningly.

"Go! Run! That's what you want. Run on!" Earl used the gun to gesture for her to run away.

Bari slowly got to her feet. She was wobbly with fear. She walked backward at first with her eyes fixed on Earl. When Earl urged her on, she turned and ran away from him. Bari ran for about twelve yards. Earl lifted his gun and pointed it at her. He pulled the trigger. The gunshot rang through the open air. Bari paused for a second; then she continued running. Earl fired another shot. It hit her. Bari fell to the ground. Within seconds, curious neighbors pulled back drapes and opened blinds and windows.

FRANKI STIFFENED WHEN she heard the first gunshot. Her heart stood still when the second shot rang out. "Please, God, no!" she screamed as she bolted across the room to the window. She grabbed at the blinds. The clip broke on one side of the rod and the blinds came crashing down to the floor. When Franki stuck her head out the window, she saw Earl turning all about wielding a gun. Bari was not in sight. "Oh, Jesus!" Franki cried. "Bari! Please be okay, oh, Jesus."

Franki ran down the stairs so fast that she nearly fell. When she got outside, the picture that faced her was like a scene from some horrible movie that she had seen before. All movement after that seemed in slow motion to her. Franki saw Bari's body lying motionless on the ground near the fence by the corner of the block. She screamed at the top of her lungs and started running toward her sister.

"Bari!" Franki called out as she got closer to her.

RICKY AND KIM pulled onto the block. He saw a man; then he saw a woman running behind him. Ricky didn't see the body lying on the ground. He didn't pay them any mind. He parked his car. "Grab the food in the back," he told Kim. They got out of the car and started walking toward Franki's building.

EARL TURNED AROUND and saw Franki. He raised his gun and aimed it at her. "You bitch! This is your fault!" he said.

Franki froze. Earl raised the gun and pointed it at her. "No!" Franki screamed.

Earl fired. Franki hit the ground. The bullet shattered the window of the house behind her. Franki realized she wasn't shot, so she frantically crawled toward the building, tucking herself close to it for shelter.

"OH SHIT!" RICKY said, dropping the bag of food that Kim had handed to him. He quickly reached in his waist for his gun. He instantly pointed it at Earl.

Earl pointed his gun back at Ricky. "Are you ready to die, too? Are you ready to die, too?" Earl yelled. Ricky kept his gun aimed.

SIRENS SWIRLED AT the top of the block. Earl quickly turned his attention to them. Ricky did, too. Earl ran into the middle of the street. Several police cars sped toward the scene. Three ambulances followed. Earl raised his gun again. He pointed it to his own head this time. He squeezed his eyes shut. His hands trembled and his body tensed. Suddenly he stopped. He put his hand down to his side. "Drop the gun!" an officer yelled. Earl smiled at him. He stood very still. "Drop the gun!" the officer yelled again. Ricky dropped his gun. Earl saw his mother's wheelchair slowly rolling toward him. His mother sat quietly in it, watching him. She raised her hands and reached out to him. She was smiling, too.

Another police car sped onto the scene coming up the one-way street in the wrong direction. Earl turned around just in time to see

Bari's motionless body on a stretcher being lifted into the ambulance. He turned back to his mother. She was still there, still smiling. Earl raised the gun and pointed it to his head. He pulled the trigger.

INSIDE THE AMBULANCE, the emergency medical technicians worked on Bari. Long tubes ran from her body to intravenous poles. An oxygen mask covered her face while the technicians adjusted switches on the machines that blinked out her vital statistics. The ambulance sped through the streets with its siren sounding. Traffic careened to the left and right of them, clearing paths.

"We're losing her," one EMT said. They rushed from machine to machine, readjusting monitor levels. Another attendant started a heart massage.

The ambulance pulled up in front of the hospital and careened to a stop. Quickly the EMTs pulled out the stretcher and ran the gurney down the ramp through the hospital's trauma unit. "She's going into cardiac arrest!" the doctor yelled when Bari was wheeled into the room. "Prepare to defibrillate." Bari's chest was exposed. The doctor placed the machine on her chest and charged it up. "Clear!" The machines clicked and buzzed. "I'm not getting a response. Again! Clear!"

FRANKI, RICKY, AND Kim rushed into Cumberland Hospital. They waited almost an hour before the doctor finally came out from behind the green double swinging doors. They could tell right away from the look on the doctor's face that something was terribly wrong. They stood up and walked toward the doctor, meeting him halfway. Franki and Ricky identified themselves as Bari's family; then the doctor spoke to them.

"Is she gonna be okay, Doctor?" Ricky asked.

"It's too soon to tell. The bullet went into her back and lodged itself in her chest cavity. She went into cardiac arrest earlier. She's stabilized now, but there are signs of hemorrhaging. . . . If there is anybody else, other family members, that you want to call, you might want to do it now."

"Oh, my God," said Franki.

"Jesus. . . ." Ricky felt weak in the knees. Kim held on to him while they walked back up to the visitors' waiting room. They sat down on a bench, Ricky with his face buried in his lap. He and Franki cried and cried some more.

"We have to get to a phone. You wait here in case the doctor comes out," he told Franki.

"Okay."

Ricky called Hazel. He was on the phone with her for a half hour telling her what had happened and praying with her. Hazel told him that she was packing her bags and coming into New York on the first flight that she could get out. She didn't think twice about flying now. She used to say that wild horses couldn't make her do that.

Ricky hung up the phone and went back to Franki and Kim. He sat on the bench with his head in his hands and his eyes squeezed shut.

"I stayed away too long," Ricky said painfully. "I should have come home a long time ago. I should have been there for my sister, for my family. God, this life is so unfair."

Kim reached for Ricky's hand and squeezed it. Without a word, Ricky squeezed back.

"You know," Kim said, in her accent, "sometimes you have to think, what price life?" She sighed as tears made a stream down her face.

forty-six

THREE MONTHS LATER Bari was sitting in her hospital room in a wheelchair by the window. She had been sitting in the same spot for an hour just staring into space. The sun didn't seem to bother her as it beamed in full force on her face. Bari barely squinted her eyes. It was as if she believed the sun's rays would render some kind of healing powers to her.

Spring was quietly creeping in and little tulip were just beginning to push up through the earth on the hospital grounds. Sprigs of fresh green grass were everywhere. Life. New life. Somehow it seemed so unfair. She knew that Earl was wrong in what he did to her. Why did he have to kill himself? Even if they couldn't make it, as hard as she tried, he still could have made it with somebody else. It pained Bari to know that he was dead.

"Knock, knock," Barbara said, pushing open the door and walking into the room at the same time. She was carrying two large shopping bags. "Are you all packed and ready for me to take you home?"

"Very funny," Bari said, real dull-like. She knew that she still faced several more weeks, maybe even months, of physical therapy before she would be released. She still couldn't walk on her own.

"I saw Franki downstairs parking her car. She should be up here any minute." Barbara set the bags on the floor.

Bari glanced at Barbara, then turned back to look out the window.

Barbara walked over to her and kissed her on the cheek. "Whoa, what's up with you? What's the matter with that face?" Barbara asked her.

"Please, Barbara, I'm really messed up today."

"Are you hurting? Is it your back?" Barbara asked, putting her bags down on the bed table and on the floor. "Isn't today your therapy day?"

"Yeah, it's my therapy day and my back is killing me, but I can deal with that. It's my soul, Barbara, and my spirit that's hurting me right now. That's what's been hurting me every day. How am I ever going to forgive myself for what happened? Earl didn't kill himself. I did it. I should have been the one to die." Bari sniffled, then covered her eyes with one hand and cried.

"Bari, please don't torture yourself like this. It's a terrible thing that happened, but you have to let yourself heal now. You *have* to."

Bari wiped at her eyes. She looked at Barbara helplessly. Bari knew that neither Barbara nor anybody else would ever be able to understand her pain. Her guilt. How could they?

Bari calmed herself, then started talking again. "I was watching the Channel Seven news at noon today and I heard about that lady in Texas." Bari was still wiping at her eyes with the back of her hand.

"God," Barbara said, almost under her breath. "I was hoping you didn't see that."

"She was killed, Barbara. Her husband, the man that she loved, shot her and killed her." Bari was shaking her head in disbelief. "It's amazing how things happen. Franki and I used to always say that when one incident happens, whether it's a train derailment, a plane crash, a pit bull mauling somebody, or anything, you end up hearing about it again and again somewhere else. Could you imagine that? Here it is, Earl shot me. And somewhere else in the world, somebody else was getting shot by her husband."

"And it's gonna happen again and again before it's over."

"Maybe it doesn't have to. I mean, all things considered, I was lucky. I'm not dead—I came pretty close, but I'm still here. But maybe I could prevent somebody else—if it's just one person—being killed. Maybe that's my calling, Barbara. Somehow I think that would help me cope better with all of this. It's the least I could do."

"Well, it certainly would be a good thing if you could help somebody else. The fact is, some people say that's what we're here on this earth for. But me, I believe that when things happen to a person maybe it's something that they need to experience, for whatever reason."

"What need would I have to experience getting shot by my husband?" Bari asked.

"I'm not saying that it's a need per se; I'm saying that maybe in a past life you dealt with spousal abuse and you did nothing about it. Maybe you had to deal with it again in this life so you could fix it. And maybe you'll keep coming back again and again until you conquer it. I believe that."

"It's those kinds of beliefs that introduced me to a lady named Zuma," said Bari.

"What did you say?" Barbara asked. She had turned her attention away from Bari momentarily when a nurse came in to glance in on Bari.

"I asked you what's in those bags," Bari said, changing the subject.

"Oh yeah, I bought you some of those awful crumb cake doughnuts that you like so much from the deli by the job. I wanted to cheer you up. Looks like you could stand to eat one right now. Oh yeah, and by the way, David and the gang said to tell you hello. Sidney sends his love." Barbara walked over to her bags and started to open up the one with the doughnuts. "Mind if I sit on the bed?" she asked Bari.

"Of course not," Bari said.

"You know how those nurses are. I don't want to make them mad." Barbara chuckled. She took out the box of doughnuts and set it on the bed table. Then she reached back into the bag and took out two small paper plates. "So what did the doctors say, Bari? It's been three months that you've been here. When do they think you'll be able to walk again?"

"They don't know. . . . I don't want to think about it. I don't want to talk about it."

"I'm sorry. I shouldn't have asked," Barbara said. She put a doughnuts onto a plate and gave it to Bari.

"Could you give me that container of milk on the tray by my bed?" Bari asked Barbara.

Barbara reached to pick up the milk. "This milk is room temperature."

"That's okay," Bari said, holding out her hand for the container.

"Are you sure you want this?" Barbara asked.

"Give me the milk, please."

"Yuck!" Barbara said as she opened the container and handed the warm milk to Bari.

Before Barbara made it back over to the bed to sit back down, the room door flew open and a dozen "get well" balloons were released into the room. The balloons flew all over the room before they attached themselves to the ceiling.

"Whoa!" Barbara said.

"Ahhh!" Bari yelled, startled.

Franki and Nell rushed into the room right behind the balloons.

"Hey, baby sis!"

"Hey, girls, what's up?" Nell asked, putting the bags she was carrying on the floor and heading over to Bari. "How are you feelin', Bari?"

"As well as can be expected under the circumstances," Bari said, deadpan.

"Careful, she's bitin' today," Barbara told them.

"Shut up, Barbara," Bari said.

"Let me hug my girl," Nell said, reaching down and gently putting her arms around Bari. "I'm scared I might break you. Is that okay? I didn't hurt you, did I?" she asked, straightening herself up.

"No, you didn't hurt me," Bari said. She managed a half smile. Franki reached out and hugged her, too.

"I don't like seeing you like this. I want you to hurry up and get better so you can get the hell out of this gloomy place," Franki said.

"I know, Franki. Believe me, I want the same thing," said Bari.

"I know you do," said Franki.

"That's okay, though; we'll just keep coming here to egg her on until she gets better," Nell said.

"Why did you two come in here like a couple of bag ladies with ten bags each, making my little room look more crowded than it needs to?" Bari asked them.

"Because, my dear, did you really think that we were lettin' you off the hook, just because you're in the hospital? It's Thursday night and we're reinstating girls' night out right here, right now. I got us some spinach artichoke dip and tri-colored tortilla chips, some wing flings and blue cheese dressing, et cetera, et cetera. We got us a spread," Nell said.

"And I bought the drinks. Unfortunately, we could only have sparkling water, since some of us are on medication and can't drink wine," said Barbara.

"Yeah, unfortunately," Nell said.

They started unpacking small bowls and aluminum-foil-wrapped goodies.

"Well, that's one way to get me out of this hospital. You all are gonna get me kicked out of here. Look at all this stuff. It smells like a restaurant in here." Bari laughed. "They're coming to get me soon to take me to my physical therapy."

"That's okay; we'll be here when they bring you back," Barbara said.

"I smell food," Ricky said, as he, Kim, and Hazel walked into Bari's hospital room.

"Looks like they're having a party in here," said Hazel.

"Mommy! You're back," Bari said.

"Yeah, I'm back. I got here in the wee hours this morning," Hazel said, hugging Bari.

Barbara and Nell stood up. They hugged Hazel, Ricky, and Kim. Ricky and Kim made their way over to Bari and hugged her, too.

"Look at my baby," Hazel said, as she stroked Bari's hair.

"Mommy, don't even start crying," Bari said when she looked into her mother's eyes.

"You know I can't help it." Hazel sniffled. She quickly dug around in her pocketbook for a Kleenex but couldn't find one. "I'm so worried about you I don't know what to do."

"Here you are, Mrs. Hunter," Nell said, handing a napkin to Hazel.

"Thank you, Nell," Hazel said.

"Don't worry about me, Mommy. I'm gonna be okay," Bari said.

"You're looking good, Sis," Ricky said.

"No, I'm not," Bari said sourly.

"You really are, Bari. If you recall, last time we see you, you were very, very sick. You don't look so good then," said Kim.

"That's true," Bari said. Then she turned her attention back to Hazel. "How long are you gonna be here this time, Mommy?"

"I made arrangements to stay for as long as you need me to."

Ricky put his arms around Hazel. "Mom is gonna be staying with

Kim and me until you get well enough to come home. We just got a little apartment over in Boerum Hill. Then she's gonna stay with you to help you get around in your house once you get home."

"Good," Bari said.

My house. What am I gonna do about my house? Bari thought. *I can't go back there. I need to get rid of it and all of the bad memories. Maybe Ricky and Kim will want to buy it. I'll consider that when the time comes.*

"We stopped by the mall and picked up some fresh housecoats and personal items for you," said Hazel. She reached into her pocketbook and took out a small brown paper bag. "And I thought you might want this." Hazel handed the bag to Bari.

Bari opened the bag and took out her posy kerchief. "Mommy," Bari said, surprised. "What made you . . . ? You never believed in this."

"I believe in a lot of things now. And I believe that those things have a lot to do with your still bein' here."

"Thank you, Mommy," Bari said, holding on to her mother's hand.

"You're welcome, baby."

The door to the room opened again and a short, round, rosy-cheeked Nurse Friedman came into the room. "I'm sorry, folks, but I have to take my favorite patient to have her physical therapy. I'll get her back to you as fast as I can."

"We're gonna hold you to that. We'll hunt you down if you take too long," Ricky teased.

"Be nice," Bari said, as she was wheeled out of the room.

"I think she's looking a lot better these days," Franki said, as soon as Bari was gone.

"Physically, she's looking good, but she's still depressed, though. I can't believe she's feeling so guilty about Earl's death. She thinks it's her fault," Barbara added.

"I feel guilty about it myself, every day," said Ricky. "Every day I want to kick myself for not pulling my trigger first. I should have been the one to kill him."

"But then you would be in jail and I couldn't handle that," Hazel said.

"So be it. I just hate that I didn't know what was going on. Nobody told me."

"Nobody knew how deep it really was. Bari kept it all to herself, believe me," said Franki.

"Well, one thing is for sure: Her nightmare is over. It's just so damn—oops, I'm sorry, Miss Hazel, it's just so crazy how things turn out. Life is a blip," Barbara said.

"It can be if you choose to live in the dark. You always must live in the light so that you can see all of the choices you have before you and for sure you will make fewer errors," Kim said.

"Is that from Confucius?" Barbara asked.

"No, that is from me," Kim said proudly.

"Look, let's not stop praying for Bari; let's keep up the faith and get her back healthy again. I need to see her walk again."

"Amen," Hazel said.

"Amen," Ricky seconded.

"Why isn't anybody eating?" Barbara asked, as she got up to put some food on a plate.

"I'm right behind you," Nell said.

And soon everybody else followed suit.

Bari was back from her therapy in no time. The smiling nurse wheeled Bari right back to the spot that she had taken her from. "Wow, looks like a party in here. You're a very lucky lady, Mrs. Jordan."

"I am, aren't I?" Bari looked all around the room at each and every smiling face. *These people love me. I deserve to be here. I have a lot to live for and a lot to give still. I'm thankful.* Bari had a smile pasted on her face and a distant look in her eyes as she sat and munched on spinach artichoke dip and tortilla chips and sipped on sparkling water. Her pain was gone for the moment.

The opening door brought her back to her reality. Dominick walked into the room wearing a bright grin and carrying a small plant from the evergreen family. He greeted everybody before he walked over to Bari in her wheelchair. "How are you feelin'?" he asked her, kissing her on the cheek.

"I feel good now," Bari said.

"Good." Dominick took Bari's hand and squeezed it. "I bought this for you. It's an evergreen plant. I want you to have it and always remember that as long as this plant is green I will be here for you. I love you; you know that."

"I love you, too," Bari said. She squeezed Dominick's hand back and they held each other's eyes for a full half minute, holding hands and sharing a mutual warmth that would have melted butter.

"Oh my, we have a full room. Hello, everybody," Nurse Kate said.

"Hello," they all said in unison.

"I just came in to say hello. How are you today, Mrs. Jordan?"

"I'm fine, Nurse, but please, just call me Bari."

"Okay, Bari," the nurse said. "Well, enjoy your company and I'll check in again with you later."

"You got it," Bari said. She was glad that her family and closest friends came out to visit her today. She needed that. She was happy that they were there, but now she looked forward to her time alone. She had a lot of thinking to do. A lot of reflecting. Earl had been heavy on her mind, and she needed to figure out a way to come to grips with the fact that he was gone. That would be the hardest thing in the world that she would ever have to do. She needed to try to understand what went wrong in his head. And she needed to think about her own feelings and what her instincts had been trying to tell her. She realized that all this time she had been making the mistake of listening with her heart. She had it straight now. She knew that starting today things would be different. *She* would be different.

E-mail Teri Denine at

tdenine@aol.com.

1. Bari and Franki were raised together in the same household by the same parents. Discuss the personality differences between them. Which girl is a mirror of their father, Jimmy, and which is a mirror of their mother?

2. Grandma Greta passed down her posy kerchief to Bari for luck and protection. Was the power of the posies any different from the power derived from the dusts and other articles Bari received from Zuma? Discuss examples where the posies and/or the articles from Zuma were helpful to Bari's life or marriage.

3. It has been said that most couples see certain signs at the beginning of a relationship that may indicate the direction in which the relationship will go. Discuss some of the early signs that should have told Bari about her relationship with Earl.

4. Is it possible to live with a person on a daily basis and not have any idea whatsoever that this person is abusing drugs? Is it possible to be completely oblivious to every sign? At what point should the lights have gone on for Bari?

5. Earl is haunted by his deceased mother's image and has become addicted to drugs as a result of it. Should he have faced his past and turned his father in? Would this have helped his life? His marriage?

6. Bari had a very supportive base of family and friends. What could they have done to help Bari get strong and take control of her life? Could they have helped her? If so, how? If not, why not?

7. Bari put her blood, sweat and tears (as she put it), and a whole lot of time into her job. If she had put the same effort into her marriage, do you think it would have made a difference?

8. At Christmas time, when Hazel, Ricky, Bari, and Franki were all together for the first time in years, Bari looked frail and stressed. Could Hazel have taken a different approach in confronting Bari about her physical appearance? What could Ricky have done to help?

9. When Earl held Bari captive at their home, could Bari have gotten away if she wanted to? How should she have behaved? What did you expect when the children were singing "Ring around the rosy, pocket full of posies..."? What would you have done that night if you were Bari?

10. Were you happy with the ending of the story? What would you have written differently? What would you have happen in a sequel?

A Reading Group Guide

For more reading group suggestions, visit
www.readinggroupgold.com
and www.the-blackbox.com.

St. Martin's
Griffin